Son of Empire

S A Melia

Dickson House

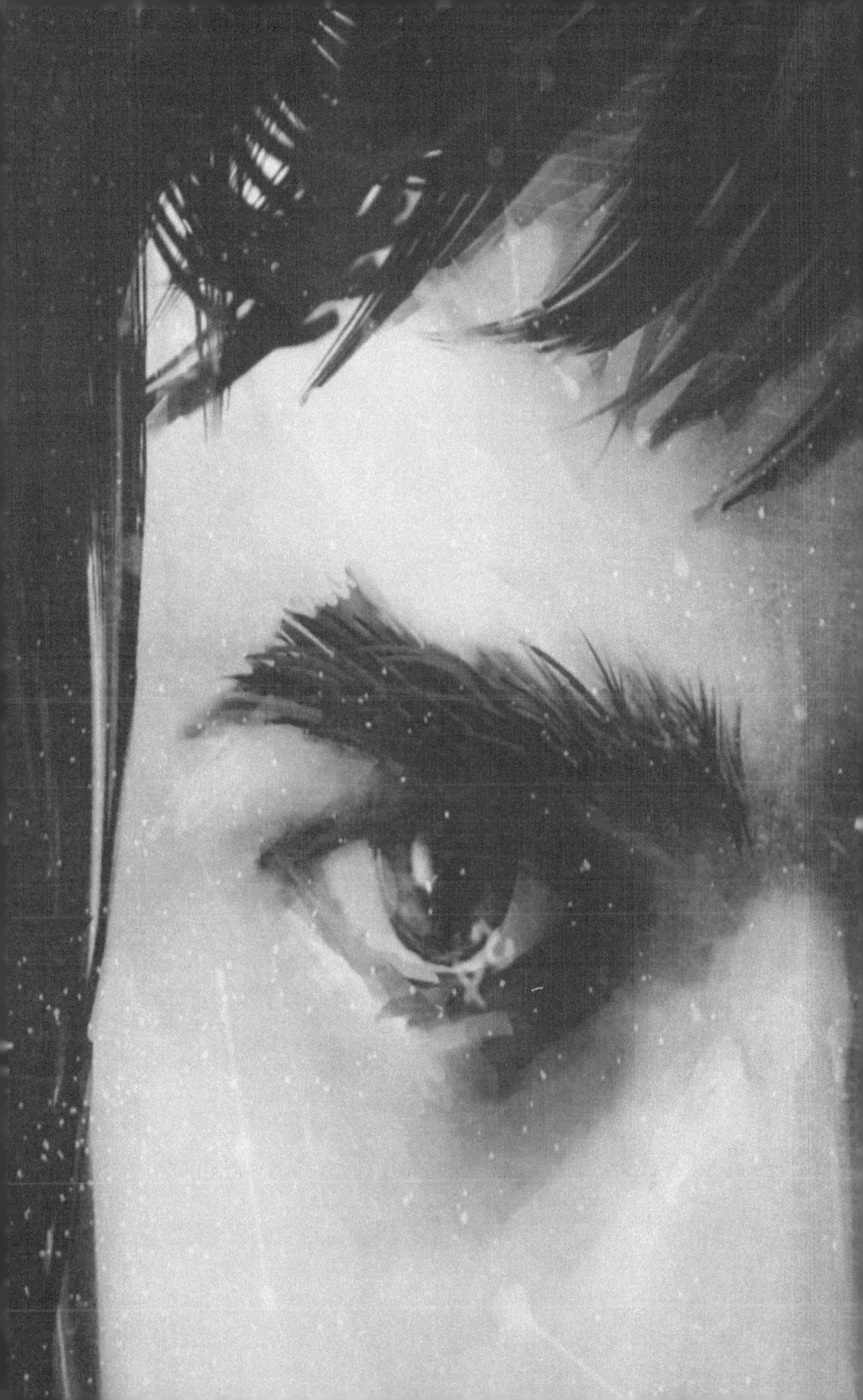

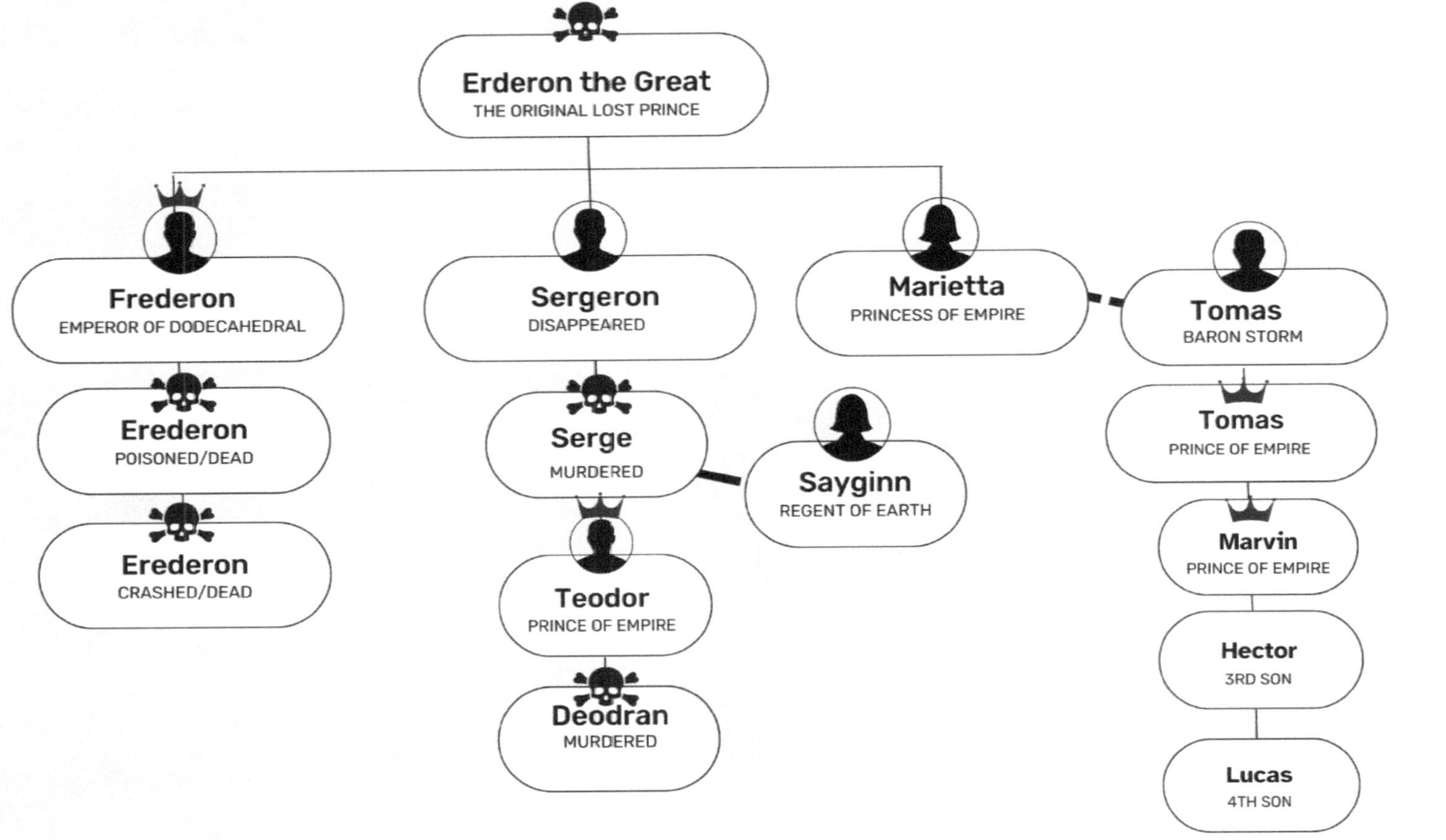
Erderon the Great
THE ORIGINAL LOST PRINCE
Frederon
EMPEROR OF DODECAHEDRAL
Erederon
POISONED/DEAD
Erederon
CRASHED/DEAD
Sergeron
DISAPPEARED
Serge
MURDERED
Teodor
PRINCE OF EMPIRE
Deodran
MURDERED
Sayginn
REGENT OF EARTH
Marietta
PRINCESS OF EMPIRE
Tomas
BARON STORM
Tomas
PRINCE OF EMPIRE
Marvin
PRINCE OF EMPIRE
Hector
3RD SON
Lucas
4TH SON

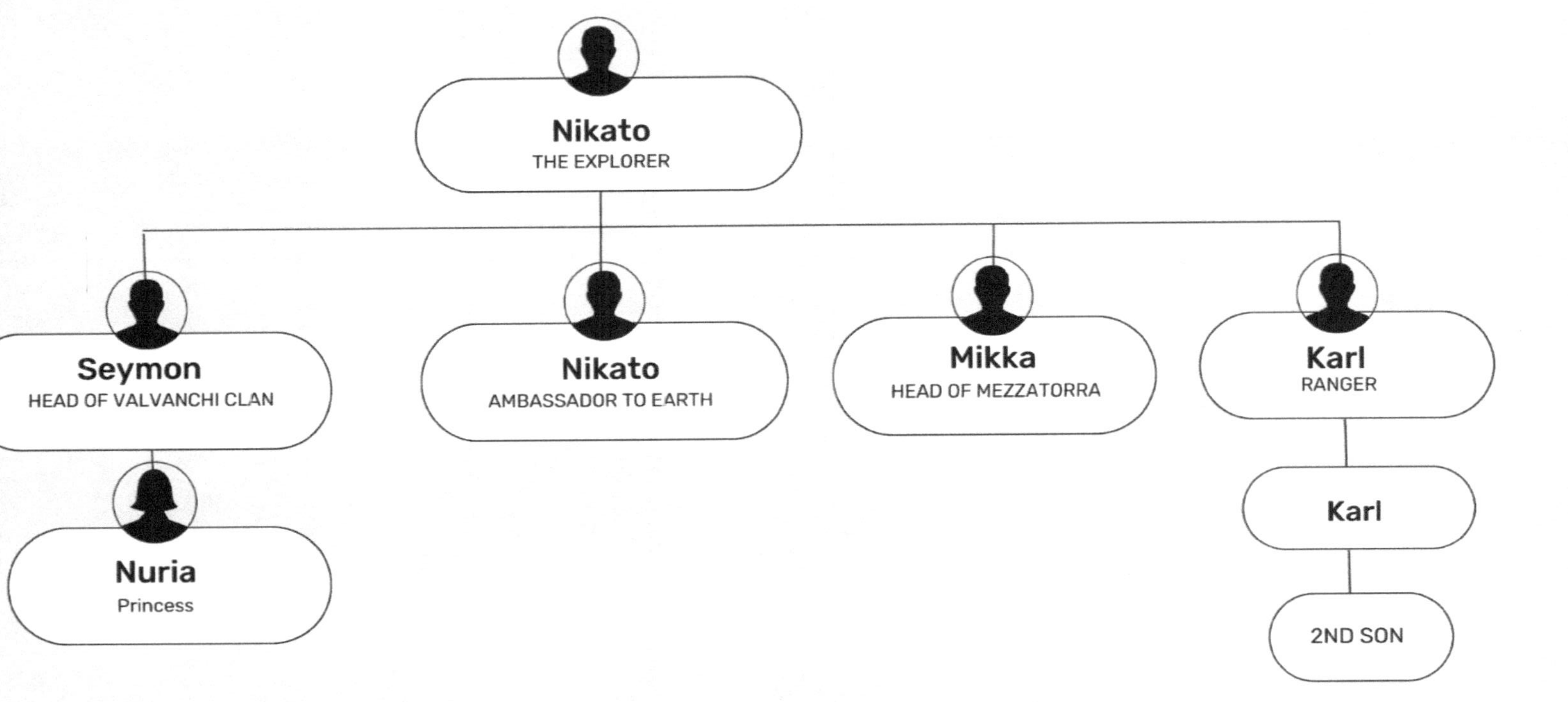

Nikato
THE EXPLORER
Seymon
HEAD OF VALVANCHI CLAN
Nuria
Princess
Nikato
AMBASSADOR TO EARTH
Mikka
HEAD OF MEZZATORRA
Karl
RANGER
Karl
2ND SON

Chapter 1

An Early Call

"Guy Erma, get yourself dressed and get to the yard!"

Guy shuddered as he woke from the nightmare. He lay blinking as his brain scrambled to restore his thoughts to the everyday. The voice, he realized, came from his communicator. Wearily, he reached to pull it from under his pillow and said, "Juke?"

Too loud! Guy felt the children stirring in the darkness of the attic. He knew better than to wake them, not when it was still dark. Had he missed his alarm? He cradled his communicator against his cheek as Jukona, a market trader and purveyor of London's finest strawberries, continued.

"I need you here, now. They have set up checkpoints on all the roads out of Domeside – the tailbacks are stretching right into the Dome; we need to get going. Grab your stuff and look lively. Mam will feed you when you get here."

The message cut out. Guy lay for a moment in the semi-darkness. It was morning. Well, almost. It was the Ascot Races. He had been due to meet Jukona at five.

What time was it now? 4:22. "Get over here," Jukona had said. Checkpoints, what was that about? Oh yes, the Prince. He had been kidnapped.

Last night, he had been dressed in black satin trousers and a red fashion shirt, serving drinks from a silver tray in the Cap of the Dome, the VIP suite at the top of London's famous Dodecahedron Dome. There had been cocktail tables designed to look like stylized palm trees, with flat tops and column bases. Someone had removed the tabletop from the tubular column. Inside, Guy had seen dirty feet wearing golden sandals, footwear of a fallen angel. No cocktails, no party hats, but Guy had seen Prince Teodor and done nothing. Chart Segat and Emperor Frederon had done nothing either.

Chart Segat was the administrator of the Dodecahedron Dome and leader of the Dome Militant space defenders, and Frederon was the emperor of the twelve planets of the Dodecahedral. Drinks in hand, they had peered down at their captive. Why would they kidnap and hold the future king? God help Prince Teodor.

Why did I do nothing? I should have – What? Shouted or pointed or something. What, with Chart Segat just standing there? Are you mad?

Squirming out from among the other children who slept in the attic, Guy went to where the night before he had stacked and folded his clothes. He picked them up, along with his boots and rucksack. He stripped off his night shorts and pegged them to a line along the wall, then headed into the bathroom. Three small toilets, including one which was permanently blocked, and three showerheads of which only the first had any real water pressure. He washed and dressed, all without switching on the one working light. He picked up his rucksack, paused, and looked inside; he hoped it might not be true, but no, he saw a pair of polished patent leather shoes.

Oh no, he groaned and reached inside the bag to remind himself. Yesterday, before the cocktail party, before the kidnap at the Cathedral, there had been the rehearsal with the Domeside choir. Prince Teodor had been there and so had Guy. They had dressed the prince as a golden angel, and Guy had stolen his shoes. He had thought no one was looking, but one person had seen. It was the prince. He had seen Guy take his shoes but had said nothing. His eyes had said: Take them if you want them.

I don't want them. I'm going to give them back, Guy told himself as he slung the bag on his back and headed down the stairs at a run.

"You hear me, Prince Teodor," he spoke aloud to the empty staircase. "I'm not a thief! I will give you your shoes back."

Chapter 2

A Cold Awakening

"The glass floor was cold. The space was blindingly bright with morning sunlight.

"Where are you?" Teodor frowned. Was that his father? Why was he so impatient?

"What day is it?" Teodor replied. "On Sunday, I will be sixteen."

"Forget that! Where are you?" Teodor rolled his stiff and aching shoulders. They had shackled his wrists behind his back using the large lead handcuffs normally reserved for securing out-of-control Borgs, so twenty centimetres of skin - from his wrists and up his forearms - were chafed and bloody. He drew his arms up to examine the damage. He wished he had some antiseptic cream, some bandages, some warm water...

"Are you injured?" His father's voice again.

"It's not bad." He looked around and suddenly felt like he was falling. He sat on a transparent floor, and beneath him was the City of London. He did fall forward, and his hands hit the glass floor. Spreading his palms and fingers wide to steady himself, instinctively he spread his legs as well. Soon, he lay starfish-like on the floor – his eyes mapped out the districts beneath him: Blackfriars, St. Pauls, and the City.

"I am lying on top of the Dodecahedron," he thought. "The Dome you built, father."

"The alien Valvanchi built it, not I. You know that, Teodor."

"But Dad, I've never been on top before. This must be the top of the Dome, but the floor is transparent – as are the sides of the Dome, so it feels like I am falling, but I'm not."

"Where are you?"

Slowly, he drew himself up to kneel so he could look around. His elbows and knees were scuffed from where they had stuffed him in a circular tube; that was yesterday. At least he assumed it was yesterday. Later they had chained him to a heavy metal shelf alongside an out-of-date cleaning droid, some half-used tins of paint, and a jumbled pile of dirty dust sheets. As if someone had recently finished decorating. So, had he been asleep? They had used drugs, sleeping fluids onto rags then pressed to his face. Was this place new? The Cap of the Dome was new – the squat flat rooms Chart Segat had built for his own use on the roof of the Dome.

"I'm in a storage cupboard," he thought, looking down once more. "A storage cupboard in the Cap of the Dome."

"Chart Segat has you."

"But father, he's the man who killed you. You and baby Deodran!"

"I better go," his father replied.

"No, please don't!"

In an instant, Teodor was standing by the black coffin on a golden dais – the high Dome of St Paul's above and behind him, the choir sang.

"'In darkness, you are never alone, for I will always be in your heart."

He hadn't cried at his father's funeral. The Press had reported that he looked in shock. In truth, he remembered little except what he watched on repeat, and he hadn't remembered this hymn until this moment. Who had chosen it?

In darkness, you are never alone, for I will always be in your heart. Had they foreseen that he would arrive at this desperate plight?

But tomorrow is my birthday, Teodor stopped himself. If I survive until tomorrow. But, I will survive. I must believe it. I must.

"I will be King of Earth!" he said aloud.

Even to himself, he sounded ridiculous – why did an entire planet need a King? Of course, the planet didn't, but the United Races required a single representative for each race at its assembly; for this role, humankind had designated an Emperor. A single man to represent the entire race, only it was never intended that he would rule.

So much power should never rest with only one man. That's what his father said.

When I become Emperor, I will give the power back to the people, Teodor thought. That's what my father wants, Teodor hesitated. Wanted. That was what his father had wanted.

Who could imagine this? Teodor sighed and bent to lick the worst of the scratches on his wrists. The warmth and saliva were strangely comforting. He licked it again. Am I a wounded animal?

Oh well.

"As your King..." he spoke aloud to the shelves. "I find these conditions deplorable." His voice cracked with broken laughter, and he realized if he didn't do something, he would start to cry. And he didn't want to cry. To cry would mean they had beaten him, and he wasn't beaten yet, was he?

He froze. Footsteps. Who was coming?

Chapter 3

A Bad Night's Sleep

"Nuria woke, and her wrists were burning. She looked down, expecting to see scabs and sores – but no, her flesh was pristine. This was why they warned you never to connect with a human.

She groaned. She had slept badly, waking with a sensation of dampness down her side and thighs. This is what Teodor is feeling, she thought. She sat up, feeling miserable, and threw her legs out of bed. At least I know he is still alive. She stood up and stamped her feet. Not because she was stiff, but it was something she felt she had to do.

I have to find him. I only need one small clue. And then I will know where he is.

Thirty minutes later, she was dressed and standing uncertainly in the atrium of the dodecahedron dome. Teodor was here somewhere, but where?

"You'd be less exposed if you were invisible, m'lady," her security droid said.

She nodded; there was a digital display to her left with a vibrant ever-changing display of flowers. She walked over as if to look, and then she disappeared. Any onlooker would just assume she had stepped to the right or the left of the display, that they had blinked and missed her. But no, Nuria was still there, entirely invisible, as she walked amidst the workers hurrying into the Dome.

"I can't be late. Not again."

"I've paid too much, but it's probably worth it."

"I'm sure she dislikes me, and I know she wants to ruin my chances."

"The guy is a jerk. She won't make him happy, like I could."

"Typical of Guy to find out about Prince Teodor."

"I need the money. Don't you know..."

Nuria spun round. Someone had mentioned the prince.

"Not only that, but he plans to use the money he'll make to save me. It's not like I need saving. It's not like I'd do the same for him."

The girl stood, looking bored, next to the serving station near the center of a cafe. She appeared oblivious to an important-looking customer who was trying to catch her attention. Clearly distracted by her own thoughts, had she really mentioned the Prince? Nuria passed behind a large ornamental shrub at the entrance to the cafe and reappeared before walking in, listening as she did.

"I mean, obviously any Intel about the prince is worth a lot of money, but how is Guy going to tell anyone without getting caught? I mean, who does he know? No one. If he tells anyone and it gets back to Chartsie, he'll be facing a Borg with a blunted blade. That's what I told him. A rabid Borg in a cage and a rusty broken blade. That's what he can expect if he says one word about the prince."

The girl was so lost in her thoughts, and Nuria was equally mesmerized by what she was thinking, that neither of them noticed each other until Nuria stood within a hand's reach of the serving girl, who suddenly emerged from her daydreaming to stare at Nuria.

"Yes?"

"Erm?" Nuria was lost for words. This girl knew something, but how was she going to persuade her to tell her?

"Did you want a table?" the girl asked then with a pert curtsey, "Princess." Nuria looked at her in surprise. "Princess Valvanski - sorry Val-van-chi, yes?"

"Yes. And what's your name?"

"Marline," the girl said and pointed to her lapel badge (it read: MARLINE). "Did you want breakfast?"

Nuria hesitated – of course she had had breakfast in this place yesterday. "I'm not hungry," she replied, and Marline's thought-response was impatient.

"Of course. She doesn't want breakfast. Now, if I could get her into the boutique, I could make some real money, and I'd not need Guy's Prince Teodor money. But if she only has coffee, I might not even get a tip. Or maybe she's so rich she tips more than she spends."

"Actually, I was hoping to visit the boutique," Nuria interrupted. She had noticed how other staff were closing in. She had to separate this girl away from the others if she was going to persuade her to share her secrets.

"We're always happy to open early for VIPs," Marline replied, checking the time. "They'll still be cleaning, but if you don't mind a bit of noise?"

"Oh no, I don't mind at all!" Nuria assured her.

"Mr. Francis, may I take the princess over to the shop?" Marline worked hard not to frown. "Oh, it has to be Francis. He was the one who tried to stop me from being the new teen model. Loulou said he only agreed because I was already a bit famous and had good credit on my modeling account. Loulou says I must be extra polite to him."

Loulou? Nuria looked around. Francis? She looked at the man with interest.

"That's not your job, Marline," he said – then in a low whisper he did not want Nuria to hear. "She can just as well walk there by herself," he nodded. The store was only ten paces or so beyond the cafe. "Someone will take care of her."

"She's only a Baby-Ski after all." Francis' thought was disdainful.

He must have been at the party last night, Nuria thought. It was Chart Segat who had insulted her uncle, calling him Valvan-ski, and then her, Baby-Ski. Was he a friend of Segat? She sighed. Of course, everyone in the Dodecahedron was beholden to that man.

"Please," Nuria started. "Ow!"

Nuria bent in two as if she had been hit, and gripped her stomach with both her arms, she stumbled.

They kicked him. Someone - Somewhere - had kicked Teodor, and she had felt it.

She gasped and grasped her knees as she struggled to stand.

What if they hit him again?

"Princess?"

The girl Marline was leaning in to check on her, and now bent to put her shoulder under Nuria's arm to help her stand.

"I'm taking her to the shop," she told Francis and the others.

"We'll deduct the time from your pay, Marline," the manager called after her.

"I'll make it up later!" Marline replied with a flick of her hair.

"Hurry!" Nuria gasped.

Someone had grabbed Teodor and forced him to his knees. Nuria walked despite the pain.

"Lean on me, Princess," Marline replied. "We're almost there!"

"Maybe she's not well-adapted to our atmosphere," Marline thought. "I heard of aliens who collapsed because of the pollution or the air or something. Obviously not Scavengii pirates, damn them, but others. Maybe the Baby-ski was not yet adapted to Earth."

"I'll make you comfortable..." Marline said, leading her inside. "And you can get a free - I mean - the boutique serves the finest teas to our clients."

Nuria felt better almost at once as she stepped inside. Better, but that meant she had lost contact with Teodor, she thought crossly, as she looked around the beautiful shop with its glittering rails of clothes. As Marline had predicted, it was empty – except for two cleaning droids. But despite the high ceiling, it was crisscrossed with electrics and tech wires; yet there was an upstairs and a balcony looking out over the atrium.

"I want to go up onto the terrace," Nuria said.

Marline checked the girl, thinking: "There are only ball gowns upstairs when I might have sold her shoes and a handbag here."

"I'd like a gown," Nuria said, "And shoes and a bag. I can fly us upstairs." And wrapping an arm around Marline's waist, she lifted them both off the ground, and spiraling up she floated them up to the floor above. Nuria knew this was breaking the rules on showing her tele-powers to humans, but it was just her and this girl. And she had to reach a spot from where she could properly connect with the prince.

"Wow!" Marline breathed as Nuria landed them on a plush sofa where they collapsed side by side.

"Teo, Teo, Teo - stay with me," Nuria muttered. "Open the window!" She added and pointed to the vast double doors. They burst open so fast, the glass shattered and filled the space, the curtains and inner veil flung violently apart, ripped and billowed high.

"No!" Marline cried and cowered at her side.

"It's ok, it's ok," Nuria said and patted her hand. "Give me a minute."

Nuria could see him, or rather she could see what he saw. Teodor was curled up defensively in a ball. When he glanced right, it was as if he was hanging in space for the entire Dodecahedral lain out like a model. Nuria found herself searching the Dodecahedral atrium, the square with its cafes and the distinctive black and white design of House Jewel. Only Teodor turned away, and she found herself staring into the cracked face of a half-human, half-machine battle Borg, and its eyes blazed red.

Nuria screamed. As she did, she lost the connection. She sat a moment on the sofa with her face in her hands.

"He's in trouble," she muttered. Opening her hands and eyes, she saw Marline staring at her.

"Teodor?" Marline whispered.

Nuria nodded once, Marline gasped then asked: "Shall I get some tea?"

Nuria nodded.

The girl stood up, straightened her skirt, and ran a hand through her hair. Comfort gestures, thought Nuria.

"You'll be able to save him?" Marline asked as she paused at the door.

Nuria gave no reply. She still had no idea where Teodor was. She had seen the Dodecahedral Dome from above, but where? What was the highest spot in the Dome?

"Maybe you can show me your best gown while we drink tea?"

"What occasion do you want a dress for?" Marline had reappeared; she now wore a smart black and white blazer over her black serving dress.

"I'm going to dance with Prince Teo at the Ascot Ball," Nuria said.

"I see," Marline replied, thinking: "Me too - if it goes ahead?"

"Really?" Nuria asked.

"She's reading my thoughts."

"My house paid for me to dance with him," she said. "I'm wearing red, but I think your color is blue, don't you?"

"Did she read my thoughts when I was thinking about Guy and The Prince? Would she pay Guy for information? She's not likely to tell Chartsie. But I might not need Guy's money if I can sell her a dress. And a bag. And shoes."

"Of course, I'm not sure I'll need the dress. Now the prince has been kidnapped."

"Don't say that," Marline thought. "I need this commission. And Guy saw him. He was alive. He said Chartsie had him. That means the Cap of the Dome."

"Is there a glass floor in the Cap of the Dome?" Nuria asked.

"She is reading my thoughts," Marline thought before she replied aloud, "Yes." In her mind's eye, she remembered the glass floor from the night before and how she and the other girls had dared each other to stand still and stare down, but how if you stood for too long you swayed and sometimes felt sick. "We try not to look down, though." She added.

"Thank you," Nuria said with a sigh. "And where is this Cap of the Dome?"

Marline walked two steps to the shattered open window and pointed skywards. Nuria walked out to stand at her side and looked up.

At that moment, a circular door spiraled open; it illuminated a small troop of Dome Militant standing on a shimmering disc as it hovered up through the open space.

"Yes, he's up there!" Nuria murmured, then as an afterthought. "Those men must be huge that we can see them so far above. "

"Borgs," Marline shivered. "Ugly brutes."

Nuria did not reply, just stood and watched until the disc disappeared.

"I will pay, Marline. I'll pay handsomely if you can help me free him."

The girl nodded.

"So, where is that disk going?"

"Well, the Cap of the Dome, but they came from the Dome Militant barracks – that side of the dome, it's all their training and living units. Jails too. Maybe he is in there."

Nuria nodded. At that moment, Mr. Francis appeared – looking askance at the open windows and the partially ripped curtains and billowing inner veils.

"I like this dress, Marline," Nuria said aloud. "Please pick out two bags and two sets of shoes. I will come back for a fitting later today." Then, pointedly to Mr. Francis, "Marline connects with me; I want her to choose all my clothes."

"The windows, the curtains," he stuttered.

"Charge my uncle," Nuria replied.

"Princess," he agreed, with a small bow.

This time, Nuria ran lightly down the stairs, paused to nod once to Marline, and left through the front door. She told her security droid to call the car."

Chapter 4

Battle Borgs at Dawn

Teodor crouched on the top of the Dome; through the transparent floor, the Dodecahedral complex was laid out beneath him. He was used to the view now, so he ignored it and listened to the approaching footsteps. It did not sound like the clipped march of the Royal Guards, nor the light steps of his mother. No, that was too much to hope for. It must be someone else. Somebody he did not know. And whoever it was, they were not his friend.

And yet, they can't all be evil, Teodor thought with hope.

"Good morning! Can you help?" he cried out. Even as he spoke, he choked on the words, for a door opened to reveal two Battle Borgs. Half-men, half-machines, these had once been heroes of the Dome Militant Space Defence Forces. They had died in combat, and the families had chosen for them to live on as Borgs – enhanced humans with metallic legs, implanted weapons, and a Communicator embedded in their brains. Men or machines, who knew? How much of their humanity remained?

And yet, they should be hard-coded to obey – but yesterday, they had ignored his orders, his pleas. Even when he had begged them to stop. Who could have reprogrammed them? Had they all been reprogrammed? Each Borg was supposed to be autonomous in battle – so surely, one would recognize and help him? It was their duty to their prince.

Teodor recognized one Borg from the previous night – that one had ignored his pleas for help. The other was new. Bitter bile rose in the back of his throat, but he swallowed it in a supreme effort of self-control. He had to escape. Maybe the second Borg? After all, the Dodecahedron Dome was a vast complex of sports and entertainment, the Cap of the Dome was mostly offices and meeting rooms. He might only be a mere fifty yards from some public space. Fifty yards to freedom. Somehow, he must escape.

He flopped down, as if in despair, even though he was calm and relaxed. With his chains hastily rearranged behind his back, he pressed the palms of his hands to the wall on either side of the metal shelf. Who said you could not fight in chains?

"Give me your hands, boy, so that I can unlock you," the Borg said. It was the new one, the one that might still obey him.

Teodor did not move.

Come closer, come closer, he urged silently.

"What's wrong with you, didn't you hear me?" The Borg bent forward. Exactly as Teodor had hoped. He threw his legs up and out, kicked the Borg under the chin, and threw him backwards. The full impact had not hit the machine on the jaw, or it would have surely killed him as shards of bone shot up into his brain. But it had been strong enough to send him spinning.

Teodor looked beyond to the second Borg. It was older, only partially a machine. He looked human. Yesterday, it had refused to help him. Why?

"I am Teodor, Prince of Earth. You must free me!" Even if this had not worked before, Teodor knew he had to keep trying. At some point, these Borgs must return to their original programming. One would surely obey.

Seemingly not today – the aging Borg, with half his face fallen away, an evil black machine gun implant in his upper arm, and needle blades in the place of nails on three of his fingers on each hand – leered down at him with a mocking salute: "Prince Teodor, it's shower time. Surely, you'd like some clean clothes?"

Teodor straightened slightly; suspicious but listening. He turned as the younger Borg tottered to his feet, trying to reattach a piece of skin that had fallen loose from his cheek where Teodor had kicked him. After a few moments of patting the flap of flesh into place, he ripped it free and threw it into Teodor's lap. Teodor stared down at the square of rotting flesh, which he could feel was cold and wet through the fine silk of the angel costume shirt. That was no mistake, when it came to accuracy – whether with blades, bullets, or pieces of flesh, the Battle Borgs of the Dodecahedron never missed. Why had he kicked the man-machine? Had he wanted to hurt it?

They want to hurt you!

Beyond the younger Borg unzipped a large canvas kit bag. Teodor recognized it as military kit designed to carry 45kg or 90kg or more of equipment into battle. The bag was large enough to…

"No!" Teodor protested, as he realized what they were about to do. He once more kicked out at the approaching Borg, but this time the machine punched him hard in the belly and kicked his legs away.

"Don't." Teodor curled himself into a tight defensive ball, as the Borg raised its metal fist once more.

"Stop!" The older Borg ordered. "I think Teodor will be reasonable. Won't you, Teodor?"

Teodor spit blood from where his head had smashed against the metal shelf and did his best not to tremble and cower as the Borg reached behind him to unlock his chains.

Teodor looked apprehensively at the large black kit bag; its zip gaped open like a mouth.

"No!" Teodor protested, struggling to his feet as his chains fell away. He backed up to the wall, trying to put space between himself and the Borgs, trying to find a way to escape. As he looked right then left, vertigo assailed him. Once again, he stood in space high above the city, and the transparent wall appeared to disappear. Without warning, he bent double and was sick.

The nearest Borg reached forward, shoved Teodor's head fully between his knees, then he picked him up and pushed him inside the black bag.

Teodor could not help but whimper.

"Please, I am your prince."

They pushed him back down so his knees were under his chin. He squirmed and twisted to wrap his arms around his legs and hug them close, as they zipped him into darkness.

What are you doing to me? Where are you taking me?

Chapter 5

A Hero's Nightmare

"Uncle..." Nuria peered into the dark bedroom. She had raced back to the Embassy from the Dodecahedron Dome, her uncle Nikato had been in a meeting, and Uncle Karl was still in bed.

Was he still asleep? She reached out to him, and his thoughts filled her mind.

Karl's dream was a patchwork of memories. He dreamt he was flying. Fast and low above the Sas Darona Savannah. Where was he going? What was he doing, flying so quickly? Then Nuria saw it. A line of white fire shot high into the sky.

Was that the shield?

Where was he? In his dream, Karl accelerated fast then braked hard. What followed was a jumble of memories.

Mezzatorra was a crashed shuttle wedged on a rocky outcrop. Too valuable to be abandoned, it was ideal for a remote centre of cybernetic entomology.

"Mezzatorra. Permission to land?"

No reply, only a babble of panicked voices and shouts.

What was going on in Mezzatorra?

"Negative, Karl, negative. For God's sake, get out of here!"

Karl looked down; he was holding a Dome medallion. He ran his thumb over the circle of letters:

Loyal to Empire, Fear only God.

The Dome Militant thought Nuria. Her uncle had seen them, but what were the Dome Militant of Earth doing attacking Mezzatorra?

The medallion morphed into a glass brick with a small ecosystem inside; soil, plants, minute flowers, and... a cloud of insects exploded outwards then swarmed towards his face and poured like water into his eyes and the passages of his nose. Nuria felt the sharp bites as they attacked the gums of his mouth and the soft tissue of his ear. To Nuria, it was as if her whole head was engulfed in flames.

LOCK DOWN SAS DARONA. LOCK IT ALL DOWN.

Nuria screamed.

"Nuria!" Karl woke with a start. "What are you doing here? What time is it?"

Karl stared at her.

"Oh, Uncle Karl, you must wake up. I have sensed Teodor, and I need you to take me to the Palace so I can tell the Regent."

"What? Have you been into the Dome already this morning? Tell me you had some security?"

"Yes, yes... but I woke up, and I had been dreaming of Teo all night, so I had to go. But I have seen him..."

Karl was already reaching for a shirt.

"Wait outside for me, I'll be dressed in two minutes."

Nuria nodded and headed to the door.

"Order a car and some security."

As he dressed, Karl walked to the window and pushed the curtain aside. The light reflected over the multi-faceted panes of the Dome, and Karl held up a hand to protect his eyes.

"Another Dome," he muttered. "Why are we doing this again?"

"Teo, he's nice," Nuria replied stubbornly.

Karl nodded. "Not a good reason," he thought. At his side, Nuria sighed. Karl smiled, but still, his gaze drifted to Buckingham Palace on the far side of the river. He remembered the golden hair spilling over delicate features, and a long, slim neck. She was a queen, and the rulers of Dodecahedral chose their consorts carefully. Karl doubted there was a more beautiful woman in the empire.

"Uncle, the car is ready..." Nuria called.

He nodded – somewhere out there, a prince was waiting.

Chapter 6

Sea Gods and Mer People

As the door slid closed, Teodor kicked his way free of the canvas bag. He heaved the zip apart with his bare hands, and he leapt to his feet, ready to fight.

"Okay, you brutes, I'm ready," he declared.

Only, he was alone.

The Borgs had dumped him on the floor and left.

Teodor took a deep breath and checked his surroundings. Tiled walls, bright taps, a triple shower, and beside it, a deep, exotic bath. He walked to the bathtub, touched the delicate multi-colored mosaic on the surrounding walls, and half-smiled at the images of sea creatures and mythical sea folk.

Running his fingers across the controls for water, oils, and perfumes, he thought, "Nice." Leaning back against the bath, he examined the room; the floor was thickly carpeted and adorned with fluffy rugs. Everything was color-coordinated — bath, basins, towels, and carpet: gold and bright magenta, the Emperor's colors. It made his mother's best silver bathroom seem dull and merely functional in comparison. Across from the bath, the wall above and around the basins was a wall of gleaming golden mirrors.

Teodor looked at his reflection and examined himself, starting with his feet. Those stupid sandals, now tattered and dirt-caked. How filthy were his bruised and scarred limbs. How ridiculous the short white angel tunic looked now that it was stained. Were those bloodstains under his bruised and bleeding face? A dirty, haggard face, shaggy hair, large scared eyes, but he told himself firmly, "No tears, no tears yet."

He pulled his glance away and noticed clothes stacked on a low stool between the dual basins. Walking over, he saw that all the clothes were black.

"Of course," he thought.

With new purpose, he stepped toward the shower.

As Teodor straightened the collar, he realized that of all the strange fashion outfits he had been obliged to wear over the years, this was by far the most extraordinary. They had provided him with a complete uniform of a Dome Militant Apprentice. If the press caught a photo of him dressed like this, it would be guaranteed to make both the tea-time news and the front page.

Funny, he thought, it's a set of black training trousers and jacket with yellow-gold details. The undershirt and laces were black but with a luminescent edge at the neckline and cuffs – gold and black - a striking but not an unusual combination. No, it was the Dodecahedron Dome embroidered on his right breast that looked so strange. He spoke the motto once more to himself:

"Loyal to Empire. Fear only God."

It meant that the Dome Militant's first loyalty was to the Emperor and the twelve planets of Dodecahedral. It also meant the only thing they feared was God, neither man nor machine, certainly not any United Races laws. What made them think they were justified in kidnapping their prince?

He sighed and, since he could think of nothing else, he picked up the stained, ripped angel costume and dropped it in a small bin. He heard an automatic door open and looked back to where he had come in. No, it was still locked shut. The movement had come from another direction. A section of the mirror had slipped away. He strolled over, glancing once more at his reflection. No, he decided, he did not look like himself – but at least he did not look like the broken, dirty boy he had seen in the mirror a brief time before.

"Calm, Teodor. Control." Unbidden, Tilson's encouragement came to mind. He straightened his shoulders and stepped toward the opening.

Teodor paused.

Dare he go any further?

On the other side was someone he knew. Chart Segat, the mayor of all Domeside and head of the Dodecahedron Dome. This man knew his mother and had been friends with his father. More than friends, it was Chart Segat who had executed King Serge's dream to build the Dome Militant fighting force. Where his father had had the vision, Chart Segat had the knowledge of how to make this come about.

So, was he free? Teodor hesitated. Was it not Chart Segat who had killed his father and brother? The bomb under their vehicle had been from the Dome Militant armory – so, as the head of the Dome Militant forces, Chart Segat was to blame; even though he had always claimed to be innocent. Still, he knew Chart Segat - surely this man would help him?

Teodor realized that he should have moved or done something. He should not be standing in the doorway. Chart Segat was in conversation with a Dome Militant soldier.

"Maybe he was free to go," Teodor thought. He looked around for an exit. There was a distant double door, with the two Borgs who had brought him standing guard. "So not that way."

Then, he glanced in the other direction. What he had thought was a mirrored wall, was, in fact, a glass wall – transparent on one side, mirrored on the other. From where he was sitting, Chart Segat had watched him as he showered.

Teodor was outraged. He strode forward, bristling with anger.

"Chart Segat, how dare you?"

The man looked up at him, glanced over to the bathroom, and smirked.

"Now, Teo - wait your turn."

He turned back to where a young Dome Militant was showing him a moving image on his Communicator, Chart Segat said.

"But this is all the evidence you have?" Chat said. They both peered at a fuzzy image on the screen. Teodor thought it looked like one frame, a still taken from a film. It was out of focus; either that or it was a ghost.

"How dare he? How dare he ignore me?" He wanted to shout, but a second voice cautioned him to be careful - after all, this man was implicated in the death of his father - even though King Serge and Chart Segat had been friends. Still, Teodor was about to demand that he be freed, when he heard the Militant say.

"I was right behind him, Chartsie. I saw him change. It was a Zaracan soldier. The explosion had injured two men. No, not men: brothers, twin brothers. I heard him gasp, swear, something. When I looked, he was right there, a Zaracan soldier. Then he switched back to being a Dome Militant."

A Zaracan soldier? Where?

"Are you telling me a Zaracan infiltrator led the attack on Mezzatorra?" Chart Segat asked.

"His idea, his plan, his leadership..." The young fighter confirmed.

Zaracan? Mezzatorra? It was the name of a base on Sas Darona. It had been much in the news; Teodor could not remember why. But was not Sas Darona in lockdown? Teodor looked at the Dome Militant youth with interest. He was tanned. Had he recently returned from Sas Darona? But how?

"Mezzatorra?" Teodor repeated aloud.

Both turned towards him.

"What?" gasped the Militant, who noticed him for the first time.

Chart Segat laughed. "He's from the Riffaut. Forgot to go home after last night's party."

Teodor decided he would pretend not to understand what Chart Segat meant, so he said crossly, "I am Prince Teodor of Earth, and this season I am wearing House Riffaut."

"He's good, isn't he?" joked Chart Segat.

The Militant had fallen silent.

"Chart Segat, may I have your Communicator?" Teodor pressed on. "I need to call my mother and tell her I am ok."

For one moment, Teodor thought Chart Segat might indulge him. He would pass him a Communicator, and he would be on his way home. Holding his elation at bay, Teodor picked up a sugar roll from the breakfast trolley, ripped off a corner, and ate it. He sensed rather than saw the Militant's surprise but ignored him. Teodor had noticed cameras pointed towards the bathroom. This revelation shocked him. He had been naked in the shower, and they had filmed him? Who had a copy of that film, those images? Was someone else watching?

He found he was coughing with indignation, choking on the sugared bread in his mouth. With raw anger, he turned back to Chart Segat.

"Chart Segat, I demand that you let me go."

The man was watching him closely. Their eyes met.

"I don't think so, Teo."

Teodor squared his shoulders. "I am Prince Teodor of Earth. You owe me your obedience."

Chart Segat snorted in contempt. "I owe you nothing."

"You there!" Now Teodor addressed the Militant standing across from him. "Pass me your Communicator. I must call my mother."

"Ignore him, Des."

The Dome Militant looked at Chart Segat. Teodor pressed on. "Des, is it? Des Parks?" Teodor knew by the look of horror on the young man's face that he was right. But was it him? Teodor had picture posters of Dome Militant blades champions in his bedroom. Only Des no longer looked like his picture.

It's the tan, he thought, and the hair. Sas Darona! Oh, I must call my mother!

"Remind me, Des. What is the oath you swore when you joined the Dome Militant? I'll tell you. You swore to serve your regent and protect the empire. So, Des Parks, give me your Communicator."

Teodor held out his hand. His fingers almost touched the coveted device. He had used the name three times on purpose. Across from him, the young guard was so startled, the jug slipped from his hand, and milk spilled over the plates and tray.

Des turned to Chart Segat. "He's not from the Riffaut, is he?"

"You may go, Des," Chart Segat murmured. The young man hesitated. His mouth opened and closed several times, until finally he said, "This ain't right, Chartsie."

"YOU MAY GO, DES."

The youth snapped to attention; the blood had drained from his face.

Teodor was elated. 'This ain't right.' A fighter, a Dome Militant had said that. 'Ain't right.' Surely, he would tell someone? Only, Teodor recognized all too well the fear in the other's face. As the door closed, Teodor realized he would soon be alone.

"Make sure Guy is ready." Chart Segat called out to the departing soldier. "Tell him to have his blades ready."

Des Parks frowned. Guy Erma, Teodor wondered, where had he heard that name? Des Parks looked from Chart Segat to himself and back again. This time, Teodor realized he had no idea what the soldier was thinking.

"Oh, and Des?" Chart Segat held up his index and thumb closed tight together in a mime that said, "Keep it quiet."

The door closed. If Teodor had hoped for some last-minute change, some chance of rescue, it had been in vain. Of course, these men were loyal to Chart Segat, and why not? Chart Segat ruled supreme within the Dodecahedron Dome. As the door closed, Teodor remembered: This ain't right.

There was hope in those three words, Teodor thought, as he turned back to Chart Segat. He would not give up. Not yet.

"This is about the Dodecahedron Debate, isn't it? Even if you force a change, it will only be overturned once I am free." Teodor stepped a little closer and tried persuasion: "My mother would be grateful if you were to free me now."

"Yes, your mother must be worried. But don't you see, Teo? Your mother only has one son to worry about. I have one hundred thousand boys and men for whom I am responsible. What will happen to them when the Dome is closed?"

Teodor paused to consider. "I don't think my mother intends to shut down the Dodecahedron, I mean the Dome." He wondered if this was a terrible secret to have revealed, so he added: "Not forever, anyway."

"And she thinks she can run the Dome without me?" Chart Segat sneered.

So that was his grievance, thought Teodor.

"I will speak to my mother if you like, but ultimately you must face trial for the murder of my father," Teodor paused, "And my brother."

Too late. He realized this last remark had been a mistake.

"I didn't kill the baby boy," yelled Chart Segat. He was referencing the terrible headlines denouncing him as a baby killer as well as the king's assassin: "I didn't kill either of them. It wasn't my men that set the bomb. Ten of my Militants were killed in that explosion. Do you think I would murder my blood? For that's what they are. These men, these boys, they are my blood."

Teodor knew Chart Segat had always denied any involvement in his father's death. To hear him speak so eloquently, to see his distress, for a few moments, Teodor was inclined to believe him.

"In that case, you have nothing to fear. " He said gently. "The courts will prove you innocent."

"Innocent. No, it's you who are innocent. Naïve! If you believe that the truth comes out in a court of law."

"Chart Segat, I am your prince and your future king. Let me go, and I swear I will speak with my mother."

"Future king! Just look at you. Without the Royal Guard, you are nothing."

"This is outrageous. The Dome Militant belongs to my father."

Out of nowhere, a hand sprang out and pulled Teodor forward by the nape of his neck. "And now, the Dome Militant belongs to me." Teodor's face was inches from Chart Segat's, as he whispered. "You think I killed your father and brother - I didn't. Who told your mother it was me? Who is advising her to unseat me during this Dome Debate? Who is it who sits in her drawing room even more frequently than yourself? Don't tell me you haven't noticed his snake-like presence, no matter how expensive are the silks he wears."

"There have been complaints from the Zaracan Democratic Union," Teodor said hesitantly, "over actions taken by the Dome Militant on Sas Darona. The agreement was for a small training base." He finished the sentence with a bit more confidence.

"Huh, you think? You believe this? Why, who told you? Who told you it was a Dome Militant bomb under your father's car? Your mother needs to stop listening to those Valvanskis and listen instead to her people, her own kind."

"I am sure my mother does listen," Teodor protested.

"Your mother! Well, if she listens... You might survive. I won't kill you, my prince, but the actions your mother takes may very well result in your death if the vote goes against me at this afternoon's Dome Debate. Who will control the Borgs? They like fresh meat, and they like to play with their meat too. So, your only question should be: How long will they toy with you, my Borgs, hey? How long before they finally kill you? An hour, six hours, a day?"

Teodor opened his mouth to speak, but no words came. He went to move, but found he was frozen to the spot. He stared at Chart Segat, yet all he could feel was horror. The mask of jovial eccentricity had fallen from Chart Segat's features, and for the first time, Teodor saw the ruthless ambition of the man. At the very last, he dropped his gaze, only to hear Chart Segat say: "Take him away."

The same two giant Borgs stepped forth. Teodor felt his spirit quail as he looked into their soulless eyes. The first Borg grabbed him and spoke. "Head between your knees."

Teodor could do nothing but comply as another cyborg appeared and tied his elbows together behind his knees so tightly his head was locked in position, before roughly turning him over. Tied up like a sack with his bottom as the base, they grabbed him by the ankles and hauled him up. Pain immediately cut into his arms from the tie: pain from the weight of his hanging body. Teodor tensed, pulling up on his arms and legs. The pain receded for a few moments, but as he released, it came back with twofold intensity. With little time to think, he was dropped into a military backpack and a capsule of sleeping salts was thrown in with him. The light disappeared as the bag was zipped closed, and he was hoisted onto someone's back.

The prince struggled. He discovered the bag had a vertical stripe of netting down one side. He pressed his face against the laces and found he could breathe clean air. The guards were moving at a rapid jog. He wrestled to find a more comfortable position, managing to free his head, but he was rewarded by a random punch that whacked his shoulder and back, only inches from his neck and head.

"Ow!" he cried out, but the only reply was another punch, this time striking his thighs. The blow also caught his hand, cruelly twisting one of his fingers. "In God's name, will nobody help me?"

Even as Teodor struggled against his confinement, he thought he heard his mother; her voice was inside his head. 'Teodor, where are you?'

He stopped moving. Someone was calling him. Through the netting on the side of the backpack, he could see he was on a cyborg's back. They stood atop the flying disk, but he could also see further. Looking out, he glimpsed Buckingham Palace through the panes of the Dome on the far side of the river. He had heard the voice coming from the palace. Goran thought-control was a form of low-level telepathy. Teodor had never appreciated it might range this far.

"I'm in the Dodeca... do-dec. I'm in the Dome, in a backpack, I'm upside down. They kicked me."

"Where are you?" The voice was like a whisper.

"Mother?"

"No, my name is Karl."

"You need to help me," Teodor said. "Stop these Borgs, free me."

"I don't know where you are. We are connected. I can see what you see, hear what you hear, feel what you feel - provided the distance is not too far, but I can't actually SEE you."

"I need to escape," Teodor pleaded.

"I know and I'm sorry," the voice faded.

Teodor saw they had descended behind the massive sports stadium, and he no longer had direct sight of Buckingham Palace. He closed his eyes and concentrated, but the contact was gone. Had she heard him? What had he said? Why had he been so stupid? He had told her about the kicking. He should have told her Chart Segat was involved. Frustrated, he moved around to find a comfortable position. The sleeping capsules had fallen close to his face. The smell made him feel sick. Another slap and a threatening growl.

"Just shut up and sleep. If you know what's good for you, you'll be quiet and sleep."

Teodor was impossibly uncomfortable. His back, arms, and legs were all at awkward angles. Despite everything, the sleeping drugs were powerful. He started to drift off.

He heard the voice one last time.

"Don't give up. I will save you."

Chapter 7

Building Trust

"So, what do you think?" Sayginn looked across her breakfast table. She did not know what she thought. Karl was tall and strong. She read wisdom and fierceness in equal measure in his face, but her eyes also wandered to his lean, muscular physique. Sayginn wondered what would happen if the Emperor walked in and found the Zaracan here. Why had he brought the girl?

Nuria Valvanchi was such a plain thing and somewhat annoying in her intensity. If only she would sit still; what was wrong with her? She was supposed to be a Princess – this girl was nothing like the polished girls of the Dodecahedral court. But she was a Zaracan.

Had the emperor always disliked the Valvanchis of Zarac? Sayginn could not remember. For many years, he had called them alien enemies and was openly critical of their interference in the affairs of the Dodecahedral Empire. Sayginn wondered if she should send Karl away or ring and invite someone else to join them. If the Emperor did discover her alone with these Valvanchis, he would be furious. She did not want to alienate him, when likely as not she would be forced to marry him very soon. Keep it business-like, she thought.

"Last night someone left this paper in my car; it was a report on Mezzatorra, and it mentioned your name. What exactly happened there?"

"We have to tell her about Prince Teodor," Nuria pleaded with her uncle in her thought voice.

"Not yet," Karl replied. "She doesn't know us. She doesn't trust us."

"But they were carrying him in a rucksack."

"They were keeping him alive; we have to be careful; she might think we planned this thing."

"Yes but,"

"Nuria, first we do this..." Karl put an end to their telepathic conversation.

"Yes, Mezzatorra was a tragedy," Karl said aloud as he turned back to the Regent. Sayginn sat in silence after Karl had told her everything. "I don't know if you know it, but Mezzatorra is the name of a crashed shuttle. Too valuable to be completely abandoned, it proved ideal as a base for research into the Sas Darona plague, in particular, the exponential multiplication of the plague-bearing flies and how to reverse or halt it. When the Dome Militant attacked—"

"There was no proof it was the Dome Militant," Sayginn cut in.

"Whoever attacked the research station, they released the plague. We had no choice but to deploy a protective fire dome fueled by monazite-9."

"Ugh, monazite-9 powered – that must be expensive."

"Not really," Karl shrugged.

"So, it's true then, there are reserves of monazite-9 on Sas Darona."

Karl did not reply; he just shook his head as he concluded. "The fire dome saved the entire region, but all those left inside died."

"Surely research into the Sas Darona plague is terribly dangerous; why would you do it?"

"What interested our scientists was the cy-sects' ability to reproduce."

"You mean the crystallization when a body turns into a colony of plague insects?"

Sayginn had taken time to research insects the night before. She had watched with mounting horror the images of animals being attacked and crystallizing into colonies of plague flies. She had not looked at the images of similar human suffering, but Karl, she knew, had witnessed just that. He had sat on one side of the fire shield while a few feet away, colleagues and friends died of the plague.

"It's horrific, yes, but it's also amazing from a scientific point of view. One insect self-replicates one hundred thousand times. This ability is something we would like to see in our miniature robots, our nanites – the gains to our industry could be..."

"But the risks?" Sayginn interrupted. "Didn't you think about the possibility of an attack by the SDLA?"

Sayginn found it hard to imagine any part of life that did not include a concern for security and the possibility of terror.

Karl shook his head. "The SDLA is made up of primitives. Our base had a secure vault. They should never have penetrated. No, someone gave the SDLA advanced explosives. And Dome medallions were found..."

Sayginn hated the word 'primitives.' The Sas Darona tribes' nomadic culture saw them hunting two to three hours a day, with many hours left to develop exquisite arts and crafts. On Earth, it was widely considered a precursor to modern human existence; some held romantic views about tribal life, ignoring the high infant mortality and short life span. Yet Karl had also mentioned Dome medallions, so Sayginn started to protest:

"You can't blame the Dome Militant just because you found a Dome medallion. You have been on Earth a few days; you can see how commonplace they are – all the boys, all the young men. There is a hierarchy. Apparently, some have special engravings, and some metal colors are particularly rare, but a Dome medallion is as much a fashion icon as a symbol of armed conflict."

"Indeed, I can see that, but on Sas Darona, and outside this system, a Dome medallion only means one thing: Dome Terror. The Dome Militant is becoming infamous for their activities around the star gates, and of late, they have been more brazen in their illegal mining on Sas Darona. The Dome must close, Sayginn."

Sayginn wanted to say Sas Darona should be part of the Dodecahedral, even if it meant the empire had thirteen planets instead of twelve; after all, the tribes were human. But she held her tongue. Instead, she drank some tea and said:

"How would you feel if the Dome stayed open, but I was in charge?"

This time, it was Karl's turn to play for time, taking a bite from his breakfast roll and stirring his drink thoughtfully.

"Unfortunately, it's not me you have to convince."

Sayginn nodded as she took a quick inventory of her feelings. It had been a long time since she had felt so attracted to any man. Here she was, drinking her tea, wondering whether he liked the pose she had taken with her cup hanging loosely on one finger. Had he noticed how her hair was loose – not pulled back, as was her habit? Did he mind that she was wearing goran jockey silks and fine wool leggings? Did he find her casual attire attractive? If the Emperor had been in Karl's place, he would have thought her pose flirtatious, perhaps even a tease. But what of Karl? Did he even like her?

At Karl's side, Nuria had stood up. "Ok enough, uncle - Teodor is in danger – we have to tell her." Nuria's telepathic rebuke was impatient.

Sayginn looked at her annoyed, so Nuria reached to grab a breakfast roll and sat down again. She took one bite, then with a frown placed it back on her plate.

"I have to tell her!" she said telepathically to Karl. He shrugged, so Nuria turned to the Regent.

"We are Valvanchi, and we have special powers. Has anyone explained to you about the power of telepathic connection?"

Sayginn looked put out; the jockeys were racing the gorans across the lawns, she should be out there with them.

"Yes, Princess, I know about the telepathic connection. You made one with Prince Teodor yesterday - when you were riding gorans. Did you think you would be such an experienced jockey after only one ride, if you were not connected to my son, who has been riding all his life?"

"Yes, I connected with Prince Teodor. And I am still connected."

Sayginn stepped away from the window and looked at Karl, who nodded once – she turned with new interest to Nuria.

"I felt him this morning," Nuria said. "I think I know where he is."

"Why didn't you say so at once?"

"We wanted you to trust us," Karl said. He snapped his fingers, and all at once, he was himself again. Tall, white, cropped hair; pale, cream skin, and eyes alight with his special powers. Across from him, Sayginn did a double take and stepped back. The change had been instantaneous, and it was shocking. One moment she had been looking into the face of a Domeside man, the next she faced an alien. Karl did not know whether he should be relieved or insulted by this more honest reaction. Clearly, his disguise was effective and convincing, but if Sayginn did like him – and he was beginning to think she might – she was less enamored with his race as a whole.

"Despite everything, Sas Darona, Mezzatorra, the United Races, we are on your side. We two; we want to save Teodor."

"We think you may have a shot of him if we could check the security footage you are collecting. I can show you," Nuria said.

"I have to dress," Sayginn said. She took out her Communicator. "Patrice, I am sending you the Princess Nuria; she has some information - we can trust her."

Nuria stood up.

"Do you know where to go?" Sayginn asked.

"Thank you," Nuria nodded and fled.

Karl was left behind. He went to leave, only Sayginn stopped him with a hand wave.

"Why were you flirting with me?"

"I wanted you to trust us, me – I'm not my family." He shrugged.

"You should have told me you had information about Teodor straight away..." Sayginn replied. "I am his mother, after all." She turned and headed back to stand looking out at her gardens, but not before adding, "What is it you want, Karl Valvanchi?"

Karl knew this had been his cue to depart, yet something had changed. She did not want him to go, and for his part, he had never seen someone so sorrowful yet so beautiful. On instinct, Karl followed her to the window and stood a moment – the morning light shining on his face.

"I thought you were supposed to marry the Emperor?"

"Marry him, give up my planets and my rule, and become the mother to four new sons," Sayginn replied bitterly then, looking at him. "Is that what you want too? Power, marriage, and sons?"

"My five-year marriage contract won't be renewed. I have two sons on Zarac 1. So no, not sons..."

Sayginn was confused by this answer. Karl sounded like he was talking to himself. Slowly, Sayginn leaned in towards him and kissed him lightly on the cheek. Karl looked a little taken aback. It was a kiss, a kiss on the cheek, but still a kiss. Then Sayginn said:

"Go with my blessing, Karl Valvanchi. Go and save my son. Do whatever it takes."

This time, she kissed him on the lips. Karl stared down at her, then quickly checked the room. He had glanced at the servants, only robots. He also looked at the door. Yes, it was closed, Sayginn thought, as she once again imagined the Emperor coming through that door and discovering her with Karl Valvanchi. It was as if she wanted to be discovered. Then, she felt his arm around her waist, and he pulled her close.

"You didn't answer my question," her voice was little more than a sigh. "What is it you want?"

He looked down at her one last time and said:

"I want what I cannot have."

And then he kissed her.

'IN GOD'S NAME, WILL NOBODY HELP ME?" Teodor's voice rang out clearly. It was like a bolt of lightning through Sayginn, who fell back from Karl's arms and spun around to look at the Dome. How was this possible? Karl wondered. But of course. The mother. Sayginn had the closest of all connections with her son. The kiss between them had triggered a strong telepathic connection.

"Kiss me!' Karl told Sayginn using his telepathic voice to compel her.

Sayginn sank into his embrace, and Karl once again connected to Teodor. He swerved, giddy from blood pumping in his head. He felt a sharp pain in the fingers of one hand. Karl's senses were overwhelmed by the smell of sickness, and -

"Sleeping gas!' Sayginn thought. Her breath came out in gasps as she saw what Teodor saw, felt what he felt.

"Speak to him," urged Karl.

"Teodor, where are you?" Sayginn asked.

"I'M IN THE DOME. IN A BACKPACK. I'M UPSIDE DOWN. THEY KICKED ME."

The words were clear enough but were jumbled together, with a quick succession of images. Then, nothing.

"Let me try," urged Karl, and he grasped her around the waist and pulled her close. "Let me tune into your love for him."

"MOTHER?" They both jolted to hear him, his voice as clear as if he stood in the room.

"No, my name is Karl."

"I need to escape..." Teodor pleaded.

"I know and I'm sorry..."

Teodor continued talking, describing his situation, but his voice seemed to spiral away from them until it was just a whisper of misery, and Karl cut in at the last moment to say, "Don't give up. I will save you."

Karl waited, clinging to the Regent and searching for Teodor through her desperate love.

"He's gone," Karl gently detached himself from her embrace.

"What do you mean he's gone?" Sayginn squealed. Karl realized she thought Teodor was dead.

"No, not that. He's fine. He disappeared out of range. I thought I saw an image of a disk transport in his thoughts, and a military bag." Karl had seen a lot in Teodor's thoughts that he did not want to tell Sayginn, not until he made sense of it. He had made a mental recording of the few instants they had been in contact and already, he had rerun the memory three times. There were faces and places, but also harsh words and rough treatment. The insights made him truly afraid for the prince. Now, more than ever, he knew he could not leave that fifteen-year-old boy to face the might and menace of the Dome alone.

"Yes, I saw the bag, and it felt like I was flying." Sayginn said.

Karl looked across the river to the Dome. He already had a theory as to why and how the brief encounter had come about. From where they stood, they could look out through the window, across the gardens and the river, and through the panes of the Dome to the Cap of the Dome.

"You know there is disk transport in the dome?" He pointed. "The disks fly up to the cap."

"He was flying down..." Sayginn interrupted. Karl stroked her hair and kissed the parting of her golden hair.

"Yes, I thought so too... But the disk passed behind one of the buildings; at this range, it would block the contact, but at least we had a brief connection."

"That was him. In real time." Again, her spoken voice; she sounded sad and tired.

"In real time. Now tell me everything you remember. Everything."

"His hair was wet. I felt that, and I thought he was wearing a Dome Militant uniform. What did you see?"

"I caught glimpses of all sorts of things in his mind. But wet hair means he probably had a shower. Clothes too, it means they are taking care of him."

"But the disks only travel to and from the Cap of the Dome. Chart Segat has his bedroom up there. And his bathroom... There are horrible rumors." She paused – panic was swelling inside her. Karl reached out to her with comforting thoughts, but she brushed them aside and replied in quiet despair: "Oh Karl, we have to free him."

"Sssh. I scanned him for injuries. There was some bruising, and he was hungry, but I think he was mostly unharmed."

She did not ask how or why, only sobbed one heartfelt sob, then, pulling herself together, she coughed and said with determination:

"We should go downstairs. They are tracking all movements. They will have monitored the disk."

At that moment, and seeing the turmoil inside her head, Karl wanted to kiss her, only he knew it was not the time. He just nodded, and they headed down.

Downstairs in the ballroom, hastily converted to a military headquarters, Princess Nuria of Zarac and Patrice Macey of Earth were standing by the desk of a young analyst. Nuria already had them looking through videos of the disk rising and falling from the circular door to the Cap of the Dome. Sayginn and Karl hurried to join them as the analysts had pulled up the most recent video. They watched two Dome Militant Battle Borgs standing on a disk floating down from the Cap of the Dome.

"Can we zoom in on that backpack?" Karl said.

"Oh, look – it's moving!" Sayginn whispered, not wishing for anyone to know what she thought until her fears were confirmed.

"Ouch!' muttered Karl, seeing a Borg kick the bag.

"I knew they hit him," Nuria said. "I felt it too, it really hurt."

"Can you feel Teo now?" Sayginn asked.

"No, he's too far away. There are too many obstacles, but when I am in the Dodecahedron, when he is in the open..."

"Regrettably, Nuria doesn't have her full powers yet," Karl explained.

"Can we magnify the image?" Nuria pointed to the screen. "Is that lacing down the side? Focus there."

Above their heads, as the camera zoomed in, a face was pressed up against the netting of the backpack. The head was upside down, and the skin distorted where the lace bit into it, but the eye was wide open, and it was a clear blue.

"Iris identification," the analyst said. Then, after a moment: "It's a match." Leaping up, he shouted: "We have first contact! We have seen him."

Every head in the room turned toward them. Chairs creaked as analysts stood up, and there was the clatter of staff running forward to look. Within an instant, a crowd of soldiers and analysts looked at the screens, now showing several views of the floating disk, its passengers, the backpack, and the face and eye peering from the side netting. A huge cheer rang out.

Patrice Macey called them to attention.

"Ok, everybody! Heads up."

He pointed up, they all turned to look. At the center of the main wall was a clock; it read twenty-three hours, fifteen minutes. It was the amount of time Teodor had been missing. Briefly, another statistic flashed across the screen in amber letters: 64%. It was the probability of finding Teodor alive. It was a life statistic. All the historical data was clear – the longer the prince was gone, the less likely it was that he would return without injury, or even at all. Karl could see the emotion building up inside of Sayginn as she looked at the numbers on the wall; then, she gasped. Patrice Macey tapped his Communicator, and the timing changed. With this new sighting, Teodor had been missing for only thirteen minutes, and his chance of survival shot back up to 83%.

Patrice nodded with satisfaction and addressed the crowd:

"Ok, everyone, get to work. This is a hot lead; we have to get on top of it." Then, to Nuria, Sayginn, and Karl: "C'mon. I'll bring you up to date."

Karl and Nuria walked with Sayginn around the ballroom, listening and watching. All the time, he was waiting for the information on the flying disk – where had it come from and - where had it gone. It turned out the disks were outside the monitoring of the main Dome systems, and only visual files were available. Analysts scrambled to rectify the issue. The only information they had was that the disk had returned into the Dome Militant Military complex, but there were no audio or video feeds available. None of the three Battle Borgs on the disk had been seen since, and none had been identified.

"Those Borgs are so old, I am surprised they are still in service," Patrice remarked.

Sayginn looked at the close-up photos. They were unmistakably Battle Borgs of the Dome Militant, with their massive metallic structure, mottled cracked skin, and mechanical eyes. She couldn't think of more terrifying jailors for her son.

"Surely, they are still cyborgs, and cyborgs are programmed to obey a direct order from Teodor. Do you think he has forgotten that?"

"Until we can identify those Borgs, we cannot know whether they are modified. The iris scan showed signs of drugs. Maybe Teodor is not entirely conscious," Patrice responded.

"He would know they should obey a direct order. He would know," Sayginn repeated. "We should send our men to check the military prison bank again."

"We did that yesterday, but there were prolonged delays in getting access. If he was there, they had plenty of time to move him," Nuria explained.

"We need to catch them unawares," Karl suggested.

"They have prisons in the Dome Militant barracks complex; he must be there," Nuria said.

"We should also send a forensics team into the Cap of the Dome. If he was up there, we should find a trace of him – particularly if he used the bathroom. If we find that, we can pin this kidnapping on Chart Segat," Patrice said. "We are still waiting for permission to gain access to the Cap; we sent a request yesterday. Freddie went there for a party, but they won't let our people anywhere near."

"Why not?" Sayginn sounded petulant. Karl was surprised that she seemed to believe Chart Segat would or should cooperate, when it was staring her in the face that he was the one who had orchestrated the kidnapping. Ultimately, he realized she thought herself a force for good and expected her people to think the same.

"See no evil, hear no evil, know no evil. They don't want us to know what goes on up there," Patrice replied.

"It should not be allowed to add lead to buildings," Nuria added. "I couldn't scan the Cap of the Dome because there was lead in the walls and floors."

Sayginn let out an exasperated sigh. Karl reached out to her with his thought voice:

"I don't need telepathy to do this. I can gain access to the Cap, and I can check the military prison."

Patrice was explaining the different legal procedures employed to force Chart Segat to comply, but Karl continued a conversation telepathically with Sayginn.

"I can go in undercover, and discreetly look for the prince or traces of the prince."

"And you won't get caught?'

"I am a telepathic shape-shifter from an advanced technological society, Sayginn."

Her eyes widened in alarm, and she glanced up at him with sudden wonder.

"They won't know what's hit them." He smiled and added. "Nevertheless, my regent, do I have your permission?"

"My permission... I'm begging you. Please." Her thoughts were brimming with delighted laughter. Karl smiled and bowed. He said his farewells and took his leave. He looked back at the door and saw Sayginn looking after him.

"Don't give the game away," he urged.

"I won't say anything; you're my secret weapon."

"I meant don't give the game away; you're my secret love.'

There was a pause, and even at this distance, he thought she might be blushing.

Patrice Macey was standing watching them; he had stopped talking a few minutes before.

"Thank you, Patrice," she said, choking on the words, but telepathically she sent a thought message to Karl. "I'll be careful, you're my secret love."

"Uncle!" Nuria called impatiently from the door.

Chapter 8

Strawberries for Breakfast

Guy Erma wiped his face with a small, ragged towel. It had been a mad rush setting up one stall on Dome Market Square for the morning crowds, then fighting through crazy traffic to set up another stall at the racecourse. Like last year, they had done it, and (Guy thought with a smile) they would probably do it again next year. The stand was perfect too, with old trellises covered by brand new boards and the awning decked with artificial greenery – all carefully washed and spruced up by Jukona's hard-working wife, whom Guy nicknamed in mock reverence: Mrs. Juke. Only one item was on sale, served in little plastic boxes, placed atop a soft napkin, plump and red, the season's first strawberries.

Guy sniffed and licked the skin of the red fruit, but he did not eat it just yet. It was one of his free strawberries and a bribe from Jukona who, time and time again, reminded him, "You've got yours. Keep your hands off the rest of the stock."

Guy chuckled and put the fruit back into a hidden container. He adjusted two of the plastic boxes to slip a third into the back row and wiped a small spot of juice from the edge of the stand. Everything would be perfect today. He lightly snatched up his strawberry again, caught the torn skin with the sharp edge of his teeth, and pulled it away. With a high circular move, he pressed the fruit whole into his mouth. As he bit down, it exploded inside his cheeks; what pleasure!

Jukona was calling him. Guy hid his exasperation as the man repeated for the third time, "Yes, sir, the stall looks beautiful." He spoke slowly and deliberately. "Fit for Chart Segat, fit for an emperor, and the Emperor is going to see her too. Prime, prime site this, right next to the staircase, where all their fine, fine lordships will pass on their way to the Imperial balconies. No other site like it on the course! Royal Ascot Weekend!" On the final words, he stretched the vowels into a fervent chant: Roooyal, Aaaasscot, Weeeeiik'n.

Guy looked up speculatively at the empty, overlapping balconies, and eyed the magenta-carpeted stairway. The stairs led up to the VIP suites. The Emperor had one, of course. Did Chart Segat have one too? Would they see him? Would he serve them? Last year, he and Jukona had a small stall far from the center – was this new location a chance thing? Had Chart Segat made the change? Did he have that power?

Guy was still speculating when Des Parks arrived. Unsurprisingly for a Champion Blades Fighter, he had a pack of fighting blades and protection gear; what he said though was a surprise.

"C'mon, I need to work out with you - check if you're as good as they all say."

"I'm working," stuttered Guy, not sure he was hearing correctly. Train with the legendary Des Parks?

Des made a show of looking around the quiet racecourse and idly chatting with stallholders. Royal Ascot was due to open to the public at 11 am – there were thirty minutes to go, and the market traders, who had arrived at six, were long since ready.

"Not now, you're not. Ask Juke," Des replied.

"Juke, can I take a break?" Guy asked.

"What for?" It was a gruff reply.

"It's me, Juke. I have to prep Guy for a blades demonstration later today." It was the first Guy had heard of any blades demonstrations; he looked up, interested. Des just shook his head, so Guy knew not to ask. Des added hurriedly, "I'll have him back by eleven."

"Ok, go on then, but no later than eleven fifteen, mind you. I know what you boys and your blades are like," Juke said with a warning tone.

"Good," said Des in an undertone. "We've got to get you something to eat."

"I have eaten, Des," Guy replied, not quite believing his luck.

"Half-a-dozen stolen strawberries don't make a meal, Guy. A fighter must start his day with breakfast. And you have a busy day ahead of you." Guy grinned. "Did you hear what happened to Seb last night?"

"Sebastian of the Riffaut?" Guy said with an affected toss of his hair, then seeing Des frown, for Seb was Des's best friend. "No, what?"

"There was you, worried about Marline, and at the same time Seb started drinking. He so annoyed Chartsie, he had him locked up."

"What?"

"Safest place for him. I know Seb is upset by this kidnapping of Prince Teodor, him being a lookalike and all, but he needs to keep his mouth shut."

"Poor Seb," Guy agreed, "and the Militants have still not been mobilised."

"Nope. I guess not." Des said, he looked glum. Both he and Guy knew the Dome Militant were the only real hope Teodor might be found. So why had they not been mobilised. "What do you want to eat?" Des asked changing the subject.

A short while later, they were munching on breakfast rolls of meat and eggs with steaming hot drinks alongside. Guy was also unlacing the pack of blades he always had stowed in his backpack. He knelt to help Des with his cuffs and calf shields first, as he was the junior fighter.

"I looked up Mezzatorra on the system," Guy said. "What is the exponential entomological investigation?"

"You don't want to know." Des changed the subject. "I need you to look at this. There's not very much footage of this young chap, surprisingly enough, but this is from yesterday. I think it is a level five display."

"I know entomology is the study of insects, but how are insects exponential? It doesn't make sense."

Guy moved his hand in the shape of an exponential curve.

"Calf greaves, Guy," Des said.

Guy bent to lace on his lower leg protection.

"Did you get a chance to look around? The system said Mezzatorra was a United Race beacon science institute. That means it was unique, doing different experiments."

"The study of Sas Darona plague," Des said. "That's what the scientists did at Mezzatorra."

"Did?" Guy asked.

"They are all dead. That's what the Dome Militant did, ok? That's all the Dome Militant ever does. Now, will you look at the screen?"

Guy said nothing. If the Dome Militant had killed the scientists, they must have had a good reason. He looked at the small screen Des had unfolded onto the table. On the screen was a youth wearing a diamond protective shirt and performing a display on a pristine, circular, blades mat, laid out on a small lawn at the entrance of Horse Guards Parade stables.

"That's Prince Teodor," said Guy. He bit his tongue. Genius, why not say something stupid? Of course, it was Prince Teodor. Who else would wear a diamond shirt?

"Training, yesterday morning," Des added unnecessarily. "There were snippets on the news, but I downloaded the whole sequence. I don't know why they always criticize him. He's at least a level five, I would say."

"Blades is not about display. It's the fight that matters," Guy replied automatically. Nevertheless, he reran the demo sequence with interest.

"Is he fast, do you think?" Guy was having trouble concentrating because of the questions racing through his head. Why was Des training him? Why today? Why this video of Prince Teodor? Did this mean the fight might be reinstated? Was the prince not taken?

"Hard to tell, the camera distorts the action. But he's strong, and he's super fit," Des replied.

Guy nodded and tried to think of something else.

"He looks a bit heavy to me."

"Maybe, but see this," Des paused the film at the first clash between the prince and the blades expert. Guy watched carefully.

"Is that Tilson? Is he his instructor too? Was this yesterday? Tilson was late, I remember, he spoke to me."

Des shook his head dismissively. He rewound the film.

"There. Tilson is hitting him there. But look, he just takes it and bounces back – then bang! He hits back. Ouch! I would not like to be on the receiving end of that."

"Show me again." Guy rewound the film and slowed it down. Subconsciously, he was mimicking with his hands the move of the prince's punch: "Oh, I see. I think Tilson could have turned a little faster."

"Well, certainly. You'd have to do so. You could not take many hits like that."

"What, me?" Guy started to protest: "Des, the fight with Teodor was cancelled. And after yesterday... Maybe he's..." Guy wanted to say dead, but all he could think of was the golden sandals. Yesterday, Guy had seen... He had seen the prince imprisoned in the base of a cocktail table. He had seen and done nothing. Guilt pinched him once again.

And I have his shoes. It had been so stupid of him to take his shoes.

For a moment, Guy was transported back to the Cathedral the day before. The prince in the golden fighting angel costume, the crowds of boisterous children, the press team demanding photos, and – in the midst of all that – the prince had seen him. He had watched him take and hide his shoes, and he had not said anything. Guy briefly hugged his backpack; the shoes were still there. Dare he tell Des?

"Taken, he's alive." Guy looked up at Des. All at once he realized Des knew something. Maybe Guy could confide in him, tell him what he had seen?

"It's not right," Guy murmured. "He's our prince."

Guy's heart leapt, for though Des did not reply, he knew from his eyes that he agreed. It was wrong of Chart Segat to have kidnapped the prince. This certainty was followed by the ever-present Dome mime for silence: finger pressed to thumb and a quick shake of the head. Don't talk about it.

Des pointed at the screen: "The display. Concentrate. We don't have much time. Do you know that presentation?"

Guy shrugged. He did know it, but why say so?

"Didn't I see you practicing it once? Or twice? Did Loulou not give you the money for the test?"

Guy shrugged. Of course, he had wanted to ask, but Loulou always seemed short of money.

"I didn't ask. Blades are about fighting, not display."

"Go on, show me." Des pointed the screen at the wall. A small image expanded to fill the white space. "Just as a warm-up. If you don't know it or can't remember it, you can copy him."

Guy hid his contempt. Of course, he could remember the examination display. But did he know it as well as the prince, with his diamond shirt and hand-picked tutors? That was the real challenge. He leapt down from his stool and bounced to the center of the available space. They did not have a blades mat, just four random items of clothing placed in a square. The room was not a gym, just a dilapidated meeting room in the basement of the grandstand. It was now mostly used for storing tables and chairs, all of which were deployed for the Royal Ascot event. Only a few broken items and the scratches across the walls remained to bear witness to its previous use.

Guy started slowly. He was watching the prince and shadowing his moves just a fraction out of sync. Within three or four steps, he had matched his rhythm and needed no further cue to continue the intricate display of turns, kicks, and balances. He saw Des walking along the line of an imaginary blades mat. The prince's film rolled on the wall above, while below Guy shadowed and mimicked him move for move. Suddenly, Guy stopped thinking and let his body do the talking. With each stretch, he reached higher and further than the prince. His long, slim limbs gave his kicks greater precision and distance. His fast spins let him slip a triple spin into a routine where the prince only managed a double. As they came to the end, Guy held the final pose just a moment long enough to prove the point, then said, "I'm better than him."

"You're better than him at blades, for sure."

The two paused a moment to watch the prince in the diamond shirt dismiss his blades instructor. He dismissed Commander Tilson, no less. Then, he called two great gorans to his side. The final image on the tape was a frozen image of Prince Teodor with two yearling gorans licking and sniffing his hands.

"Life's not fair," Guy muttered.

"Life's NOT fair," agreed Des. "On guard?"

Guy laughed and spun out of the way as Des bore down in a fast, hard attack. Their blades clashed, and they parried. Careful to stay within an imaginary circle, they dueled back and forth. Des sometimes pressed home a hard attack. Sometimes he relented, allowing Guy to make his attack before defending himself against Guy with elegant ease. They were both laughing as Guy's Communicator rang out. Momentarily distracted, Des used a jab to knock the blade from Guy's left hand and put his dagger to his neck:

"Do you yield?"

Even though he was beaten, Guy was grinning from ear to ear. He felt such a dizzying sense of elation. He was in a blades fight with his hero, Des. Even to have lost the fight, it was still a dream he had long imagined. Now it had been a brief reality; only, it was over all too soon.

Juke's voice was shouting from Guy's Communicator.

"I need you back here now, Guy. I said quarter past, not half past, not quarter to twelve. Get a move on."

Guy smiled grimly.

"I yield."

Des nodded.

"You're in decent shape. Oh, yes, and a message from Chartsie. You're to join the party again tonight."

"Loulou said she did not want me to work tonight."

"Chartsie said 8 PM."

"Yes, but!"

"C'mon, Guy! If you want to get into the Dome Militant, you'll do whatever he says, hey? Whatever he says. You hear me, whatever Chartsie says. Or he'll throw you to his Borgs."

"No, he won't."

"Won't what?"

"He won't throw me to the Borgs. He said so. I think he knows who my father is."

"Well, maybe," Des admitted. "He and Loulou go way back."

"I think Chart Segat is my father."

"He told you that?"

"No, but..."

Juke was shouting again.

"Get back here now, Guy Erma! I warned you."

Des was grinning as he pushed Guy towards the door.

"Whatever Chartsie says, Guy. Whatever he says. You have to do it."

Chapter 9

The Glass Palace

The west entrance of the Dome was often nicknamed the 'Glass Palace,' with its two transparent walls shedding bright sunshine in rippling rays onto the compound, and a magnifying glass wall opening onto the swimming complex. Nuria came out of the lift and stared at a three-meter-high scantily clad teenage boy walking across the east wall.

"He must be a model," she thought, as the image rippled and disappeared. Nuria stared and saw a small figure continuing to stroll around the edge of the leisure pool. She breathed again as she understood the illusion. At her shoulder, Karl looked around the lobby, at the many information computers, three-dimensional representations, and maps of the Dome. High on his right was a vast, ever-changing events schedule, and underneath a row of ticket machines, the sign read "Seven Levels of Sport and Pleasure."

Neither Nuria nor Karl were interested in the public areas. Both knew these were being monitored by AIs. Nor did they intend to penetrate the military levels, busy with Dome Militant fighters. If Prince Teodor was being held there, then he would not go unnoticed nor unaided, at least, so said both Regent Saygun and Prime Minister Macey. Both clung to the hope that the majority of the Militant were loyal to the Empire, and by that, they meant King Serge and his son Teodor.

The focus of Karl and Nuria's mission was the black areas. Those areas within the Dodecahedron Dome where there were no cameras, and no one was quite sure what Chart Segat had put there. King Serge might have known; he had worked hand in hand with Segat building the Dodecahedron, but of course, Serge was dead. He had taken any secrets to the grave - maybe that was the reason he had been killed?

Earlier they had discussed their plans with Karl's elder brother, the Zaracan Ambassador to Earth: Nikato Valvanchi.

"Try not to do too much damage," Nikato had said. "And no casualties."

"We will need tech support," Karl said.

"And weapons," Nuria had added.

"No weapons," the Ambassador replied. "If you can't do whatever discreetly, and only with your powers, then don't. Just brief the Regent and let her send in the Royal Guard. We do not, and I repeat NOT, want a fight of any kind with the Militant in their own Dome, do you hear me?"

"We're outnumbered," Karl agreed.

"And Nuria, your role is to sit quietly in some coffee shop and scan for the prince; you will pass information back to your uncle and nothing more."

"But I might not be able to sense Teo from a coffee shop," Nuria protested. "I have been working on a Dome Militant Admin look."

Nuria waved a hand down her body and instantly transformed into a youthful Dome Militant administrator, of which there were thousands throughout the Dodecahedral and Domeside. "Uncle Karl needs me to connect with the prince."

"Your uncle plans to enter a Dome Militant jail," Nikato replied. "You cannot follow him there. Your father would be furious if he thinks I let you walk into such danger."

"How can it be dangerous, if I am with Uncle Karl?" Nuria replied.

"I am giving you Zed," Nikato added, ignoring Nuria. Zed was the young librarian who had helped Karl the day before. "He's a tech-head." Karl was unconvinced.

"What if we run into these so-called incorruptible Battle Borgs of Dome?" Karl had asked. "They are the ones who appear to be detaining Prince Teodor."

"Do what you must. Human casualties zero," Nikato had said. "And Nuria you will have an escort, stay out of trouble."

While Nuria strolled through the Dome with her normal security and a 'so-called' tourist guide, Karl had shape-shifted into a human at the embassy; he pulled on worker's dungarees, adorned with a badge that said "Prime Air-Conditioning." It was standard procedure for Zaracan diplomatic missions to assure their services, so they owned several small businesses, including an air-conditioning team. Now, they were using some of their uniforms to gain access to the Dome. Two Zaracan guards were similarly disguised, as Karl had said he only wanted three men in total, but unexpectedly, three further men climbed into their transport as well. These appeared to be actual air-conditioning engineers; their Prime Air-Conditioning jumpsuits were stained at the knees and elbows.

"Who are they?" Nuria asked in a whisper.

"Where are you going?" Karl asked them.

"We do have a job to do," one replied. "Unless you require our services as well." He slapped his hip, where his weapon was concealed.

Karl looked at Nuria, who shrugged. She reran the briefing from earlier. Her uncle, the Ambassador Nikato, had not mentioned that real work would be going on alongside the rescue. Had he? The plan had been for the tourist guide to lead Nuria and Karl to where there was a market for local art, along the outer wall of what was the Dome Militant prison block. If Nuria sensed Prince Teodor, then Karl had the air-conditioning uniform and pass, so in theory, he had access to most of the Dome. If there was a problem, he could call on Zed to open any doors he did not have clearance for. So, why had someone sent these three extras?

"I thought the bill of works was a fake?" Nuria said. Something was out of place. Nuria could sense it. Why was this not mentioned at the morning briefing?

"It's a cover, allows us to hang around until you need to leave." The man seemed to be implying he was wasting time. "I'm Alton. Just give me a call. We will be ready whenever you need to leave."

"Okay," Nuria muttered. They had arrived at the open market for art, which stretched for about half a mile, with dozens of small stands competing for attention. Nuria knew that she must have a cover, so the intense concentration she needed to listen for Teodor did not look strange. So, she said to her guide, "Isn't this art beautiful? I must look at everything. I am going to walk right to the far end and then..."

She stopped.

'I can feel him,' she sent telepathically to Karl. 'He's right here. Just beyond this wall.'

'What state is he in?'

'He's sleeping - do you want me to try and wake him up?'

'Yes, I should be able to sense him once he's awake,' Karl replied, then aloud to the others. "Okay, I'm going in."

"Follow us," Alton, the leader of the three air-conditioning engineers, replied.

"I'll take the Princess somewhere more suitable," the tourist guide/embassy secretary said.

"I want to stay here," Nuria complained.

"It's not a safe quarter. I mean pickpockets, but if Karl is going to attack the Prison, well... you need to be far away from here, Princess."

"Go," Karl urged her, then with telepathy. 'Go find somewhere quiet where you can sit. I will connect with you the entire time, so you will see what I see.'

"Yes, go," Alton echoed, and his voice sounded firm.

'I'll need an open window to maintain the connection,' Nuria complained to Karl, then she remembered the high balcony on the front of House Jewel and the room full of ball gowns. "I have to go pick up a dress anyhow," she told her guide, then with her thoughts. 'Good luck, uncle.'

Chapter 10

Watching from Buckingham Palace

"We are calling the suspects A1, B1, C1. We cannot identify them yet, but they belong to Chart Segat. Of that, we have little doubt," Patrice briefed Sayginn. Karl Valvanchi had left an hour ago. Sayginn had only left the operations room; now she and Patrice undertook one last turn around the monitoring stations. After the initial excitement of the disk, there had been no further sightings of Prince Teodor. Most likely, he was securely locked away inside the Dome military complex, somewhere they still could not access.

"Which brings us back to the question of motive," Patrice reflected. "Segat said he wanted a seat at the table on the future of the Dodecahedron Dome. But did they just do this to catch our attention, to make us listen?"

"He also said he did not kill Serge."

"He has said that all along," Patrice said. "Maybe we should have listened."

Another image appeared.

"This is Des Parks, Dome Militant. He was seen leaving Segat's apartment about six minutes earlier," Patrice said with satisfaction.

"Do you think he might have seen something? Can we bring him in for questioning?"

"Not with this evidence. If we see any of the suspect Battle Borgs, we will grab them and run a diagnostic on their key programming. But this Des Parks? He's human, only eighteen. Still, if he shows up at the Royal Ascot racecourse, we intend to grab him and persuade him to help us with our inquiries."

"Persuade?"

"There's a small radio station at the racecourse, it's no longer used, but there are a couple of sound-proof rooms where we'll start inviting individuals in for a little chat."

"No!" Sayginn said quickly. She knew what Patrice meant by this euphemism. He was talking about beatings, even torture. Otherwise, why bother with a sound-proofed room?

"Regent, there is always a little bit of horseplay. The occasional fight when the Royal Guard meets the Dome Militant."

Sayginn's head was spinning. They would try to cover up the questioning as some inter-military unit skirmish. Should she protest?

She glanced over and reminded herself of the images in the maintenance corridors. During the kidnap, the Militant Battle Borgs had used snake droids to cut Royal Guards and cy-wolves to shreds.

"No, Patrice, we cannot use their methods. We must be better than that."

"And I promise you, I will give him every chance to prove his loyalty as he helps with our inquiries," Patrice Macey replied.

"No, Patrice, what we need to—" If she had been about to say more, she stopped. "What's that?"

She pointed to an image displayed on a small screen on the far side of the wall.

"That..." Patrice peered at the code displayed across the bottom. "That is a random surveillance flying drone. Its current location is..." He checked a number on a console. "Royal Ascot."

"Yes, but what's that?" Sayginn reached forward to tap on the screen.

"Oh, it looks like a couple of Militant youngsters. Blades-fighting."

"What are they doing?" Sayginn could see what they were doing. She just wanted someone to confirm what she was seeing.

"Well, it looks like they are copying Prince Teodor's blades display."

"Yes, but that was Teodor yesterday," Sayginn said. "Those training session recordings are never released. So that video has been hacked," she paused. "And I recognize that one. What's his name?" She felt her pulse race. She did know that youth, and she knew when she had seen him.

"Let the computer ID him," Patrice said, then tutted. "Unregistered. Domeside orphan. Could be anyone."

"Not anyone!" Sayginn was shouting as she remembered: "He was with Chart yesterday, and Loulou at the Clinic. He's the one who was due to fight Teodor at blades!"

"And the other one is Des Parks," Patrice said, reading the screen. "Last seen leaving Chart Segat's personal chambers."

Both Sayginn and Patrice had moved closer to the small screen; others turned to look. The images of the fight multiplied and expanded across the screens.

"That kid fighter, is he any good?" asked Sayginn.

"Well..." Patrice hesitated, then said, "Teodor is strong."

Sayginn had a sudden insight. She had seen Loulou at the Clinic with Chart Segat. It was well-documented in the popular press that she was Chart Segat's mistress, but the youngster had been there. Sayginn had seen Loulou at the Festival of Fashion, and fleetingly, she remembered the dazzling display of blades along the length of the catwalk. This boy had been there too. And what had the Emperor said? One or both of those children is said to be Loulou's love child. She had seen the boy with Chart Segat as well. So, this boy was close to Loulou, or even Loulou's son. He was also known to Chart Segat.

"Rewind it. They were talking beforehand," Sayginn said. She was looking at the youth. This film was black and white, but still, there was no ignoring the shine on his hair, the light in his eyes. There was also something familiar about him.

"There. While they're eating. Is there any audio?"

"No, this feed came from a mini-droid. We can try to lip-sync it," an analyst suggested.

"Of course, speaking with their mouths full," muttered Patrice, peering at the black and white images, "That bit there. Where they are pointing at Teodor on the screen."

"Why this sudden interest in Prince Teodor?" Sayginn asked. Patrice shrugged.

"His disappearance is all over the news," Patrice said.

"Why hack a film of him fighting today, when the fight in the Dome was canceled last week?"

"Here's the audio transcription," Patrice replied with a shrug, and he pointed to the scrolling text. "I would not like to be on the receiver end of that."

"That doesn't make any sense," Sayginn said, impatience rising within her like boiling water. These two boys, both in Chart Segat's inner circle, they had to know something.

"The lip reader does not always match exactly with what was said," Patrice explained.

"Oh, what did the other say there?" Sayginn replied.

"The machine can't lip-read the back of someone's head."

"This is impossible, just bring them in..."

"Sayginn, we've got nothing to go on. Wait, look." He pointed again to the scrolling text. "Well, certainly. You'd have to move – you cannot take hits like that."

"What does it mean?" Sayginn groaned.

"They are talking about taking hits, it's blades fighter speak." An analyst suggested.

"A hit is like a punch, a slice is a cut," one of the others volunteered, and as he did, he mimed a punch holding the handle of his blade.

"Wait a minute..." Patrice rewound the tape. "Look there, in the video they are watching, Teo punches Tilson."

They watched and, though the image was a shadow on the wall, the painful wince on Tilson's face was all too obvious.

"And then the audio..." Patrice pressed play.

Well, certainly. You'd have to move – you cannot take hits like that. Patrice pressed pause. "Okay," he said uncertainly.

"Is he talking about Teo hitting him?" Sayginn said. "Are they training to fight Teo?"

"Let's carry on."

Again, the other boy spoke from the nod of the back of his head. Then came a pause, while the other ate and drank before finally he said:

Taken. He's alive.

"What!" Sayginn squealed.

"Okay, okay, I'm going to rewind," Patrice said. He replayed the tape and waited for the lip sync.

Tolkien, he's a liar.

"Hold on," Sayginn was desperate now. These boys knew something. "That's not what it said the first time; rewind it again."

Taken. He's alive.

"He knows something. He must have seen Teodor."

"That's exactly what we need," Patrice agreed. "They do know something. This a live feed from the racecourse. We have their IDs. We'll find them."

He turned to Sayginn.

"Whatever they know, we'll know it within the hour."

Chapter 11

An Adventure on a Summer's Day

It had been a sunny day in early spring when Teodor strolled back from the goran stables, and that's when they jumped him. A handkerchief was pressed to his face; his legs were kicked from under him, and a sack was pulled over his head. Later, when he woke, he was sick for a full five minutes – throwing up all the food from the previous twelve hours. The mock kidnap was meant to be as real as possible, but on that occasion, he had escaped.

"What you have to understand," his father had said, "If you are kidnapped, the last two minutes are the most dangerous. I can get within two minutes of rescuing you. Just as I come within shouting distance, they will kill you out of hand. It won't be fair. It probably won't be particularly clean. It will be quick. Whether a double shot to the head or a knife to your throat, you'll be dying as I cover the last fifty yards to free you."

Loosely bound in a cave, Teodor remembered how he had known he was beside the palace lake. He had waited until his captors became relaxed. One was on a call. The other was away taking a leak. Quiet as a shadow, he had crawled from his prison. Before he had gotten many yards from his cell, his father, the king, had sprinted forward to pick him up and carry him away.

"Inevitably, I will know where you are being held. We will have all communications monitored. Anything said – even on shortwave radio, even by semaphore – we'll hear, we'll see." Teodor remembered how his eyes had been blue and full of laughter. His father had been merry that day, though what they discussed was deadly serious.

"The city will be locked down. The planet will be closed. The Star Gate will be shut. Unless they are very quick, their only option will be to sit tight and hope. But they will not be able to hide for long once hundreds of cy-rats and thousands of cy-roaches are deployed."

"Cy-roaches!" Teodor said in disgust.

"Military issue, top secret, very fast, very dangerous." And he ran his hand up Teodor's leg and across his chest like an insect. Teodor squealed, his father laughed, and they wrestled for a few moments. Teodor remembered how his father had lifted a finger for silence.

"The thing is, cy-roaches will be programmed to your scent, your DNA, your fingerprints. Whatever it takes. We will find you."

"So, I just wait?"

"Have you been listening?"

"You said the last two minutes were the most dangerous."

"You have to escape! You don't have to go far. You just have to be clever. You have to get out! Chances are, my men and I will be camped just outside, waiting to liberate you."

Teodor nodded and leaned in to sit cheek to cheek with the king.

"I will escape, father. I will escape, and you will be waiting."

A prescient memory, Teodor thought, and a welcome change from the nightmares. Once again, he awoke in pain. He was lying on his side, his elbows tied behind his knees, and his head twisted at a cruel angle on a concrete floor. He struggled a little, then peered around. It was an old-fashioned cell, with concrete walls and floor, metal bars on three sides, and he could see into neighboring cells. There was someone there. That someone had said something, and now he spoke again.

"So, are you awake now?"

Teodor saw a face bent down to his level, looking through the bars. For a moment, Teodor thought he was still dreaming, for the face looking at him was his face.

"If you scoot over here, I might be able to help. I've got this." He held up a small knife. Teodor could not decide whether he moved more like a worm or a bug. Still, he crawled using his elbows and knees until he was pressed up against the bars. The youth with his face reached through, slipped his knife inside the plastic tie, and started to cut.

"Well, it's cutting. But it's tough. It might take a while. Can you bear it?"

"Yes. Please carry on..." Teodor rasped; for the first time, he was aware of how thirsty he was.

The youth set to it with renewed concentration. In the end, it only took a few minutes. Teodor sat up and rubbed his arms where the binding had cut into him, all the while patting and shaking the circulation back into his legs.

"Take it easy," the other said.

"Who are you?" Teodor asked.

"Well, I'm Teo. Prince Teodor to you," he said with a laugh. "No, my real name is Sebastian." Teodor nodded for him to continue, and Sebastian did. "I said something Chartsie didn't like, so they had me locked up here all night. I hope they haven't forgotten me. I'm dying for a hot bath and a proper sleep – in a comfortable bed, you know."

"Chartsie?"

"I told him he should free Prince Teodor. I was quite drunk; you can see I'm the Prince's lookalike, and it's a good living. People pay us for all sorts." He hesitated. "You'll find out soon enough."

Teodor was dumbstruck. His head swam, and he felt a bit sick. He tried to remember when he had last eaten and he tried to think where he could be sick in this tiny cell. Most of all, he tried not to think of what a Prince's lookalike might be called on to do.

"Do you mean..." he asked at last.

"Waiting on tables, serving drinks, being decorative at parties. That's what I meant," Sebastian hesitated, then changed his mind and joked instead: "It's surprisingly well-paid." He peered at Teodor through the bars, "I don't know you, do I? You're not the Riffaut, are you?"

"I wear House Riffaut," Teodor replied.

The youth looked at him a few minutes longer. "You haven't had surgery, have you?"

Teodor shook his head. "You have?"

"Cheekbones," he replied and pointed.

After a moment, he sat down close to the grille and took Teodor's hand. "That was me, yesterday at the Cathedral. I posed for the official photos wearing the angel costume. I could tell you could not bear it. Do you remember?"

If Teodor was shocked at the familiarity of his touch, the warmth of the hand seemed like electricity spreading right to his heart. He closed his hand around Sebastian's.

"I'm Teodor, Prince of Earth. Yes, I do remember you. It's just that – well, I do want to support Domeside fashion – but that angel costume." He trailed off.

"A bit OTT," Sebastian agreed.

"But I think I've seen your photos before. You model my clothes; do you enjoy it?"

"I think so. It depends. Earlier in the season, the designers had in mind for you to wear a lot of lime green. We did this whole photo-shoot. At the same time, they were talking about you fighting Guy Erma. I just said: 'A boy who is a blades fighter would never wear lime green.' And when they saw the photographs, they were angry because I looked so sulky, but ultimately, they redid the collection. You only had the one green outfit in the end."

"A green blazer, so bright it practically shone in the dark." Teodor laughed as he replied. "Yes, I saw it. I told them to put it back in the wardrobe."

"Did you? I wish I had seen that. I knew I was right."

"Bright green!" Teodor laughed. Sebastian joined in, side by side in neighboring cells, they sat and laughed, fingers intertwined through the bars.

"I was due to fight Guy Erma, you know? Do you know him?"

"Yes, everyone knows Guy Erma!"

"Everyone knows Guy Erma?" Teodor asked. "Yes, I think I saw him." He hesitated, thinking about how his shoes had been taken. "Is he any good?"

"Who?"

"Guy Erma, is he any good at blades?"

"My God, yes. He spins like the wind and bites like a goran. None of the juniors can stand against him."

"And he likes Maths," Teodor added. "I definitely want to meet him."

"I'll tell him."

"Tell him I want to meet him with a blade in each hand."

"Go Prince Teodor," Sebastian laughed and added: "Look, if I do get out of here, I'll tell them I saw you."

A glimmer of an idea occurred to Teodor.

"Maybe we could swap places?"

"We have to get you out," Sebastian agreed. "But for you to wait tables for Chartsie? No." Sebastian thought, then said: "I tell you what. You could pretend you are one of us. Most of the Militants don't know you've been taken by their lot. Just find one who doesn't look too bright and then tell him you are from The Riffaut. Eight of us have your face. Tell him you have a photo-shoot, and if they don't let you go, you won't get paid. And if that doesn't work, say: I'll give you a cut. Can you remember all of that?"

Teodor paused, then said. "But please sir, I'm not him. I'm The Riffaut, and there is a camera crew waiting. If I get paid, I can give you a cut."

"Good accent. But you must say: The Riffaut, no one calls it House Riffaut anymore."

"The Riffaut, got it. How much is a cut?"

"Well, this weekend you're likely to get eight to ten thousand, so a cut is at least five hundred. That's good money for the Militants."

"Ten thousand is very good for a weekend's work; why the top prize at Royal Ascot is only fifteen."

"If you got it, you got it," Sebastian replied with a wink, before adding. "And you have definitely got it."

"Ok. Thanks. I'll remember," Teodor hesitated. The dread was settling in again. "If I get out of here."

"You'll get out. The Dome Militant of Dodecahedron is loyal to the empire, Teodor. I don't know what Chartsie thinks he's doing. You're our prince. You're our blood."

"It was a Dome bomb that killed my father." In his mind, he could clearly picture the two explosions. He also remembered the one coffin, how his mother had buried the two bodies together.

"They were hugging – they were in a hug when they died. I can't separate them." She had wept as she tried to explain.

"Actually," Teodor hesitated. "It was the second blast that killed them. The first bomb – the Dome bomb – injured them but did not kill them. The shield on the car kept them alive. It was the second blast..."

"The second bomb was not Dome Militant," Sebastian interrupted.

"No, it wasn't even from within the Dodecahedral Empire. No one knows where it came from. My mother thinks the Dome Militant brought it in from somewhere."

"Dome Militant spacecraft only operate within the twelve. The United Races will not give them keys for any other Star Gates."

"Well, we won't know anything until there is a trial. Chart Segat has to be brought to account."

Sebastian moved uncomfortably.

"What happens to the Dome and the Dome Militant if Chartsie is locked up? Can you wait until I get paid at least?"

"I don't know. I honestly don't, but I'll think of something."

"Sssh. Did you hear that?" Sebastian did not need to say anything more. Tense now, they both sat listening. They could hear doors opening and footsteps.

"Someone is coming," Teodor whispered. Unexpectedly, he sounded hopeful.

✦

Karl entered the Dome Militant prison, something he never in his life hoped to do. To get there, he had followed Alton and the other Zaracan 'air-conditioning engineers' into the Dome Militant complex. Clearly, their human appearance was working as were the uniforms. Dome Militant security had barely looked at his pass. The small group had headed confidently into the complex until finally at a junction they had paused.

"Through there and on the right," Alton had said, before adding. "Good Luck."

Even as he entered, he heard voices amplified by Nuria's telepathy.

...It was the second blast that killed them. The first bomb – the Dome bomb – injured them but did not kill them. The voice was loud.

"That's him, that's Prince Teodor," Nuria cut in using her thought-voice.

"Ssh, Nuria," Karl said forcefully. "I need to focus." There were three guards sitting at desks in the entrance lobby all were looking at him with interest.

Karl reached to his belt, found and released some autonomous gas pellets. They whizzed and spun around the small space, exploding into the faces of the startled guards and causing them to keel over, fast asleep.

Karl walked around each one, taking their weapons from their hands, lowering them to the floor and checking for a pulse.

"Three Dome Militant down – no casualties. Zed, open the prison cells so I can look inside."

He continued along the corridor and double-checked each cell in turn. They were black steel, lightless cells. Clearly, some of the inmates had not seen daylight – or even light – for a while. You could tell by the way they froze at the sudden opening of the doors. Teodor was not there.

But Karl could still hear Teodor talking.

It was the second blast that killed them.

Where was he? Karl concentrated. He looked carefully at the black metal cubicles. He had seen a concrete cell with metal bars. The prince was not here. But he was close. There was a door on the back wall. Locked.

"Zed?" Karl said. Sat in the distant control center in the Zaracan Embassy, Zed heard him, and the door clicked open.

Beyond was a narrow spiral stairway. Karl could not see the bottom. He released two small flying droids that had been folded away in his pocket. They zipped down into the darkness. Karl checked his Communicator to see what the droids saw. One droid was destroyed on arrival, but the second started relaying images.

A table with some half-drunk coffees and a newspaper, three chairs, and a Battle Borg pacing, weapon in his hand. Behind the Borg, Karl saw another row of cells. These were older cells, dungeon-like. They had grille-style locked doors, and a key hooked up to the wall alongside each one. Karl listened in again to Teodor.

Chart Segat has to be brought to account.

He was so close. These had to be the cells where Teodor was being held. Karl looked again at the droid-relayed image. Just one Battle Borg. Just one. In his elation, he had let slip his disguise for a moment, then quickly he shape-shifted back to become a Dome Militant soldier and pulled his medallion out of his shirt onto his chest. He set off at speed down the stairs and landed with a light leap at the bottom.

Not one Battle Borg. Six Battle Borgs of the Dodecahedron Dome Militant. He saw at once they had used a magnet to turn the droid and keep it pointed away from them. Karl brought his blades up. He threw both blades in different directions simultaneously. One Borg staggered as the blade was buried deep into its skull. The other just reached up and caught the blade after it had bounced off his head plate. Now he spun it back towards Karl. Karl avoided the flying blade, but the five remaining Borgs were closing in. He disemboweled the nearest Borg with a lethal blast of fire at close range. The Borg keeled over. But another grabbed Karl from behind.

Two down, two engaged, Karl was aware of the other two Borgs racing towards the cells.

Towards the prince, thought Karl. Teodor!

"What is it?" Sebastian asked. Teodor had leapt to his feet and was frantically pacing around his cell.

"I think they're coming. They're coming for me."

Sebastian stood up. They both looked to where the noise of a fight, crashing metal, and a scream could be heard through the door.

"They are only fifty meters away," Teodor said and hesitated. What was it his father had said? It won't be fair. It will be quick. Whether a double shot to your head or a knife to your throat, you'll be dying as I sprint the last fifty yards to release you. "I have to get out."

"There's no way out," replied Sebastian.

All at once, the door to the cell flew open; a Battle Borg stood in the doorway. It stared at Teodor free from his bindings and leaped in to grab him.

"No!" Teodor yelled and dodged. "Let me go!" He ran forward, ducking under the arms of the Borg, making for the open door. Too slow; the second Borg grabbed him and tossed him over his shoulder, and then they were off, running at breakneck speed. Teodor screamed and kicked until he felt the sharp bite of an injection into his neck and saw a black rucksack being opened. This time, the drugs were quick. He thought he heard someone shouting his name.

"No," he whispered. "I don't want to die."

His eyes went dark. He was falling.

Two live Battle Borgs, thought Karl. I can take two. They were carrying something. That something was kicking.

That's him. That's the prince.

Karl leaped into the path of the lead Borg, blades up and ready. The machine lifted its metal fist like a battering ram. He sprinted towards Karl with Teodor over his shoulder. Karl loosed two fighting blades, but the Borg ducked swiftly. With the other hand, the Borg lifted Teodor by the scruff of his neck, using him as a shield. Its other fist was still pointed forward, ready to ram Karl aside. Desperate to save Teodor, Karl reached up to grab him but was met with the Borg's metal fist hammering into his chest. Karl was thrown back, flat against the wall. The Borg carrying Teodor managed to force its way through, and Karl went to chase him.

However, his pursuit was interrupted when he found himself pinned to the wall by two blades held across his neck, thrown by the last remaining Borg. Out of the corner of his eye, he saw that the Borg carrying Teodor was running through the door and up the spiral staircase. For an instant, Karl thought of Teodor, but then he felt the blades cutting into his skin, and all he could think of was defending himself. He pressed his hands hard against the wall; he leveraged his feet up, and kicked out into the Borg's abdomen. As the it staggered backward, Karl grabbed the handles of the blades at his neck, and spinning free, launched them in a deadly pirouette. The last Borg fell as its head was severed from its body.

Karl looked along the corridor to where Teodor had gone, but he had missed him. Then he noticed movement in the cell beyond. Hope surged in his heart. Karl rushed to the cell, finding exactly what he had seen in Teodor's thoughts: four connecting cells, all with grilles in place of walls. In the third cell, there was a youth who looked remarkably similar to Prince Teodor. A lookalike.

"What's your name?" Karl asked.

"Hi, I'm Prince Teodor of Earth," came the reply.

"No, you're not," Karl said.

"He's alive," the youth said.

Karl swallowed and reached out to feel.

"Yes," he agreed. "Alive. Just."

That was something to be grateful for... Despite everything, the Borgs had not killed Teodor.

Turning back to the lookalike, Karl pointed into the next cell, where the plastic ties lay cut and abandoned on the floor.

"He was there, wasn't he?"

The youth peered around Karl to the carnage in the corridor beyond. His mouth fell open, but he said nothing.

Karl Valvanchi coaxed: "Do you want to get out of here?"

"Yes, please."

"Ok, then tell me everything."

"Zed, I'm heading up to the Cap of the Dome." Karl said as he closed the door to the prison behind him.

"Ok," came the cautious reply.

"And I'm taking Nuria with me. Her tech skills are quite good, but she'll need you for the passcodes and entry algorithms."

"I see," the young man replied, but he sounded hurt.

"It's not that you can't help Zed, it's just that Nuria has the connection, and we can't go on like this. We can't just run around hoping to find him. We have to locate him; we have to go to the source."

Chapter 12

The Midnight Blue Gown

She was not very talkative, Marline thought, this Valvanchi princess. Strange really because her family were all diplomats. And that's what they did, didn't they? Ambassadors and Embassy staff, weren't they talking all the time?

Nuria had arrived in the shop about an hour before, and other than asking for the windows to be opened, had been quietly thoughtful. She had agreed to refreshments and a fitting for her new dress, but beyond that, nothing.

"It's like she's a million miles away," Marline thought, and she looked critically at the girl before her. The princess was wearing an evening gown of midnight-blue silk, patterned with blue roses; it had a tight, fitted waist. With it, she wore a wide full skirt that was ruched and lifted at the back into a bustle. The blue perfectly matched the tint of her eyes, and her skin looked pearly white next to it. When she had not moved or said anything for almost a minute, Marline approached. The other model and sales assistant were huddled in the far corner, whispering. Marline had been a bit shocked by their casual rudeness towards the young alien princess. It would not surprise Marline if the girl hated this dress. But as she looked into the girl's face for a clue, she saw a single tear run down her cheek.

"Princess?" Marline sought around and found a box of tissues. She passed one to the girl, who nodded gratefully and blotted the tear away. Marline could not help but feel sorry for her. She had come to House Jewel alone, if you discounted the two huge Zaracan robot guards who never let her out of their sight. So now, she stood alone looking at her reflection in the glass.

This is not right, thought Marline. A girl should have a mother when she's choosing a ball gown.

"My mother is dead," came the reply. Marline looked into the sad face. She had not seen the girl's mouth move, but she was sure she had heard her speak.

"Telepathy," the girl replied with one word.

"Useful," Marline had swallowed her initial shock – after all, she knew the Zaracans were telepaths - so why not make use of it?

"Why useful?" Nuria asked, still talking with her mind.

"The other girls say it's treason to speak to a Valvanski, I mean Val-van-chi." Marline was careful to pronounce the name correctly inside her mind. The girl smiled gratefully.

"So do you hate this dress?' Marline asked, she was smiling this was something you should never say to a customer, but telepathy was like a secret conversation. She could say what she wanted.

"Not hate it, no, but I was supposed to wear this to the Royal Ascot Ball. My uncle had arranged for me to dance with Prince Teodor." Then she explained further. "He has a dance card, so only a small number of girls are asked to dance with him, but my uncle got me a slot. And, well, now, we don't even know if he's alive. The ball might not be cancelled, but either way, it's not going to be the same."

"Well, the Dome Militant have been recalled now. If he's in the Dome, they'll find him."

"It was the Dome Militant who captured him in the first place."

"No, it wasn't." Marline's thoughts were loud and angry. "Nobody from the Dome Militant was involved in this. I know all those guys, they come here drinking in the evening, so we girls know what they're saying, and they're all saying the same thing." Marline was emphatic. "The Dome Militant did not do this. But they will find him; I can promise you. I bet you right now some soldier or fighter is just about to free him. He'll be home by teatime, and the ball tomorrow night, well, it will go ahead as planned."

"Well," Nuria spoke aloud for the first time, sniffing as she concealed her tears, "I guess I have to have a dress then."

"Yes, you do, Princess."

"Should this not be full length?"

"Are you looking for marriage, are you?"

"No, I'm too young."

"You're too young, and Prince Teodor is too young. So, you wear a short dress."

"I won't be marrying Prince Teodor," Nuria replied, "I don't even want to."

"Well," Marline laughed inside her head. "You must be the only girl in London, the only girl on planet Earth who thinks like that."

Nuria laughed. The two girls smiled at each other a little shyly, but inside their heads, they were full of joy.

"Do you think this dress suits me?"

"Yes, but the fit isn't perfect. Can I introduce you to Janie, the lady who made this dress?"

"This dress is handmade?"

"Handcrafted, Princess, all these dresses are unique creations of craftspeople. Also, if I were you, I wouldn't use those blue accessories, too much matching. If it were me, I would be looking at this coral-coloured bag and shoes, and you need shimmering tights as well. We don't want people to look at your legs, but we have these new tights which are spun with threads of pure crystal. I just love them; they look and feel like pixie dust." As Marline waved forward the seamstress and walked around the shop picking out accessories, she started to feel more confident. She wanted to help this young princess, and she felt sure she was the best person in Domeside to do it.

❖

Nuria already liked this girl very much for her practical turn of mind and kind advice. She was also appalled at her avaricious intent of persuading her to spend a vast amount of money. At that moment, she heard the tinkling of bells as the door opened, followed by a wave of gasps. Glancing down the stairs, she saw her Uncle Karl – still dressed as an air-conditioning engineer standing uneasily in the doorway.

He needs me.

"Marline," Nuria said, turning to the girl. She had seen Karl too. Nuria saw not just disappointment but something close to panic on her face. "You choose, I will have this gown, and two of everything else. All the accessories you can think of. And thank you – you are the best salesperson ever." Then, as the head of the store approached, Nuria repeated. "I will have the gown and two of everything. Marline must choose. Only she knows what I like." Nuria nodded to Marline, who beamed in delight as Nuria sped down the stairs.

"You have to come," Karl said in fast Zaracan, holding out a rolled flight suit. "Say your goodbyes and come with me."

"Uncle was right about the prison," Nuria said once the door had shut behind them. "I would not have been much use against those Borgs."

"You located him. He was just there," Karl sighed. "Just there and I missed him."

"Six Borgs though, uncle." Nuria replied.

Nuria looked thoughtfully up to the Cap of the Dome. "How many are up there, do you think?"

"You know how to be invisible?" Karl asked. Nuria nodded. "And you have your basic shapeshift?"

"Yes, yes." She replied.

"If things go wrong – I'll cause a distraction - you head straight back to the embassy." Nuria nodded, then side-by-side, they headed across to one of the vast column-supports of the Dome. A full three yards wide, as they passed behind the pillar, they simultaneously disappeared, and heading to a corner, they slipped on their flight suits. Then, they waited.

Soon enough, a circular opening appeared above, while below, a disk took off from the atrium. Karl and Nuria leapt into the air and spiralled up, before accelerating ahead of the disk to disappear into the very Cap of the Dome.

Chapter 13

A Meeting at Royal Ascot

Guy was adjusting the display of strawberries when he heard the beeping. He ignored it at first, then looked up and saw a droid pointing in his face. It sounded an alarm, and a red light flashed on its casing. He looked at the droid and then looked back, wondering what or who the droid was focusing on. Clearly, it was not the stock of strawberries, neatly presented in pretty tubs. Guy reached up to switch off the droid, but it dodged away. He then saw the emblem on its casing: Royal Guard. Across the plaza, the red and silver uniforms were coming.

Panicked, Guy ducked under the stall tables. He materialised about five metres away and ran. Obviously, he could not outrun a flying droid, but he did want to get away from the Royal Guard. Only, where to go? He looked up and realised there was only one place. He raced up the carpeted stairs to the VIP suite where Chart Segat was entertaining his guests. As he reached the door, he saw with relief that Chart Segat was still welcoming his guests. Guy tried to slip through the door, but he was caught and pushed back by a Dome Militant.

"Whoa, Guy! Where do you think you're going?"

"The droid, the droid. It's after me!" Guy shouted, panicked. He made so much noise he attracted the attention of Chart Segat, who looked over indulgently. However, his smile faltered as half a dozen Royal Guard arrived in the lobby to his VIP reception. One guard marched boldly forward to grab Guy and pull him away from the Dome Militant.

"Chartsie!" shouted Guy in despair.

"What's going on?" Chart Segat said.

"This boy needs to answer some questions. It's by order of the Regent."

"Ok, but he is Dome Militant. And he's underage."

Guy glanced at Chartsie – what had he said? Was he a Dome Militant now? Now that the Regent wanted to question him? Did Chartsie know he knew? Did Chartsie know he had seen ... the dirty blood-stained legs wearing golden sandals in the confined column stand of a tubular cocktail table. Is that why the Regent wanted to see him? But how could she know?

"Well, you can accompany him, but we have executive orders. This boy is to be questioned."

Chart Segat tutted and waved forward four more Dome Militant. In tight formation, the Dome Militant, Chart Segat and Guy were escorted from the VIP suite to a small meeting room in the racecourse business centre. The first and second floors were guest suites for the races, but the basement had been taken over by the Royal Guard. They had installed a further monitoring station with screens and terminals. Analysts and communications experts all worked under large images of Prince Teodor in a variety of guises, including a photo of him in the angel costume from the day before. A photo that Guy realised was actually an image of Sebastian. He frowned briefly, but he was pushed onwards.

It had taken twenty minutes for Sayginn to reach Royal Ascot from Buckingham Palace. A change of clothes had taken six of those minutes, but at least her transport was fast. Patrice had arrived ten minutes earlier. He reported they had already found one of the two Domeside boys. Des Parks had been 'invited for a chat' – in an underground soundproof room.

"Go to the Royal Box, act normal. I will brief you as soon as I have something." Those were her orders, Sayginn thought. So here she was, greeting her guests. Drinking something alcoholic? She passed the drink back to a waiter.

"I need coffee," she told him. He snapped to attention and fled.

It felt better to see someone jump at her command, a rush of calm swept through her. She managed a smile and some small talk with one of the Barons and his wife and walked out onto the balcony. She told herself she was not looking for the other boy. Instead, she saw Chart Segat.

She knew he would be there. But here he was, promenading with Loulou on his arm. That vile man walked through the crowds, basking in his status as celebrity leader of the Dome. Women swooned. Men fawned. Boys ran errands. Loulou, the most beautiful woman on all Earth, had her hand twisted around his arm. Sayginn watched him now, mingling with his guests, lots of Dome Militant uniforms, and sports celebrities. He was listening to one, joking with another, always a quip, a comic look or a laugh. Did the man never stop? Then there were the girls. Sayginn watched the younger, more excitable girls crowding around Chart Segat. And who was that? Simon Sorrow, that sleazy billionaire space robot magnate and owner of three Domeside nightclubs. Still, he was younger than the Emperor; she reminded herself. The group disappeared up the stairs to one of the VIP boxes.

She breathed again and nodded in thanks at the coffee the servant brought. Her Communicator flashed once. A message from Patrice.

"We've found both boys."

"I will come at once."

"Sayginn, please stay where you are."

"Patrice, just tell me how to find you."

Chart Segat did not once let go of Guy's hand. Both he and Guy were looking right and left as they assessed and understood the effort the Royal Guard had deployed to find the prince.

"Is this him?" the man in the suit asked. "Chart."

"Patrice," Chart Segat greeted the minister. "This is Guy Erma. He's Dome Militant, so he's under my protection."

"Are you his father?"

"No Patrice, I am his fairy godmother. I am Chart Segat, mayor of Domeside, commander in chief of the Dome Militant. Since this boy has no father, he is my responsibility. What do you want with him?"

"I am Patrice Macey, prime minister to Regent Sayginn, head of her government and commander of the Royal Guard." Patrice replied unnecessarily, drawing himself up to his full height. "This one needs to answer some questions."

"Not without me, he doesn't," Chart replied, before adding. "He's only sixteen."

"Very well, you can sit in."

Guy, Chart Segat and the three others were led into a small meeting room with a blacked-out, mirrored wall. Even as Guy wondered if the room was being monitored through the mirror, he saw Des, shirtless and chained to a chair. His shoulders were red with lash marks. There were cuts under his eyes and across the bridge of his nose.

"Des!" cried Guy and ran to stand at his side.

"So, you two know each other?"

Guy looked up at Patrice Macey and panicked. Chartsie and the Dome Militant were standing in the entrance, looking wary. None of them acknowledged Des or even seemed to recognise him. By their defensive stance and the way their hands cradled their blades, he could sense their anger.

"What's going on here?" Chart said. He tried to sound cheerful, but somehow did not quite manage it.

"This boy is withholding information about the kidnapping and whereabouts of Prince Teodor," Patrice said.

"Are you quite mad?" Chart replied.

"These two were filmed discussing the prince's location this morning," Patrice said, and as he did, he scrutinised Chart Segat, who looked shocked before he replied with bluster.

"That's impossible."

Guy had a sudden doubt – he and Des had talked about Teodor during training, had they been overheard? What had he actually said?

"Watch," Patrice said.

On the screen was the film, showing Des and Guy in conversation. Patrice pointed out the blades and the video projection of Prince Teodor.

"So, the boys were training at blades this morning. I don't see how that is relevant," Chart said. Guy glanced up at Chartsie. So, he thought, Chartsie's trying to cover up for us. But this does look bad, training to a video of the prince the day after he was kidnapped.

"Why this sudden interest in Teodor?"

"Well, maybe if the Prince had not been lost in the cathedral yesterday?"

"It was Battle Borgs wearing Dome Militant uniforms who grabbed Teodor yesterday. Can you explain that Chart?"

"Don't!" Chart screamed. "The Dome Militant should have protected their prince. If it had been us, the prince would be here – he was due to race, wasn't he?"

"Stop!" Patrice shouted back. "You forfeited your right to protect our Kings when Serge died."

"I did not kill King Serge. I did not kill the baby prince!" Chart Segat shouted.

"Then you won't mind if we fully investigate all and any leads we have on the whereabouts of his son. I think one of these two boys, or both of them, know something." Patrice rewound the tape and showed a small segment of conversation where only one side could be heard. "Look!"

Guy saw they had rewound to a section where Des was eating and drinking. Des looked away. Were they trying to embarrass him? Who looks good when they are eating?

Tolkien, he's a liar.

The audio transcript offered helpfully. Patrice sighed but rewound the tape.

Taken, he's alive.

"Taken, he's alive," Patrice repeated with satisfaction, then to Des. "All I need from you Des, is for you to tell me why you said that."

One of the soldiers now turned Des around, and Guy struggled not to react as he saw how his face was bloodied and bruised. As if the marks on his back were not enough. Still, Guy could not help but wince when Des ran the tip of his tongue over a bleeding lip. That must hurt, he thought.

"I am Blades Fighter Des Park. ID number H59941 of the Dome Militant, and I demand legal counsel."

God, Des was brave, Guy thought. Name, rank and number.

"What about you?" Patrice said, spinning around. Guy realised with a start that he was talking directly to him.

"Do you want legal counsel?" Patrice nodded to the film on the wall. "You've got Chart Segat as your Fairy Godmother – sorry, Parental Guardian. Can you tell us what you were talking about?"

Guy froze. Now what? He knew it was his turn to be brave. Brave and silent, just like Des. He just hoped they did not beat up his face, he was meant to be working today.

"That audio transcript changed," Chart interrupted. "It's unclear, and we cannot hear what Guy says at all."

Guy looked again. Chartsie was right. They must have used a miniature camera; those things were notoriously unreliable. Was there even an audio feed?

"Guy was facing away from the camera," Patrice said, and he sounded friendly. "But maybe he could help us out and fill in the missing conversation?" He held out an open hand of welcome. "Can you remember, young man?"

Guy looked at the screen. He knew perfectly well what Des had said. The way he mimed for Guy to stay silent. They had been talking about the prince, no, not exactly talking. Guy had realised Des knew something. He had wanted to tell him about the gold sandals, but what had he said exactly? Had they said Teodor's name? Guy watched the short clip of the film again. It was not clear what he and Des were talking about except for the last phrase.

Now the screen showed some analytics:

Lip-sync accuracy check.

Taken, he's alive   55% accuracy score.

Tolkien, he's a liar   45% accuracy score.

The two percentages jumped out at Guy. So, they were not sure which of the transcripts to believe. It was almost 50/50. Suddenly, he knew what to say next.

"Des said Tolkien, he's a liar."

"Of course, he did," said Patrice, looking down on Guy with a wry smile. "But can you remember what you said before that? I mean, who is Tolkien?"

Guy hesitated. He had not thought this through. He glanced around for inspiration. Chartsie was just behind him, in front of him was Des. Someone was missing. Tilson. Where was Commander Tilson?

"Tilson," Guy said slowly. "What Des said was: Tilson is a liar."

Both Des and Chart Segat looked over at Guy, waiting.

"Tilson, he's a liar," Guy repeated with more conviction. None of the Royal Guard looked like they were going to refute this. The lip synchronisation was clearly not perfectly accurate.

"Right, and who is Tilson?" Patrice asked.

"Commander Tilson is a senior blades instructor in the Dome. He's my teacher, and he's Des' teacher." This might work, he thought.

This hope didn't last long. There was a sudden harshness in Patrice Macey's eyes.

"Ok, that's plausible, but what were you saying here? What did you say before Des said: Tilson is a liar?"

Guy looked at Des. Did he remember? What Guy had actually said was, Teodor is our prince, and what he had meant was, it wasn't fair to kidnap a member of the royal family. Not when he was the only one, and King Serge was dead. And the Dome Militant... That's it, Guy thought. It's the Dome Militant.

"I want to join the Dome Militant," Guy said. "I'm sixteen, and I want to become a blades fighter."

"I'm sure," Patrice glanced at Chart. "And we can talk about that later. Right now, I need you to help me by remembering what you said before Des said, Tilson is a liar. You tell me, and Des here goes free, and we all go back to the Ascot Races for a lovely day out. Wouldn't you like that?"

Guy nodded. Out of the corner of his eye, he could see Des's tied hands, his thumb and index were pressed tight in the familiar mime, the one that told him to shut up. He had to keep quiet. He also had to say something. What was the last conversation he had had with Des, before today? Unbidden, he remembered Marline sitting on the edge of the jacuzzi.

"Well?"

Suddenly, the words rushed out of Guy in a clutter.

"I said Tilsonwastellingme... No. Tilsonwasbraggincos hehadkissedMarlinelastnight."

"Sorry, I didn't catch that?"

Guy found he was blushing. At his side, Des looked at him with incredulity.

"It's a bit embarrassing because Tilson is our teacher, and we should not have been talking about him."

This lie seemed to work, but still, Patrice was unrelenting.

"Ok, but I'd still like to know what you said."

"I'm sorry and all..." Guy started apologising to Chart. He did not know why. In turn, Chart looked startled and nodded towards the interrogator.

"Yes, so you have apologised." Patrice said. "So now tell us, in a lovely clear voice, what you said."

"I said," Guy paused and swallowed, not quite believing what he was about to say, "I said: Tilson was bragging he had kissed Marline last night, and Des said: Tilson, he's a liar."

The Royal Guard paused. Even Chartsie seemed a little taken aback, Guy thought. Finally, Patrice said, "Who is Marline?"

"She's my half-sister. She's a model from House Jewel."

"Of course, she is. And the party?"

"Chart Segat's party in the Cap of the Dome last night."

Guy was emphatic. No one could contradict this simple fact. Tilson was a blades instructor. Marline was a model. Both had been at the party. Whatever he had said was irrelevant. The whole lie was a particular construct of several truths, and as such, undeniable.

"Convenient," Patrice said. The interrogators seemed to know when they were beaten. They looked between themselves and shrugged. Chart Segat quickly stepped forward and pointed to where Des was still bound to the chair:

"I don't think you'll object if I get this young man to a doctor. You know he's only seventeen?"

"Eighteen," Patrice growled.

"Unregistered," Chart Segat hissed back.

The two stood glaring at each other.

"He can go," Patrice said at last.

The Royal Guard untied Des and helped him up. They handed him his shirt and jacket.

"Nice tan," sneered one.

"Des has been training in the southern mountains," Chart shouted angrily, as he quickly escorted both Des and Guy outside. "Quick thinking, kiddo," Chart said to Guy in an undertone.

"Thank you, Guy. That was clever of you," Des breathed.

Guy's elation at this praise was short-lived. As they stepped into the corridor, the door of an adjacent room opened and in the doorway was Regent Sayginn. As Guy glanced over at her, he realised she had been watching him and Des through the mirrored wall.

"I know you," she muttered, clasping her two hands together, squeezing her fingers so hard her knuckles were white. "You're Loulou's son."

Guy paused, sensing something was really wrong here, but with Chartsie's heavy hand on his shoulder, he knew better than to reply.

"Guy has no mother or father," Chart replied.

Sayginn ignored him. Guy noticed she deliberately averted her gaze, ducking under his stare as she went down on one knee to gently stroke Guy's cheek. Her finger was so soft, and he found himself wishing she would never stop. And yet her hand was shaking.

"Teo is sixteen tomorrow," she said and Guy wondered if anyone else had heard. He looked up at her. She wasn't like either Loulou or Marline. There was a soft openness to her face, which was unlike the hard grimaces and glamour smiles of the Domeside models. "Have you seen Prince Teodor, Guy?"

Guy's heart raced, and he was sure Chartsie could feel it too. He swallowed nervously and glanced up at the man, but the Regent gently took his chin and turned his face back towards her. "Well?"

She wants to know so badly, Guy thought. And I want to tell her. So, I won't lie, but what can I say? Once again, he relied on the truth. "I saw him in St Paul's Cathedral yesterday morning. I was his understudy, playing the part of the angel in rehearsals. I saw him in costume, but then I left. I had to go to maths."

"I see. I did not realise you were there as well," Sayginn replied, her voice trembling and her eyes filled with accusations. She thinks I'm part of it, Guy thought. And why not? Did she remember him from the clinic yesterday? Had she seen him at the Festival of Flowers? He had seen her at both, and of course, he had seen Teodor twice as well.

"I left just before," Guy explained. "Before the explosion."

"We don't know what happened to Teodor, you see?"

Guy nodded, his heart still pounding. The only thing he could think of was the dirty golden sandal and the crumpled shadowy form at the base of the cocktail table. The only thing he could feel was Chartsie's hand heavy on his shoulder. He looked to his left and caught a glimpse of the band of gold on Chartsie's finger. It was etched with words in bold capitals like teeth, both inside and out. Inside it read: Fear only God. Outside it read: Loyal to Empire. Guy swallowed nervously: Loyal to Empire, Fear only God: the motto of the Dome Militant.

"Have you seen him?" Sayginn insisted, and this time Guy could see the tears in her eyes.

Please don't cry, he thought. And it was all Guy could do to shake his head briefly. He wondered if she could see how he was trembling from this effort. Guy knew he had seen Prince Teodor and not just in the Cathedral. Could the Regent tell by looking at his face? He wanted to tell her he would help if he could. He would save the prince given a chance. Rescue him, whatever it took. Only, Chartsie was standing so close that Guy could feel the warmth of his body at his back.

"I am Loyal to Empire." This was the oath, the words of the Dome Militant. "I Fear only God."

He looked imploringly at the Regent. Surely, she would understand that he was loyal to her, that he loved the empire. She must understand that he wanted to help, only Chartsie repeated. "So help me God."

The moment was interrupted. Sayginn rose abruptly, and after turning away from both of them, she spun angrily back, and this time snapped at Chart.

"What about you, are you loyal to empire? Do you fear only God?"

"I am, I am loyal to empire." Chart replied.

"Then perhaps you can update me on what the Dome Militant has done to find my son." Her voice was anguished.

"Is this a formal request for the Dome Militant to help in the search and rescue of Prince Teodor of Earth?" Chart replied mildly.

"Does there need to be a formal request?" Sayginn was shouting, screaming even. "He is your prince. He is your future king. He is your future commander in chief."

Patrice placed a hand on her elbow. Sayginn glared at him too.

Chart shrugged as he said: "Then I will, of course, mobilise the Dome Militant at once." He glanced around a little disparagingly at the amount of tech the Regent had at her disposal. "You know you only had to ask, Sayginn."

"Let them go," Patrice snapped, holding up a hand lest Sayginn say something more.

Sayginn and Patrice stood and watched as Chart Segat, with both his hands on the shoulders of both Guy and Des, made a quick retreat.

❖

"You should rest, Sayginn. You're not yourself," Patrice started to say.

"No, my only son has been kidnapped. I'll not rest. Why would I be myself? Are you saying I should not care?"

Patrice shrugged, then said. "Guy Erma. At least, we know his name."

"Well, whatever his name, he was lying. That was as plain as the nose on his face. But it's also clear he belongs to Chart Segat. The other one, Sas Darona, you think?"

"Not sure how he got back. Sas Darona is in lockdown," Patrice muttered.

"I don't want to know," Sayginn replied curtly. "Sorry, I did not mean that. Pick him up again after this weekend. For now, just keep close tabs on them. One or all of them should lead us to Teodor."

Her steward had come alongside: "They are waiting for you in the changing rooms, my lady. The three o'clock race."

Sayginn checked the time. Karl had said he would free her son, what had happened to him? How much longer before Teodor was free?

Her steward coughed by way of a reminder. Patrice came up to her. He glanced at the time.

"Are you sure about this? Are you sure people will understand why you're racing?"

"I will try and make them understand," Sayginn hesitated, "And if nothing else, it will give us more publicity. More headlines."

"What? Regent races while son in captivity?"

"Regent races in the name of her captive son."

Patrice sighed. "Ok, I'll go and sit with the press team and make sure they get it right."

Sayginn headed off flanked by her steward and bodyguards.

"Oh, and Sayginn," Patrice called after her. "You had better win."

Chapter 14

A Last Race

S ayginn stood tall before the mirror in the jockeys' changing room. She breathed deeply, willing the anxiety of the day away. She stretched high, so she could almost see her pulsing heart below her ribcage. Pushing her palms vertically upwards, she reached higher, lifted onto her toes, then released – her body falling forward into the crouched position she would take on the goran's neck. She let her head hang loosely down, and her vision framed her lower body. She clenched her legs, felt the electricity ripple, and saw the muscles move under the flesh. Slowly, she rose again to her full height.

Deep breath, slow whistling release.

I have to win. I have to win, for Teodor's sake.

Her eyes turned to her riding gear. She leaned over, picked up the leggings, lifted one foot and rolled them up. Black leather boots, snow-white woolen riding half-pants, wide black leather belt, generous red and white silk shirt, and the silver crown proudly emblazoned on the back. Checking the straps on her helmet one last time, Sayginn pulled it on and adjusted it, lifting the visor so the crowds would recognize her face. She turned to find her butler and jockey waiting. They nodded their approval.

"The press is outside?"

"As always..."

Sayginn stepped out and went down to where Blue Barbrina stood. A rumor spread through the crowd as people noted the Regency colors. They checked the silver embroidery and looked up into the famous face: the Regent was to ride Blue Barbrina. The rumor became a murmur as the words were repeated from one to another: the Regent is to ride Blue Barbrina! Then came an excited yell: ride her, win with her! The crowd moved, closing in on the barrier to see for themselves. A news presenter stepped up to talk to her.

"I am dedicating this race to my son, Teodor. He is not here today. He was taken yesterday. We have not gotten him back. I don't know where he is. But I do know that he loves these gorans, and he would want Blue Barbrina to win. So, Teo, if you are watching this, I am racing for you, my love. I want to win for you."

The crowd cheered once more, and Sayginn noticed, with wry satisfaction, that the odds of Blue Barbrina winning were improving. Reassured and energized, Sayginn led Blue Barbrina briskly into the starting gates. Only then, as the runners lined up, did the crowd's roar start to fade. Sayginn remembered her pledge to win. She wondered if that had been reckless. She checked the competition: they all seemed so young. For the most part, these jockeys were in their early twenties. Paulio, one of the oldest and most experienced, was only thirty-two. Each goran was different in size and coloring, and vaguely the same weight – although the parameters were extremely broad. Only one rule was strictly enforced: all gorans had been born within the same two season, two years ago. All the runners in the Royal Ascot celebrated their second birthday within one week of the race. Sayginn thought of Dark Daniella; her cubs were due in the next few days. There would be six goran cubs, the vets had said, one of whom, thought Sayginn, will race this race in two years' time.

Blue Barbrina growled in a deep voice, as if reminding Sayginn to keep her mind on the contest at hand. Or maybe it was antipathy to Imperial Rina, who was being forced forward into the neighboring box. Sayginn noticed how the Emperor's goran was foaming at the mouth, her yellow eyes watering, and upon looking back, she saw the cause: the red lash marks on the goran's back and haunches. Lowering her visor, Sayginn now leaned over Blue Barbrina and started an insistent and persuasive monologue: "See Rina, Barbrina. We must beat her to survive. She is the enemy above all enemies. See Rina, and beat Rina, my beauty." Blue Barbrina let a sharp, angry growl escape. Sayginn looked around; they were under starters' orders now. She crouched forward, tensing her thighs, knees, and ankles. Then she whispered to Barbrina the familiar words she used to start a race.

"Time to start Barbie, ready? Time to start, Barbie. Ready. Time to start. Go!" The gates shot up, thick hind legs propelled sleek bodies in a dive up and forward. They were away!

In the first straight, Sayginn concentrated on increasing Blue Barbrina's speed. She paid no heed to Imperial Rina's initial head start. Red luminous speedometer figures shone inside her helmet. Blue Barbrina accelerated to 55 km/h after five bounds, 65 km/h after seven. The winner would be the goran who reached its fastest speed first, then maintained it for the three circuits of the course. Blue Barbrina was coming up fast on the first pointed bend. This would be the most dangerous, with the gorans still on top of each other in a densely pulsing pack. Some lesser felines reached out claws to injure the stronger players. Blue Barbrina fended off one such blow with a swooping paw push within her coursing movement. But on the inside, Imperial Rina caught Blue Barbrina's left jowl with a subtle flick of her hind limb. Blue Barbrina pulled back, somewhat miffed at the taste of her own blood.

With urgent words, Sayginn tried to mold her pain into anger. Barbrina needed little encouragement, as they came out of the curve; the red digits flashed 70k, then 71k, then 74k, 78... 76... 79... 74. In rhythmical pounding movements, Blue Barbrina caught up with Imperial Rina and matched her speed for one circuit, at last inching past her rival as they entered the third.

Sayginn felt panic fringe her surge of excitement. Blue Barbrina was stretching her advantage with every stride, and she was a body's length ahead of Rina and two lengths ahead of the rest of the field. Coming into the last bend, Imperial Rina closed in on the inside. Even as Sayginn urged Blue Barbrina on, she heard her screech, and she threw her head back in such a way that Sayginn nearly fell. With a lightning glance over her shoulder, Sayginn saw with her vicious claw, Imperial Rina had opened the soft fleshy paw-pads of Blue Barbrina's right rear leg. Then Imperial Rina was upon them, pouncing from the right, rising onto her rear legs and lunging forward with strong front paws, as if to push Blue Barbrina out of her path. By chance, the smallest of her talons locked into Sayginn's tensed thigh. As Imperial Rina pulled back, she ripped away a fragment of muscle; Sayginn's scream could be heard in the Imperial boxes. Spectators stared helplessly at the images of the conflict at the bend.

Blue Barbrina reacted to Sayginn's pain, lashing up and out at Imperial Rina. Sayginn shouted quick encouragement and Blue Barbrina leapt forward into the race again, even as a third goran went to pass them. Blue Barbrina streaked ahead at 75 km/h. Imperial Rina, her bottom jowl now ripped in four irregular cuts and hanging away from her toothy jaw, chased Blue Barbrina with evil growls and hisses.

Yet there was no catching Blue Barbrina as she bore her wounded rider to the safety of the arrival post. She raced past the screaming masses from Domeside, ever stretching the distance between her and Imperial Rina. Her gait was a shade lop-sided, blood spotted the front rows on each excruciating impact, but the red digits never dipped below 74 km/h as she took the final bend to cross the finishing line, five lengths ahead of Imperial Rina.

It was a victory the likes of which had not been seen at Royal Ascot for many years, and the crowd loved it. Two equally matched gorans, a bloody fight, a severe injury and a victory for the underdog. The cheering and screaming continued unabated even as Sayginn cantered to a stop. She smiled and waved in her triumph. Beneath the bravado, she was concerned to feel Blue Barbrina's limp become more marked. At her call, a vet tended the paw even as Blue Barbrina stopped. Sayginn's sodden riding pants were almost black with her seeping blood and had left a dark stain on Blue Barbrina's snow-gray coat. Blue Barbrina turned and dropped her head to sniff the wound, and then, before Sayginn could move, her thick tongue swished out and licked the length of the fifteen-centimeter incision. Her saliva was warm and seemed healing. Sayginn fondled the beast, roughly scratching her behind the ears, and gazed with love into her dark eyes.

As they announced her name, Sayginn stepped onto the podium unaided and stood straight, as the Emperor placed the gold medal around her neck. Then both turned to watch the Regent's colors being hoisted to the sound of 'God Save the King.' As the last fanfare sounded, Sayginn could feel the throbbing of the leg wound like a drum in her head. The music ended, and she smiled, but it was a feeble effort. She pinched her thigh to hold the burning at bay just a little longer.

As they filled her arms with a huge bouquet, it was as though they had given her a heavy sack. She first sighed, then sank to the ground, seemingly overwhelmed by the weight of the flowers. As she passed out, her last thought was bleak:

The time was 3:24 and still no news from Karl Valvanchi.

Chapter 15

Of Sandals and Shorts

"This is Nuria Valvanchi, together with Karl Valvanchi. We have accessed the Cap of the Dome and are currently searching for forensic evidence of Prince Teodor in Chart Segat's bathroom."

Nuria stood at the center of the gold and yellow bathroom and looked in amazement at the mosaic tiles depicting a fantasy of sea-people and mermaids. Behind her, Karl hung a neat sign on the outside door handle. Cleaning. No entrance.

"Nanites," he said and took out a silver tube from his pack. Untwisting the top, he poured small silver beads across the floor. Nuria stepped up onto a small footstool, while Karl leaned back against the wall and watched. With their silver casings, they looked like a wave of ball bearings rolling autonomously across the floor. As they had no on-board processing capability, they were constantly broadcasting their findings back to a central processor.

"Is this Chart Segat's bathroom, do you think?" Nuria asked. Karl shrugged. "Why do we think Chart Segat is involved? He was a long-time ally of King Serge."

"Serge was murdered," Karl replied.

"And they want to get rid of Segat at the Dome Debate? So that's it, Segat wants to stay in power?"

"And keep control of the Dome Militant. You saw what they did at Mezzatorra."

"I saw your dream about Mezzatorra. I thought it was just a nightmare," Nuria replied. "I was going to read your report."

"Yes, you should. No, actually, don't read the report. Thing is, the Dome Militant is out of control, not just on Sas Darona. Around all the star gates heading in and through the Dodecahedral, they are a menace."

"Good job they don't have the gate keys to leave Dodecahedral space then," Nuria replied.

"They are not likely to get any either, most people believe it was a bad idea to give the humans keys to their own star gates, let alone access to other systems."

"Huh," Nuria was about to say something when the display refreshed. "Oh! The nanites have found him. They have found traces of the prince's DNA."

Karl strode over to look at her screen, where the display had created a map of the bathroom. The traces of Prince Teodor were numerous. Several partial footprints had been identified on the floor, his hair was caught in the plughole, and traces of his blood were found in the grout between the tiles. The nanites were overheating with excitement at the contents of a small bin.

"Is there something there?" Nuria said and walked over.

"Stop!" Karl pushed her back and instead went to pick up a piece of cloth; gently shaking the nanites to the floor, he discovered a pair of short shorts.

"Oh!" Nuria cried. "Those are the gold shorts. From the angel costume." She dialed up another image, one of Teodor from the day before – she quickly showed it to Karl, who nodded and picked up a handful of nanites and placed them on the material, further information started to scroll down the screen:

Sweat

Positive ID: Prince Teodor.

Sewage

"Sewage?" Karl wondered.

"Sample sewage?" Nuria said to the nanites.

At once, the number of links to Prince Teodor doubled as the nanites identified all the traces from before Teodor had washed.

"Can we use this in an investigation?" Nuria asked, showing the screen.

"Technically, it's an illegal search," Karl replied.

"I'll save the data anyhow." Nuria wondered whether the evidence they were gathering could be used in any investigation. She guessed they would call it an illegal search. Yet, how else could they secure the evidence when the Dome Militant barred both the Royal Guard and the Police from the Cap of the Dome? Nuria meticulously saved the data and checked the camera droids were filming the scene in an orderly and methodical way. She started to dictate again. "We have found the clothes that Teodor wore on capture. There is no doubt these are his clothes. They match the description of the angel costume. Also, there is DNA on the clothes. This places Prince Teodor in this bathroom in the last six to eight hours."

"Chart Segat's bathroom," Nuria added as an aside to Karl, and she shivered.

"He was fighting to escape a Borg last time we saw him," Karl reminded her.

"And we'll keep on fighting too!" Nuria replied.

"Finish your report. See if you can reach him."

Nuria nodded, quickly dictated the last of the findings, then combined all the data and sent a backup to the embassy. Then, she closed her eyes and reached out with her telepathy.

"I can hear him breathing," Nuria told Karl, then added. "But it's not enough to know where he is."

"They will have drugged him again," Karl said.

Nuria nodded. Drugged was better than being beaten unconscious, another unspoken option, but she added. "But it's not enough to know where he is."

Karl glanced at her and nodded once. Then with a command, she called the nanites back into their carryall. She briefly checked the number was correct, zipped up the small bag, and replaced it in Karl's backpack. They checked their reflections as Dome Militant staff, then Karl said.

"Invisible, Nuria."

She disappeared, and when Karl felt her hand in his, he left the bathroom, taking the cleaning sign as they went. Beyond was the great salon where Chart Segat liked to entertain. No one seemed to notice or care what one solitary Dome Militant soldier was doing or that he appeared to have two shadows at his back. The large space was a hive of activity as decorators, artists, and special effects engineers transformed the space from a sparkling silver beach paradise to a dark dungeon, complete with human robots acting out terrible tortures and suffering. Karl felt Nuria tugging impatiently on his hand, so he stopped staring and walked into the small office; he plugged a comms bullet into the nearest console.

"Get going on this, Nuria."

"It will take me a few minutes to clear security," Nuria replied, and reappeared disguised as a young Dome Militant admin. "But I think we are on Chart Segat's private network. Well done, Karl."

"Copy everything," Karl said, then added: "And I'm going to need the code to control those Battle Borgs."

"Deciphering it right now."

"Hurry up. We're going to need it."

Chapter 16

The Dome Debate

The army aircraft descended into the back courtyard of Buckingham Palace. During the two-minute flight, Sayginn had recovered from her faint, but the brave face she had displayed on the podium, a mere façade for the press and her people, was gone. She strained and gasped as her entire body quivered in pain. The landing was smooth. Even as they touched down, the Royal Guard lifted her onto a stretcher. Doctors ran forward, crouching under the rotating blades, then jogging beside the stretcher – across the landing area and into the palace.

The medical clinic was on the first floor, so the stretcher hovered vertically up the stairwell and over the banister, while medics and Royal Guards ran up the stairs. Finally, Sayginn reached the white-tiled sterile center, where doctors cut away the soft wool riding pants and cleaned the surrounding skin. The wound was deep. The bone had been scratched. Still, no expense would be spared to heal the Regent. Medics fitted a healing droid to her leg. Over the next hour, this sophisticated machine would accelerate the growth and regeneration of her flesh by using chemicals and proteins. Even as the droid clamped shut around her thigh, the pain fell away like a dark cloak; Sayginn saw nurses preparing a bed.

"No," she growled, "I will not rest. Get me a change of clothes. The pain is gone."

"Your Highness, for the leg to heal..." The doctor was concerned but not surprised.

"I have no time for rest, doctor," she replied. "The Dome Debate."

"Then at least use a hover chair until the droid is finished. Sayginn, you must not walk." She nodded briefly, the doctor turned to his staff, "Prepare a chair!"

Patrice Macey had arrived, he looked relieved to see Sayginn was conscious.

"Still no news?"

"No, but we have more help now. Why don't you come and see?"

Sayginn steered the hover chair to the top of the stairs. "Here goes nothing!" She said as she tipped the chair down, in fact, she was fine. She hovered down to the floor below. As she turned into the ballroom, she realized something had changed. At the center of the desks was a huge three-dimensional representation of the Dome; it was drawn in gold, red, and blue lines of light – a mesmerizing apparition. As Sayginn watched, the graphic spun and expanded, focusing on the Cap of the

Dome. There, Sayginn saw two green avatars moving around the area. She steered her hover chair around the display and in doing so, saw Nikato at a small table. Nikato was controlling the graphics.

"Regent Sayginn," he said, rising to his feet. "Those green shapes represent Karl Valvanchi and Nuria. They have found evidence of Teodor, as you suspected, in Chart Segat's bathroom. And they have been successful in accessing the computers."

"And this?"

"This graphic is drawn from the Dome's files. For the first time, we have a full map of the black areas. We can track Karl Valvanchi and Nuria, and through this terminal, we are receiving all their reports and data."

"And Teodor?"

Nikato shook his head. "Nuria can't get a fix yet. He may be drugged or unconscious."

Sayginn stared at the Ambassador. They were counting on finding Teodor through the young Princess Nuria's mind-to-mind contact. Only, seemingly it did not work if you were asleep. Asleep or unconscious? Oh, what have they done to you, my Teodor?

"Karl will find him and get him out. I know he will. We'll be able to watch their escape on this graphic. It will be like we are there."

"Five-thirty," Patrice repeated, without expression.

"I have to leave now," Sayginn murmured. "The Dome Debate."

Patrice nodded once. "We will go together."

"Good luck, Regent," Nikato said.

"I have the votes," Sayginn replied and smiled as she left.

"Yes, but they have your son," Nikato murmured, and he shook his head as the door closed behind her.

As Patrice climbed into the car behind her, he said, "Don't listen to Nikato."

"I..." Sayginn hesitated. "He has threatened sanctions."

"They would not dare. Teodor is gone. We can appeal to the United Races."

"Can we?" Sayginn asked. "How long will that take?"

Ashes, she thought, all lies in ashes. Even with Teodor kidnapped, her duties remained unavoidable. All Sayginn wanted to do was to lock herself in the palace with a screen and Communicator. She wanted to pore over the footage from outside Chart Segat's offices. She wanted to check the known prisons of the Dome and the military establishment. Of course, she had people doing this and everything else she asked for. She had more analysts, cyborgs, and robots considering every practical option and following it up; meanwhile, she had to do her duty. Her duty involved turning up at all the pre-planned events, to show herself undefeated and unbowed by this most terrible of attacks. Sayginn was just not sure she could do this anymore.

Patrice looked at her strained face and patted her hand.

A short while later, Patrice and Sayginn entered together into the huge competition gym. In the light and shadows of the Dome, the conference table had been set up at the center of a circle of blades mats. As the delegates arrived, they passed pairs of Dome Militant engaged in highly-decorative, extraordinarily-complex display fights, while Dome Militant soldiers in shining uniforms lined every pathway and stood to attention along each wall. Sayginn looked along the line of sharply dressed young men. There was no denying this was an excellent fighting force.

Behind the wall of Dome Militant, ropes held back the crowds, and large screens so everyone could watch. The Dodecahedron Dome Debate was planned as a spectacle as exciting as the Ascot Races. It was expected that the different parties would fight their corner as ferociously as the gorans had raced their race. In the car, Sayginn had looked over the notes of her speech and remembered the brave phrases she had agreed weeks before. Her heart failed her, and she abandoned the papers on the seat of the car and walked on empty-handed.

Arriving last, Sayginn took her place at the head of the table. When she looked down the line of delegates, her supporters on the right seemed quiet, subdued, and uneasy. Everyone had expected this debate to be canceled. Sayginn realized it might have been preferable because it was unclear what this charade might achieve. In the end, Sayginn had insisted the debate go ahead because she felt in her heart that this was the key to Teodor's survival. Now she looked at each of the faces, no longer seeing individuals but the baronies they represented. Those owing their wealth to Emperor Frederon were backing Segat, while those indebted to her late husband, King Serge, would vote for her.

"The Emperor still believes in Chart Segat," Sayginn thought.

Segat spoke first. Sayginn and her supporters listened, as grim as death memorials. Across from them, even their opponents were subdued, as if shamed into silence. The vast man joked, exclaimed, shouted, and gestured, but his audience was unmoved. When he concluded with a blistering attack on the Royal Family, there was no response, neither applause nor rebuke. He sat down in silence with no one offering any further comment or discussion.

Patrice Macey stood up, bowed to Sayginn, and said simply: "We still have no news of Prince Teodor. It is thirty-one hours since he was kidnapped. We do, however, have these pictures from this morning."

Patrice showed the film of the Battle Borgs on the flying disk entering the Cap of the Dome and the close-up shot of Teodor's face where he was upside down inside the black rucksack.

There were shouts and exclamations from around the table. All turned to look at Segat.

"Well, Chart," Patrice said. "Do you recognize these Borgs?"

"Are you accusing me?" he replied.

"No. I only asked whether you recognize these Borgs, since the disk is traveling between the Cap of the Dome and military units within the Dome Militant. Both of which you know well."

"All I will say is that if you re-elect me to the post of Dodecahedron Administrator, I will do all in my power to find these Borgs and free the prince."

"Ok, I would just like to point out to the committee that we shared this intelligence with Chart Segat's office this morning, and they have already had five hours to trace the Borgs."

This time, Segat snapped. "Let's vote, Regent."

Sayginn realized she was stroking her thigh where the claw wound was aching. How could this be happening? The Valvanchis said... Chart Segat said... Patrice said... Suddenly she felt a little woozy. She found she could do nothing but stare at her opponent.

"Give me back my son," Sayginn muttered. If Segat heard her, he did not acknowledge her. Sayginn moved to the podium and pulled herself up. "Since the death of King Serge, we have seen the Dome Militant managed by Chart Segat. At first, yes, this was extremely helpful, but now, what do we have? Reports of piracy! Reports of theft. Reports of scientists slaughtered as they undertook vital research. And these young men who trust their futures to the Dome Militant, should they be put under the power of this man? This man, who continuously jokes about how he will 'throw badly behaved boys to the Borgs.' Rumors continue that kids have been forced to fight those monsters with blunted blades. Maybe we don't have any proof, the truth is, we just don't know. Maybe it is just a Domeside legend. But not my son."

"This morning, we saw evidence of my son held against his will by Battle Borgs. My son is not just anyone. He is not just the only heir to King Serge. He is not just the only heir to Emperor Frederon. He's a clever, talented boy, who has worked tirelessly for years to achieve the education and skills he needs to lead these great institutions."

"And if this is how Chart Segat treats my Teodor, the finest of his generation, what hope then, for the young men of Domeside? That they will be treated fairly? If I were to have control of the Dome, I would treat each of these fighters as if he were my son. Their well-being, education, and the full development of their talents – so they may go on to make useful contributions to our great empire – that would be my primary concern. For a fairer, gentler Dome, put me at the helm. Put me at the helm and help me find my son."

As she sat down, Segat said. "Give me the Dodecahedron Dome," he waited until the cameras turned towards him and sneered. "Your son will survive."

It was out-and-out blackmail. Sayginn blanched, and her supporters looked equally appalled. No one dared make eye contact with either Sayginn or Patrice, and certainly, none dared look at Chart Segat.

Each of the fifteen delegates had a black switch in front of them and two lightbulbs on their desks, red and green.

A green light was a vote for Chart Segat to continue as Dome administrator.

A red light was a vote for Sayginn to deselect Chart Segat and take over.

On the screen above their heads, a countdown started, and each of the delegates reached for their switch. As the countdown reached zero, the delegates voted. Sayginn had closed her eyes. Then she opened them, it was easy to count the votes. Down the left side of the council table where her supporters were, there was a line of seven red lights. On the right of the board table, where the supporters of Emperor Frederon and Chart Segat sat, there was a line of seven green lights.

As was her prerogative, Sayginn had the deciding vote. She had sixty seconds to vote and decide the issue.

It was the moment, she thought. This was what she had envisaged during all those months of preparation. She would vote and Chart Segat would lose 8 votes to 7. Only now, she sat with her finger ready to vote, with the count at 7 vs 7, and her own vote the casting voice, and all she could think was: Please God, just free Teodor and I will vote the way you want.

She looked around the vast gym. The double doors were maybe one hundred meters away, an entrance where her son could make a smiling appearance. For some reason, she imagined him in the suit and shoes he had worn the day before, appearing at her shoulder and kissing her on the cheek. Then she corrected herself and tried to imagine him in the angel's costume with his hair carefully curled, running toward her with a shout of delight: "I'm alright Mum!"

She kept looking, but there was no movement in the crowds surrounding the council table, and all the doors remained firmly shut. A single tear ran down her face, but she kept looking, hoping beyond hope. In her mind's eye, another vision; she saw Teodor in ripped clothes with a dirtied face and scared eyes, dumped before her, crawling out of a narrow black kit bag. She blinked and looked around her. On her side of the table, all her supporters were staring at her. Patrice Macey offered her a handkerchief. On the right side of the table, her opponents, none of them were making eye contact.

Segat coughed. "Regent Sayginn, I do recognize one of those Borgs, and, therefore, I will go so far as to guarantee Prince Teodor will be sleeping in his bed in Buckingham Palace tonight if I am re-elected." It took a few moments for what he had said to sink in, so he repeated himself, "If I am re-elected, Teodor will walk free tonight."

"Sayginn, you must vote..." Patrice pointed to the clock; there were less than fifteen seconds left. Sayginn had fifteen seconds to decide. Red to vote with her supporters. Green to re-elect Chart Segat. All at once, Sayginn started to cry. At first, it was two quiet tears running down her face. Then her breath started to come out in gasps, and she was sobbing. Sayginn reached up to her face as if she herself could not believe what was happening when suddenly her body convulsed into loud howls. Too long had she kept this grief pent up. Not only for Teodor but for Serge and Deodran as well.

"Give me back my son!" she cried, and her voice broke with anguish. "Give me back my son!" This time, it was a howl. She had lost all awareness of where she was. "Where is my husband?" she wailed. "I want Serge."

Patrice stood up, looking ashen. "Sayginn! Please, Sayginn."

"No, no. Teo! Teo! Give me back my Teo!" Sayginn was no longer herself, sobbing and wailing.

How long she stood there, she would never know. A siren sounded, and all the voting lights went out. The sixty seconds allocated for the casting vote had expired. Now the vote would have to be run again. Above the table, a new countdown began. Sayginn sat sobbing into a handkerchief, as Patrice tried to comfort her. Segat stood up to address the council. He looked shaken.

"Yes," he said. "We all still grieve for Serge. Serge was my friend too. He put me in charge here. He trusted me. He would trust me to do the best for his son and the empire." He paused, then he raised his finger in defiance. "Vote for me and Teodor will be free tonight. Let's vote."

The committee reached for their voting machines. The lights flashed on. This time, the outcome was clear.

There were fourteen green votes in favor of Segat and one red vote for Regent Sayginn. The Dodecahedron Dome Debate had been lost. Sayginn was the only one who had voted for herself to take power in the Dodecahedron; all fourteen other members had voted for Segat to continue as administrator of the Dome. He rose to assume the posture of triumph, and around the gym, the assembled men and women roared.

Sayginn stared unseeing at the result displayed on every screen. She was still shaking and weeping. "My son. Give me back my son."

Chapter 17

The Wine Cellar

When Teodor awoke, it was dark. This time, they had left him with his hands tied, but his legs free. He was cold. The floor was freezing. The air was chilly. His vision cleared, and he saw a brass plaque. He recognized the name and, looking around, he saw his prison. It was not a cell, but a wine cellar. He looked at the badge again. This was not just any wine cellar. This had been built by the finest craftspeople on the planet, who had also installed the wine cellars at Buckingham Palace. Teodor remembered being shown around by his proud father. The wine cellar perpetually maintained the wine at the ideal temperature, while protecting it from fire, explosions, rats, and even insect infestations.

"I will deploy ten thousand cy-roaches to find you," his father had said.

"Cy-rats and cy-roaches won't make it inside here, Father."

Then, he saw something that made him smile, and he started to crawl across the floor towards the wine rack, then twisted and squirmed until he managed to grab hold of an abandoned bottle opener. It was a spiral corkscrew with a sharp point. It took a while, but after a long struggle, Teodor cut his ties and found himself free again.

With a sigh, he shook out his limbs, then rolled, crawled, and finally stood up. He walked to where a leather armchair was placed next to a tasting table. Teodor relaxed back and rolled his shoulders against the padded chair back. A short while later, he stood up, went to a rack, and picked out several bottles of wine and read the labels. He was hoping he might recognize a wine his father would drink, but he knew this was foolish – it had been two years since he sat beside his father at dinner. He remembered how he would pour a little wine into a small glass and tell him the name.

"Taste this," he would say. His mother would protest, but his father would reply, "He needs to learn good wines, Sayginn." Then to Teodor. "Never drink much, just drink the best."

Teodor turned the wine bottles one at a time until he thought he recognized one, then he used the corkscrew to open it. Next, he ransacked a little sideboard and found a glass. He danced a little jig when he discovered some packets of nuts. He placed all the items on the table and then decided to check for his captors.

The only light in the wine cellar came from a high window. It was dappled light, as if reflected off the water, and it fell in a small triangle high in one corner of the cellar. Teodor knew this was deliberate to protect the wines; it also meant that most of the cellar was in darkness. Silently, Teodor now crept around, looking. There was only one entrance, and it was shut. He walked up to the door, pressed his ear to it, and listened. Dare he try the handle? If he did, his captors would know he was standing behind the door. Then what should he expect? More drugs, more ties, more blows? Silently, he retreated to the armchair and table, poured himself a glass of wine, and settled down to eat the nuts.

"Here's to you, Dad!" he said, raising his glass. And that's when he saw it – a high grill on the far wall. That might be his way out.

Chapter 18

Preparations for a Party

J uke dropped Guy off outside House Jewel and held off giving him his money until the doorman came down to the car.

"Now, hand this in and make sure they mark the amount correctly against your name. You worked hard today."

As Guy climbed out, Juke grabbed him by the arm. "Chartsie said he'd get you a place in the Dome Militant?"

"Yes, he has."

"He'll want something in return, you know that?"

"Yes. He wants me to fight."

"Do you know who?"

"It won't be Borgs," Guy joked. "He said he wouldn't throw me to the Battle Borgs."

"And you believe him?"

Guy hesitated. Did he believe Chartsie?

"Look, Guy," Juke continued and nodded towards House Jewel, "They've offered you a job here, right?"

"Yes, they said I could model."

"So? It's not factory work – it's well-paid. You might even get some travel if you play your cards right."

"Yeah, but... you know they call the girls courtesans?"

"Yes, I know that."

"Do you know what they call the boys?"

"Don't listen to that gossip. Those fashion girls and boys have a choice. Sure, some of them advance faster with the right patron, but not always. You're good-looking and clever. Just look at Sebastian. No one tells him what to do."

"Sebastian always wanted to be a model. He likes the clothes, fabrics, design, all that stuff."

"Sounds like you know the lingo too."

"I want to join the Dome Militant. That's always been my goal."

"Okay, Guy, I understand. I've heard it before. Chartsie... Well, you've made a pact with him. And don't shake your head at me."

"No, Juke, really..." Guy wondered how to convince him. "I think Chart Segat might be my father."

"Really? Well, I suppose Chartsie and Loulou go way back, but listen. When it comes to it, think for yourself. Not the Dome Militant. Not

House Jewel. Not Chartsie. Think of only one person: Guy Erma. Got it? That's how you might make it."

Guy nodded, speechless, his heart thudding. There was nothing he could say. Juke patted his arm. "Go on, get going."

The doorman had spotted the money in Guy's hand. With a genial smile, he accompanied Guy to the front desk, where they let him in and into a small back office.

"What do you have for me, Guy?"

Ten minutes later, Guy was heading out again. Just ten pounds in his pocket, but almost a thousand marked against his name. He checked the time, then reached into his pack for his running blades, locked them onto his feet, and sprinted towards the Dome.

Loulou turned and smiled as Guy emerged from the bathroom, wrapped in a thick warm towel. She pulled him into a hug and helped dry him. Both ignored the commotion in the changing rooms. The spacious room was filled with glamorous young people preparing for a night in the Dodecahedron Dome, with sly appraisals and the inevitable gown mishaps that characterized this unique gathering of professionals, commonly known as Chartsie's court.

"Look," Loulou said, pointing to the perfume 'Dagger,' a gift Guy had given her on her birthday. "Smells nice, huh?" She arched her neck, and he sniffed appreciatively with a smile. "Now we need to get you ready. You've got a new outfit for tonight, see."

Guy eyed the clothes apprehensively. They were covered in cellophane, but what he could see involved far too many white and red sequins.

"Do I have to wear that?"

"Chart Segat sent the instructions himself. Anyway, you'll look very striking. Remember, the Riffaut have Teodor's contract this year, but who says they will have it next year? Everyone noticed you last night, and I want to make sure they keep noticing you."

"Like Chart Segat notices you?" Guy whispered.

"Shh now, he's a good man. Let Dana dry your hair, and then we'll do your makeup."

"Makeup?"

"Erederon, Guy, think Prince Erederon."

As the girl dried and styled his hair, Guy's thoughts wandered to a bright morning.

Two weeks before, Guy had gone down to the kitchen and persuaded the staff to let him take up Loulou's tray. At the time, he had still been canvassing Loulou, persuading her to talk to Chart Segat about the Dome Militant. So, he had cajoled and charmed the kitchen staff to lay on some breakfast extras – then added a few flowers he had picked from the attic window box.

He had entered her bedroom as the sun came up, and while the doctor was still in attendance. Loulou had barely glanced at him as he came through the door and directly pointed to a small table. She was, therefore, startled when he climbed onto the bed to kiss her good morning.

"Guy!"

The doctor coughed, somewhat impatiently. Guy saw he was holding a small piece of skin-coloured cloth. No, that wasn't cloth, it was artificial skin. Guy turned to take a proper look at Loulou and saw that the right side of her face, from the hairline to the chin, was a mess of small cuts and black bruising.

"Loulou!" Guy was upset.

"Oh, don't you worry," she had said, "The doc will have it repaired in no time. Did you bring me that beautiful breakfast?"

"Yes, I made it myself."

"My lovely boy!"

"Hold still." It was the doctor, and the small tool in his hand hissed. Leaning with his head against Loulou's neck Guy felt every twitch even as Loulou did, he knew the tool was like a pricking needle. It would repair the skin well, but it was painful, nonetheless. But not once did Loulou flinch or draw away. Guy knew he should say something.

"I wish I was... you know..."

"Wish what?"

"I wish I was your son."

"You are... (gasp!)" She grabbed Guy's hand and squeezed it in sudden pain. Guy saw the doctor was working close to the outline of her eye. "Oh, I've said it now!" Loulou said, breathing hard. "I should have told you long ago. I am your mother."

"My mother?" All at once Guy was kissing every part of her, her ears, her neck and her hands.

"Hold still, Guy," Loulou scolded,

"But you are my mother?"

"Do you think I'd take a chance with Chartsie's temper for anyone else?"

"Chartsie did that to you?"

"I should not have told him. Or I should have told him a long time ago. I don't know why I lied to him." She sighed. Guy was appalled. Who dared lie to Chartsie, and why? Loulou saw his expression: "You were such a beautiful baby. I just wanted to protect you. I... Oh, why did I force her?"

Loulou fell silent. She tried to look away, but the doctor put a hand to her chin and turned her face firmly back in place. Guy saw him applying jelly to a bruise that was already a touch yellow above her eyebrow.

"Force who?"

"Oh, I've told Chartsie now, so you might as well know. I swapped you. At birth. I swapped you with Marline. I forced her mother to take you. I said I needed a girl. I said it would not make any difference. I said I would swap you back. I said so many things, but I was lying; all I wanted was to keep you alive."

Guy watched the tears running down Loulou's beautiful face, even a drop of yellow snot dripped from her nose. The doctor had paused in his work. He handed her a damp cloth. She wiped her face gratefully and took a moment to breathe. The doctor set to work again. He was working on the last three cuts that Guy saw looked like scratches from finger-nails.

"Marline is your daughter..." Guy mused.

"No, no she isn't. That was another lie. But it was to protect you. He could not know he had a son. He would have killed you. He would have killed Marline, even though she was only a girl – but Chartsie..." she sighed, "Chartsie talked him out of it. Oh, he was so good that night! Whatever anyone tells you. Chart Segat, he's a good man."

Guy's head was spinning.

"Who would want to kill Marline?" he asked.

"No, no, no." Loulou was shaking her head. "Sssh. Chart Segat, he knows now. He'll take care of it. Chart Segat always takes care of his boys."

"What? Did he say I could join the Militant?"

Loulou laughed a little sadly, then hugged him to her neck once more and whispered: "I only wanted to protect you, Guy." Guy did not know what she meant, and could not think what else to ask.

As the doctor finished, Loulou thanked him. She rose from her bed and washed her face, then went to sit in the window seat, taking the tray of food with her. Then she waved Guy to her side, before pulling him into her lap and kissing him.

"Hmmm, let's see this breakfast. Will you share it with me?"

So, Guy sat with his mother on that bright morning, sharing buttered croissants and hot tea, while she told him of his birth and showed him a few photos of his baby years. For thirty sun-filled minutes, he had thought this was the happiest day of his life.

"Of course, this will have to remain our secret. With my career, I cannot have an illegitimate son, what would my customers say?" Guy nodded; of course, he knew this – it was the same for all the children born of models, their very existence always denied.

"I don't mind that. And I will tell no one."

"It doesn't matter whether you do. You are not registered, so no one will believe you."

"Will you register me now?"

"I don't know, Guy. I'll do what Chart Segat tells me." Guy did not reply. Everyone said Loulou had Chart Segat wrapped around her little finger. No one knew what Guy knew. Chart Segat beat Loulou; he took out his anger with his fists on her face and her body. She had tipped Guy's chin up to look into his eyes one more time:

"And you should do the same. Whatever Chart Segat asks, you must obey him. If not, he'll throw you to the Borgs."

Guy started to laugh, then stopped. Loulou was deadly serious.

"Whatever Chartsie says, Guy, do you hear me?"

"They had finished drying his hair, and the girl fussed with the shape and layering of his curls. Guy glanced at Loulou as she stood with the hairdresser, who produced some hair spray and a small pair of scissors. Guy paused for a moment. He found himself looking up at her face, searching for some trace of the cuts and bruises he remembered so clearly. Was that a small imperfection close to her hairline? Otherwise, the artificial skin had done its job; there was no sign, no scars at all. Except it struck him suddenly that the scars were all inside. Beyond the perfect skin, the perfumed hair, the painted lips, beyond that was a scarred, battered, and frightened woman, and this was his mother.

"Loulou?"

Loulou bent down, for he had spoken in barely more than a whisper.

"Is Chart Segat my father?" Guy whispered.

"Guy, what are you talking about? Is that what he told you?"

Guy hesitated as he tried to remember, then said, "He said I was to be tested aboard the Emperor's yacht, so I thought..."

Loulou smiled and interrupted him: "Tomorrow, right? Well, you'll know tomorrow. No more guessing. As for Chartsie, whatever he says, Guy, do whatever he says." Guy hoped the sudden fear he felt did not show. "And make sure you win," she added, "...or else he'll throw you to his Borgs."

"No, he won't do that."

"Just make sure you win." She smiled a brief, tight smile and bent to kiss him. He lifted his face to kiss her back. The kiss was over in an instant, but Guy held her gaze a moment longer.

"I've always loved you," Guy told her.

"You're going to be late."

"Goodbye, then."

Guy paused to look back a moment at the doorway, to see Loulou watching him leave. She had been his mother for less than a month, and already Guy knew it was over.

It was a short walk from the changing rooms to the Cap of the Dodecahedron Dome. A short, steep climb up a metal stairwell that hung high in the rafters of the Dome. As he reached the last short flight, there was a platform; Guy paused to look down at the busy center below. It was a complete view down inside the Dome. Unlike Chart Segat's room, you could hear the crowds here. The wind blew up, bringing with it all the smells and flavors of the crowds and restaurants below.

Guy looked down at the clothes they had given him. He was wearing a brand-new fight-protection suit and, over it, a red chiffon blades uniform. They had kept the sequins to a minimum. Just a red gem at his neck and a constellation of sparkles across the shoulders and along the tunic hemline, but otherwise, it was a blades uniform. Well, Chart Segat had said it was a fight. A demonstration fight, Des had said.

He remembered the white chiffon and gold they had used to make the angel costume Prince Teodor had worn. Did he look like a prince? At this height, thought Guy, it was easy to imagine you were an angel. Standing on the narrow stairwell, high above the Dome looking down on all creation, Guy was that lone guardian angel – strong, silent, ready for any fight yet alone. All at once, Guy was afraid. He gripped so hard onto the metal rail his knuckles shone white through his skin.

"I don't want to go!" he said. There must have been half a million people in the busy Dome that Saturday evening, but no one to hear him.

"I don't want to," he whispered. Footsteps. He looked back, Marline coming after him. She was wearing heels, but she ran nonetheless, albeit a little unsteadily. As she came up to him, she hugged him hard.

"Oh Guy, oh Guy," she said. "You're going to get into the Dome Militant. I know you are."

Guy nodded just once. He certainly hoped so. She looked him up and down, "Are you fighting tonight? Is it a display fight?"

"Yes, well, I don't think they have given me these clothes to throw me to the Borgs," Guy replied, glad to say aloud what he had been thinking.

"No, no. They only throw losers to the Borgs."

"Chartsie said he would not be throwing me to the Borgs. He said so."

"Well, if Chartsie says so," Marline agreed. "You have to do whatever Chartsie says; you know that?" She paused then added. "Do you get paid?"

"What do you mean?" Guy asked.

"Well, I was at a party last night, and they paid me four thousand five hundred."

Guy looked at her, astonished.

"Marline," he said. "Why do you want this money? I mean, really?"

"I want to be free," she replied. "I want to be free of all this. And to do that you have to have money. I've started making my clothes. They are House Jewel fashion now, but one day, there will be a House Marline. That sounds good, doesn't it? House Marline. I will have tons of money, and I will be free to do whatever I want."

Guy thought of Loulou, the best-paid model in Domeside. Was she free, he wondered? Was she happy?

"House Marline," Guy repeated, thoughtfully. It sounded highly unlikely, but still, he replied: "That's a great idea, Marline."

"And you're so good-looking, I'll want you as my first model."

"Now come on, Marline. You know I'm joining the Dome Militant."

"Why can't you do both? Guy Erma, fashion model and blades fighter. Hey, why not?"

"The guys would kill me; that's why. The other guys of the Dome Militant would kill me. They hate the fashion models."

"Yeah, yeah, they're just jealous about the money."

Guy just shook his head, "Yes, well. I'm not interested in money."

Marline nodded. She reached up to push his hair back over his ear. The scent of her! He clung harder onto the rail, as he felt his entire body sway, as if hit by a wave. He looked up at her. She was taller than him, but maybe only because of the heels. With her make-up done, and dressed in the finest House Jewel fashion, she was the most stunning new girl of Old Fleet Street. And she had been his friend for such a long time.

Guy felt awkward now because he knew he was supposed to kiss her. She was only a short distance away, but he just did not know what to do next. He reached to take her hand and eased a fraction closer. He looked up at her and, unless he was mistaken, she was nervous too. This was much harder than he had thought it would be.

Remember, she is only Marline, he told himself.

With this thought, he felt the warmth spreading through him. He rose onto his toes and ever so carefully, he kissed her. Pressing his lips to hers, but concentrating hard, so their teeth did not clash, their tongues did not touch. The sensation was overwhelming – waves of heat followed by walls of cold. The softness of her lips lit an inferno in his heart. As they parted, he was breathless.

"I love you," he whispered, and he meant it. She stood a moment, looking down at him. She blinked just once, and while she did not speak, her eyes told him her reply. Then she batted her lashes and stamped her foot, reclaiming her usual pose of sophistication. With a spin that set her skirts flying one way and her curls another, she set off to leave:

"Bye then, Guy!" she said, blowing him a kiss. "Make sure you win!"

Guy smiled and climbed the last four steps to his destination."

Chapter 19

The Gilded Cage

In the Cap of the Dome, the event planners had left, their work finished. Karl, disguised as a Dome Militant, with Nuria as a small admin at his side, looked around with interest at the new decor. It was gruesome in parts, but now, they were bringing in various goran fur rugs, small sofas, and large reclining bags. The finishing touches were all in gold, silver, magenta, and red velvets. This was a night of fabulous entertainment in preparation.

It appeared that the night would commence with blade fighting. A large, gilded, circular cage had been installed at the center of the space. One of the disk-jets rose directly up inside the blades cage.

"That's clever," Nuria murmured and pointed.

A special blades mat had been manufactured in two concentric pieces: a large fighting circle and, at its center, a small black rug to fit on the disk. The decorators were checking the fit of the two rugs. The central rug was not correctly aligned, so as the disk rose up into it, it jammed. The two technicians stretched out on the floor and tugged at the rug until it fit correctly. With shouts and rapid withdrawal of hands, the disk smoothly moved up into the floor. The join between the disk rug and the circle rug fitted so perfectly that the join all but disappeared.

"Neat," Nuria commented. "But what's it for?"

They watched as one of the production team, clearly excited about this detail, jumped onto the disk and shouted instructions:

"Let me try it. Let me try it." The engineers lowered and then raised the disk, while the event-planner posed and turned as if he were a blades fighter.

"I think the fighters are going to enter that way," Karl pointed at the disk.

"It's going to be an epic night," a waitress said, coming alongside. "The cages fold away after the fight, and the party carries on."

"Only one fight?" Karl asked and looked over to Nuria.

"Well, the running order is Victory Dinner downstairs, and then a private party up here, which starts with a fight." Nuria paused as both of their Communicators beeped. They checked.

"Tsk," Karl said. The Dome Debate had been lost. Chart Segat had been voted into power for five more years.

The next call was from Nikato.

"Pack up your stuff; you're coming home."

"Nikki?"

"You've done a great job with the Dome computers, but you can analyze the data back at the embassy."

"No, Nikki. I have to find the prince."

"She betrayed us, Karl. Chart Segat has been voted back into power."

"No, she didn't," Karl replied. "She had to save her son." He turned to Nuria.

"Teodor – does he fight with blades?"

"Yes, yes, of course."

"Is he any good?"

"I guess... Why do you ask?"

"I know where he will be tonight."

Nikato interrupted him: 'You must come home."

Karl took on a child-like tone:

"Oh, please, Dad, just a few more hours!"

"Ok, you stay if you must, but bring Nuria back to the Atrium. Alton and his team are waiting there; they can bring her back to the embassy."

"No," Nuria protested. "I have to stay..."

"Hey, whatever this is," Karl waved around the room. "It's going to be dangerous."

"But I can help."

"Yes, you can. Go show the Regent what we found here. Tell her she must keep sending her forces into the Dome."

"But the Royal Guard... the Dome Militant, they hate each other."

"We need every man, every pair of eyes, every robot... Tonight, we must find him." Karl paused and looked at the gilded cage, which was now fully in place.

"At least we know where he's going to be."

"Oh god," Nuria whispered, looking at the black line of the fighting mat.

"She will believe you. Now go."

Chapter 20

Conflicting Orders

"Patrice, we have a call from the Dome," Patrice Macey walked to the large screen. Regent Sayginn had retired to her suite. The doctors had recommended a sedative to help her rest. Patrice was alone in the ballroom, with the rescue operation to oversee.

"We have to bring the prince home," he told his men. "That is our only mission. We have to get him home."

He walked over to look at the large screen. Static, then Chart Segat appeared.

"Patrice!" Chart looked surprised. "How is the Regent?"

"She is resting," Patrice replied.

"Well, we will get her son back. I promise you, now that I have power, we will get him back."

"If it had been up to me, you would not be in power now."

"Well, Patrice, the Dodecahedron Dome Debate decided otherwise, and since I am an administrator of the Dodecahedron, I wish to lodge an official complaint. We, in the Dome, have been subjected to an unfair attack. Yesterday, we provided you full access to all of the facilities. Today, we recalled the entire Dome Militant to search for the prince. So why did you send in an attack team in secret today? Three of my prison staff have been attacked."

"I have no knowledge of such an attack," Patrice replied, but he knew Chart was talking about Karl Valvanchi. He had already seen the tapes, including a brief interview with the lookalike.

"Patrice, I pledge myself and the Dome Militant to find and secure your prince. I want him on the throne of Earth just as his father was. I also want to restore his reputation as one of the finest of our young people."

"How will you do that, Chart Segat?"

"Well, I don't wish to spoil the surprise. But consider it a gift to you and the Regent. The prince will be free. He will be alive. But if my men have to defend themselves and our young King from unprovoked attacks, who knows who might get hurt in the crossfire?"

"I will not withdraw my troops until he is found," Patrice said. "That is an entirely unreasonable request."

"Of course, but think about my request. You should be worried about your prince's security," as he said it, he laughed salaciously, "Particularly as the night is growing dark, and here in the Dome, the parties are starting. Who knows where the little prince may end up? What fun he might be having, or about to have?" It was a clear threat, and Chart Segat was no longer laughing, "If you want him back, you should first withdraw your troops."

Patrice switched off the communication, turned, and gave the order.

"Withdraw all the Royal Guard from the Dome. They are in danger."

"What about the prince?"

"The Dome Militant and Chart Segat are looking for him," Patrice replied.

The call cut out. "I might have just killed him," Patrice thought. From this moment onwards, Teodor was truly on his own and at the mercy of Chart Segat and the Dome Militant.

Nuria raced up the staircase to the bedrooms of Buckingham Palace. She had just listened to Patrice Macey order the exact opposite of what her uncle Karl had wanted. Where was the Regent? She was the only one who could overrule Patrice.

She saw a doctor and nurse coming out of a small room.

"I wish she had taken the sleeping pills..."

"She agreed to rest...." The nurse agreed.

"At least an hour. Stay by the door, don't let anyone in."

The nurse nodded and went to move a small chair.

Behind her, the bedroom door opened, then shut.

Ten minutes later, Sayginn appeared fully dressed at her door. Inexplicably, Nuria Valvanchi stood beside her.

"I have to redeploy all my forces into the Dome."

"Your highness," the nurse protested.

"My son needs me."

Chapter 21

Silk Balaclavas

"Get dressed."

It was a blades uniform of beautiful blue silk. Even the emblem on the front was familiar.

After all, I always wear House... the Riffaut.

The balaclava, also made of blue silk, with only three holes for his eyes and mouth, was less welcome. He looked up at the Battle Borg and said resolutely, "I'm not wearing that." He crossed his hands over his chest.

The Borg did not reply. With a simple gesture, he grabbed and pushed Teodor's arms down. There was no resisting the brute force he used. Despite himself, Teodor had to let his arms fall to his side; the Borg did not even notice the look of anger on his face. Instead, he reached for him with blades protruding from his index finger and thumb. With an economy of strokes, the Borg cut Teodor's clothes from his body. At the very last, he sliced through Teodor's shirt with a fast cut just a fraction too deep and left a long, thin, red line down his torso.

"I can't fight injured," Teodor gasped.

The Borg looked at him and turned away. When he returned, he had a disinfectant spray in his hand. He sprayed down the length of Teodor's body. The wound started to close. He sprayed again. Teodor winced but fought to stay silent. The treatment stung, like a line of fire running up the length of his body. Had the Borg noticed, wondered Teodor? Would a Borg recognize courage?

"Get dressed."

This time, Teodor complied – resisting these machines was clearly futile. He nevertheless looked for any cameras, but he remembered the Borgs could broadcast anything they saw, so maybe someone was watching. So, when the Borg presented him with fighting boots and jumping blades, together with cuffs and calf greaves, Teodor cried, "I protest at this treatment; I am a prince of Earth."

The Borg turned away. He had not, Teodor noticed, given him any hand blades.

"There you are, Guy, and very fine you look. Come and sit by me."

Chart Segat had been welcoming his guests. Now he drew Guy Erma to a red chaise-longue tucked away in a narrow corner. As they sat down together, Chart tugged on a drawstring, and a curtain fell closed. Guy found himself alone with the mayor of Domeside, and all at once he could think of nothing to say. Chart Segat; he told himself, the one person he had to impress to gain his place in the Dome Militant.

Say something!

But it was as if his tongue and jaw were frozen closed. Instead, Guy found himself scrutinizing the pores of the man's skin, and the small scar close to his ear. Was that the mark of repair surgery? And that smell? Urgh, it was a whiff of strong spirits on his breath.

"What have they done to your face?" Chart Segat mocked, lifting Guy's chin to look closer.

"I think they wanted me to look more like Prince Erederon."

Chart Segat pulled out a handkerchief, licked one corner, and reached up to clean the eyeliner from Guy's cheeks.

"Eyeliner was something of an affectation Erederon adopted in his twenties." Guy moved uneasily from left to right but willed himself not to flinch at this unexpected familiarity. "You don't need eyeliner to look like him," Chart was saying. "Why should you? Tonight, we'll remove the last obstacle. Tomorrow, we'll get you tested on the Emperor's yacht, and then you'll be on your way."

"You are talking about the ID tests, aren't you?" Guy spoke at last. He had had time to think about what tests Chartsie might mean and had concluded that the only tests that were illegal were blood and DNA tests. "You want to prove my mother is Loulou?"

"That's right," Chart Segat replied, his voice dripping with mockery.

"And are you, my father?" Guy blurted out the words, relieved to say what he was thinking. Hoping, indeed, for if Chartsie was his father, how could he possibly refuse him a place in the Dome Militant?

At first, Chart Segat appeared lost for words, then he replied. "Is that what you think? Is it not obvious to you? It's been obvious for a while, even without the tests. Oh, you'll find out soon enough."

Why don't you just tell me? Guy thought, biting the inside of his cheek to contain his anger. Why all the hints? Who did he look like? Suddenly, Guy remembered Dana the hairdresser had said: "He could pass as a young Erederon?"

Erederon? That was the dead prince, the last son of Emperor Frederon. No, that was not possible, a dead prince would not be able to help him get a place. Guy was so disappointed; he stammered, "But I thought you were my father."

Chart Segat laughed loudly. "Tomorrow!" he said. "Tomorrow, Guy."

Guy was appalled; how could he bear this?

"You need to concentrate on the fight." Chart Segat waved down at the red silk combat uniform Guy was wearing. "You know, I am expecting you to win."

With each word, he jabbed Guy's shoulder with a pointed index. "Win!" he repeated. The word 'win' was like a jolt, not through Guy's shoulder, but his entire nervous system.

"Of course, I'm going to win," he replied defiantly, and probably a little too quickly, he added as an afterthought. "Who am I fighting?"

Chart Segat just laughed and laughed, finally catching his breath before saying: "Yes, I am sure you will win."

"I could beat a Borg, too," Guy said recklessly.

"Could you now? Well, don't worry, I won't do that to you."

"I will do anything you ask, Chartsie. Anything."

Guy thought Chart Segat would laugh at him. Instead, he looked at him steadily for several long minutes:

"Listen, Guy, if you want to do something for me, then tell them I did not kill the king or that baby, Prince Deodran. Tell them that. Make them understand I am not their enemy."

Guy just stared at him, what did he mean? Chart Segat sighed.

"Go on, time for you to go." He shouted: "Des, are you there?"

Des came through the curtain. He looked both anxious and embarrassed. Guy saw Des look him up and down, and he seemed relieved at what he saw.

"You know what to do?" Chart Segat asked. Des saluted his fist to his heart and waved to Guy to accompany him.

"Oh, Guy?" Chart Segat called as they left. "If you do lose badly, I might still throw you to my Borgs, do you hear me?"

Whatever else, the Battle Borg was meticulous in his preparation. He watched the man check his calves, his cuffs, and correctly adjust his boots and foot blades. The equipment was of excellent quality, too. Now that he was ready, Teodor longed to feel the weight of the daggers in his hands. Another Borg arrived, with a short message:

"They are ready."

They handed him a blue silk balaclava; Teodor hesitated. It will be hot, he thought. It will block my peripheral vision and dampen my hearing.

"Put it on," the Borg said. Teodor glanced up. The machine would or could force him if he did not comply. He sighed and pulled the blue silk headpiece into place.

The Borgs had extended their running blades, and they ran on each side of Teodor, holding him by the elbow. It was a tight, secure grip from which Teodor knew he could not escape. They passed from the wine cellar out of the maintenance tunnel, across the Dodecahedron Dome's central atrium. Crowds milled around to and from restaurants and entertainments, watching on large screens. They laughed and applauded to see the two Borgs and a blades fighter dressed for the Riffaut. Teodor wanted to make himself known. Only he was wearing a balaclava, and they were running fast. They passed through the atrium in a few instants. Then, they were standing on a disk, and rising up through the Dome on a jet of fire. Teodor found himself looking over to see Buckingham Palace in the distance. Calling out with his thought-speech in his head:

"Mummy, can you hear me?"

"My prince, I hear you."

"Mother?"

"No, my name is Karl Valvanchi, and your mum sent me to rescue you."

Chapter 22

With Blades in Both Hands

Guy stood on the edge of a fighting mat, waiting. He looked around the Cap of the Dome. For once, the views – both out over the city and down below into the Dome – were obscured. The crowd was three deep with Dome Militant. There were very few civilians present, and no juniors or apprentices – just a host of fighters stood around the gilded fighting cage.

Confidently, Guy walked to the stool prepared for him. He looked across at his opponent's place, but it was still empty. So, he took up his steel and set about sharpening his blades one last time.

It would be the first time he fought with non-blunted blades. He polished the spine of the dagger with the ball of his thumb. He had received scratches and nips from training blades, but this was different. These blades were sharp. What would it feel like to be cut during combat? Des came up and offered him a clean cloth to polish his blades.

Guy looked again at his red costume and said, "I'm fighting to represent House Jewel. Why?"

"Well, it's a bit of a gimmick, I suppose."

"And who am I fighting?"

"Take a guess."

"I'm too nervous to guess."

Guy picked up his hand blades and spun them with his fingers on the palm of his hand.

"And if I win, do I get to join the Dome Militant?"

Des did not reply. With a fanfare, the lights dimmed. Guy saw the crowd disappear into the shadows as the lighting changed. A spotlight illuminated the blades mat; it was a silver circle of light at the centre of the cage. To Guy's astonishment and shouts from the crowd, the floor opened up, and a disk floated into place. At the centre were two tall Dome Militant Battle Borgs, and – held firmly between them – was a fighter dressed in blue silks, emblazoned with the emblem of the Riffaut.

Guy saw the Borgs discreetly release cufflinks as they floated up through the floor, but most of the crowd saw nothing, for the cyborgs quickly concealed the chains within their armour plating. They handed the youth his blades and marched sharply away. A small figure was left standing, blinking in the light, peering beyond the gilded cage to the shadowy figures beyond, uneasily lifting his leaping blades from the theatrical mist that rolled across the floor.

At least, he is young, thought Guy. He had had a moment of doubt when he thought he might have to raise his blades to fight a man or even a Battle Borg, but no, his opponent was a youth. But who could it be? Guy had already fought and beaten everyone his age in Domeside. The boy was wearing blue silks. They bore a familiar emblem.

"See?" said Des. "The Riffaut. You're fighting the Riffaut. The gimmick is that some say you look like a young Erederon, and the Riffaut are all modelled to look like Teodor. It's Prince Erederon vs. Prince Teodor, that's the gimmick."

"But we're wearing masks..." Guy could not think what else to say.

"Well obviously. Or did you think that was actually Prince Teodor?" Des joked.

Guy looked at him.

"What if it is? What if that boy is the prince?"

"Don't you want to fight?"

"No, of course, I'll fight. I mean, it can't be the prince, can it? It's just a gimmick. Only I can't think of anyone from the Riffaut who takes his blades that seriously. None who could stand against me, in any case. Sebastian gave up months ago."

"In that case," Des replied bluntly, "You should have no trouble winning. Because guess who the loser has to fight?"

He nodded where one of the two Borgs had walked around to stand by the scoreboard.

"There's going to be two fights?" Guy asked nervously.

"No more questions," Des said. "Just concentrate on this fight."

Des was already looking across the room. He seemed anxious, Guy thought. Why? And if his opponent was a model from the Riffaut, then why was he guarded by Borgs?

After a moment or two, the youth wearing blue silk saw Guy. He looked at him carefully, then drew himself up a little straighter. Their eyes met, and for one small instant, Guy thought he saw fear. The look changed; resolve replaced fear. The other pushed his shoulders back. He nodded just once. Without further hesitation, his opposition took the last two steps and sat on the stool prepared for him. He was ready. The fight could begin. Des put a hand on Guy's shoulder, and Guy gave him back his steel.

Guy looked curiously across at the other youth once more. He was wearing a mask. A balaclava of blue silk.

"What? Does he not have a second?" asked Guy.

"There," Des murmured, and they both watched as Tilson stepped up.

❖

"Tilson." Teodor smiled at the familiar face.

"Calm, Teodor, control."

"May I use your Communicator? I need to call my mother."

Tilson avoided looking at Teodor as he replied, "No time for that, my prince. You must prepare yourself for a fight."

"I will not fight," Teodor said resolutely. "They cannot force me."

"They can force you. If you don't fight him, they'll give you another opponent." Tilson nodded grimly to the nearby Borg.

Teodor shook his head, a brief shake of disbelief.

"I won't fight."

"Fine. Don't fight," Tilson seemed to agree, but then he nodded to the crowd. "Don't fight and they will call you chicken, and this time they will have seen it with their own eyes. Are you chicken?"

"I am not."

"Well then, prepare yourself, that young man is quite a champion."

"Is it Guy Erma?"

"You know him?"

"Everyone knows Guy Erma," Teodor replied with a smile. Out of nowhere hope sparked inside of him. "At last!"

"At last?" Tilson replied.

In that instant, Teodor was exhilarated. Maybe this was not as bad as it could have been. A blades fight, he could control. A blades fight, he might win.

"Finally. I'm glad to meet him with blades in my hands."

"That's the spirit," Tilson replied. "Now go."

As the numbers started to count down on the fight clock, Teodor stood up. He was ready for a fight. Across from him, Guy Erma took his place. Teodor looked over at him. As they had said, he was slim and perhaps a little taller. They also said he was fast, thought Teodor; time to find out. He watched the numbers on the clock decreasing, and as the countdown continued, questions ran through his mind.

Five

Was he doing the right thing?

Four

Maybe he should just refuse to fight, would that be the right thing to do?

Three

So, this boy spun like the wind and bit like a goran? Did he?

Two

And what if Teodor lost this fight? What then?

One

There was only one solution; he must win! Yes!

Guy bounded forward. The other fighter looked strong, confident even. Who could it be? There was no one from the Riffaut who could raise a blade to him. Guy could tell it was not anyone he had fought in the Dome blades championship or any other fighter he knew. The build was not familiar, and the eyes were so clear and blue. So, few people had blue eyes in Domeside, who could it be? Guy bent into a defensive posture. He decided to try a few passes just to test him, and then he would attack.

Teodor spun three times in a fast progression of pirouettes, closing the gap between himself and his opponent. In doing so, he gained momentum and knocked aside the blade Guy offered by way of defence, and spinning in close, brought his closed fist and the handle of his blade down hard to strike Guy in the ribcage, just under the arm.

Teodor would have hit him firmly above the heart, a semi-mortal blow, but at the last moment, Guy turned aside. Not fast enough to avoid the hit entirely, but enough to reduce the impact.

Under Teodor's hand, Guy shook and sidestepped a fraction before bringing his blade up. But it was a feeble defence; Teodor caught and pinched his wrist and twisted his arm up and behind his back. He was forced off-balance, into a painful fall forward off his leaping blades and onto his knees. Carefully now, Teodor placed the point of his blade to the back of his opponent's neck.

"Do you yield?"

Above them, on the scoreboard, the result flashed green under the Riffaut icon. Teodor had won the first round.

"I told you not to let him hit you!" Des was exasperated.

"I don't know who he is!" Guy gasped. "God, that hurt."

"Of course, it hurt, we looked at that this morning."

"This morning? But we were looking at Prince Teodor," Guy said shakily. "Ouch!" Des was smearing jelly on the red marks on Guy's ribcage. He scanned it quickly, as well.

"It's not broken, but your ribs are bruised. It will hurt bad tomorrow. Right now, you must fight."

"Ok. I'll fight. I'm not afraid. But why we are wearing masks?"

"Look, Chart Segat is over there. Just concentrate on the fight."

"Des, something is not right here."

"Will you stop thinking and just fight?"

Karl Valvanchi stood in the shadow of Chart Segat's throne. Carefully, he reached inside the man's mind. He listened in on a whispered conversation Chart Segat was having into a minute microphone.

"'So, help me God' does not mean anything. I need that promise in writing. I want to a guarantee of my ongoing management of the Dodecahedron. A contract to provide specialist support to the Imperial Army and a free hand in everything else. And you get the Regent to drop all charges against me in connection with Serge's death."

Karl could only hear one side of the conversation.

"Well yes if you want him tonight. If not, well, my Borgs have been very restless recently. I might have to throw them a tidbit, maybe two tidbits. Yes, both of them. Your nephew and the one you have not tested yet."

"Well, persuade her to bring the marriage forward to tonight. I will only be convinced once you have made her your wife."

Karl Valvanchi pulled his mind probe back. He couldn't bear to hear any more. He knew he should listen to the remainder of the conversation, but whoever Chart Segat was talking to, it did not sound good for Teodor, or, for that matter, for Sayginn. He had to get this opponent out. But how?

The Dome Militant were so numerous; he was alone. If his disguise should slip... Still, it was a carnival atmosphere. The men were mostly laughing, drinking and betting. Did the Dome Militant realise they were watching their prince?

Karl took the time to reach out and shake the bars of the gilded cage. He used a sensor to test its materials. There was neither entrance nor exit to the cage. Either you were locked inside, or you were outside. He examined the hinges where the walls of the cage were joined.

One way out was through the disk transport, Karl thought. In fact, it was possibly the only way out and the only way in.

Teodor let Tilson tighten his greaves, as the left one had come loose. He was watching the medication applied to his opponent. The fight remedies always worked immediately but were not without pain, either immediately or the next day. Teodor remembered how satisfying it had been to land his punch at the centre of his opponent's chest.

"I hit him," Teodor told Tilson, elated. "Did you see how I hit him?"

"Crack a rib or two, why don't you?" Tilson said in jest, but his tone was fierce. Teodor knew he was proud of what he had seen.

"I thought he was fast."

"Calm, Teodor, control. He is fast. You caught him by surprise. Don't expect to get past him so easily next time."

"If I win, will they let me go?"

"I don't know, my prince."

"But you can get me out of here?"

Tilson hesitated again.

"I am Dome Militant. I have to follow my orders."

"But who gives you your orders, am I not your prince? Your future king?" Teodor paused as he considered who might have higher authority.

"Look over there, my prince."

Teodor could see nothing through the shadows, except the cameras spinning through the mist.

"I can't see," Teodor realised there were actual cameras. "Is this fight being broadcast? Is everyone watching this?"

"Not everyone, only a select audience."

"But who?"

Tilson shook his head and changed the subject.

"Get your blades out, my prince, the countdown has started."

Teodor saw the numbers flashing. He picked up his blades resolutely.

"If I win, I get to go home, right?"

"Just fight, my prince, just fight."

"Best out of three or best out of five?" Teodor asked, without turning.

"Five," replied Tilson. "Now go."

Teodor paused just outside the circle. He knew what he was going to do. He had to win three points out of five to win outright. As the count reduced to one, he stepped into the circle. As the zero appeared on the screen, Teodor ran two steps and leapt high in a tight somersault, so he landed almost on top of Guy Erma. Just in time, Guy stepped back, rocking as he fought to stay within the circle.

Now, Teodor drew himself up to his full height, with his blades high above his head, points directed down, towards his opponent. He let out a yell of defiance and realised at the same instant he had waited too long. Below him, Guy Erma was moving, bringing a blade up towards Teodor's belly. Teodor swung his right blade down in a circle of fury. He knocked Guy's blade aside and caught the top of Guy's thigh with the point of his own blade. For a minute, it caught inside the fibre of a protection suit.

Uh-oh, Teodor thought. As he pulled his blade free, orange and blue lights were flashing around the arena. Guy Erma twisted free from Teodor and Teodor wisely spun the other way. Taking a defensive pose, he circled the mat opposite Guy Erma, trying to make sense of the flashing light.

FIRST BLOOD the screen read.

Teodor looked at his blade. It was red. He had cut his opponent. More than that, Teodor realised, Guy Erma was wearing a protective suit, where Teodor had none, just silks against his skin. He looked at the small amount of blood on his knife and immediately had a terrible foreboding. If his opponent should attack him back, he would be in trouble.

"Then finish it," he heard the voice within his head. His father goading him as ever, to higher levels of perfection. "Finish it."

Teodor raced across the mat once more and was pleased to see a startled look of disbelief on his opponent's face. He attacked with three heavy blows, one from top right, one up and under from bottom left, right hand and round again in a horizontal slice. Finally, a swinging kick from the left. It was the textbook level-5 attack star except for the last kick. In a display, the kick came from the right since you would be off-balance and a kick from the right was the more difficult. In this fight, Teodor brought his left to bear. He had the satisfaction of watching his jumping blades catch and jam into Guy's blades. Now, the other boy was falling and, at the very last moment, he reached up to grab Teodor and pull him down after him, but his fingers could not find purchase on Teodor's silks or his sweat-drenched arms.

In an instant, Teodor knew Guy was trying to grab the shielding he should be wearing on his arms, and not just the naked flesh. If Teodor had been wearing any protection, what might the outcome have been? Instead, Teodor let himself fall back onto his bottom into the blade ring, while Guy was propelled across the mat and out beyond the black line into the gilded fence beyond. Guy had landed outside the ring. He had lost.

"Two," thought Teodor, satisfied.

His jumping blades were still caught up with Guy's so, as the light lit up to announce his second point, Teodor leaned forward to disentangle them. In doing so, he reached to pull Guy Erma up into a sitting position.

"You alright?" he asked amicably. He could see Guy Erma had been winded by the fall and was gasping to catch his breath. "Take it easy," Teodor urged.

All at once, Teodor felt a little sorry for Guy. He could hear the crowd booing and jeering. While it meant nothing to him, he guessed these men must know Guy.

Didn't everyone know Guy Erma?

"Guy Erma, I'm glad to meet you."

The other looked up at him, trying to read his face behind the mask. "You know my name?"

"They said you were a great blades champion," Teodor said a little sadly. Had he even believed a Domesider could beat a prince who had had hundreds of hours of tuition with the best tutors on the planet? He saw him glance with angry eyes at the score, as they both rose up on their fighting blades. Guy turned and spat angry words in Teodor's face.

"It's not over yet."

Teodor watched Guy Erma stalk back to his stool. Now he knew he should be worried.

❖

"C'mon, Guy, what is your problem?" Des shouted. "That was a classic move. You left yourself wide open, and he took you down. Where is your head?"

Guy pulled off the balaclava and ran his hands through his hair.

"I can't concentrate with this thing on." Des gave him a towel. Guy gratefully wiped his face. He pushed his fingers into the bridge of his nose and massaged the soft flesh there.

"I have to win one point." Guy groaned. "I have to win at least one point."

"You have to win the next point," Des reminded him darkly. "C'mon, everything he has done so far has been textbook. Now you know how strong he is. Go in there with some true Domeside flair. Try a reverse spiral, or the up, over and double-back. But expect him to have studied all the well-known moves. So, he will have a response. Just be careful."

"Not if I take him at speed. He'll be lucky if he sees me coming."

"That's the spirit. Now go in there and get him."

Guy stood watching the numbers counting down to the start of the fight. Around him, the crowd was quietening. The score was ominous: Two—Zero. Either Guy would win the next point, or the fight would be over. No one in the room was ready for the fight to end just yet.

"Go on, Guy!" he heard a voice yell.

"Get him, Guy!"

The shouts warmed Guy. At least some of the men still believed in him. Even though it had been a pretty poor fight so far, some of them still thought he could win. He was fighting for House Jewel and the Dome. He had to win. He kept moving on his blades, maintaining the warmth in his muscles. He looked over at his opponent; he looked relaxed. And why not? He was ahead on points.

The lights flashed to zero, and both moved. Guy saw his opponent was trying to get away around the perimeter of the mat, apparently anticipating a direct attack, and assuming a defensive pose. Not quick enough. Guy was on him and inside his defences before he had his blades up. He had his opponent trapped; one blade pushed up under his chin. At any moment, he could stab up into his face. His opponent had frozen. It was enough to win, but Guy was not satisfied yet.

Guy drew his other blade back. He intended to slice away the silk tunic from the left side of his opponent's body, just above his heart. It was a winning blow. Non-lethal, since he expected the other to be wearing protective body armour, but a final winning blow. He signalled his move with a minute flutter of the blade, which had the men around the cage on their feet and roaring. Louder than all the others, one familiar voice. Chart Segat shouted:

"Kill him, Guy! Just kill him!"

Guy smiled. Too late. In playing to the crowd, Guy had waited too long. He saw real terror in the other's eyes. All at once, Guy saw blood on the point of the blade under his opponent's chin. Guy knew he had not cut him. No, his opponent had pressed his chin down onto the blade, knowing the sight of blood would distract him. Why? All at once, Guy saw the clumsy kick. A desperate knee was rising to his groin. Guy twisted aside. So, the knee impacted his hip. As Guy moved, his opponent reached to push the blade away from his chin and then turned away. Guy brought his other blade up, slicing out. He felt something soft against his blade's cutting edge. Softness, he was not familiar with.

He had little time to check, for his opposition was still spinning. He was trying to put some distance between them. Guy reached out casually with one foot, tripped his opponent and watched amazed as his opponent fought to keep his balance. He tumbled into an awkward forward roll, still desperate to get away. Guy saw his chance when the other failed to rise from the floor. Flying through the air, he landed square on his opponent's chest. Then, Guy had both blades crossed across his neck:

"Do you yield?"

The lights flashed the score above them. Two—One. One screen was flashing Second Blood. The crowd around the gilded fence was going mad. A voice cried again:

"Kill him, Guy!"

Guy smiled grimly; it had been a quick win. He wondered why his opponent had fought so hard right to the end. At the same time, he was aware that the body underneath him felt different. He removed his blades from the other's neck and took them both in one hand. It was a traditional sign of peace. With his spare hand, he gently patted the other's chest.

"Take it easy," he said with a smile. Then he patted him a second time. Either this fighter was wearing ultra-thin protection, or he was naked under the silk. Guy started to stand, but stopped when he saw the wound, where he should have been wearing synthetic leg mail. There was a long, narrow cut from his groin to his knee. Guy reached to help the other up. But the fighter in blue just ignored his outstretched hand, neatly sprang to his feet, and with a small limp, went back to his place.

As Guy returned to Des, he heard his opponent gasp. Tilson would be applying the skin healing spray; Guy knew well how much that burnt – doubly so, close to one's groin.

Good, he thought, his opponent would be weaker for it. He still had two points to win.

"Well done," Des said mildly. "A bit untidy, you should be careful about playing to the gallery. This is not a display match, but you nailed him in the end."

"I think he's only wearing light mail."

Des hesitated, glanced across the fighting mat to the opponent, then replied quickly.

"That's his choice and not something for you to worry about."

Right, thought Guy, pulling off the balaclava. He sat looking across at his opponent. He had to plan his next move carefully. He should expect his opponent to come out fighting fast, wanting to win the point and end the match. The other had taken his balaclava off as well. He was towelling his cheeks and eyes, then pushed his hair back with one hand. The move was familiar, as was the face. For a moment Guy was confused, could this fighter be from the Riffaut? As Guy watched, a huge Battle Borg came up, and there was a brief altercation. The cyborg went to force the balaclava back on him. In the end, his opponent pulled the blue mask back on himself. He looked truly miserable. Guy looked at the red mask in his hand and sighed, then pulled it on. At least they both agreed on one thing: the masks were a pain.

The countdown started. Guy stepped up to the edge of the mat. He looked at the score and reminded himself: he had to win this point. Otherwise, he was out. He saw how the other moved his right leg a fraction slower than his left. Guy decided on his attack. As he spun in on the right side, he realised the limp had been a trap. The boy in blue silks had both blades up, and he was arching down on Guy. Guy was impressed. He cursed himself not to have anticipated such a simple ploy. They engaged in a fast blades' fight that saw Guy back up a couple of steps before, with elegant ease, he increased the tempo and saw his opponent tensing in concentration as he replied.

Aha, so my speed is causing you a problem, Guy thought. I will remember that.

He eased off, throwing up one last arching blow that sent the other leaping aside. Guy had the space for another attack. Kicking his jumping blades over his head, he spun in with his blades down to reach and cut his opponent's legs. The other saw him coming and responded by twisting back in a handspring. For an instant, they were in mid-air, heads down. They slashed at each other, and their blades met, then they both spun away. Guy was quicker to find his feet and pirouetted forward, blades outstretched. This time, there was an entirely satisfying tearing noise, as he split the red silk from the left shoulder blade down across his opponent's back to level with his kidney.

Guy paused as the crowd's cheers hit him like a wave. Blood was pearling up through the silk, where he had sliced into bare skin. So, his opponent was wearing no protection at all! Why then, was he fighting with un-blunted blades? Guy was on the defensive, because the cut, while impressive, was not a win, and across from him, his opponent charged back.

Their blades clashed. Guy was hard-pressed as the other rained down hard accurate blows. Each one was heavier than the last. All threatened to unbalance him. The edge of the mat was awfully close. Guy checked over his shoulder to see whether his foot blades were in or out of the black line. When he looked back up, he saw the punch and felt the wind of it passing close to his cheekbone. He had spun ahead of it in a tight spiral, bringing his hand blades up with determined accuracy. In an instant, he had one point pressed to his opponent's heart, while he drew his second blade level with his eyes.

Had he stepped outside of the mat as he spun round? He was so close to the edge. He saw the other looking down at his feet; he was inside. Just. He might have put a blade outside as he turned. In fact, he was sure he had. Eye to eye, both were panting as they waited for the referee. Either Guy was disqualified, or he had won.

As the lights lit up Two - Two, Guy saw frustration flash in his opponent's eyes, followed by anger. Guy stepped back quickly. This time, there were no words to say. Guy quickly backed to his stool.

"This is not a fair fight," Guy told Des. "He's not wearing any protection at all."

"Not your problem," Des replied shortly.

"I stepped off the blades mat."

"Did you? I didn't see it. You were bloody fast; that's all."

"They can't repair that cut across his back with skin spray."

"Again, not your problem."

"So, he has to go into the next round injured and without protection?"

"I'm sorry, Guy, but you have to win."

"Sorry for what?"

"Sorry for him."

Des nodded to where the other fighter leaned against the stool and panted with pain. Guy looked over and winced in sympathy. Both looked to where an extension had been flashed up; it would be three minutes until the next round. Des picked up Guy's gym jacket and helped him pull it on, closing the zip to his neck. Pausing to place his hand on Guy's shoulder, he said:

"Stay warm and conserve your strength, you have to win."

"...the time of his life."

"Regent Sayginn, I have hacked a secret comms channel. It's beaming video from the Cap of the Dome," Patrice said.

"On screen."

All around the ballroom, the screens flashed black for a few instants until the same scene appeared on each. On the largest display, the multiple images amalgamated to create an enormous 3D film. In the Cap of the Dome, in Chart Segat's private space, a gilded fight cage had been erected. Men stood three or four deep, yelling. On the blades mat, two small fighters – one wearing blue, one wearing red – were engaged in a blades fight.

"What?" said Sayginn. "Who is that?"

As they watched, the fighter in blue was cut with a sharp blade. He screamed. On a nearby screen, an analyst was running an ID check against a still of the screaming face.

"Iris scan. One hundred percent match. It is the prince!"

"I don't understand!" cried Sayginn. "Chart Segat promised to free him. Now he has him fighting like a caged animal. We have to get him out of there. We have to go now. They can't stop us from accessing the Dome. Patrice, send your men. Go."

"Regent, wait, there's something else."

"What? Tell me quickly."

"The images, the reason I was able to hack them. They are being broadcast into this palace. They are being received and played on a screen on the first floor in the west wing."

"Frederon!" Sayginn said with a snarl. "Frederon is watching this match."

Sayginn did not wait – she just accelerated the hover chair up the stairs and along the corridor. Patrice and the others raced to keep up. She burst into the salon without invitation and kept going until she found herself staring at the Emperor, who was resting on a sofa, watching the blades match on a large screen. He was laughing with his entourage as she arrived.

"Do you think this is amusing?"

"House Jewel vs. House Riffaut," Frederon said. "Of course, it's amusing."

"No, it's not." Sayginn could not find the words, because she could see on his face that the Emperor knew what she was going to say.

"You should never have cancelled the fight, Sayginn. Look at your son; he's having the time of his life."

"They are going to kill him. He's fighting without protection! And against someone who everyone agrees is a far better fighter than him."

"Well, you should have more confidence. He seems to be holding his own quite well."

"How did you get this feed? Why didn't you tell me if you knew?"

"Chart Segat," Frederon replied crisply. "Some of us still believe in him." He stood up. "Don't get peevish, Sayginn. I said to him that a good fight might do Teodor good. Although I had expected him to return him first."

"Frederon, how could you? Chart Segat killed Serge and murdered Deodran, how could you?"

"No, he didn't. Why would Chart Segat and the Militants plant those bombs? Look, this conversation is getting boring. We know where Teodor is. We have always known where he was. I presume you are sending your men over to retrieve him. I'll go with them. Chart Segat will not deny me. I will bring him home."

In the corner of the room, a door spontaneously opened, then closed. Sayginn looked and frowned. So, Princess Nuria had been listening – this was a conversation she did not want relayed to Ambassador Nikato. Yet for now, she needed the aliens. At least until she got her son back.

"You'd better bring him home, Frederon; you better."

Chapter 24

A Small Diversion

Karl Valvanchi glanced guiltily over his shoulder as he heard the crowd of men roar with bloodlust. He was no longer in the Cap of the Dome. He had made his way to the disk transport control area at the back. He hadn't wanted to let Prince Teodor out of his sight, but with the prince locked inside a gilded cage, Karl could think of only one plan to get him out.

Guy Erma had won another point. The match was going to five points. Good, he had more time. There was a three-minute extension too. Right, even more time. He paused as he saw the close-up of the deep, long cut across Teodor's back.

"I have to get the prince out," he muttered tersely. "But first, I have to disperse those Dome Militants."

Karl walked up to the control panel. Within seconds, the keyboard lit up at his touch. He spoke using comms back to the embassy.

"Zed, I need your help. Please don't disconnect this line."

"Sure, Karl, I'm right here. What do you need?"

"Open these."

Karl pointed, and at once, three compartments sprang open. Inside, there were neatly racked weapons and a stack of what looked like coiled steel ropes: snake droids.

Karl picked up a snake droid and examined it with a grim smile.

"Just a small diversion."

Chapter 25

Of Droids and Disks

"Let me take a look, see if I can do anything," Tilson said.

Teodor stood, gripping onto his stool. The cut across his back burned. He knew that climbing onto the stool would tear his back further. He took a few steps, then halted as Tilson examined and probed his back carefully. Even the remnants of his silk vest brushing against the scar were excruciating.

"I can give you morphine." Tilson hesitated, as both knew the drug would slow Teodor's responses.

"Against him?" Teodor asked. He couldn't imagine anything worse than being even slightly slower when facing such an opponent.

"Well, it's not ideal. Can you fight through the pain?"

"Do I have any choice?"

"It's only one point, Teodor. You still have the strength to defeat him. Take your time, find the opportunity. I've asked for an extension. Come and sit, rest for a few moments. Take some aspirin. It will dull the pain." He handed Teodor a glass of water with white specks. It was fizzy water too, absorbing the medicine quickly into his bloodstream. Grateful, he removed his balaclava to drink.

"I'm just taking my medicine," he said, as the Battle Borg stepped up beside him. The Borg had already picked up the balaclava and was pushing it toward Teodor's face. Teodor brushed him aside. The machine persisted. Teodor emptied the glass in one gulp, just in time before the Borg knocked it from his hand. The Borg attempted to force the mask onto his face again.

Teodor glanced down at the shards of glass scattered beneath his stool. He noticed how quickly Tilson had moved to avoid its fall. Then, picking up his blades, Teodor grabbed the facemask from the Borg's hands. With a swift motion, he sliced the silk into narrow shreds that floated to the ground. The Borg stared at him in disbelief, processing the action and searching for a solution. Teodor leaped down from the stool, out of the machine's reach. The Borg followed him, but as he leaped within the black circle of the blades mat, the Borg halted and lost its direction.

Teodor turned his face toward the light and deliberately brushed his hair back from his face. Let them look at me, he thought.

Let them see who I am.

Then, as the silks brushed against his injured back again, he had an inspiration. He reached across his body and sliced the blue silk with the Riffaut logo from his body. Now, he stood wearing only black shorts, black boots, calf greaves, and cuffs. There was no disguising how vulnerable he was, or who he was. With a blade in each hand, he was their prince and their future king. Unprotected, unyielding, he was ready for the fight. Would anyone believe, seeing him standing there, that he was Sebastian or any other model?

Closing his hands around his blades, he pushed one fist into his hip and let the other hand fall straight by his side. He squared his shoulders and looked beyond the gilded cage. See me, he thought. See me and recognize my father, who always stood like this when making tough decisions. Lifting his chin with pride, the crowd fell silent.

Look at me and be afraid, for I am the last surviving prince of Earth.

"That's Prince Teodor," Guy exclaimed, looking across with his mouth agape.

"Who did you expect?" Des murmured.

Guy gazed down at the blades in his hands and then back at the prince. It was what he had dreamed of. If only the prince was wearing armor. If only their blades were blunted. If only they were not wearing such ridiculous balaclavas.

"I can't do this," Guy muttered. "It's not a fair fight."

Des ground his teeth in frustration. "Do you want to face a Battle Borg with just a blunted blade in your hand?"

"Sorry?" Guy looked astonished.

"The Borgs are right there. What do you think will happen after this fight?"

"Chart Segat said he wouldn't do that to me."

"If you end up in the Dome Militant, the guys and I might be able to protect you. But if you lose this, expect Chart Segat to throw you to his Borgs tonight. Chartsie and his men will be out for blood later this evening. Your blood. You have to win."

Guy stepped away from Des. The color had drained from his face, and his hands felt cold. He squeezed his blades to restore circulation.

"He won't do that to me," Guy replied.

"Oh, won't he?"

Guy glanced over his shoulder. From here, he could clearly see Chart Segat in the massive armchair that served as his throne. Around the fence, the men were silent, uncertain. What should he do? What should any of them do? He looked at Des one more time.

"Loulou and I can't help you with this," Des said. "You have to win."

Don't think about Chart Segat. Don't think about House Jewel. Don't think about the Dome Militant. Think only about yourself, Guy Erma, and you might survive. Guy heard Juke's advice clearly. Think of yourself.

"I know. I will. I'll win."

"Go for it, Guy."

Guy stepped up to the edge of the mat. He looked at the prince and felt a twinge of sympathy. Prince Teodor couldn't know how much he needed this victory. In any case, he was a prince; he was bound to be ransomed, rescued, and saved. He would be safe tonight.

While Guy Erma was an unregistered Domeside orphan. Who would protect him?

"This still isn't a fair fight," Guy said to himself, glancing at his armor and then at the questionable referee. "I have to win, yes, but let it at least be a fair fight." Suddenly, the countdown started, and Guy knew what he needed to do.

Nine

Reaching up to his ears, he pulled the mask off and sliced it in two on the edge of his blade.

Eight

With his left hand, he cut the tunic from his body, not even watching as the red silk fell to the floor.

Seven

He unfastened the buckle at his neck.

Six

He released the buckle at the center of his chest.

Five

He reached across to the buckle on his hip.

Four

With a fluid motion, he discarded his protective vest and stood across from the prince. Yes, he still wore chain mail shorts that stretched down his thighs, but there was nothing he could do about that now.

Three

He ran both hands over his face, pushing his black hair back. His Dome medallion gleamed at the center of his chest.

Two

He spun both blades across his palms.

One

He stepped up to the fight and, with a new resolution, faced his opponent. The crowd at his back was screaming their approval.

Now, thought Guy. We are equal. He looked to see if the prince had noticed. Teodor gave a smile of approval. Guy nodded in return and leapt forward to engage him. With new enthusiasm, they jumped into the fight and met in a clash of blades that was fast and accurate. Guy forced the pace and realised that Teodor did not seem to have slowed noticeably. He probably had not taken morphine; Guy knew it was the last thing he would do at this stage.

The flying blades were very decorative. They were equally matched in height, strength, speed and accuracy, as they spun across the mat keeping in close contact. Guy enjoyed the challenge. He had rarely faced such an equal opponent so close to him in age, but as he dodged a punch Teodor had added at the end of the last parry, he remembered this was not some demonstration.

Guy dived to the floor. Disappearing out of Teodor's reach and causing him to topple a little, Guy was already swinging his leg across the floor and slicing Teodor's jumping blades from underneath him.

Teodor fell forward, trying to throw himself bodily on top of Guy, but Guy had anticipated this and reached up to Teodor's shoulders. He rolled him over and pushed him down onto the floor and onto his back. Teodor screamed. In an instant, Guy knew he would win, and he went to leap on top of the prince, only the prince brought his leg up. Guy's momentum propelled him onto the prince's knee. Guy cried out as the knee punched into his belly, and it was all he could do to roll away. He lay panting on his stomach, glancing around to check as the prince was clawing the floor to pull himself up to his feet.

I have to get up, thought Guy. At that moment, the floor on which he lay fell away.

Guy dropped. He realised, astonished, that the disk transport was in motion. A circular door in the floor was opening. Guy scrambled to his feet. The metal floor on which Guy stood was sliding away, opening up an abyss into the Dome below. Instinctively, Guy moved away from the drop. But the disk was closing itself away and very soon the floor would disappear from under his feet, and he would fall! He looked up. Above him, the prince was staring over the edge looking down at him.

To Guy's unending wonder, the prince immediately reached down to grab his hand. Guy leapt up but not far enough, rocking on the edge of the large circular opening. At once, the prince wrapped an arm around his waist and steadied him.

The prince hauled Guy up onto the fighting mat. Guy glanced down and immediately felt sick. He had nearly fallen, all the way down to the floor of the Dodecahedron Dome. It did not bear thinking about. He turned his back on the opening.

The prince was not moving; he stared into the abyss that had opened in their fighting arena. Why had the door opened? Guy could hear the men shouting. "What now?"

Was this supposed to happen? The scoreboard read two—two.

Should he fight on?

Teodor backed away. He grabbed Guy by the arm and drew him away from the opening. Guy glanced over his shoulder: another disk was coming up from below. There was nothing on it – well, no people anyway. Was that a piece of rope?

What about the fight? The clock was still ticking. He glanced across to Des, to see what he was doing. Then, out of the corner of his eye, he saw something move.

The prince?

The prince leapt on top of him. Guy knew such a body tackle was not strictly legal, but apparently, the prince wanted to win. Guy fought to bring his blades up, but the prince wrestled him to the ground.

"Stop it!" the prince shouted.

Guy wriggled, desperate to free himself. He was not going to yield. He was not going to lose!

"Stop it!" the prince cried. "Look!"

The prince had yanked his head, pulling his hair back and forcing him to look.

A snake droid. Above their heads, bullets were spiralling out into the Cap of the Dome. The shouts from beyond the golden cage had turned to screams, noise, and smoke confusion. Someone was attacking them!

"Stay down," Teodor insisted.

"We need to get under it," Guy said.

"Yes, I know. Go!"

On elbows and knees, they crawled onto the newly-arrived disk platform and underneath the snake droid. They cowered in its shadow, safe as above their heads, bullets spiralled in all directions.

"What in God's name is happening?" Guy muttered.

All around them, the metal of the gilded cage was rocking and exploding. One panel was hit at the join and started to topple. A second followed suit. In a matter of seconds, the entire structure had collapsed inwards.

"I think someone is trying to rescue me," the prince muttered.

Guy was barely listening. He looked for Des. Des was flat on the floor, was he injured? He looked for Tilson; it seemed like Tilson might have escaped when the cage was destroyed. The Battle Borgs were both down. One was still twitching, but the other clearly dead.

"A rescue?" Guy repeated.

The lights had gone out. Guy could see that the crush of men who had been pressed up against the gilded cage had dispersed. Chart Segat had disappeared from his vast throne. Some had fallen. Some looked injured. Some were crouching between these bodies, either hiding or trying to escape. Some men tried to shelter in the bathroom, but a long volley of fire shattered the windows and mirrors. The men threw themselves to the floor. And still, the snake droid was shooting.

"Some rescue," Guy snapped.

"Yes, well, beggars can't be choosers," Teodor replied.

Guy glanced at him and could not hold back a cough-like laugh: "You're not a beggar... Sir."

The prince looked at him. Almost at once, his anxiety melted away. He smiled briefly. Guy felt him relaxing, and first checking for his blades, the prince reached over and said into his ear: "I suppose not. But you can call me Teo, Guy Erma."

"You know my name?"

"Everyone knows Guy Erma," Teodor smiled just once. He went back to peering out at the room, and then added: "I have to get out."

"We both have to get out." Guy pointed up at the digits glowing on the underside of the snake's head: "That's a five-second fuse."

Teodor nodded and pointed to the bathroom. "That's an iron-clad jacuzzi. Can you run?"

"It's shooting everything that moves."

Teodor pointed to the shrinking bullet tail of the snake. "Ten, nine, eight..." He counted down the last rounds. "Ready?" Guy nodded. "Five, four, three, two, one."

The last bullet had been shot. They rose up on their blades and sprinted across the space. Around them, the other men were moving too, heading to the exit or throwing themselves flat on the floor behind couches. Guy and Teodor jumped as one into the jacuzzi bath and stayed under the water. Above their heads, they saw the light flash gold, then back to black. Then they resurfaced, coughing and spluttering.

"I don't know why you think this is a rescue; that thing almost killed us," Guy protested.

As they watched, the disk transport started moving again, and what remained of the snake droid disappeared. Something else was coming.

"I need to get out fast. Is that the door?" Teodor said. Suddenly, he grabbed Guy by the shoulder and put a blade to his neck. "Decide now: will you help me?" He pointed at the door.

"The Dome Militant went that way," Guy said. He reached up to push the blade away and looked to see Chart Segat had retreated into the next chamber. Soon, he would come back with Dome Militant on all sides. All around, the Dome Militant were starting to stand up and dust themselves off. No one was looking at them, yet. Teodor stared fearfully at the uniformed men.

The double door slammed shut into Chart Segat's face. The locks slid closed. Who was controlling the doors?

"Will you help me?" Teodor insisted, pushing the blade back under Guy's chin.

Guy reached up to the blade. The edge was sharp when he tried to push Teodor's hand away. The prince did not yield.

Could he mean this? Guy thought. After everything, he was going to be killed by his prince.

"I have to escape," Teodor insisted.

Guy tried to think, what were the odds of them getting out of the Dome from here? It had to be possible, didn't it? But if he helped the prince escape, how much more trouble would he be in?

"Whatever Chartsie says, you obey him." He remembered Loulou's flat warning. He did not need to hear what Chart Segat was shouting from the other side of the door to know what he wanted. He saw Teodor looking nervously in the same direction.

I am on my own, Guy thought. I have to decide.

"There is another way out," Guy looked straight at Teodor, "But it will be dangerous, us being so wet."

"You swear to get me out?" Teodor replied.

"Will there be a reward?"

"What kind of reward?" The prince sounded surprised.

"I want to go with you to Buckingham Palace."

"Oh." Teodor was clearly relieved. Both turned to the sound of shots. The Militant were shooting the hinges off the double door holding back Chart Segat.

"Tonight," Guy insisted.

Chapter 26

Flight from the Dome

In the Cap of the Dome, another disk-jet had appeared. As it rose up through the floor, all around, small groups of Dome Militant were crouched – blades in hands, watching. They relaxed when they saw the disk was not bearing another snake droid but a single Dome Militant warrior, with blades in both hands.

Shape-shifted once more, Karl scanned the Cap of the Dome. He realized at once that the prince was gone. So, his plan had worked. Zed's smart programming of the snake had succeeded. None of the Dome Militant had been injured, but the cage had been destroyed and all the Borgs were dead.

What had happened to Prince Teodor? He scanned for DNA traces, and a trail of blood droplets flashed bright orange in front of his eyes. He followed their footsteps to the great bath. There, he paused a moment – looking at the blades, greaves, and calf protection abandoned at the side of the jacuzzi, in puddles of water. Glancing over his shoulder, he heard Chart Segat giving loud instructions, rallying the Dome Militant. Karl paused a moment, picked up the abandoned blades equipment, and hid it in his pack.

No need to leave any clues for Chart Segat, he thought grimly.

From the bathroom, the trail was easier to follow. Clearly, Prince Teodor was not alone. Karl made his way along the dark space between the bathroom wall and the outer pane of the Dome, looking out onto the city – and found the open panel into the infrastructure of the Dome itself. An opening into a crawl space that threaded its way through the verticals and horizontals of the Dome. Quickly now, Karl reattached the grille and tightened the screws. As he came out of the darkness, he bumped into a Dome Militant Guard.

"Did you see them?" the young man asked. "Did they get out through the verticals?"

Karl paused and theatrically looked over his shoulder. He could see the soldier was dying to get into the space himself.

"They're not there," he replied.

"Do you mind?"

Karl stepped aside; he thought there was something remarkably familiar about the young man. Before he had time to think about it, he heard a voice.

"Des, are they there? Can you see them?"

It was Chart Segat coming up close. Karl slipped away. From the shadows, he watched. Des shaking his head as he reappeared.

"The grille was locked tight. If they had gotten out that way, they would have left it open behind them. Besides which, they cannot climb with blades' gear on."

"Prince Teodor could never climb as Guy does," Chart Segat said. "They must be hiding somewhere. Fifty to the man that finds them. C'mon, Des, they can't be far."

Karl Valvanchi smiled as he listened. So, the prince had got away, and the Dome Militant had no idea where he was. But Karl knew how to find him. He sent out a loud thought message:

'Nuria, I need you to help me find the prince again.'

'Uncle, I'm in Buckingham Palace.'

'Find a balcony or get up on the roof... Send me your location, and I will boost your powers.'"

***

Teodor realized he was climbing down the very structure of the Dome. Inside the verticals that supported the large pentagons that made up the Dome, there was an intricate trellis of connected triangles. It was not wide. It was easy enough to find hand and footholds. Only, it was best not to look down. The drop beneath them, the sloping abyss right down the side of one of the highest pentagons of the Dome, was frightful. Beyond the next junction was a vertical descent. As Teodor thought of a long straight drop, his foot slipped, and he found himself hanging by one hand. He must have yelled out because, below him, Guy looked up.

Teodor peered down at him, realizing how far he had fallen behind. He reached up above his head with his other hand. He wanted to catch hold with both hands but found he could not reach. He tried to lift one of his feet up to a strut, but the distance was too far. He tried his other leg. The pain in his fingers was excruciating, but he could not let go. Then he felt Guy underneath him. He looked down. Guy was pushing his shoulder up between his legs like a seat and propelling Teodor upwards. Teodor reached up again. His second hand caught. Mercifully, his right hand found a strut. He was pulling himself up and off Guy. Guy kept climbing until they were alongside each other in the confined space. Guy reached up and stroked Teodor's hair.

"You haven't got the hang of it, have you?"

"I can climb," Teodor said. "I'm not afraid." But he knew that he sounded afraid, very afraid. Had this Domeside boy noticed?

"Do you know the song 'Goran Rider'?"

"Goran Rider?" What was this now?

Guy started singing: "He was a no-good Goran rider. What more can I say?"

Of course, Teodor had heard it, even though he was not supposed to listen to music on the radio. The girls played it in the stables. The tune was catchy, and Teodor realized he knew the words, so he joined in: "He made me laugh, he made me sigh and then he rode away!"

"Great song!" Teodor yelled.

Guy grinned and swept the hair from his eyes.

"Ok, so watch! He was (right hand) a no-good (left foot) Goran rider (pause).

What more (left hand) can I (right foot) say? Now breathe." Then Guy changed his voice to mimicry: "It's imperative to breathe."

Teodor laughed. He was thinking of the choirmaster in the Cathedral, how he was always scolding him: "It's imperative to breathe, Prince Teodor."

"Did he say that to you too?" he asked Guy.

"He said it more often to me. I was your understudy. He always made it clear I was nowhere near good enough."

"I'm sorry about that," Teodor said, "I'll ask for someone else next time."

"What? Who? He's the head of Cathedral music."

"In that case, I will tell him he is too busy and important. I am sure he must have some underling who ..."

"Ok, can we reorganize the Cathedral music team another time. Now watch... He made me laugh (right foot), he made me cry (left foot) and then (left hand) he rode (right hand) away."

"Breathe!" they both said together. Was this what it meant to have a friend? Teodor wondered.

"Ok. Try it."

Teodor started singing:

"He was a no-good Goran..."

"You need to sing louder..." Guy shouted up at him.

"Won't someone hear us?" Teodor said, he was right to wonder, no?

"No, can't you feel how cold it is? We're climbing down the outside of the Dome. No one can hear us."

Teodor reached to press a hand to the wall. It really was freezing. Of course, he was climbing down the vertical of the Dodecahedron Dome, how else did he expect to escape?

"This is crazy," he muttered, then with more conviction, he sang.

"... Goran rider. What more can I say? He made me laugh. It works..." Teodor exalted, then started singing again. "He made me sigh - whoops wrong hand."

"Once you get started, you can't stop until you reach the bottom. And sing a bit louder. It helps. The song blocks out everything else."

"You mean the fear?" Teodor said cheerfully because he was no longer, in any way, afraid.

Guy smiled. "Well, if you were afraid, I expect it would. Do you want me to shimmy past, so I am below you if you need me again?"

They were down in less time than Teodor would have thought possible – just two verses of the song 'Goran Rider.' They sat perched at the intersection, peering down the next long vertical.

"It's a long way down." Teodor said. Another long narrow chute which he had to climb down.

"Don't worry about it." Guy replied. "We're not going all the way to the bottom, but you can see it's dangerous. Won't be a problem for us?"

"No mistakes, huh?" Teo replied cheerfully.

"Mistakes, us?" Guy replied. "It's not as far as it looks. We need to keep going because it won't take them long to realize where we are."

"Oh?" Teodor stiffened as he thought this through.

"We don't want them waiting for us at the bottom."

"No, we don't," Teodor said, glancing back up where they had come from. "Let's get moving."

"Don't look down. I know I don't."

Teodor took a breath and started to sing again.

"Louder," called Guy, joining in. They continued, quickly moving hands and feet in turn – until Guy led them out of the trellis into a more conventional air-conditioning tunnel.

Now Guy shot along, sliding on his hands and knees like a supersonic slug along the polished metal surface. Teodor threw himself after him. He caught up with him, only to hear him counting.

"Five, or is that six?" Guy was talking to himself, and Teodor saw him shaking the grille, but it did not budge.

"Go back," he whispered to Teodor. "It's the fifth exit. I think I miscounted." Teodor nodded and backed up as quickly as he had come. It was not far. Guy squeezed past to the previous air-grill. He reached to shake it, and it came away in his hand.

"Phew!" Guy said. He let the plastic grid drop below him. Teodor sighed with relief. He sat back and banged his head. He turned and saw a strange sight. Screwed to the inside of the air conditioning tunnel was a glass brick. Inside, he could see soil and plants, and movement. There were insects inside the brick. He peered closer. It was an entire miniature world inside what looked like an industrial glass brick. He looked again. There was a metal device mounted to the side, and then he noticed the screws. The screws attaching the glass brick to the wall were shiny and brand new.

Then he heard a voice inside his head:

"Where are you, my prince?"

"Nuria, is that you?" Teodor asked, then as he peered into the miniature world across from him, he said. "Have you seen this weird thing?"

"That's a poison pill," cut-in another voice, a male voice.

"Poison pill," Teodor muttered. "Nuria, what is this? Don't they make these on Sas Darona? Does that mean plague? I thought Sas Darona was in lockdown." He leaned in to look at the markings visible on one end of the glass brick.

"Don't touch it, just tell me where you are."

"Here," he thought, then looked down into the changing room. "Here."

"What's that? Oh, now I see you." Nuria said. "I have the location, uncle; I am sending it to you now."

"I will be there shortly, my prince," Karl concluded.

***

"Did you know there's a poison pill up there?" Teodor said, jumping down to where Guy had opened his locker.

"A poison what? Forget that," Guy said, ignoring how Teodor pointed up at the tunnel. "Look, I thought this might happen," Guy told him. "I thought I might need to make a quick getaway." He laughed bitterly. "But I only have one set of spare clothes." Guy's hands were shaking as he reached up to take down the trousers.

"Look, you wear the sweatshirt and pants. I'll wear the t-shirt and jacket. I've got these," he pointed to his leggings. "It will look like I've been training."

"Just look," Teodor insisted, and Guy clambered up the lockers to see what Teodor meant.

"That's new," he said with a frown, showing Teodor the image. "It wasn't even there yesterday."

"Ok, well that's something." Teodor was pulling on the shirt, grateful to have some clothes to wear, and looking beyond Guy to the locker. "Are those my shoes?"

"Yes, I took them," Guy stopped. He had been about to say, 'To keep them safe,' but he knew this was a lie. "I am sorry I took them. I don't know what came over me. Please take them. I don't want them, honestly."

"Oh, I don't care." Teodor grabbed the shoes. "They're mine." He closed his eyes and breathed in the smell of polished leather. "Mine." He muttered. Just even a touch of new polished shoes made him feel stronger.

"I wanted you to have them back. I promise," Guy said. "And I want to help you. You're my prince. I'm loyal to the empire, you know?"

"Loyal to the empire, fear only God," Teodor nodded in approval. "It's a good start." Then, lacing the shoes: "Thank you, Guy Erma. So, how do we get from here to Buckingham Palace?"

Perplexed, Guy shrugged. "Yes, I guess that's where we're going," he said, partly to himself, before adding. "Can you wear your running blades with those?" Guy asked.

"Yes," Teodor turned them over. "They have the grooves here."

"Here, you can have my best blades," Guy said. "I can make use of my training pair."

"We need to be fast?"

"Yes. And I never walk anywhere. None of the Militants do. We don't want to draw attention to ourselves. So, we move, and we move fast."

Guy was already standing at the door. Quickly, Teodor followed.

"It's clear. Now let's go."

Only it wasn't. It wasn't clear.

From the double door, a troop of Dome Militant were charging around the curved perimeter. Guy tugged Teodor, and they raced away from them. They were a good distance ahead when Teodor glanced back.

"Battle Borgs!"

Guy looked over his shoulder. Borgs pushed through the line of Dome Militant. Then the shooting started. Guy was behind Teodor.

"Faster," hissed Guy. "We have to go faster."

He leaned into a sprint, head down, his running blades flying. As he did, a shot rang out. It hit Guy's Communicator, just centimeters from Teodor's back. Guy saw Teodor glance at the mangled metal on Guy's wrist, but neither stopped. They pushed on faster, stretching their legs to lengthen their leaps.

They passed another double door. Out of the corner of his eye, Teodor saw movement. Not more Dome Militant? The door burst open behind them. It was a single black-clad soldier. He did not follow Guy and Teodor. Instead, he knelt combat-ready facing their pursuers.

Who is he?

Teodor checked to see if Guy had seen, but Guy sprinted forward, only stopping as he reached the far end of the circular corridor and a final double door. He stopped, holding the door open. Teodor came up alongside him. They glanced back. The Dome Militant had slowed, cautious to see one of their own standing guard, but the Battle Borgs kept coming. As Teodor watched, the single guard metamorphosed.

No longer a Dome Militant guard, he was a tall man with white cropped hair, who stood up and drew himself up to face the huge Battle Borgs alone. He reached an empty hand out towards them, and the Borgs stopped. It took them a few steps to lose their momentum. Their weapons sagged and the light dimmed in their eyes. The Battle Borgs came to a complete standstill just a meter ahead of where the man stood.

"Who was that?" Guy whispered, turning accusingly towards Teodor.

"I think my mother sent him to rescue me."

'Just run.' The voice in Teodor's head was an order. 'Just run and don't look back.'

A sudden explosion of power sent the frozen Borg tumbling, even as the Dome Militant were thrown left and right like leaves on a breeze.

"I need to get out of here," Teodor said.

"What is that?" Guy said, crouching defensively.

"I don't know what he is." Teodor pushed them both through the door and pulled it closed. There were stairs before them.

He's lying, thought Guy. That's Killer Valvanski. He knows it, and I know it. So, the Regent sent Killer Valvanski into the heart of the Dome. The Militants would just hate that. They would never forgive her.

For a moment, Guy had a doubt. So, who was he fighting for? He thought he was helping his prince. But if his ally was Killer Valvanski, did that make him a traitor? He looked at the sweat pearling around the edge of Teodor's face. He saw the fear-filled way Teodor swept his hair back from his face.

It's not his fault, Guy thought. He's just trying to get home. Ultimately, I'm not yet a member of the Dome Militant either, I have to think of myself. Suddenly, Guy was overtaken with urgent fear:

"Let's get out of here. Can you do this?"

Teodor looked around. Guy had leapt down an entire flight of eight steps to an interim landing on the square staircase. Teodor nodded a little nervously and threw himself after Guy, accurately landing beside him, but also grateful when Guy reached to grab his arm and steady him on landing.

"Let's go," Guy murmured and led the way. They made their way down the stairs in massive bounds that took them down flight after flight of steps. In a matter of minutes, they made their way down eight or ten stories. Guy pushed open the doors, and they stepped out into the competition blades arena. He pulled Teodor after him as the prince looked up in wonder at the huge panes of the Dome and the light and shadows cast over the competition gym even at night. The night illumination was redder and somehow more deadly than the morning light. Guy sighed. Two Dome Militant guards were standing inside the doors. Now they looked up and recognized him:

"Ah, Guy," said the first.

"Benjy!" Guy exclaimed; hand outstretched. He was as round as he was tall, and Guy knew he was one of the very first Dome Militant. Since he rarely put in any time at the gym, for several years he had been rewarded with duties at the guard posts in the car park or the back entrances of the stadiums. Now he stepped forward with a clipboard.

"I have a note here to return you to the Cap of the Dome if I see you."

"Not me!" Guy replied, but behind him Teodor gasped. The fat soldier glanced at Teodor then turned to look at Guy:

"What did you do this time? The call came from Chart Segat's office itself."

Guy shrugged and tried to smile.

"Hey, Benjy, you know me. A bit of this, a bit of that. Ain't nothing illegal, mind. You know that."

"I know you." Benjy reached to sweep the hair back from Guy's eyes, pushing his head back a little to look in his face.

"And I know Chart Segat, or rather, I know things about Chart Segat I wish I didn't." He bent down and whispered in Guy's ear: "So just you get out of here, and don't come back tonight, do you hear me?"

As Teodor leaned in to hear the whisper, Benjy noticed him again. He looked at him for a minute, then screwed up his eyes in concentration:

"And I know you," he clicked his fingers, as if trying to remember. Guy stared. Had Benjy recognized the prince? He had to find a way to get Teodor out too.

To his surprise, he heard Teodor say. "Sebastian, my name is Sebastian. I'm from Ho... the Riffaut."

"That's right, one of them lookalikes," the other guard said. "You should be at the party upstairs, no?" Guy winced – was Benjy going to send Teodor back?

"No," Teodor cut in, and then to Guy's infinite delight, the prince said: "I have a client back at the House. A good customer..." Guy checked. Yes, Teodor had Benjy's full attention now, but did he know what he was doing?

"I can give you a cut if you let me get there on time," Teodor said.

Now Guy was struggling not to laugh. He wondered if the cameras had picked up this exchange. No one would ever believe this. He could hear Sebastian roaring with laughter inside his head.

"The Riffaut pays you on Monday, right?" Benjy replied. "Well, make sure you come and see me, or the next time I see you, you'll wish you had."

Guy felt embarrassed for Benjy and his blatant greed. Teodor looked a little pale. Guy watched Teodor nod once.

"I will come back on Monday."

Benjy went back to his chair and picked up his newspaper. It was a sign for them to carry on.

"Quick thinking, kiddo," Guy whispered, then with a laugh. "I can't believe you said that." Teodor blushed.

"Don't you dare tell anyone," Teodor told him. "I'm not a fashion model. I'll never be a fashion model, but I met a boy called Sebastian in the cells."

"That's right. He was shooting his mouth off last night at a party. I know Sebastian. But I'm not a fashion model. I'll never be a fashion model. Ever." He glanced back, Benjy was staring at a screen. Guy knew he was doing his best not to see where they went – so he added. "We should run."

Guy led Teodor in a sprint along the full length of the back wall, all around the vast competition gym. Then they were out the far side, and out onto a broad curving avenue that led down to the atrium. As the door closed behind them, Guy paused to take a breath and started down at a more leisurely pace. The avenue was crowded. The atrium below them more so. It was time to mingle with the throng.

"Do you realize how much money you just promised to Benjy back there?" Guy asked, as they walked in measured leaps, careful not to draw attention to themselves. When Teodor did not reply, he added: "You know how much Sebastian is earning this weekend?"

"Of course, you and Sebastian are friends?"

"Oh yeah, we go way back," Guy said. "Even from before he had the surgery."

"Well, he did mention the money. He suggested that if I pretended to be him, I should offer the Dome Militant a five per cent cut, about five hundred, which is a lot for a Dome Militant."

Guy paused. He quickly did the calculation, and the resulting number was a shock. "Ten thousand? I did not know it was that much."

He did not speak for a long while, instead concentrated on weaving his way through a large crowd in the atrium. There was a crowd of people fifty deep trying to leave the Dome.

"The Dome is in lockdown," Guy told him. He was looking at how all the entrances had been closed, and long lines of people were queuing. Guy saw that it was the teenagers who were being actively searched, and not too kindly either. The men and women were being ignored. He looked over to see if Teodor had seen it too. The prince looked dazed and weary – so close to freedom, yet so far.

"They are checking everyone on exit," Guy explained.

Teodor nodded. Guy could see he did not understand. "They're not all like Benjy."

"We need to get out," Teodor said, his voice pitched high in panic. "If we stand here much longer, they will find us. They will take us."

"I know that" Guy said, taking his hand and squeezing it. "I know how we can get out too. It's just that the person I know who will get us out is not on duty yet."

"We can't stay here."

"No," Guy sighed and looked around. "We need to hide." Across from them, the crowds, lights, and music of Bistro Jewel seemed to beckon.

"Are you hungry?"

"Starving," Teodor admitted. "But if we can get back to..."

"Just now we need to hide. Come with me."

With their heads down, Guy and Teodor entered the busy Bistro Jewel. Guy had had a word with the head waiter as he came in, and he had been pointed towards the staff door. There was a dance act performing on the staircase stage. Most eyes were on the girls and their colorful costumes. Guy led Teodor through the staff corridors, towards the noise of the kitchens, until...

"Hi, Guy! Have you finished for tonight?" It was Marline.

"Hmm... hmm," replied Guy, then: "You look cute!"

She had changed into a short, red tutu, with a black corset, and a striped overskirt ruched up to reveal her legs and underclothes.

"They charged me fifteen hundred for this dress. Can you imagine? The first time I've had to pay. Still, I'll get four thousand two hundred for the party. I had to pay for the shoes too," she sighed. "I hope he notices me."

"Who?" Guy asked.

She preened a moment, then added: "I was at Chartsie's table for dinner, and I have been invited to Simon Sorrow's Ascot Party. It's themed as Space Pirates." She pushed out her hip to show a fake sword.

"Guy," Teodor hissed, miming the need for speed.

"Simon's saying he'll invite some of us girls to his island. You know, Paradise Bay?" She nodded seriously. "It's well paid because it will be a whole week away. I'm hoping he'll pick me."

"Guy," Teodor insisted, so Marline noticed him, and she was annoyed to be interrupted.

"Aren't you two supposed to be upstairs? Didn't Chartsie ask you to work?" She asked Guy but she also glared at Teodor.

Oh no, thought Guy. Because he could think of nothing else, he reached up, turned her face toward him and away from Teodor. However, Marline was not easily distracted. She turned again to look at Teodor. She was assessing him with a trained eye. Guy decided he would have to take the risk.

"I too want to be free, Marline," he whispered. She took a last look at Teodor. Then she turned back to Guy; her face was grim.

"They are looking for..." she hesitated, "for all the Riffaut models."

"I'm not," Teodor said.

"I have to free him," Guy pleaded, silencing Teodor with a nudge.

"And he's going to pay you?" Marline asked, "How much?"

"More money," Guy searched for an answer. "More money than you earn in a year."

"Hold on," Teodor countered, "How much..." he quailed as Marline glared at him.

"Marline should get a cut," Guy added. "At least 10%."

"15%" Marline said firmly. "So, listen, Des is on duty from seven in the bistro tunnel. He always lets us girls sneak home for a snack or change of clothes. He'll let you through."

"Yes, I know."

"You'll need to hide, and you'll need a distraction." She nodded to where Chart Segat had entered Bistro Jewel, and Loulou was standing to greet him.

"Can you do something?" Guy asked.

"Yeah, but you need to keep him out of the way," Marline said.

Teodor was standing frozen, staring at Chart Segat through the serving window.

"Don't worry." Guy said, he reached up to kiss Marline on the cheek, then took Teo's hand. "Let's go!"

"Good luck, Guy," Marline called after them.

"Was she your girlfriend?" Teodor whispered to Guy.

"Yes."

"How old is she?"

"Sixteen."

Teodor frowned.

"But Simon Sorrow is about a hundred years old."

"I know, but Marline wants to be very rich. And Simon Sorrow is rich, you know?"

"She knew Chart Segat."

"Everyone in the Dome knows Chartsie," Guy replied with a sigh. "Don't worry; she won't tell. She's my best friend."

"Can she really help? Help us escape?"

All at once, there was a loud drumroll from the performance area. A loud voice called out:

"And for the first time tonight. The one. The only. The youngest face of House Jewel, said to have the narrowest waist of all our girls. I give you: Marline."

"Oh yeah!" Guy murmured.

"Does she?" Teo stared, for Chart Segat was turning to look at the stage.

"She's really good," Guy said, then added. "Watch out!" The chef was coming towards them: "Now hush, let me do the talking."

Oh, I met him on Magnolia Way, and I was just a girl...

Teodor glanced back once to check. It was Marline, she was singing. *She really was very pretty*, he thought.

Chapter 27

Soap Suds

The Borgs had stopped. Zed had done it again; he had isolated the code Karl needed, to stop the Borgs. Only now Karl faced two dozen Dome Militant guards. As he stood before them in his natural state, he could tell that they recognised him. Their only confusion was finding him at the heart of their Dodecahedron Dome.

That won't last long, thought Karl. As he watched, he saw one, then another of the Militants reach for their blades.

Time to go. Karl dived through the doors and down the stairwell where he had seen Teodor escape and sprinted in pursuit. He shape-shifted back to a Dome Militant as he ran, but he was aware this might no longer protect him. Still, at the entrance to the gym, the two door guards barely looked at his ID. He headed across the gym and out to the atrium. The scene that greeted him was chaotic.

The last games had just finished, and crowds were making for the exit. At the same time, the Dome had gone into lockdown. All the doors out of the atrium were shut or heavily staffed, and Dome Militant were demanding the IDs of everyone. There would be no escape through those doors.

'Nuria, can you sense the prince?'

'I can't, not now you are inside a building. If I was there, maybe.'

'Stay where you are, the Dome is dangerous tonight,' Karl replied. 'Tell Sayginn to send every man she has. Teodor is on the run, but with luck, he might stumble into the right hands.'

'I thought you said Guy Erma was good,' Nuria replied.

'He certainly knows his way around the Dodecahedral, but he only one boy. He can't do this alone. Nor can I. Tell Sayginn. Send everything.'

***

Teodor found himself wearing a hat as well as an apron, and he was washing dishes. He had a little brush for scrubbing, and a deep bowl of hot water and suds.

"The deal is," Guy explained. "We wash dishes until Joe arrives at seven. If we can clear this backlog, we'll get one hot supper to share for free. Let's do this — we've less than ten minutes."

Teodor looked around the busy kitchen.

"Hiding in plain view. And your girlfriend, can she sing that long?"

Teodor glanced back to where the crowd clapped and sung along.

He was a no good goran rider, what more can I say...

"Oh yeah!" Guy danced a few steps. "She would sing all night, if they let her."

Teodor nodded – he too danced a few steps on the spot, but one of the kitchen cooks shouted at them, and they both turned back to their work.

"I should call my mum," Teodor said.

"You can't," Guy said. "They are all on the Dome network. They would recognise our voices straightaway. They would come straight for us. Look, we're safe here. Three exits see. They think we're trying to escape out; they won't be looking for us here."

They worked on. Behind them, the crowd cheered, and the host said. "Sing us another one, Marline?"

Teodor felt uneasy. Surely the simplest thing was to call his mother? He glanced around the kitchen; there were three doors he could see, but could he trust Guy? Teodor looked at the burnt Communicator on his wrist. Guy had saved his life, not just once, but in the climb down as well. They were mere metres from the exit of the Dome. He watched as Guy's Dome medallion slipped out from behind his apron. Guy caught it before it dipped into the soap suds.

"Why are you helping me?" Teodor nodded purposefully at Guy's medallion, still in his hand. "You're one of them, aren't you?"

"Not yet," Guy replied firmly. It was true he was not yet a Dome Militant. Teodor wanted to believe him, so waited. "I want to join the Dome Militant. I want to join it very much. I'm the best blades fighter of my age in the Dome, and..."

"You're good at maths," Teodor finished thoughtfully. He spoke slowly now. Hc had to discover the truth. "So why would you not get a place?"

Guy paused, then shrugged.

"Because I'm an unregistered orphan from Old Fleet Street. I don't know who my parents are. And if you're unregistered, well, no Black and Gold. Unless... Well, Chart Segat said if I..."

Guy hesitated.

"If you what? What did Chart Segat want?"

"It wasn't a fair fight tonight," Guy said. "You being without protection. Both of us fighting with live blades."

"Yes, that was Chart Segat, he organised it that way," Teodor agreed. He added in a conciliatory way: "You didn't know."

"No, I didn't know until I cut you. Look, I'm sorry..."

"Don't change the subject. Tell me about Chart Segat." Teodor could see that Guy might have turned and walked or even run away, but they were chained to that spot by the fact they had to do the dishes. Teodor took a pan and rinsed it, to give Guy time to breathe.

"I think they hoped... I believe Chartsie thought I might kill you. When I went to knife your heart, I thought you were wearing protection. If I had cut you..."

"I pushed you aside, though," Teodor recalled. "Just."

"I didn't want to kill you. I honestly thought... I have never fought anyone without protection before. I mean, it's Dome Militant rule number one. You fight blades – you wear protection. Not even the champions fight..." Guy faltered, "Well, you hear stories of fights to the death, but I thought they were just that: stories."

"Guy, this is not about the fight. You were forced just as much as I was. I can see that. But even when you knew I was unprotected, even when you saw I was your prince, you were desperate to beat me. You must have known there would be consequences if you hurt me."

Guy did not speak for a few moments. He was shaking his head in denial, but not saying anything. Teodor waited. He was starting to wonder whether he should have trusted Guy at all.

"They told me I had to do what Chart Segat said. Whatever he said," Guy hesitated. "And if I did not..."

"What? What would make you consider killing your prince?"

"He would have..."

"What?" Teodor insisted.

"He said he would throw me to his Borgs. He meant to..." Teodor stared at him, willing him to tell the truth. Something he could believe. Guy flinched under his gaze, then continued with new conviction:

"He would have locked me in that cage with two, maybe four, cyborgs. I would only have a blunted blade. He would have watched as they tormented, then killed me."

Teodor interrupted and he spoke as if he was in a dream. "He would throw you to his Borgs. The only question, then, is how long before you died? An hour, six hours, a day?" Guy swallowed nervously. So Chartsie had said that to the prince too. "I didn't think he meant it," Teodor concluded.

"I didn't think he would do it, either. Not to me. But there's this boy, Des. He's a friend of mine. He won the Dome Junior Championship and the Emperor's medal. That was three years ago. He was just sixteen. Chart Segat sent him to fight the Battle Borg." He looked at Teodor. Now the prince had to know, too. "Des was wearing his victor's gold, and some basic protective gear, I think. They let him have his hand blades, but still, they made him fight for his life. Fight for his life for nearly three hours." Teodor reached out to steady Guy, held his arm firmly, as Guy swayed and blinked back tears.

"Des Parks? I know him," repeated Teodor. "I have his poster..."

Guy nodded slowly, but then he stopped. Teodor was pointing.

"Des Parks," he repeated. Guy turned to see Des standing looking at them.

"Marline told me I'd find you here."

Teodor and Guy exchanged glances. They were caught.

Des nodded to Teodor: "What's he still doing here?"

"The Dome is on lockdown." Guy replied. "Chef said he would give us a fried supper if we washed these dishes."

All the dishes were done now – they had cleared the wash station. Teodor dried with hands with something akin to pride, as he looked at Des.

"You said: That's not right Chartsie," he added by way of reminder. "This morning, remember?"

"Yes, I did," Des replied, then briefly he saluted with his fist to his heart. "Come, I'm on duty in the bistro tunnel."

"And you'll help?" Guy asked.

"Chartsie wants both of you back upstairs," Des told him.

"Please, Des. I did not win the fight."

"No, you didn't." He shot a glance of admiration at Teodor. "But you didn't lose either. I guess you both have to get out. I guess I'll have to close my eyes a moment while on duty?"

Des sounded fierce, but he winked at Teodor.

"Get your supper to go and come with me. Where are you going to go?"

Teodor saw Guy hesitate. "Buckingham Palace," he replied.

"All the bridges are closed." Des said.

"We'll have to use the south tunnel then," Guy winced at the prospect.

"You'll only get in by Old Fleet Street., Des told him. "And only if you get there quick."

Teodor wished he knew what they were talking about. Old Fleet Street was a long avenue through Domeside. Was that the shortest way out?

"Go up to the attic now and eat your supper. You'll think of something. If you're quick, and if the tunnel goes all the way under the river as they say..."

"You're talking about the old underground railway," Teodor interrupted. "Yes, it comes out near the stables. My father told me."

Des lifted his hand, and pressing his index finger to his thumb, mimed for silence.

"Why are you helping me?" Teodor asked. "If Chart Segat wants us upstairs."

"Chartsie is not always right. And you heard what Guy just told you." Des reached down to tug at his trouser leg. Teodor saw that where he should have a human ankle, he had a metallic cyber implant. "I only wear the skin when I'm training." Then, with a nod to Guy. "They did it to me; they'll do it to him." Des pointed at Guy. "He's got no mother and no father. Just like me. Just get him out of here and don't send him back. You have to protect Guy, Prince Teodor. Promise, King Teodor?"

Teodor was pale, as he finally understood. They were both speaking the truth. Teodor knew what he wanted. They needed his protection as their prince. He had to help them.

"As Imperial Prince of the Dodecahedral, and your future king, I do swear I will protect you, Guy Erma. So, help me God."

It was an oath. Both Guy and Des saluted him, fists firm against their hearts.

"So, help me God," they replied.

Teodor nodded in reply. He could not fail now. In his head he heard a voice:

'Run, Teodor. Run.'

Chapter 28

Alliance Ended

"Frederon – where is my son?"

Sayginn knew she sounded like a banshee, but why not? Hers was the desperate scream of a despairing mother. The Emperor had just arrived back from the Dome alone. He stood a moment, speechless, at the bottom of the stairs. Sayginn sped across the ballroom on her hover chair. Now she was on the first step, barring his progress. Her grief knew no bounds.

"You promised me. If I agreed to marry you, you would give me my son."

"Sayginn, calm down. Let's step into the library, shall we?"

Inside the dark room where the lights of the Dome served as the only illumination, Sayginn manoeuvred herself forward on the chair, aiming punches at the Emperor while he ducked out of the way. She wanted to hit him. To kill him. This was all his fault. And she hated him. The emperor stumbled back till, perched against a table, he caught her fists and held them.

"You promised me, Frederon, you promised me."

As he continued to hold her arms, Sayginn sat, helplessly weeping. At last, Frederon went to pour himself a drink.

"Chart Segat does not know where he is. The Militants are looking for him. Looking for him for real now."

"Looking for him for real. You're saying Chart Segat, and the Dome Militant have had him all this time?"

Frederon nodded.

"Chart Segat used the Battle Borgs. Somehow, he reprogrammed their base loyalty routines. They did whatever Chart Segat told them."

"And you knew?"

"Well, I did not know they would use Battle Borgs – Teo must have been terrified."

Sayginn could barely breathe, for waves of anger and despair were running through her.

"My only son, Freddie. He was all I had left. My son."

Sayginn could stand it no longer. She put her face in her hands and sobbed. After a while, Frederon sat down on a footstool nearby, drinking slowly.

"You were always so independent. Your son was your weak spot. I thought if I showed you. I thought you would see how you needed my protection."

"But why, Frederon? Why?"

"Chart Segat said there was a lost prince. Not one of mine; a baby boy who had been fathered by Erederon. I wanted to believe. I thought I could trust him. I wanted you to be my wife. I wanted my son's lost prince to be real."

"And Teodor?"

"An heir, a spare," Frederon said somewhat wistfully, before adding forcefully: "I never meant any harm to come to him. Chart Segat was supposed to take and hold him – hold him for twenty-four hours. I was right. In that time, you did agree to become my wife. I don't know if it started going wrong from the beginning, with the shooting in the Cathedral. If I had known..."

"But what happened to him, Frederon? Where is Teodor now?"

"He escaped. There was an explosion, and he escaped."

"But how?"

"He had that boy with him. I don't know what Chart Segat did to either, or in fact both, of them – but they ran like scared rabbits. It looks like they made it out by climbing down the columns of the Dome. They have had some help. Whom did you send in there? Is it Killer Valvanski?"

Sayginn did not reply.

"He is slaughtering them. He detonated a snake droid in the Cap of the Dome, and then he attacked the Dome Militant at a bottleneck at the top of some stairs. Who knows how many he has killed; how many he has injured?"

Sayginn said nothing. She picked up a picture of Prince Teodor from a table.

"Sayginn, he hacked the Dome computers. Chart told me they think he got everything, and then he set viruses that deleted everything else. It's complete chaos over there. We should assume he knows."

Sayginn reached to take a picture of Serge and Deodran.

"Now he knows about the small war Serge and Chart initiated – that you turned a blind eye to – on Sas Darona."

"Serge did not start any covert war. And I have not turned a blind eye to it. The humans recognise Zaracan sovereignty on Sas Darona," Sayginn muttered.

"Yes, and I am sure the Valvanchi will believe you after this," Frederon said. "Chart says he will use the Battle Borgs to bring the prince back, but you must call off Karl Valvanchi."

"Call off Karl Valvanchi? Of course."

Frederon wrapped his arms around her.

"Sayginn, darling, please. Just let me handle it. Chartsie trusts me." He held her there and then said, with new compassion and eagerness. "He can see. We're in this together now. I will find him. Then tonight, we will celebrate, just you and me, man and woman, and tomorrow, we will be married."

Sayginn placed the photo of Serge and Deodran face down on the table, perhaps hoping they had not heard what the Emperor had said.

She was left holding the picture of Teodor, holding it tightly in two hands. The door burst open behind her.

"Regent Sayginn. We've found him. It's an exact match. Three cy-roaches and cy-rats! They have beamed in his location. I think we can get him out."

Sayginn looked up. She briefly kissed Teodor's photo, then turned to Frederon.

"Marry you? You still think I am going to marry you afterall this? I would not marry you if you were the last man left alive."

After he had left, Sayginn spoke aloud to the room.

"Ok Nuria, if you are there, show yourself."

The princess materialised.

"You don't need him, you have the protection of the Zaracan Democratic Union, Regent."

"That's good to hear!"

"I have a message from Karl. He says Teodor is running. We need to send in everything. Hopefully, one of us will find him before they do."

Chapter 29

Meal on the Rooftops

With a small pack of food stowed in Guy's backpack, Teodor and Guy sprinted along the maintenance tunnel that connected the bistro to Old Fleet Street, and up the eight flights of stairs to the top. All the doors into the main house were closed, and – as they raced through the attic workshops – the rooms were dark, with only moonlight shining down on the tidied tables. At last, they found themselves in the small attic bedroom, picked their way through the sleeping children to a high window and climbed out onto the rooftop balcony. From here the Dome filled the sky, Domeside – with its bright avenues – was laid out below them, the black stretch of river, and beyond (Teodor thought, more hopefully), the lights of Buckingham Palace. It looked a long way away.

"I still can't quite believe we were up inside that thing. We climbed down from the top." Teodor nodded towards the Dome. "How on earth did you ever find such an exit? You must have been petrified."

"Not really, I have to climb it with ropes twice a year during the Spring Sweep; most of the kids know how to do it. Obviously, most don't use it to escape from Chart Segat."

"Ah, the Spring Sweep. I was going to that one year, but my mother decided it was too dangerous. I think my father wanted me to have a go. It's to do with cleaning the inside of the Dome, isn't it?"

"Yes, they have to send droids up to do the actual cleaning, but the droids can get lost or keep going around in circles, so they send us kids up to lay down the ropes."

"But is that strictly necessary? Could they not just programme some super droid? And why do they need new ropes?"

"The ropes have to be replaced each year because the cleaning deteriorates them so badly that they can break. As for the droids, they're expensive. Kids are cheap and quick. I can climb to the top of the Dome in less than thirty minutes. It's cheap kids and ropes versus expensive cleaning fluids and droids. If a droid goes round in circles or gets lost, it not only wastes time, but also costs more in terms of battery power and cleaning fluid. I think they did a study to show that by laying the ropes, kids can cut the overall cost by about forty per cent." Guy hesitated. "Besides, it's great fun. It's become one of the great Domeside traditions. They always lay on a fantastic lunch afterwards."

"You don't get paid?"

Guy shook his head.

"There's a big fuss if you make the fastest time. But, of course, going fast is dangerous."

Resolutely, they both turned their backs to the Dome. There were no chairs, so they sat cross-legged on the floor. Guy shared out the food with careful precision. For several moments, they just ate. The food was only partially warm, but they were ravenous. Teodor wiped his face on the paper wrapping, while Guy rubbed his hands on his pants and peered down.

"Des was right. They have locked the bridges."

Teodor looked back to the entrance to the Dome. Security was tight – everyone, whether coming in or going out, was being searched. Where was the Royal Guard in their red and silver uniforms? Why hadn't his mother sent them to find him?

"Shouldn't we be moving?"

"Eat first; we're going to need to be fast." Guy replied.

Teodor saw something move. It was a glittering beetle. He reached to pick it up. It was a cy-roach. He let it nibble on a cut on his finger and then, suddenly he snapped it between his finger and thumb, and the cy-roach curled up into a small, blinking metallic ball. Teodor slipped the blinking ball into his pocket and repeated the process with another cy-roach, placing it into Guy's pocket.

"What's that?"

"It's a beacon. They will see it and know you are one of the good guys."

"And that?" A large rat had raced over the roof. Teodor picked it up and let it nuzzle the cut on his neck.

"This rat is telling the Royal Guard exactly where I am."

"Great," Guy said, but he sounded unconvinced. He pointed at a double line of Dome Militant who jogged purposefully out of the Dome. About forty in all, he thought. They were coming down Old Fleet Lane; so not far. Their helmets reflected the moonlight, making their legs and arms look like black spiders. "They know where we are."

"Des?" asked Teodor.

Guy's face darkened. "I hope he just told them straight out. You know he would not have had much choice."

"Would they have beaten him?"

"Even if they did, he would only have told them the minimum. He will have wanted to buy us some time. If they search the house from top to bottom, we'll have time, but we must get moving."

"But how?" The line of Dome Militant had split into three; they were entering by several places. "They're coming in on all sides."

"It's dangerous," Teodor nodded, he held and stroked a cy-rat. With regret, he placed it down on the ground. Guy said, "Follow me."

"Look!" cried Teodor. Across the river, three hover cars took off from Buckingham Palace. Guy shook his head.

"They won't get here in time. We have to go."

"They know where we are," Teodor said. "They know we're alive."

"C'mon, we need to stay that way."

Guy leapt over the high railing and landed lightly on the roof. Bending low, so his hands touched the floor, he ran along the ridge to the first chimney. He shimmied around and over it, then waved Teodor forward. Teodor was already over the railing, and he followed as quickly he dared, using his hands, as well as his feet to balance. They climbed around the chimney stack. There was another ridge. Feet facing forward, they slid and gripped their way down the last slope to the roof's edge. There they paused. Guy stood on the outer edge, looked down, then over to the next building. The roof overhung the road, but there was still a gap onto the next building. Guy checked briefly with Teodor. He ran a few steps up the tiles before turning, running, and leaping. He had landed firmly on the next house.

"It's not bad," he called. "Just take a run at it."

Teodor did as Guy said and threw himself through the air. He was relieved to feel Guy grab and pull him in, then the shooting started. From a window in House Jewel several floors below, a Dome Militant Battle Borg leant out and shot up at them.

"C'mon!" yelled Guy, and taking Teodor by the hand, he climbed the ridge and over the top. The shots followed them, with tiles exploding close by and fragments rushing by their hands and feet. They leapt over the far side; only, it was slippery. Guy used his feet to break his descent down the far side. Not so, Teodor – he was unbalanced by a blast under his feet and fell over the edge, landing on his behind. The tiles were as sleek as a child's slide. Guy reached to catch him as he slipped past, but lost his foothold, and fell on top of Teodor, and the two rolled fast, across and down to where the two steep roofs met at right angles. Teodor caught a foot in each of the two gutters and braced his back into the corner. He pulled Guy over towards him, even as the prince flailed on the very edge.

Teodor was wedged in the corner of the sloped roofs. Guy screamed as he looked into the emptiness, seemingly unaware of the two arms hugging and rolling him onto the next roof. Teodor jammed his own feet and kicked Guy's trainers into the gutters. The fall stopped as soon as it had started. Teodor reached out to touch Guy as he shuddered and wailed in fear beside him.

"C'mon, get up!" Teodor cried.

Guy shook his head in a negative, shuddering reply.

"Calm, Guy. Control!" shouted Teodor. "Say it! Calm, Guy, control!" The trembling slowed to a quiver, and Guy stared towards him.

"Calllmmm..."

"Calm, Guy! Control!" Teodor bent over Guy, who nodded and swallowed, then he sat up and shouted: "Calm, Guy! Control!" His voice was clear and strong.

"C'mon!" yelled Teodor. "Let's go."

Guy now followed Teodor as they quickly ran along, then up, the last pointed roof. The two were quick because they had to be. Bullets ricocheted as they came over the rim and slid down the far side. Cy-rats ran alongside them. Teodor saw one rat leap high in the air, in the path of a bullet. It fell down dead. That bullet might have hit him, he realised. Unexpectedly, a Dome Battle Borg stood on the flat window top; but as they approached, there was a blur of fur at his ankles. He went to kick away the rats, and suddenly, he was falling. Guy snatched the rifle from his opening hands. The leap was not as small as either would have liked, but then, they didn't have enough time to worry. They had made it to the roof of the Riffaut.

All around them, crisscrossing bullets multiplied. Hiding in the shadow of the small box window, Teodor realised it would be impossible to escape over to the flat roof, while they were so hemmed in by lethal exploding munitions. He looked round. Just three Battle Borgs on House Jewel, while two more had appeared on the far side of Old Fleet Street.

'Is that all?' thought Teodor. 'Where are the Dome Militant?' Guy fired at all of them at random. Teodor saw him fire over the heads of their attackers.

"It's all right, Guy. Those aren't Dome Militant; they are Borgs."

"Borgs?" Guy peered out. "They have reprogrammed the Borgs?"

"I think so. Come on."

Teodor knew it was time to take the initiative when a head appeared above them and to the right, next to the Riffaut's chimney.

"Give me that!" He grabbed the rifle and leapt onto the flat window box. First, he downed the Borg by the chimney, even as it dived into the road. Teodor sent a volley of shots to the right. One Borg was hit, and two others on House Jewel's roof dived for cover. Finally, Teodor aimed an arching blast across Old Fleet Street. Satisfied, he grabbed Guy by the hand. Both ran up and over, and down onto a flat roof.

Another Borg.

With the rifle under his arm and pointed ahead, Teodor fired with cruel accuracy. Beside him, Guy flinched, as what had been a man fell underfoot. Teodor grabbed Guy by the hand and together, they leapt over the prostrate form. Guy curled his ankles and knees high as the destroyed Borg reached up to grab his legs. Cy-rats bore down on him, pinned to the ground, the Borg screamed. Teodor did not even look. He fired ahead once again. Guy squinted at the hard-set youthful features. Was not Prince Teodor reputed to be delicate and gentle? He was known for his charity works and his shy singing in the Cathedral. Teodor glanced towards him. Guy was shocked by the fierce flame in his blue eyes.

Left, right, left, the race was not over. They leapt onto the far, steep roof, a box window, then onto to the Pleasure Palace, across another roof, another leap. The two now risked all to escape. Climb, slip, brake down, leap, then run. Panting, Teodor led the way, tightly holding Guy's hand. Always sprinting, steep upwards incline, toes digging desperately into the slope, his heart pounding lest his well-worn boots should slip! Over the top, gauging the landing even as they fell. Knees bent for maximum deceleration if it was sloped, landing in a desperate sprint if it was flat.

A voice called out inside Teodor's head:

'Go Teo, go! Don't look back! Don't slow down. Go! Now your only hope is in speed.'

He looked to where Guy ran beside him, exactly level with him, matching him pace for pace, leap for leap. He wondered that they should be so equally matched in strength and determination. In the wind of their acceleration, he thought he could hear the words of a song Guy was murmuring.

"It's better than spending a life without riding the Whirlwind, Domeside Whirlwind."

The race stopped as abruptly as it started. Teodor and Guy found themselves looking out into the emptiness of three broad avenues: Beacon Place, Domeside Avenue ahead, Old Fleet Street curved to the left and the river. Teodor was angry as he looked down into the emptiness; there would be no escape from this building, either down onto the road or back the way they had come! He had taken a wrong leap! Hiding behind a metallic air-conditioning system, he looked back to see that their pursuers were in some disarray, seemingly fighting amongst themselves. Guy tugged on his sleeve, and pulled him to the top of a metallic fire-ladder:

"Look! Old Fleet Street, and it's still unguarded. He did it. Des kept his mouth shut. We must run."

Guy skidded down the last line of tiles and leapt onto a metal fire escape. Then, he powered down the metal stair. Teodor, spurred on by his words, chased him hard, so they landed almost on top of each other at the bottom. Guy led them back into the darkness of the narrowing alleyway.

"Help me with this." He had a hand on a sewer cap. They heaved it open, and below, was a ladder. Teodor hesitated, he thought grimly of his earlier experience in the sewers, but Guy just said impatiently, "Just go down a bit. I'll need your help to pull this cap back."

Teodor did what he was told. He climbed down a few rungs but stayed up the top of the ladder. Once again, they were squeezed together in a narrow space, as Guy slipped down beside him. Together, they pulled the cap back over their heads. Guy sighed with relief as they finally got it to fall flat into position.

"That should buy us a bit more time. By closing the entrance, they won't be sure where we've gone."

"Can the Cy-wolves smell us?" said Teodor.

"No, the Dome Militant don't have those, but they will guess soon enough. Time to get our blades back on. Switch on your torch."

"How far is it?"

"I don't know."

"How do we find our way?"

"We keep going down until we get to the lowest level and then we look for the tunnel."

"Is that it?"

"There are these," said Guy, shone his torch up at a strange, ancient gargoyle. It looked out of place, as if it had been moved and cemented upon the smooth wall as decoration. "There are more of them as you go lower. We are looking for one that is shaped like a fish. The tunnel we need is itself very damp. Some say it's flooded further down. I don't rightly know. Anyway, it's our only chance."

"The floor is uneven."

"I know, but I don't want to take my blades off yet. We'd be too easy to catch."

"We'll stick together."

Chapter 30

The Thames Water Way

"They're in the sewers," Nuria pointed. She and Sayginn stood side by side, in front of the laser representation of the Dome and its surrounding areas. Teodor and Guy were represented by two red avatars with red beacons beating at their hearts. It was the signal from the cy-roaches in their pockets. Karl Valvanchi appeared as a green avatar. All three were tracked on the illuminated map. This also included, the Dome Militant and Battle Borgs, who appeared as a host of grey shapes milling in-between.

"If they can make it to this tunnel, they might go all the way under the river."

"No, we need to get them out before that," said Sayginn. "That tunnel is ancient and not in good repair. Also, look how complicated the route is. How would they find their way in the dark?"

"They're going so fast," said Nuria.

"They're running on blades. It's not very safe. It's not easy even on the flat and straight ground, through narrow corridors, round blind bends and with uneven flooring."

As they watched, the two avatars seemed to tumble over each other. There was a pause, and then they set off again.

"Oh!" Nuria said. "Oh no."

"What?" said Sayginn.

"They've taken a wrong turn. Oh, look at those Dome Militant, Battle Borgs too."

Sayginn peered at the map graphic and the trajectory of her son.

"Oh no..."

Nuria looked at the screen, then closed her mouth, stared out the open window as she sent him a message.

'Uncle Karl, can you see this? You've got to hurry up. You've got to get there first.'

"I'm on my way." Karl's thought voice was warm and calm — it echoed around the room. Sayginn heard it and felt it spread through her mind and body.

Using small, efficient, accurate leaps, they made their way along the maintenance tunnel. Half-way along

Guy opened another grille, and they lowered themselves into an older passage beneath. They heard footsteps even as they dropped through the hole. Guy scampered back up the ladder to close the grille, and Teodor climbed back up to help. They were both crouched in the darkness, as heavy boots passed overhead. Guy kept taking the lowest path. The tunnels kept getting darker, smaller and lower. They heard gunshots behind and above them, along with the echoes of running feet.

The gargoyles began to multiply. Now, they looked like they belonged – sticking out just above head height from the crumbling walls. Now, the tunnels were cleaner. There were fire exit signs, colourful posters advertising Ascot Weekend specials and bright yellow lights.

"This is the touristy bit," muttered Guy. As they turned a corner, they found themselves face-to-face with two Dome Militant Battle Borgs coming down from above. Guy threw himself backwards, stretching his body across Teodor's and pressing him against the darkness of the wall.

The Borgs kept coming. Guy fumbled at his neck for his Dome medallion.

"Don't!" Teodor warned. "You're wanted too."

Teodor looked back along the corridor, which was narrow and straight. Even if they ran, they would be easy targets. He turned back when he heard a thump. There, at the Borgs' back, was a man with white hair. He had leapt down the stairwell. Now he raised his hand. The Borgs stopped. The man turned towards Guy and Teodor. Teodor put up his hand to shield his vision from the bright lights shining like lasers from the man's eyes.

"Karl Valvanchi?" Teodor wondered.

The man looked at them both, then nodded meaningfully up the stairs. They could hear the sound of boots approaching, soldiers or Borgs, more were coming. All at once, Karl pointed at a black door marked 'Private' across the corridor. The lock clicked and the door sprang open. Teodor quickly pointed his torch down the tunnel and found a fish gargoyle beyond.

"Go!" Teodor urged Guy, pushing him forward.

Keeping as much distance as they could between themselves and the alien, they leapt neatly down the indicated tunnel and looked back relieved as the door slammed and locked behind them. As gunfire resumed, they turned and sprinted down into darkness.

"That was too close," Guy said.

Teodor reflected that Guy might be referring to the Zaracan soldier, as much as he was of the Dome Militant.

"I think – no, I don't think, I know – that was Karl Valvanchi."

"Great, that's supposed to reassure me?"

"Perhaps not, but at least we know which side he is against."

They raced on. The tunnel now ran steeply down and with every leap, the air felt damper. Teodor touched the wall with relief: at last, they were under the river.

❖

Karl Valvanchi counted five frozen Dome Militant. Unsurprisingly, all were Borgs. The men of the Dome Militant were noticeable by their absence. Ever since he had left the Dome, it had been the same. He saw them running purposefully to orders, but he also saw them hold their blades and not throw them.

Loyal to Empire

The Dome Militant knew they were in pursuit of their prince. Karl had a feeling that most of them thought this was wrong. So, they had stepped aside, turned away, and let him slip through their ranks. Without their tacit complicity, he would never have got to this tunnel, to this position, to face off against the Battle Borgs.

He was trapped. There was only one way out and, at the top, were the Dome Militant. They had let him in, but would they let him escape?

He took one last look at the fallen Battle Borgs and headed off through the same door Teodor and Guy had taken. His fate would be the same as theirs. If they escaped, he would escape. If they failed, he would fail.

❖

Guy stopped. The tunnel was old, narrow, slippery and slimy. Now they ran through water. Just when they thought they could go no longer, the tunnel dipped again. The passage was now full of water.

"We have to go on. There's still air," Teodor said, striding into the flood.

"It's still going down," Guy replied.

Teodor took the time to look at the slope in the tunnel. With the water at this level, it would be entirely submerged in just a few metres.

"Let's look."

They carried on, until they were submerged to the neck, and still the tunnel descended. There was a sign on the wall. It read: 'Thames River Tunnel Administration.' Across these words, the line of the water was clear. From the second 'n' in Tunnel, the words disappeared in the water. Guy reached up to cling onto the edge of the metal sign. Thankfully, it did not move. He could feel his legs being dragged and pushed by a strong current, ebbing and flowing.

"I'll try to swim," Teodor said. He grabbed the torch between his teeth.

"Don't go far," Guy replied.

Teodor just shook his head and dived. Alone in the dark, Guy pulled his own torch up out of the water. It flickered. He gave it a shake. He was trying to read the inscription on the side. Were these fully waterproof? He fiddled with the torch for a while, then started to wonder about the prince. How long had he been underwater?

Just then, Teodor re-emerged with a smile.

"It's not far. C'mon."

Guy shook his head briefly.

"You can't swim, can you?"

"Not well," Guy admitted.

"Hang on to my waist and kick with your legs. Like a battlement kick we do in training, can you do that?" Guy nodded. "Oh and hold your breath. It's not far."

Under the water, still wearing their blades, they were stretched out like a long eel. Guy held firm onto Teodor's hips and then realised he was in the way of Teodor's legs. Guy drew himself up, so his head rested on Teodor's backside. As Teodor's legs kicked the water beneath, he thrashed with his own legs, wishing this was over.

The tidal movement was stronger underwater, and they were rolled up against the wall. Guy lost his grip on Teodor and desperately reached to grab his waistband, only to feel Teodor reach down, grab him, and hook his hand into his belt, then they were swimming again. When the wave came again, Guy held on tight, feeling them turn and twist in its curve, hugging hard onto Teodor and kicking as hard as he could. They spun once, then twice, and finally, righted themselves again. At least Guy thought they were the right way up. He found himself fighting to hold his lips tight together, but his nostrils flared in fear. At any time, he felt he might burst if he did not breathe – then he felt something different.

Teodor had his feet on the floor. Guy reached his blades down to touch the ground as well. Next, they were both powering along, legs pumping, arms wrapped around each other. The floor curved upwards. They were stumbling out of the water, Guy slipping at the very last, so they tumbled to the ground, Guy's head falling onto Teodor's chest. They lay a few moments in the shallows, breathing hard and looking at how light from their torches reflected on the water and radiated around the new tunnel. Neither noticed that the beacon lights had gone out of the cy-roaches in their pockets.

Karl burst up out of the water and gasped for breath. Behind him was a sign. It read: Thames River Tunnel Administration. From the second 'n' in Tunnel, the words disappeared into the water.

"Damn."

He reached down to his feet and pulled out the Borg. It was not breathing. It was not moving. All its systems were waterlogged. In effect, it had drowned. Karl dived into the water again. He came back up a second time, dragging the other Borg after him. It too had drowned.

He stood looking down where the tunnel disappeared under water. Both Borgs had followed him. Then both had dived into the tunnel after the boys. Both had died in the murky waters. He paused. He checked his records. He scanned the maps inside his mind, looking. He connected with the graphics in Buckingham Palace.

For a moment, he touched Nuria's mind as she and Sayginn paced alongside the large three-dimensional image. The cy-roach beacons had gone out. The two small red avatars had come to a standstill here.

He would have to dive again. This time, he would have to search for bodies.

He sat down in the water. His head in his hands, he despaired. Dead? Both dead? Were there bodies just a few feet away in these dark waters?

Karl was careful to shield his thoughts, for he knew Nikato was listening. In his mind's eye, he saw Nikato at a terminal, staring at an unchanging screen, not daring to look at either the Regent or his niece, both pacing impatiently around the large graphical display.

Karl heard something and looked around. A patrol of six Dome Militant had arrived in the tunnel. They were men, not Borgs. They stopped, taking it all in. The tunnel sloped away into the water. The two drowned Borgs. Karl Valvanchi sitting with his head in his hands. He looked at them. He took a breath. Not able to think of anything to say, he stood up, took three deep breaths, set aside any weapon, tool or gadget he did not need – placing them on dry ground at the feet of the Dome Militant, as he dived once again into the water.

Guy coughed and spluttered while Teodor coughed, laughed and stroked his hair.

"Oh, that was good," said Teodor.

"I thought it was not far."

"I didn't believe that you would go."

"It felt like we were in a washing machine."

"Yes, but couldn't you feel the waves were propelling us upwards? It was harder swimming back to get you."

"I see," Guy sounded doubtful. "I'm happy to believe you."

Teodor pushed Guy off him, then helped him to his feet. They both stood to shake and tried to wipe the water from their limbs. Guy shivered.

"We can't stop here," said Teodor, pointing his torch up. The tunnel rose steeply now. "Let's run."

It was exciting to know they were coming out. This spurred them to run faster than their ebbing strength should have allowed. The tunnel on this side of the river was different. The fish gargoyles were less frequent or had been removed. Frequently at junctions, they found the tunnels had been blocked by a new building. After a while, emergency lighting came on, and it was clear the tunnel was used on occasion for maintenance. Finally, they stood at the junction of three passageways.

They pointed their torches up at the roof, looking for signs. The only fish gargoyle they could find was back the way they had come. The three tunnels were otherwise identical.

"There!" said Teodor at last. He pointed his torch at a small painted tile some way down the tunnel on the left. "The symbol of my house, these will lead us to the palace."

They followed the tiles along a narrow corridor. From the occasional lone tile, it became a line of tiles, and then a mosaic. Ladders led up from the tunnels as well. Each ladder looked new and was marked with numbers. Teodor climbed one, but leapt back, disappointed.

"Locked. The covers are locked. Oh, where are the cameras?"

They continued two more ladders. Teodor climbed to try the covers. The same result, the covers were locked. How would they get out of the tunnel? They had reached the end wall. Teodor looked back the way they had come and climbed the last ladder again. Guy found and opened a panel in the far wall. There was another tunnel, a crawl tunnel. It looked older, but it had older painted tiles as well.

"Ok," said Teodor. They pulled the panel shut behind them. They crawled along until they found a ladder. This time, the top was bricked up: no exit.

"Keep trying," said Guy, and they crawled on. The tunnel arched right, ever damper and older. They could see three lines of light from three separate openings. Teodor was meticulous. The first did not budge. So, he climbed to the second. Guy was amazed to hear the metal move. He looked up and saw Teodor haloed in the faint moonlight.

"Thank God."

When Sayginn and Nuria arrived in the tunnel, the Dome Militant were using their divers. They had tied ropes to the divers and given them lamps attached to their heads and their hands. After the first team had come back empty-handed, they had sent back to the Dome for younger men. As they watched, two fifteen-year-old Dome Militant Juniors were being roped up to be sent into the tunnel.

"So young," muttered Nuria.

"So small," explained Sayginn, "they are trying to see if a smaller person, like Teo, might have swum through."

"It's narrow, and the current will tumble you," the first man was saying. "Try to stick together, but if you can't make it, there's no shame in coming back. Try it once to get your bearings. If you feel ok, you can go back a second time..." The captain lowered his voice to a whisper "...to look for the bodies."

"They're wearing black," one confirmed. The captain nodded.

"Is there a way through?" asked the other.

The captain shook his head, then, glancing up again at Sayginn, "We don't know."

Karl Valvanchi, with a Dome towel draped over his shoulders, moved to stand closer to Sayginn and Nuria. She looked at him but said nothing. The boys dived.

The Dome Militant milled silently around. They had removed the drowned Battle Borgs before she arrived, but she had seen the photos. She had watched one group of divers enter the tunnel and reappear. Karl Valvanchi had explained in detail what he knew of the narrow turbulent waters.

"Teodor is a good swimmer," Sayginn repeated for the ninth time.

"I'm sure he made it," Nuria said, before adding, "But I can't sense him through water."

Karl nodded. Commander Tilson was standing a short distance away. Sayginn turned to him.

"Guy Erma, could he swim?"

Tilson stood unmoving. He closed his eyes for a moment.

"He could swim a bit. It's not on the school curriculum. He's lived by the river all his life."

Sayginn squirmed. She could feel her concerns echoing through the Dome Militant men at her side. They too were waiting – waiting for the body of one of theirs to be retrieved from the depths.

The first diver returned. He was the slimmer, taller one. He stood a moment, gasping for breath. He shook his head.

"I couldn't see them."

Nobody moved. The captain spoke to him.

"Yes, I'll go again. I'll just wait on Tony."

He looked back towards the entrance of the tunnel. They all looked back. The second teenage diver had not returned. The captain looked at his watch. He waded through the water to where another of his men was holding the end of Tony's rope. It was still spilling out, and it was shaking. The captain peered down at the water.

The lines went slack. For several moments, nothing moved. The captain strode over to pull the lines back. He gave orders to the other man to do the same. Now the rope was coming back quickly, rising through the water, and then they saw the light.

The second Dome Militant diver strode up and out of the water.

"I made it through, I got to the other side. The tunnel is not completely blocked. You can swim all the way through. And we looked on the way back. No bodies. I am sure there are no bodies. They must have made it." He grinned then continued. "And there are footprints on the other side. You can see where somebody came out of the water. I was sure I saw two sets of footprints." The diver looked excited. "They made it. They escaped."

Both turned to look up at Sayginn. Tears were running down her face. Nuria reached to grab her hand.

"He made it." Nuria said.

"Teodor is a good swimmer."

"They both made it," Tilson said, and he looked relieved.

Beside him, the Dome Militant cheered.

"Ok," said the captain. "That's sounds splendid. Now, we need to get a fixed rope in place, and then, we can go and have a proper look. So, this time, Tony, I need you to..."

"I must get back to the palace," said Sayginn hurriedly. "Come Nuria."

"You don't want to wait until they make all the checks?" Karl asked.

"No, I know he made it through. He'll be home now; I want to be there to greet him. Come with me."

Karl nodded.

"Let's go."

Chapter 31

Blue Barbrina at Rest

"Thank God," Guy smiled as he watched Teodor disappear through the hatch. He followed, as agile and quick as his fast-ebbing strength would allow. Eagerly, he looked up and peered through, and repeated Teodor's words, though not his sentiments.

"Oh God."

The hatch had opened up into the stall of a giant goran. Seemingly at its leisure, it was sprawled majestically across its bed of artificial straw. The ice-white snow goran had its head and ears up, and watched them with keen interest. As Guy appeared, it bared its fangs and growled.

"Barbrina, Barbie baby," Teodor soothed the giant cat. "He's my friend." Then, over his shoulder, "Secure the hatch, Guy; I'll just keep her calm."

"Ok." Guy pulled the lid back in place. He felt immensely safer now the tunnels were closed behind him. "I can't lock it."

"I'll do that," Teodor said. Looking and talking to the goran, he backed towards the sewer cap and then tapped a shut code on the keypad lock.

"It's jammed now. No one can get in."

"How do we get out?" Guy asked.

The snow goran had its great paws stretched out across the entrance.

"It's ok. I'll talk to her. She's exhausted anyhow after this afternoon's race." Guy realised Teodor was talking about the giant goran. He watched with amazement as the prince walked calmly up to let the beast sniff, then lick, his face and neck. "She'll want to get your scent, as well. C'mon."

Guy had no intention of going anywhere near the huge animal. He knew only too well what they were capable of, but Teodor was urgently beckoning to him. "She won't relax until she knows you're also her friend."

"But I'm not her friend," Guy muttered as he reluctantly edged forward.

"Give me your hand."

Guy reached ahead of him. Teodor offered his hand up to the great goran's muzzle. Guy felt himself sweating as he imagined the beast biting down on his arm. He feared spending the rest of his life handless. The giant sniffed the air, looked straight at Guy and roared! Guy fell back to the floor and froze.

"She's not happy," Teodor murmured. "Look, we'll just sit a while. She'll calm down and then we can go."

Not happy? Guy wondered. Was Teodor joking? Inwardly, he groaned as the prince sat down in the crook of the goran's elbow and tugged Guy down beside him. He watched in dismay as Teodor snuggled into the deep fur of the goran's chest, pausing only to check on Guy.

"Lean here against me. If she smells me on you, she won't touch you. We'll get you a telepathic link tomorrow."

"I'd rather keep my thoughts to myself," Guy muttered, unimpressed by the idea of surgery to allow him to spend time with giant gorans; what good was that in the real world?

"And you can keep that thought to yourself as well," Teodor replied with a smile. Guy wondered if he was also telepathic. "No, it's only a goran safety link, not full telepathy. It's to save you from being mauled out of hand."

"Save me from being mauled?" Guy asked. "Could you not have thought of that before you brought us up here?"

"Sssh, don't upset her. Stay calm." Teodor yawned.

"But she wouldn't hurt you. It's ok for you."

"She might if I did something particularly stupid."

"Like what?" Guy asked.

"Like bringing an ignorant Domesider into her stall. Now just relax, will you?"

Guy snorted in disgust. Ignorant Domesider indeed. He looked up and saw the goran was staring at him. Her glare was not in the least friendly. So, gingerly, he let himself lie back against the goran, angling himself so his head rested on Teodor's shoulder. Teodor immediately put an arm around him and pulled him closer.

"I'm just going to close my eyes a moment, and then I must find a Communicator. I need to call my mother."

As Teodor relaxed, Guy let himself breathe in the aroma of the snow cat. He decided it smelt like a slightly damp dog, but it was comforting, and the fur was silky smooth. He smiled as the giant rested its head on its paws. The monster did look a lot more relaxed. He saw it looking at them both, but more specifically at Teodor, and there seemed to be a twinkle in that gaze.

Guy glanced up at Teodor to see if he had noticed, then he stopped, appalled. Teodor was fast asleep. He looked at the goran, who was still calmly watching, or maybe guarding them and the far door. There was no choice. He lay back deeper into the fur, leaning his cheek against Teodor's shoulder, and closed his eyes.

Chapter 32

Waiting for News

Sayginn paced round and round the giant graphic of the Dodecahedron Dome. On the screens around the ballroom were maps of the tunnels under the palace, and analysts were scanning footage from a hundred new camera placements – as well as audio feeds.

Nuria was sleeping on a little sofa. Karl and Nikato were in conversation with the captain of the divers in the river tunnel.

"No, we have been through this a dozen times, and the passage is now completely lit. Their bodies are not there. Both made it."

"I'll use nanites and cy-roaches," said Karl.

"Nanites are not a technology the Zaracans had shared before," Nikato lamented.

Karl shrugged.

"Sayginn, can you get me down to the tunnel at the other end of the water? From this end?"

"Yes, yes, you're right," she said distractedly. "I sent some people, but yes, go help."

❖

The late news channel interviewed Chart Segat.

"So, you think the prince is dead?" the newscaster insisted.

Chart Segat sighed. He gave every impression of knowing something tragic, but not being able or permitted to speak of it.

"Those poor two lost boys," he repeated.

The news then changed, and another reporter summarised:

""he only thing certain is that Prince Teodor, heir to both the kingdom of Earth and the empire of Dodecahedral, was last seen entering a deadly tunnel under the river. Whether he drowned or not, has not yet been confirmed. He was accompanied by the young blades champion and Dome Militant Junior, Guy Erma, who is also feared drowned."

Frederon stood on the balcony, looking down at the ballroom below. He slapped the balcony rail in frustration.

"Where are they?" he growled.

Chapter 33

Dawn in the Stables

When Guy opened his eyes, it was morning. A girl crouched down beside him whispering to Teodor. Guy moved unsteadily. He realised the girl must be a servant – judging by her clothes, she looked like she worked with the gorans. Both Teodor and the girl reached to help him.

"Don't rush now," urged the girl.

"Stay close to me," added Teodor.

All at once, the Communicator on the girl's wrist sounded an urgent alarm. They all tensed, and the giant goran sat up quickly, clearly perturbed. For the first time, even Guy could see it looked grumpy.

"Yes?" the girl whispered nervously. She watched the goran with fear, but at the same time, she was practically standing to attention. Guy noticed Teodor looked annoyed.

"Is he there? Is the prince there?"

Guy thought he recognised the voice.

"Mother!" protested Teodor and pulled the Communicator towards him.

"Give me a visual," the voice insisted. "Are you hurt? Tell me what you see, girl!"

"No, my lady, he's ok. He's completely filthy." She whispered. Behind them, Blue Barbrina started to pace. Teodor reached to touch the girl's arm. She nodded. At last, a Communicator, he thought briefly – then spoke in a whisper.

"Mother, Barbie does not like Communicators, so I am switching this off until we get out of her stall."

"Teodor, don't you dare!"

Teodor switched off the Communicator and reached out to steady Guy.

As the giant goran wound back and forward, she rubbed up against them, licked its jowls and snorted, the stable girl looked frightened but determined. Holding firm onto each other, Teodor got them to edge first one, then several, steps towards the door.

At the entrance, two other girls had appeared. As soon as they saw Blue Barbrina on her feet, they stopped running and, with a balletic grace, started to glide towards her – each taking a different wall of the stall. The goran watched them both approach, its head turning from left to right.

Guy found himself behind both Teodor and the two girls. He relaxed a fraction and watched as the tallest of them reached a hand to the goran's muzzle. Then, Teodor and the second girl reached up their hands, too. As Guy watched, the snow cat snorted one more time, then sank back into the hay, and even rolled over on her back. The girls laughed in gentle purrs and leant forward to scratch its chest. Teodor took Guy firmly by the hand and led him quickly outside.

"Was that telepathy?" Guy asked when they were finally outside.

"Low-level mind control, not like..." Teodor hesitated. "Not like we saw earlier... em... last night."

The girls came out of the stall. As quiet and smooth as ghosts, they closed and carefully locked the low door. They shuttered the top opening. As the last latch slipped into place, all three squealed.

Guy jumped. He saw the girls had concealed their excitement until this point because of Blue Barbrina. Now they went wild, they hugged and kissed Teodor. Guy laughed with the girls as Teodor took turns to kiss, hug and squeeze each one – blushing a shade pinker with each embrace.

For the first time, Guy thought, Teodor seemed perfectly relaxed – crowded around as he was by the slim stable girls. He exchanged nonsensical conversations with them. These appeared to revolve around three key facts:

One, he was alive.

Two, he was back.

Three, he had slept in the stables with Blue Barbrina.

As Guy listened, he realised that, to these girls, nothing was as dangerous as a night with the great snow goran. They were full of advice and warnings, should he ever decide to do this again. The principal advice seemed to be that he should never sleep alone.

Guy bit his lips as he tried not to laugh, while Teodor listened carefully to each of them and encouraged their shy kisses and quick hugs.

"And this is Guy Erma. He's my friend. He helped me escape."

The girls looked at Guy, as if for the first time.

"At least you brought us a handsome one."

In a few moments, each of the girls, in turn, had kissed and hugged Guy, causing him to turn bright red. They giggled, and Guy laughed and laughed.

"And here's my mother," Teodor sighed, and the girls slipped away.

"So," whispered Guy. "Are those all your girlfriends? I mean, how many are there?"

"Yes, I mean no, well not exactly." The Regent rose from the car. "I'll tell you later."

There was no time for Guy to ask anything more, because Teodor was walking towards his mother. Regent Sayginn gathered Teodor in her arms. She hugged him for a long time with her eyes closed. Her face had a look of relief, then she kissed him on his hair, his forehead and, briefly, his lips.

"You're alive!"

Sayginn glanced at Guy, then back at Teodor.

"That was a good blades fight; you did well."

Teodor nodded just once.

"I didn't win, though," Teodor said. "Mother, may I introduce Guy Erma? He helped me escape."

"Ah, yes!"

Guy had the distinct feeling the Regent was not entirely delighted to see him. He remembered, with a sinking feeling, their last encounter in the interrogation room – in the basement of the Ascot racecourse. She, too, recognised him. He had not exactly lied to her, but he had not told the truth either. Did she know that? Her welcome was cordial.

"Welcome to Buckingham Palace, Guy Erma."

"Mum, what day is it?" Teodor said and climbed into the car. "I lost track - is today my birthday?"

Sayginn laughed. "Is that why you escaped, to eat birthday cake?"

"I escaped as soon as I could," Teodor replied. "I lost track of the days. It's not been easy...erm."

"I know, I know, I'm sorry." Sayginn paused. "Of course, you lost track of time, well it's Sunday, and yes, it's your birthday. You're sixteen today. Now let's get you both to the medical centre."

"And later they'll, there'll be cake?" Teodor asked hopefully. "It does not have to be cake, but I'm ever so hungry."

Chapter 34

Interlude. Diplomatic Exchange

From: Ambassador Nikato Valvanchi II, Earth

To: Ex-Ambassador Nikato Valvanchi I, Zarac 1

Father,

I regret to inform you that, at the Dodecahedron Dome Debate, Chart Segat was confirmed for another five years in power. So yet again, and despite our efforts, the humans refused to listen to our guidance.

I am now proceeding to Phase 2, as agreed.

Nikki.

From: Ex-Ambassador Nikato Valvanchi I, Zarac

To: Ambassador Nikato Valvanchi II, Earth

My son, you have done well under very difficult circumstances. I think this kidnapping has undermined Chart Segat more than anything else he could have done.

Under his leadership, I do not believe the Dodecahedron Dome will pose any credible threat going forward. The Regent is bound to restrict him in every way possible.

We also have undeniable proof of their actions on Sas Darona. I have no doubt the Regent will put an end to Dome Militant activity there as well. The Sas Darona problem will, therefore, be at an end. Be patient.

You will be rewarded for your work. I am proposing that you become ambassador on Freyne. I hope the Council will agree.

Do not proceed with Phase 2. I repeat. DO NOT PROCEED.

Your father.

From: Ambassador Nikato Valvanchi II, Earth

To: Ex-Ambassador Nikato Valvanchi I, Zarac 1

URGENT

Father,

I regret to inform you; one device has been activated. The technical readouts say it was triggered by an excess of heat.

Therefore Phase 2 is now underway. Request permission to proceed at once to Freyne.

N
From: Ex-Ambassador Nikato Valvanchi I, Zarac
To: Ambassador Nikato Valvanchi II, Earth
This is very distressing news. I have informed the Council. They are also saddened but have decreed Phase 2 should continue as planned.

The Council have also confirmed your new post as Ambassador on Freyne.

This is a promotion – well done, my son.
Your proud father.
P.S. Does Karl know?
From: Ambassador Nikato Valvanchi II, Earth
To: Ex-Ambassador Nikato Valvanchi I, Zarac 1
Father,
Please confirm if I should include my brother Karl in the Council's plans. He is, afterall, only a military commander.
N
From: Ex-Ambassador Nikato Valvanchi I, Zarac
To: Ambassador Nikato Valvanchi II, Earth
Negative. Do not inform Karl.
He will be more use to us if he is innocent.
Your loving father.

Chapter 35

Home Sweet Home

"How did you scratch your leg?" the doctor said as he examined the back and side of his calf.

"I slipped when running across the roofs, I think it was then..." Guy replied.

"Well, I need to run some tests, it might be infected." The doctor swabbed the cut and placed the bloodstained cotton into a medical analysis unit.

"Is it serious?" Teodor asked, coming over and pulling tight a white robe as he did.

"I just need to check for any infection." He walked to a cupboard and pulled out an egg-shaped drone, setting it in motion.

"What's your favourite food?" Teodor asked Guy and handed him an identical robe, but Guy did not reply.

"Blood test?" he repeated.

"Will it take long?" Teodor asked the doctor, picking up on Guy's concern.

"Well, does Guy know who his parents were? It's quicker if we already have a relative's DNA."

"My mother was..." Guy hesitated. "Do you have lots of records on file?"

"Almost the entire population..."

"Look up Loulou and Marline from House Jewel. That's Louise Gem Erma, and Silver Marline Erma, House Jewel, Old Fleet Street."

The doctor entered their details.

"Yes, I have both, they are recorded as mother and daughter."

"But that's just it. Loulou is not Marline's mother. She's mine."

The doctor looked surprised and peered in at the records.

"Well, it could be. Marline has only ever been tested as Loulou's child, and the results have never identified a father, which would be surprising – unless of course - if you tested for the wrong mother."

"So, you could find out Marline's real parents as well?" Guy asked.

"As well?" the doctor looked confused. "I will need permission from the Regent, these tests are still illegal."

"Oh, give it to me," Teodor said, and he pressed his thumbprint to the security screen. "Plus, the results are for my eyes only – I'll share them with you Guy."

"Yes, but..." Guy interrupted, wondering what would happen if Teodor found out his father was Chart Segat.

"Don't worry – when we know, we'll decide what to do next. Your real parents should be prosecuted for not registering you at birth."

"Oh," Guy said uncertainly.

"How long will it take?"

"About three hours," the doctor said. "I'll programme the drone to come find you when it is done. I'll give you some interim tablets for now, and personalised formula once I have the full DNA scan. I only get the scan; I won't know who your parents are."

"Thank you," Teodor said.

"Yes, thank you," Guy added after a moment.

"So, shall we go eat? What do you like, Guy?"

"Eggs and peas." Guy replied. "That's my favourite."

"Not a big Domeside pie?" Teodor asked. "My favourite is a nice, plump steak."

"I had Domeside pie on my birthday. It was a special treat. I was twelve." Guy stopped himself. It had indeed been an incredible outing. Loulou had taken him to lunch in the bistro and ordered for him the most expensive dish on the menu: King-size Domeside Pie. Guy had been so excited; he could hardly eat. He turned to see Teodor waiting.

"How about if this morning you have the best breakfast Buckingham Palace can provide?" Teodor said, then to a nearby servant: "Ok, we'll have brunch as soon as it is available. All the trimmings, and pudding too." The butler bowed and headed off.

The prince and Guy Erma had stopped at the top of the stairwell above the ballroom. They were distracted by the bright laser display of the Dome. "What's that?"

Below was the palace ballroom, with its horseshoes of hurriedly assembled workstations, walls of screens, cables, men, more screens and more men.

"I think these are the guys who were trying to find us. Me." Teodor said and sighed. From below they had been spotted. Applause broke out, as men called out and cheered.

"I'd better go down and say a few thank yous."

"I thought we were going to shower, then eat."

"Duty calls. You go if you like."

"No, I'm ok. I'll come."

Guy walked beside Teodor and watched the prince change again. Here was a politician in the making, working his way around the room, remembering names, and asking questions – accepting congratulations and laughing at anecdotes. Guy thought he saw the Teodor he knew for a few moments when they were shown the cy-wolves. Teodor bent down to pat, talk to and hug the giant creatures, but then he was back on his feet – talking to their captain, asking about casualties and praising their bravery.

⬡

"This is terrible, you know?" Teodor was showing Guy a news article about his mother at the Dome Debate. "My mum breaking down like that. See, she cried in front of her council." Teodor sighed, for Guy did not understand. "She'll never be able to rule now. Not properly."

Teodor placed the screen aside, switching off its content. The far door had opened, and their guest entered.

"Welcome, Princess. We meet again."

Nuria had been brought up to Teodor's chambers after a tense exchange with Regent Sayginn. Teodor had wanted to spend the entire day with Guy, but his mother had rung him twice to insist he receive the princess – something he had only agreed to do once his mother relented, saying he did not have to get changed.

"Well, Princess, may I introduce Guy Erma?"

Guy was on his feet at once and saluted the girl Dome Militant fashion, fist to his heart. Teodor paused when he saw this, then continued a little uncertainly: "Princess, I am afraid you will have to excuse my companion and me. We have had a tiring night, and we are still at our leisure." Teodor was talking about the track suits they both wore. "If you think our attire is unsuitable, I will call my butler at once."

"My prince, on the contrary, please do not make any change on my account. On my planet, we sometimes spend time outdoors on the beach in casual clothes, and it is very relaxing. I am grateful just to spend any time with you after such a terrible ordeal."

"Well, thank you." Teodor had not wanted to change in any case. "And thank you," he glanced sideways at Guy before continuing softly, "Your voice inside my head was a great comfort when I was in captivity."

"Oh, let me just hug you," Nuria said, and she threw her arms around him. Teodor looked surprised but he softened as he clasped and hugged her back. "The privilege was all mine, not that it was not terrifying, I mean are you alright?"

Teodor pulled back a little, "You were with me all the time? In my mind?"

"Not all the time," Nuria said apologetically. "My powers are... I'm not an adult, and buildings, and distance," she shrugged embarrassed. "Plus, they drugged you much of the time, I tried to send you dreams, to get you to wake up, to remain conscious, but..."

Teodor had stepped back now but was still holding her hands.

"I had many dreams of my father while I was being held captive, was that you?"

Nuria shrugged. "I'm not sure how it works, but I wanted you to be strong, to remember who you are, and try to escape."

"Yes, yes," Teodor replied, remembering how his father's words had reassured him. "Thank you Nuria. I am in your debt." He bowed his head and touched his heels together in a small salute.

"Oh, it's nothing," she replied, blushing with pleasure. You could kiss me though. Teodor stared at her in astonishment. I've done nothing but think of you these past 52 hours.

"52 hours?" Teodor replied aloud. "You mean, well yes, I suppose it was just two days. It felt much longer." Then leaning forward, he kissed her on her hairline. Thank you, Princess.

They stood a moment looking at each other, both a little flushed yet nervous, both wondering what comes next? Teodor spoke first.

"We were about to eat some cake – will you join us?"

"My prince, nothing would give me greater pleasure."

"Guy was incredibly brave today," Teodor said. He could sense Guy had been staring, and also that the Domeside boy was annoyed, with reason, Nuria had broken their fleeting time together.

"Yes, my uncle Karl told me."

"Killer Valvanski is your—" Guy stopped himself, for both Teodor and Nuria looked at him in shock. He took a breath and said: "I mean Karl Valvanchi is your uncle?" It seemed unbelievable that a powerful military man like Karl should have a family.

"He helped us escape," Teodor reminded Guy. "Karl Valvanchi is a great warrior, he protects the tribes of Sas Darona, is that not true, Nuria?"

"Well, he's my uncle, and I have visited him on Sas Darona."

"You've been to Sas Darona?" Guy was astonished. "I thought it was in lockdown."

"Yes, but I am Valvanchi," Nuria replied as if that was the only explanation needed.

Teodor nodded a moment, so the Valvanchi could pick and choose which United Races rules they followed. Guy however was less circumspect.

"I thought there was plague on Sas Darona?"

"No. It was contained with fire domes around Mezzatorra," Nuria replied.

"So why the planet wide lockdown?" Guy continued.

"Because the SDLA raided the base and stole eight poison pills. My uncle says the Dome Militant helped them."

"Pah!" Guy replied dismissively.

"Hold on..." Teodor interrupted. "Did you say poison pills? That's a glass brick with plague insects inside fitted with explosives, right?" Nuria nodded once, so Teodor hurriedly continued. "I think I saw something in the air-conditioning tunnels of the Dome, I thought I saw a poison pill."

"That's not funny, Teodor," Nuria replied. "Tell me exactly what you saw."

Teodor described their climb down the Dome architecture. How they had found the open grille and how he had banged his head and thought he had seen a glass brick.

"It seemed new – or newly installed. The air-conditioning was filthy, but the screws on the poison pills were bright and clean. That's what I found so peculiar."

Nuria's mouth dropped open in sudden shock, and then she said. "A batch of eight poison pills was stolen from a place called Mezzatorra on Sas Darona. It was an SDLA attack, but my uncle thought they were assisted by..." She glanced at Guy. "By the Dome Militant."

"That's not possible!" Teodor protested. "The Dodecahedral Empire recognises..."

Guy held up a hand to stop Teodor. "Des was on Sas Darona for six months last year and," he paused, "this year too. He just came back," he said in a small voice. "He mentioned something about Mezzatorra, and said he wanted to speak urgently to Chartsie about it."

"Des Parks?" interrupted Teodor. "I saw him earlier, he was talking to Chart Segat this morning. He said..." That's not right, he said. "He was showing Segat some photos, and yes, I remember now, he mentioned Mezzatorra, but I didn't hear all of it. What did Des say about Mezzatorra?" Teodor asked Guy.

Guy remembered the mime Des had made, urging him to be silence. Unconsciously, he pressed his fingers into the 'keep quiet' mime as he changed tack: "The Dome Militant has four separate bases. I mean, it is the one planet outside the Dodecahedral where we have keys to the star gate."

Teodor noticed the movement in Guy's hand and gazed at him thoughtfully. "Yes, Sas Darona is closer than the Emperor's planet, and the human tribes there could also be related to us. That's why the Valvanchi gave us the key. And to train the Dome Militant, but four bases? Did my father know?"

"I think so. There is masses of space. The Zaracans know that."

"By rights, it should be part of the Dodecahedral Empire," Teodor said.

"But by United Races law, it is under the protection of Zarac," Nuria replied.

"It is in our space – geography dictates it should be ours," Teodor insisted.

"Point is," Guy said at last. "The point is – and despite everything – why would the Dome Militant place a poison pill within the Dome? The Dome is our home. I mean, does anyone know what the plague might do in a neighbourhood like Domeside? It does not make any sense."

"Chart Segat," Teodor replied. "Who knows what he is capable of?"

"You're wrong, Teodor. He told me to tell you he did not kill your father or your brother. He told me he did not do it, and I believe him. And this poison pill accusation, it is just stupid. Why would Chart Segat destroy the Dome, it's his life's work."

"Maybe, Guy." Teodor said, then added. "Your mother only has one son. I have to worry about ten thousand men and youths. That's what Chart Segat told me. It was the one thing he said that rang true."

"Are you sure you saw a poison pill?" Nuria asked. "Because if the Dome Militant assisted the SDLA in the theft, as my uncle thinks..." She paused and changed her mind. "But I agree with Guy. It still makes no sense, why would the Dome Militant place a poison pill in their own Dodecahedron Dome?"

"Let's forget it. My mother says I spent seventeen of the last thirty-six hours out of my head, all drugged up. Maybe I just imagined it. Right, pudding anyone? I think we all need some chocolate. I am sorry if I spoke strong words, Princess."

"My prince, you are passionate about your people and your empire. I admire that. But yes, cake sounds good."

Teodor cut the cake and passed around slices, spoons, and dished out extra cream and strawberries.

"I'm trying to feed Guy up," he confided in Nuria. "You know what? Everyone had told me before I met him, he was skinny and fast. They said he spun like the wind and bit like a goran. So, I figure if he were less skinny, he would be less fast. I might beat him."

"Not likely," replied Guy, and they all laughed.

After they had eaten and were sitting feeling very full and rather silly. Nuria sighed and pulled out her communicator.

"I should call my uncle about those poison pills."

Teodor held out a hand to stop her.

Not yet. I might be wrong. I was drugged afterall. Enjoy your cake.

Very well my prince, but Guy Erma is not the only one getting fat today.

I'm not fat, Teodor replied.

"My prince, a message from your mother." A uniformed butler had approached them. "Guy's mother has asked for him to be returned home."

"Pardon?" Teodor replied, astonished.

"Your mother asks that Guy be returned to Domeside as soon as lunch is done, Sir. So, if you will allow me, my prince, I will call a car."

"Wait!" Teodor replied.

Two floors below, Sayginn sat on a little sofa with Karl Valvanchi, sipping a glass of white wine. His hair was wet from when he had used her bathroom, and he was dressed only in a towel.

"I have asked them to send you some more clothes," Sayginn said, sitting on the edge of the sofa a short distance from him. "They won't be too long."

Sayginn knew she should not stare, but Karl was almost naked, and the smooth flesh of his shoulders and chest was just a tantalising stretch of the arm away. She knew she should not think about it, so she said something at the front of her mind.

"I'm not sure about that Domesider."

"He's just a boy," Karl reassured her.

"I'm not sure he is a suitable friend for Teodor," Sayginn said.

"He is a great little blades fighter."

"Yes, but if he lives here with us, there's bound to be speculation. He's just too handsome, too alluring, in all the wrong ways."

"Sayginn, he's from Domeside. You think he's good-looking; it's not his fault. Blame his father or his mother."

"And who are they, I wonder? I should have him tested, discover the worst, I guess. Chart Segat has sent me three messages saying he wants him back. Doesn't that tell you something?"

"Don't send him back to the Dome."

"Why not? Why wait until he is comfortable? Will it be easier when he is used to the palace? For him, or for Teo? No, I will give the instruction." She changed her voice and touched her communicator: "Tell Teodor to send Guy back to the Dome after they have had lunch." She switched off her communicator and sighed: "Now I feel better, now I can relax."

"Good," said Karl. "Have some more wine."

"You make me feel like I'm overdressed."

"Well, you are."

"But Karl—"

"You invited me to your private rooms, to shower and wait for new clothing. How many bedrooms are there in this palace?"

"Well, with the emperor here..."

"And you have nothing better to do? Like spending time with your son, for instance?"

Sayginn flushed.

"He's resting."

Another steward came quietly into the room with a trolley of food. He started setting the dishes on a rotating table alongside the bed. The table was on a huge pivot, so it could be rotated across the bed to allow for eating at your leisure.

"I asked them to prepare you an Imperial bed banquet. You eat it in bed with your fingers."

"I have heard of this." Karl paused and looked straight at her, "Well, we have time. Now that Teodor is safe, we have plenty of time."

Chapter 36

Return to the Dome

"My prince, it is your mother's instructions for one of the house cars to return Guy Erma to Domeside, his mother is waiting for him." The Butler repeated.

"That can't be right?" Teodor replied, he looked shocked.

"Your mother says Guy must return to the Dodecahedron Dome after lunch. A car is waiting downstairs."

The Butler left as quickly as he had arrived, and Teodor spent a few fruitless minutes tapping on his communicator.

"It's no use. Mother has switched her device to private. I can't contact her. I don't want to send Guy back to Domeside," he explained to Nuria.

"Yes, but if his mother…"

"I don't have a mother," Guy growled.

"And I promised Des I would not send Guy back to the Dome. A sworn promise." Teodor hesitated; he felt the fear again. It chilled him, and he looked at Guy. "Do you think Des is all right?"

"We should check on him."

"And Sebastian, do you think?"

Guy shrugged. "The guys from the Riffaut who were also Dome Militant would have watched out for him. There's Marline too."

"Yes," Teodor replied, remembering the short red tutu and the pirate hat and sword.

"Who?" Nuria said with a frown.

"We're talking about all the people who helped us escape," Teodor explained. "Look, Guy, I can't argue with my mother." Guy gave him a look of disbelief. Teodor paused. Dare he disobey his mother? He considered this when suddenly a solution presented itself: "Ok, I cannot disobey a direct order, but she does not have to have it all her way. I'm going with you to the Dome. And we're not going alone. I want a word with Chart Segat. And I want the Dome Militant."

"What do you want with the Dome Militant?" Guy asked curiously.

"I want them; that's all. The Dome Militant belong to the King of Earth, and in his absence, his regent."

"What are you going to do?" Nuria asked.

Teodor stood a moment deep-in-thought. "The Dome Debate was lost because of me, but I think I can change that. I want to have a word with Chart Segat; that's all." Then, looking at Nuria, he apologised. "I'm sorry, Nuria. We're going to desert you."

"Oh no, you're not, because I'm coming too. The first thing we should do is check on this poison pill," Nuria said, "We need to see if it is real."

"Yes, we must and then I must speak to Chart Segat. And we're not going alone."

About fifteen minutes later, they were sitting together on the back seat of a large car. Teodor had decided they should dress for the occasion. So Nuria had changed into a white dress with a rainbow belt and her hair flowed in rainbow colours. Guy had picked a tailored black suit and matched it with a blue shirt, which he wore with the neck open, and the collar turned up. With his hair gelled back in place, even Nuria gave him a second look. Mostly, though, Nuria was admiring Teodor, who had changed into his dress uniform of red and silver, together with a ceremonial cap. The two huge golden gorans had been persuaded into the car. They seemed content enough to curl up at their feet. Teodor never stopped touching and talking to them, even as he chatted with both Guy and Nuria.

"My father told me that the Dome Militant belongs to Earth. They protect our planets. They used to be our personal bodyguards. That's why the blades championships started. Each year, the Dome Militant would compete for the twelve places in our personal bodyguard."

"Yes, I remember," Guy said. "It wasn't just the men. There used to be a competition among us boys for two of us to be around you and Deodran. Well, before..."

"Before Deodran died," Teodor finished and squeezed Guy's hand. "It was the Dome bomb under the car. My mother replaced the Dome Militant with the Royal Guard. But it was never as good. Not really. Anyway, my mum backed off from the organisation of the Dome Militant as well. And I understand, as for a while I too blamed the Black and Gold, but then it became apparent there was another bomb."

"The second bomb was nothing to do with the Dome Militant," Guy said passionately.

"Well," Teodor hesitated, "We don't know who was responsible for the second bomb."

"The Dome Militant did not place the first bomb either," Guy interrupted. "Yes, it was a Dome device, but we didn't put it there."

Teodor took his hand and squeezed it.

"I want to believe you, Guy. I want to believe you. In fact, I do believe you. And when I saw the Dome Militant last night, it was not them who were chasing me. It was not them who imprisoned me. No, every single human I met within the Dome — you, Des, the man in the tunnels, Sebastian, Marline. Everyone wanted to help me."

"Chart Segat told me to tell you that he did not kill your father; he did not kill your brother. And when he says that, he means the Dome Militant did not do it."

"But Chart Segat did kidnap me. And he now controls the Dome Militant. No, I must control the Dome, or my mother must. I intend to convince Chart Segat to give up his powers. I just need to say a few words."

Teodor sat in silence, Both Guy and Nuria looked at him with curiosity, but before they could ask anything more, Teodor said, "Nuria, can you connect the three of us telepathically?" The girl hesitated. "We don't know what awaits us in the Dome. If you would agree to boost my basic goran telepathy, well, it might be useful."

"She hasn't got the powers to do that," Guy said. "Does she?"

"I have," Nuria said. "And of course, I will offer my power to you, my prince. I will provide any assistance you require."

"Thank you, Princess."

Nuria moved to sit between Guy and Teodor. She then stretched out her arm and nodded to Teodor. He smiled and wound his arm around hers until the palm of his hand pressed against her. They both looked at Guy. He wrapped his arm around both theirs and grabbed both their hands in his. For a moment, they clung to one another.

"Close your eyes, Guy," Teodor said. "Look for the light."

Guy closed his eyes and saw a line of white light. He bent to look into the light, and suddenly he could hear them. He could hear Teodor's and Nuria's thoughts.

'Can we use telepathy now?'

'Yes.'

'Can you hear us, Guy?'

'YES!'

'I was thinking, if Guy shows us the changing room, I want to take a look to see if I indeed imagined that poison pill. I know I saw something; maybe you could take a look.'

'Well,' Nuria replied. 'we should get some pictures... But I mean, I honestly could not think of a worse place.'

"Worse?" asked Guy, and he had spoken aloud, he was so alarmed.

'Well, the exponential rate of expansion of the cy-sect population. It will accelerate in the damp air-conditioning tunnel.'

There was a pause, until finally, Teodor shared a final thought:

'Let's hope I was dreaming, then.'

Finally, Teodor spoke aloud for the first time: "Here we are. Guy, show us the way."

They were never going to pass unnoticed. Not with thirty-six Royal Guard men and cyborgs, eighteen cy-wolves, not to mention two huge gorans, accompanying them. Still, it was the three young people at the centre of this crowd that attracted the most attention. The crowds cheered and applauded as they passed. In the changing room, Teodor got one of the Royal Guard cyborgs to lift him first, then Nuria afterwards. After she had been placed on the ground, she stood for a few moments in complete silence.

"I have to..."

'Be careful who you tell,' Teodor warned.

'We don't want a panic,' she agreed.

'We don't know who has the release code,' Teodor muttered.

'It will be Chart Segat,' Nuria said.

'If so then Des will know,' Guy cut in. 'I could ask him.'

'Good idea,' Teodor replied.

'I'll talk to Karl, but I'll tell him it's a secret.' Nuria agreed.

Teodor nodded. Men from the Dome Militant had pushed past the Royal Guard to see what Teodor was doing. Their captain saluted, fist to heart.

"My Prince!"

"Captain." Teodor replied. "I escaped using this tunnel last night, and I found a biohazard behind this grill. You and your men should secure this area and make sure no one interferes with it."

"Sir, yessir." The man looked bemused.

He thinks you're mad, Guy said.

He'll find out soon enough, Teodor replied. Let's go.

"Dome Militant. Your prince, your prince!" The captain called out as Teodor went to leave, as one the men clad in black and gold fell back and snapped to attention. Teodor nodded and led Nuria by the hand, and waving Guy to follow.

'Teodor, there may be more than one,' Nuria whispered.

'What makes you say that?'

'That raid on Sas Darona I told you about. Eight poison pills were stolen.'

'You say the shield went up, didn't it?'

'Yes, a fire shield dome contained the plague but everyone inside died.'

'Teodor, what are you going to do?' Guy's thoughts were loud.

'How easy are they to destroy, Nuria?'

'Oh, there are several ways. Finding and isolating them is key.'

'And if we have the Dome Militant to help us...' Teodor reflected, yet another troop of Dome Militant snapped to attention as he passed. 'Ok, I have an idea. I must have words with Chart Segat.'

"Guy Erma! That is against Union rules," a loud voice called out to them. Teodor looked over. Standing on a table to get a view of them over the heads of the crowd was Sebastian. He leapt down from the table and pushed his way over to meet them. Teodor shook his hand energetically, but Sebastian still wanted to talk to Guy:

"You wearing the Riffaut is just unfair competition."

Guy burst out laughing and replied:

"What do you expect? I had to borrow some of Teodor's clothes."

Without asking, Sebastian buttoned Guy's jacket closed and adjusted his collar. He stepped back with a critical look.

"Better. Now you look almost as fabulous as me. You'll put me out of a job."

"That's alright because I have another job for you," replied Teodor.

Guy nodded meaningfully. Sebastian turned around slowly.

"My prince?" Sebastian bowed.

"I want you to come and work in the palace as my personal valet. You know the clothes I like, so I want you to pick out my choices every day." Sebastian was momentarily stunned, but then he replied.

"I am very expensive, Sire."

Teodor laughed then. "I should hope so. Only the best for a future King, don't you agree?" Then Teodor lowered his voice and continued: "You see, I was able to use the trick you told me, the one about pretending to be you. It helped me escape the Dome. This would be my reward to you, if you want to accept it."

"Thank you, my King. I think I will probably accept." Sebastian replied with a half bow.

"Sebastian," Guy interrupted. "Do you know where Des is? I mean, what happened to him?"

"Ah!" Sebastian's face fell. "He's not so good. He was also in the cells. He was still there this morning when they freed me. They had given him a good kicking. It depends on how soon they let him go to a surgeon. As you know, the longer you leave an injury, the harder it is to heal."

Teodor nodded.

"Guy, take ten of the Royal Guard and go and release Des from his cell. I will go ahead. I want to speak with Chart Segat. Where is he, Sebastian?"

"He's in the competition gym."

"Ok, you go with Guy. Tell them you are working on my direct orders. Free Des and bring him to the gym as well."

'Don't take any nonsense from anyone,' Teodor added in a firm thought voice.

'I won't,' replied Guy.

"Wait!" said Guy, just as Teodor turned to leave. "Sebastian, have you any idea where Marline is?"

"She left with Simon Sorrow last night. She's gone to his South Sea paradise. Lucky girl."

"Ah. Ok. Fine, I just wanted to see her," he said, his heart had sank through the floor at his feet. So, he had saved the prince, but he was too late to save Marline... where had she gone?

'I will help her also, Guy.' Teodor said, using telepathy.

Guy nodded: 'I'll go and get Des.' Already telepathic speech seemed natural and useful. Guy and Sebastian set off at a run.

'Guy! Don't say anything about Mezzatorra or poison pills until we get to speak to him alone.'

'Agreed.'

The enormous competition gym was the scene of a vast demonstration of the Dome's best blades fighters. Only five blades' mats were in use, but the hall had taken on a carnival atmosphere. There were stalls around the edges selling food. Seating was raised around the five remaining blades mats; more seats were set up on the balcony that looked down onto the gym, but none of the seats was allocated. People seemed to be moving around freely, sometimes pausing to watch a blades fight, more often just milling around.

The entire gym seemed to be in movement. Beyond the central areas, groups of fighters and youths were giving displays of blades throwing and gymnastics, to the delight of crowds who had come in from across Domeside and, indeed, the entire capital. The beautiful models of Old Fleet Street wandered, surrounded by admirers, while small groups of off-world visitors clung close together – taking photographs of the Battle Borgs.

Chart Segat had had his large chair moved down from the Cap of the Dome and installed on the platform where, the day before, the Dome Debate committee had met. A host of colourful guests surrounded him, and of course, Loulou stood motionless in his shadow. Teodor walked straight towards him. He still had his two Gorans with him, plus a dozen Royal Guard and cy-wolves. But it was the gorans that caused the crowds to gasp and part. Only Chart Segat feigned not to notice his approach, and instead, seemed intent on watching two men fight at blades.

"Chart Segat," Teodor called out. The fight stopped. Slowly, around the gym, the fighters and apprentices, the onlookers and fashion-lovers turned to look at Prince Teodor, who was standing in their midst in his full uniform, with two huge gorans at his side.

"Chart Segat! You called, and we came. You said you wanted Guy back."

Teodor saw Chart Segat look lazily at him. He seemed to count the Royal Guard, then relax a fraction – before calling out in a bored voice:

"Prince Teodor, how good to see you. You are, as always, welcome in our Dome. Even an unannounced visit. But your cats must wait outside."

Teodor did not reply. He touched the minds of his giant gorans, and they both roared. It was with some satisfaction that he saw the crowd – including Dome Militant – back off a little. Even Chart Segat looked perturbed. Conversations stopped, and Teodor realised that everyone was now turning to watch this encounter between himself and Chart Segat.

Good. I hope they all watch and take note.

"Chart Segat, the only reason I am here is to tell you that Guy Erma will not be returning to the Dome."

Chart Segat smiled. He stood up and drew himself up to his full height. He looked behind him and drew Loulou forward to stand alongside him.

"But Guy, he belongs here in Domeside." Chart Segat nodded at Loulou, implying but not saying that she was his mother. What he did say was, in fact, a complete lie: "He is Dome Militant Junior, did he not tell you?"

"Don't lie to me. Guy said the lists of Dome Militant Junior would not be published for another month. And I came here to tell you, you may have won the Dome Debate, but you will face trial for my kidnapping and the murder of my father and brother."

"Thing is, Teodor; you have to have proof for such an accusation."

"Oh, I am happy to bear witness against you," Teodor added.

Chart Segat had walked back and towered over him. He is still trying to intimidate me, Teodor thought angrily. He used his telepathy to nudge one of the golden gorans. The yearling obediently leapt up and landed his two paws on the man's shoulders. The goran's weight was enough to knock the man over and pin him to the floor. On a sign from Teodor, the goran roared into Chart Segat's face. His jaws and lips brushed Chart Segat's features. The goran's breath blew Chart Segat's hair back from his face.

"Teodor!"

Teodor spun around to where he saw Emperor Frederon standing up from another gilded chair alongside the blades mat. As he rose, the two young tiger goran cubs bounded along at his heels, then seeing Teodor's golden gorans, they started to hiss and snarl. The Emperor reached down with his black varnished nails and pulled·them back.

"Uncle!" Teodor was surprised at first. Both his gorans looked up, their faces showing the puzzlement and curiosity that Teodor managed to mask. His mind was spinning. What was the Emperor doing here with Chart Segat?

"And who have we here?"

"This is Nuria, she is…" Teodor paused. Nuria, who had assumed her human appearance for their trip to the Dome, now snapped her fingers. She no longer wore the white dress and rainbow hair. Her clothes had changed to a slim uniform in turquoise and white; her hair similarly had turned white with two thick stripes of turquoise running through it. These were the battle colours of the House Valvanchi. Nuria knew well the antipathy that the Emperor had for her race, and was, at this moment, advertising her allegiance to the highest clan: the Valvanchi. In this garb, thought Teodor, she hardly needed any introduction.

"This is Princess Nuria Valvanchi. She is the granddaughter of Nikato Valvanchi, the discoverer and unifier of the Dodecahedral Empire."

Frederon just snorted.

"Unifier indeed!" And one of his tiger gorans leapt towards Nuria, claws out.

Teodor gave a telepathic nudge to one of his golden gorans, who smoothly curved his body around Nuria, and lay across her feet. The tiger cub hissed at the larger beast but retreated.

"My work counts for nothing," the Emperor continued. "I knew your grandfather. Other than postulate the possibility of a link between our planets, he didn't do anything to forge the union. I created the empire, the Great Dodecahedral Empire of the Twelve!"

The Emperor, Teodor realised, was talking to the Dome Militant, not just to him. Some of the men even started to cheer, but as Teodor turned to look at them, they fell silent. Most now looked distinctly shame-faced. Teodor gazed up at his uncle. So, Frederon wanted to control the Dome Militant as well. Teodor swallowed, wondering if he dare proceed. Simultaneously, both he and the Emperor saw the flash of metal in Chart Segat's hand. Chart Segat was reaching up to knife the other golden goran.

"No," Teodor cried. It was a shouted imperative and the goran, with its wild instincts directed by Teodor's thoughts, moved faster than Teodor ever could and with a strength and deadly precision Teodor could barely imagine. The beast swiped at the blade and sent it spinning across the floor. Its claws passed close to Chart Segat's nose and cheeks.

"Let him go free!" the Emperor ordered. "You will need this man if you are to rule the Dome."

Now Teodor was outraged, "My uncle, he took me captive. He beat me. He starved me. He would have killed me."

"Obey me, Teodor. Free him!"

Teodor hesitated, for Frederon was his Emperor, dare he disobey him?

Just then, a shout came from behind. Guy, Des and Sebastian were charging through the far doors on blades. Guy was alongside Teodor in a couple of giant leaps. He bent to take off his blades and bowed to the Emperor in one smooth move.

"My uncle, may I introduce Guy Erma. He helped me escape from the Dome."

The Emperor turned his hawkish gaze on Guy Erma. Teodor did not notice for he had turned to greet Des, "From this day forth, you will be my personal bodyguard if you accept..." He said in a whisper.

'Help me, Teodor,' Guy whispered.

Teodor turned to see that not only was the Emperor still staring at Guy, but Chart Segat had stood up and had brushed himself off.

"This is the boy, is it not?" The Emperor said.

"Yes, Guy is a good boy. Guy is one of us." With this quip, Chart Segat had once again assumed his authority. The Emperor was smiling. Men were laughing. Chart Segat was already back in full power.

'One of us?' thought Teodor.

'He's just trying to split us up.' Guy replied with panicked thoughts. 'Don't believe him!'

Now Chart Segat placed a heavy hand on Guy's shoulder. Teodor saw Guy visibly pale. He seemed to shrink as well. More than that, Teodor noticed the ring Chart Segat wore, with letters like teeth spelling out the words: Loyal to Empire, Fear only God. He looked saw Frederon and Chart Segat exchange glances. Suddenly, Teodor was chilled to his very soul.

'Chart Segat is loyal to the Empire,' thought Teodor. 'He is loyal to my uncle Frederon, the emperor of all twelve planets of the Dodecahedral. Why? Why did Chart Segat kidnap me on Frederon's orders?'

'Frederon was going to pardon him for King Serge's death.' Guy replied. 'I heard him say so. Frederon said he would give him full control of the Dome Militant.'

'Chart Segat betrayed me. On Frederon's orders.' Teodor repeated. 'If he stays in control of the Dome Militant, he will betray me again, my mother too. There will be more bombs under more cars, and we will not last long.'

'You need the Dome Militant. You need them, Teodor.' Guy pleaded.

'If they are loyal,' Teodor replied.

Chart Segat still held Guy by the shoulder; now he bent to kiss him. Guy's thoughts turned into an anguished howl:

'Please Teodor, you swore to protect me. You swore as a prince!'

Both golden gorans roared. Remembering his promise, how with hands wet with soap suds he had sworn to protect Guy Erma, Teodor realised the time had come. He had to deliver on that promise.

"Chart Segat, let go of Guy Erma." Teodor ordered. "He is not coming back to the Dome." Chart Segat laughed and shook his head, so Teodor continued, "You will give up the Dome Militant. If you do not give yourself up, you will be arrested for my kidnapping later today." Still, Chart Segat had his hand on Guy's shoulder. With an impatient stamp, Teodor stepped forward, took the hand, and lifted it away. "Give yourself up now, Chart Segat. This is my last warning."

Chart Segat laughed, glanced at the emperor and winked. Teodor looked over; the emperor was not laughing.

'Now,' said Teodor.

'Kill him!' urged Guy again.

'Don't kill him,' replied Teodor and closed his eyes. 'I close my eyes for a moment while on duty, I will not watch what happens next.'

The two gorans leapt forward. Teodor pulled Guy aside, and the emperor backed up fast. Not so Chart Segat, he was flat on the floor. One large golden goran had pinned him to the ground. The other roared. Chart Segat threw both his arms up to protect his face.

Teodor stood over him and said so that everyone – all the Dome Militant and most notably the emperor – could hear.

"Chart Segat, you organised my kidnap using Battle Borgs. You detained me without food or communicator. You drugged me and beat me as often as you saw fit. You then threw me unprotected into a cage to fight for my life. You threatened to throw me to your borgs to fight for my life with only a blunted blade."

"Yes, but Teo," Chart Segat was pleading from the floor. "May I call you Teo? I never..."

"You also threatened to throw Guy Erma here to the borgs."

"That was a joke," Chart Segat protested.

"Three years ago, you threw Des Parks to the borgs."

There was a murmur through the ranks of the Dome Militant, a few cries quickly stifled from the crowd. Teodor took a moment to look at his people. Each and every soldier was armed. The other men and women stared at him. Teodor could feel their quiet anger, or was it desperation? All were looking from Teodor to Chart Segat to Frederon. They seemed wary of pledging any allegiance until the fight between these three was played out.

"But..." Chart Segat started.

"You will never throw anything or any boy to your borgs ever again, do you hear me?"

"My prince, I...."

"You will never throw anyone ever again."

'Now,' thought Teodor. 'Don't kill him!'

With one swift bite, the gorans took each of Chart Segat's arms in their mouths. Their teeth cut cleanly through flesh and bone above the elbows on both arms. The goran spat out the hands and forearms, sending them spinning away from him. Then both gorans leapt daintily away as Chart Segat's arms fell wide, with blood gushing out on both sides. The Dome administrator lay flat on the floor, his two arms wide like the red arms of a cross.

"Never again will you hand anyone to your borgs for torture," Teodor spoke with grim satisfaction. He nodded to two medics, standing at the side of the blades ring.

'They will give him arms,' Guy hesitated.

"Take him away. But not his arms. Cyborg implants only. As a reminder," Teodor repeated. As he spoke, each of his gorans picked up Chart Segat's hands and forearms and greedily started to chew the flesh from the bones.

The emperor looked down at Teodor. Cold respect glinted in his eyes, but he said nothing. Frederon knew that these young gorans were entirely under Teodor's control. If Teodor wanted to rip Chart Segat apart, he could not have chosen a better weapon. Dome Militant men had run forward. Teodor nodded, and tourniquets were applied. A stretcher zoomed in.

Teodor drew himself up to his full height. "The Dome Militant belongs to the Crown," he told the gathered men.

"Really?" The emperor said. Teodor turned to see fury in his hawk-like eyes. He saw the emperor was on the point of grabbing Guy. Teodor pushed the Domesider behind him, and they both stepped backwards out of the emperor's grasp.

'Hold your ground, Teodor,' Guy told him.

Teodor stopped and looked straight at the emperor.

'Why does the Emperor want you?' Teodor replied.

'He wants the Dome Militant,' Guy replied.

'I want the Dome Militant,' Teodor replied.

'No, you need the Dome Militant,' Guy reminded him.

With this thought firmly in front of his mind, Teodor stepped forward to confront the emperor.

"The Dome Militant belong to Earth, and Earth is ruled by the regent, my mother."

"Your mother was going to be my wife. Only now I think she will shortly be tried for treason herself," the emperor replied slyly.

"I beg your pardon?"

"Look..."

The emperor pointed his communicator at the screen. An image appeared on this one screen, and then quickly multiplied across every screen in sight. It was a moment before Teodor recognised his mother, because she was wrapped in the embrace of a man, and that man was Zaracan. Teodor's mother Regent Sayginn of Earth was kissing Karl Valvanchi.

"Oh my," Teodor heard himself say, glancing around at the many men who were looking up at the screen with interest. He caught sight of Nuria putting a hand to her face in fear. He did not know what to think. His mother caught on camera kissing Karl Valvanchi. As they fell apart, she looked flushed and breathless.

'She's kissing Killer Valvanski...' Teodor heard Guy's thought clearly and knew all the Dome Militant thought the same.

Mostly she was completely unaware of the crowd of people now watching. Already men around him were starting to whistle and shout foul words at the screen.

'She does not know we're watching,' Teodor replied and turned to shout at the emperor: "How did you get these pictures? My mother's room is a black room. There should be no photography."

"What does it matter? Your mother and Killer Valvanski. And everyone within the Dodecahedral is watching. I would not be surprised if she does not have to resign her position permanently. More importantly, how could the Dome Militant ever respect her now?"

"The Dome Militant have sworn..." started Teodor. Then, distracted by something on the screen, he said. "Oh, for goodness' sake, switch that off." But the images played on.

Helplessly, Teodor looked over to Nuria, 'Can you help with that screen?'

"The Dome Militant has sworn allegiance to the empire," the emperor concluded smoothly. As always, every time he spoke, the crowd was attentive, they listened. "So maybe I..."

"NO," Teodor yelled. Impressively, all the screens turned black. The largest screen exploded off its hinges, before falling slowly down the wall to the floor. Just slow enough for the crowd to scatter ahead of it.

'Ooops,' Nuria apologised. 'I told you I have not been fully trained in telekinesis. Mostly I just drop things.'

The giant screen rocked, and looked like it might fall forward, but in the end, it settled at an angle with a single wire connected above to the network.

They all looked at Teodor. Even the emperor was silent.

'The regent will never control the Dome Militant, not now,' Guy said.

'Maybe, but they cannot belong to Frederon.' Teodor replied, then he spoke aloud.

"You will not take the Dome Militant." As Teodor spoke, the two gorans leapt to his side and roared with blood-splattered mauls into the emperor's face. And then it happened. Only Teodor saw it. Only he and the emperor were aware of it when it happened. The emperor stepped back. Just one step back, but the emperor had yielded ground when faced with Teodor's anger. Teodor looked up at the emperor in triumph. He nodded once and his golden gorans leapt forward and ripped the throats from the two tiger goran cubs, leaving them broken at the emperor's feet. The emperor did not even seem to notice. He took a further three steps backward and sat down.

"The Dome Militant protect the six planets of Earth." Teodor said stepping forward. He strode up three steps to the centre of the raised platform. "They belong to the king."

'Teodor don't do this,' Guy suddenly realised what Teodor was going to do.

'I have to do this,' Teodor replied. 'If I don't do this, I cannot protect you. I cannot protect any of us...'

Teodor spoke in a loud, clear voice, looking at all those gathered in the great hall, as he said with conviction.

"The Dome Militant belong to the king of Earth."

'And I swore to protect you, Guy. This is how I protect you.'

Putting one fist against his hip, Teodor drew himself up to his full height:

"I, Teodor, son of Serge..."

The emperor looked up at him and frowned. Teodor swallowed and started again.

"I, Teodor, son of Serge... do claim this planet and its dependencies.
To rule as is my right,
to the benefit of my people,
as guided by our democratic institutions,
and proscribed by our laws.
So, help me God."

The silence continued long after Teodor had spoken the oath. Frederon said nothing. Teodor saw he was looking around the gym, trying to sense the mood of the crowd.

'Say it again,' urged Guy.

With more forcefulness, and putting greater emphasis on each word Teodor spoke the oath a second time, gazing calmly at his uncle, the emperor:

"I, Teodor, son of Serge... do claim this planet and its dependencies.
To rule as is my right,
to the benefit of my people,
as guided by our democratic institutions,
and prescribed by our laws.
So, help me God."

'Now kneel!' Teodor thought fiercely, looking round the assembled men.

'Of course,' replied Guy softly, and before Teodor could stop him, Guy knelt before Teodor and, taking his hand, pressed it to his forehead:

"Hail Teodor, King of Earth."

Nuria went down on one knee and said in a loud voice:

"Hail Teodor, King of Earth!"

It had less of an impact than it should. In fact, a ripple of anger ran through the Dome Militant at the sight of the Valvanchi girl kneeling at his feet.

'What about the Militant, why don't they kneel?' Teodor thought.

'Give them a second, Teodor. They are just getting used to the idea. What about the borgs?' Guy directed his thought to Nuria: 'Give our powers a boost, Princess. We need to control the Battle Borgs.'

Nuria complied and throughout the gym, the giant metal men went down on one knee:

"Hail Teodor, King of Earth!"

'The Dome Militant are still not kneeling, Guy.'

'One more second, Teodor...'

The emperor was no longer smiling now. The Dome Militant looked nervous. Guy glanced back at Sebastian and Des. Quickly now, they both bent to one knee:

"Hail Teodor, King of Earth!"

At this, the Battle Borgs, still kneeling, bent their heads and repeated:

"Hail Teodor, King of Earth!"

'Now see,' Guy said.

As Teodor watched, first one by one, then in groups, men and women, in family groups or with their friends, went down on one or two knees. On the podium behind them, Loulou had knelt, and with her a large crowd of models. Then all the young girls were kneeling, and with them their companions and children. Now it was the turn of the Dome Militant. First soldiers, then lieutenants, when a captain knelt his men knelt with him. When Tilson knelt, half the room shadowed him. Finally, the entire room of Dome Militant knelt and proclaimed:

"Hail Teodor, King of Earth!"

When they had finally fallen silent, at the very last, Emperor Frederon rose and with a small, slightly mocking, bow:

"Hail Teodor, King of Earth."

There was silence around the gym. Frederon glanced around at the vast crowd of Dome Militant and Domeside people, and joined in the shouts:

"Hail Teodor, King of Earth. Hail Teodor, Head of the Dome Militant."

All at once the crowd was released. The crowd roared and screamed their approval, as with one voice they started to chant.

"Hail Teodor, King of Earth. Hail Teodor, Head of the Dome Militant."

Teodor glanced one more time at Frederon. The emperor looked relaxed and even applauded him. For once Teodor felt the emperor was perhaps entirely on his side. He pulled himself up to his full height and waved at the crowds. All through the gym, the Dome Militant were falling into rows under the command of their captains. The civilians fell back until the Dome Militant, fully ten thousand strong, stood in neat rows across the gym, and in great circles all around the high watching balconies, and even out into the atrium beyond.

Teodor looked at them. For a moment, it felt like he held his breath. As one, the Dome Militant saluted closed fist to the heart. Then they raised their voices:

"Loyal to Empire, fear only God."

The sheer force of their greeting was overwhelming. For one terrible moment, Teodor felt himself to be four-years-old again. His body rocked backwards. He felt a hand at the small of his back. Guy Erma, standing at his side, had reached to steady him. And he had done so without anyone noticing.

'Thank you, Guy!' Teodor thought gratefully.

'Just do your job!' Guy replied grimly.

Without further hesitation, Teodor saluted his troops, and they replied:

"Hail Teodor, King of Earth."

The emperor said, "So, King Teodor, you have your command, what are your orders?"

The first part was easy, thought Teodor. He needed to replace Chart Segat, and he could think of one person who would be ideal for the job.

"Tilson, Commander Tilson." His instructor stepped forward and knelt to kiss his hand.

"Please, can you head up the Dome Council?"

"Of course, my King, but what are your commands?"

Teodor was quick to reply. "I want to reinstate the Dome Militant as my personal guard. I want both Des and Guy to be part of that guard. I want the Battle Borgs returned to their barracks and their programming fully checked for interference and..." he stood a moment, considering.

'I want Dome Militant places to go to Domesiders. I wanted it to be illegal to work as a fashion model before the age of eighteen, or better still, twenty-one. I want the Dome to be a fairer, gentler place, but how?'

'Don't forget the poison pills,' Nuria sent him a thought reminder.

The emperor saw his hesitation and was quick to step forward. He went to place a hand on Teodor's shoulder. Only the nearest goran growled, and the emperor hesitated but continued.

"Of course, strictly speaking, you cannot be king without the agreement of the barons. I will confer with them, on your behalf, over the next few days; they may decide that because of your youth..."

Teodor immediately understood the implied threat. The emperor had more influence with the barons than Teodor did. He would dictate their opinion. He would deprive Teodor of his crown and his power. Teodor felt his anger rising. At his side, both his gorans were growling and hissing now.

"I am sorry, my uncle," Teodor replied, "but there will be no time for that. You see, this planet is under threat of extinction. And you are in extreme danger. As my emperor, my lord and my uncle, I urge you to leave this planet as soon as you can."

"I'm sorry, Teo?"

"Yesterday, when I escaped from the Dome, I found this in the air-conditioning tunnels of the Dome. Nuria, please show us the pictures and explain."

Nuria pointed her communicator at the screens. Though cracked and smoking they lit up with images. "This is a poison pill found in the air-conditioning tunnel above changing room..." She hesitated.

"Changing room on the seventeenth," confirmed Guy.

"I have information from my uncle, Karl Valvanchi." Nuria continued. "He has confirmed this is one of eight poison pills, stolen from a place called Mezzatorra on Sas Darona."

"Thank you," said Teodor. "What we have to do now is check the infrastructure of the Dome and locate and isolate this and any other poison pill. Guy, please explain."

"Twice a year, the Dome has a Spring Sweep, when droids are sent through the tunnels to clear any blockage and disinfect all surfaces. Teenagers lay the ropes for the droids to follow. The next clean is due next week."

"So," concluded Teodor, "I must ask that this Spring Sweep be scheduled as soon as possible this afternoon. I will lead a team in setting the ropes to guide the droids. It is imperative that we work together to find the poison pills, deadly planet killers that they are, and then isolate and neutralise them. So, you see, my emperor. In this, our hour of danger, for your protection you must go."

Emperor Frederon looked at the glass brick buzzing on screen, then back to Teodor. "The Dome Militant did not do this," he confirmed, and then he glanced where Chart Segat had gone. "Did he?"

"That is not the point, my uncle." Teodor replied. "However, I will provide you with a Dome Militant escort to speed you to safety."

Frederon was still looking at the screen.

"Tilson," Teodor gave the command. "Your best men to escort the emperor."

Frederon bent down to Teodor on leaving. He nodded briefly towards Nuria as he whispered. "Those Valvanski have betrayed you, Teo."

Chapter 37

A Dome of Fire and Light

So it was that later that afternoon, Teodor climbed out of the Cap of the Dome to stand alongside Guy and Nuria and look out over his city. The sky was bright; almost silver. The sun appeared larger than Teodor had ever remembered. It hung low in the heavens, and soon there would be a rainbow of colours above them, and the sun would set. The sky was full of noise and movement. Shuttles from the Dome were taking off and returning in quick succession, the Dome Militant were being evacuated, and from other parts of the city, hover cars were taking off, forming multi-layered queues, like a cloud of locusts waiting to pass the security posts.

Below in the street, people filed out of the houses, they carried possessions and children. They joined long queues, which snaked towards the exits of Domeside. Teodor could see it was still good-humoured and orderly; Dome Militant had control of the security posts, and the people trusted it would be safe.

Using Dome Militant as security for the evacuation had been the first and best decision of the day. The second decision, to announce a problem with the Dome's power plant, was more controversial. The population were more bemused than afraid at the order to evacuate, and the exodus had the feeling of a cheerful carnival.

Teodor did not have long to reflect on what he saw. Guy showed him how to attach the rope to the top of the Dome, and then they both climbed down a short ladder. More boys and girls were arriving at the top every minute, and there was only a limited amount of space atop the Cap of the Dome.

On the fourth level of the Dome, a team of Zaracans worked with Dome Militant, as they deployed robots throughout the air-conditioning system. Karl Valvanchi was in command. He had set a table against the wall and then stacked screens alongside it. Each screen relayed images from small robots that now travelled through the air-conditioning system. Around the small room, a dozen different air-conditioning grilles were propped against the wall. As Karl watched, two technicians primed a small sphere-like machine with a large camera eye on the front and back. Using the remote control, the men made the camera rotate a full circle and then hover left and right. They directed the robot into another air-conditioning tube. These machines were proving to be robust and fault-free; all the better, as the job would be completed more quickly.

Without warning, Karl broke into a chill sweat, as he recalled Mezzatorra. Again and again, the faces of his colleagues appeared before him, and he remembered the row of corpses laid out under the tall tree. How high would they stack the corpses if the Sas Darona plague broke out in the heart of London? He leant in towards the screens. At any moment, the monitors might show another pill, but this time, it might be broken. Would there be any hope then, even in fast and furious flight?

Karl wished he was blissfully ignorant of the poison pill threat and possible subsequent plague. Those around him only worked with such calm efficiency because of their fearless innocence of what might come, whereas Karl himself felt true fear. How could he stop his hands from shaking, as he manipulated the robot? Why could he not bring himself to examine the signals?

I am Karl Valvanchi, Captain of the Zaracan army. I will not tremble like a fearful child.

He took a breath and focused on Sayginn and her son. They depended on him to find and neutralise these poison pills, so he had no choice. With renewed vigour, he scanned the information relayed from the robots.

"You must come with me to Zarac 1." Karl had said earlier to Sayginn. "You need to escape this terror."

"But what about my people?"

"Make up an excuse, say you were invited to the fifth birthday of my son; we consider the fifth an important milestone."

"If I go, Teodor will have to stay. The people must have a leader."

"Then Teodor must go."

"Teodor and Guy..."

"Teodor, Guy, his entire little gang," They laughed. Sayginn had watched, with growing alarm, as Teodor bestowed ranks and honours on those who had helped him.

Suddenly, Karl stood up and went down on one knee at her feet. He kissed her hand. "Let me stay with you, Sayginn. I will stay, and we will fight this evil together."

"But how?" Sayginn asked. "How can you stay?"

"It is the right thing to do," Karl replied. "I fear I may have caused this."

"But how?"

"I'm not sure but..."

"Sayginn," Patrice walked in uninvited, looking flustered. "Apologies." He nodded to Karl. "There is growing panic in Domeside – we need to maintain the calm to maximise the evacuation effort."

"We need to show them there is nothing to fear," Sayginn replied.

"Nothing to fear?" Karl murmured.

"I have an order to pick up from House Jewel," Sayginn said.

"You can't go in to Domeside," Karl replied.

"We can send in a convey and a troop as security." Patrice confirmed.

"It will only take thirty minutes in and out, but the news coverage should buy us several hours of calm."

"That would make a big difference," Patrice agreed. "I'll organise it."

"Sayginn-" Karl protested.

"I will only risk what my people risk, and if I can help a few more escape..."

In the light and shadows of the Dome, in the giant competition gym, everything had changed. No longer a competition space, the blades mats had been hastily rolled up; desks and screens had multiplied, as had Dome analysts – as they monitored the feeds from the droids searching through the structure of the Dome. Two Dome Militant had found Guy as he emptied his locker and asked him to follow them. Guy was led to a small meeting room. Des was already there, and Guy knew something was different, but not yet what. He looked around apprehensively.

"Ah, Guy, why so worried?" Tilson said with a smile. "Here, this is for you. You've earned it."

Across the table, Tilson pushed a black jacket trimmed with yellow-gold; the breast pocket embellished with the outline of the geodesic Dome and embroidered with the words: Dome Militant JUNIOR. He then handed him a leather-bound manual and, wrapped around the thick book, a brand-new Dome medallion.

Guy reached to touch the inscription with trepidation and looked up at Tilson:

"For me?"

"You've earned it. And I have had them prepare your entire battle travel kit as well." He pointed to a large black backpack with his name. Attached to it was a standard pack containing shiny new blades. Alongside was another larger carryall, inscribed: CAPTAIN DES PARKS, Dome Militant.

"Captain?" asked Guy, Captain was two grades higher than Des' previous rank.

"Well, it's only right for the prince's bodyguard," Tilson said. Des just grinned. Tilson continued: "Ok, we don't have much time. They will be lighting the firewall soon; then you'll be evacuated, and then there will be a planetwide quarantine."

"You were explaining about the evacuation," Des said. "You said Freyne would be dangerous."

"Yes, the Imperial Court is deadly to prince – no, King – Teodor. The Barons are forever conspiring to replace him with their sons."

"I thought Teodor was the heir?"

"Yes, but the Emperor has the choice – he can choose Teodor as Son of Empire, or he could choose someone else in his extended family."

"But Teodor has supporters too?" said Guy.

"Yes, he does, and they will become more vocal and more evident as he grows older. He will have to marry at sixteen because he also needs sons. Don't ever forget that. The more sons Teodor has in the Imperial nursery, the safer he'll be. But he knows that too. He has been well trained."

"There are Dome Militant at the Imperial Court – they are assigned mostly to transport, and more are evacuated there. I have given them orders about Teodor's safety, so trust them, and only them."

"What about the Imperial Guard?" asked Des.

"Not to be trusted," Tilson replied curtly. "Frederon had a hand in Teodor's kidnapping – he was trying to force the Regent to marry him. Chartsie was wrong to help the Emperor. But Sayginn was wrong to threaten to close the Dome and prosecute Chart Segat for King Serge's murder. Frederon promised to pardon Chart Segat, but the Dome Militant did not kill their king. The plain fact is the Dome Militant did fail that day. Both our king and that baby prince were murdered; ten of our own also died. Those murders weakened Earth and its six planets. Only Teodor can restore it now. He must quickly step into his father's shoes. I know he's young, but he might just be ready. He will need your help. You must always be loyal to him. Only him.

"As for these poison pills," Tilson sighed. "Treachery from the Valvanski, I think, though I am not sure how. Des here was at Mezzatorra. Des, you must be sure to tell them. Not today, of course, but Guy and Teodor must learn what you know."

Des nodded grimly. Tilson looked at his watch. Guy's Communicator buzzed.

"It's time," Tilson muttered. "Now, go." He walked them to the door, and at last he said, "I am Loyal to Empire; I fear only God."

"So, help me God," Guy and Des replied together.

With a last nod, they set off running on blades.

❖

There was a message from his mother; Teodor saw she was headed into Domeside, so he must leave the Dome.

At his call, Des and Guy raced out of the Dome military quarters, with light packs on their backs. Sebastian joined them from the Riffaut, jauntily jogging down the steps. He held a piece of parchment in his hands.

"Turns out I am one of Riffaut's very own lost sons," he said, showing Teodor his birth certificate. "There were always rumours, but I did not know until today."

"You hang on to that," Teodor whispered back. "That paper, that inheritance, is worth a fortune."

"Don't I just know it?"

Sebastian laughed a little bitter, a little relieved.

"Do you still want to work for me?" Teodor asked cautiously, looking at the turmoil on the steps of House Riffaut. Models and staff were leaving, lugging enormous suitcases and bags stuffed with clothes. "Maybe your future is here now?"

"No way, Teodor. I'm coming with you. I can always come back here."

"Stay visible," Patrice Mavey had said to Teodor in his message.

So, with Des, Sebastian, Guy and Nuria, he jogged on running blades down Old Fleet Street. Teodor held Nuria's hands.

"Use the connection," he whispered.

"I thought I could do this without help," she said, even as she wobbled and stumbled, she sighed. "Ok!"

She reached to touch Teodor's mind.

"Not me, Guy!" he urged her. She glanced over to the Domeside boy, who was so sure and fast on his running blades. She nodded once, and within moments, she was sprinting ahead with Guy and Teodor racing to catch her.

They had arrived at the vacuum tunnels. Teodor casually stripped off his outer clothes and then they passed through the heat x-ray, while he walked with the others in their underpants, through the vacuum tunnel and out onto the square. As Teodor pulled his clothes back on, he looked at the lengthy line of people waiting to be checked and evacuated through the tunnel. Ahead of him, Karl Valvanchi tested a small firewall device.

"We need more evacuation tunnels," he said.

"They are coming," Karl replied.

"When is the shield going up?" Teodor asked.

"Soon," Karl replied. "Your mother will be coming out of Domeside soon."

Teodor frowned at Karl. He looked over the crowds pouring out of Domeside in all directions.

"My mother is back at Buckingham Palace, no?"

Karl checked the time.

"Yes she will be!"

"Then, the shield must go up to protect London."

"Yes," Karl agreed. "The city. You should give the signal." And he climbed up to a platform from where he could look down on the crowds.

Teodor frowned, but then walked over to the engineers, he waved the others, Guy, Des, Nuria and Sebastian back. He spoke quietly with the lead engineer who nodded.

"Fire the Dome!" He shouted.

At Teodor's feet, a line of white fire shot high into the sky. It was followed at two-metre intervals, in a circle around the Dome. From the crowds and inside the city, there were shouts and some screams. Teodor and the others looked up and watched how the fire curved in high above the Dome, searching and weaving – until at last, it connected. One by one, the lines of fire found their destination, and connected in one huge star of light, high in the sky. Their trails of light were like the frame of an old umbrella. Then the fire buzzed, hummed and spat out the sparkle. Finally, starting from the top, it spread. White hot lines of light were starting to spread and multiply. Starting from the top, it was a vast spider's web – its arms and arches increasing and interconnecting in an exponential fashion. The base was enclosed in a dome of white, pulsing light.

As Teodor stared up at the fire dome, his Communicator beeped.

"Teodor, they are moving the gorans tonight. I asked them to bring it forward. Just in case." Teodor read his mother's message with a grateful smile; why had he not thought of that? "They have asked if you or I could lend a hand."

Teodor knew this was a ploy to get him out of Domeside and back to the palace – but this time, he did not resist.

"Karl, they need me back at the Palace."

"Just go," he replied. "You too, Nuria."

He led his small group of friends to a waiting hover car: "Guy, I'll give instructions to my staff, but I'm counting on you to help Des and Sebastian settle in."

Chapter 38

The Fireplace in House Jewel

Karl Valvanchi stood at the front of the lecture theatre, explaining Sas Darona plague. It was the same talk they had given him when he had arrived on Sas Darona all those years before. He even used the same slides.

The first slide was an image of an insect biting into human flesh. He explained what they were, to a crowded room of Dome Militant, Police and Royal Guard. All listened in silence and without moving.

He showed the image of the larva and the cocoon.

The men were so still that he could hear them breathing.

"Crystallescence," Karl said. He opened his mouth to try and explain but words failed him. So, instead, he showed them a slide with the diagram of the hollowed-out cocoon, and the minute insect inside.

He stood for a moment, looking at the men across from him, and many cameras were beaming his talk throughout the city. His hands were cold. His mind was blank. There were no words, he thought, no words at all.

"Look, I'll show you."

He stood a few moments, dialling up some information on his Communicator; then he pointed it at the screen and the cameras.

There she was again. Sonia, as seen by himself, as filmed by his helmet camera, still in the long grass behind the shimmering shield of fire.

"I saved one," Sonia showed him. A brick made of industrial glass and within it a mini-world of plants, soil, water and five or six insects, all mounted on the side of a small explosive.

"Cy-sects?" he'd asked unnecessarily.

"This is Mezzatorra," Karl told the crowd. He fast-forwarded the tape to double and then quadruple speed.

At first, Sonia had moved a little restlessly, but she had been moving; towards the end, she was still, as still as a statue. Finally, she seemed to doze, her body and face almost unrecognisable, just the shape of Sonia, not Sonia herself. In the setting sun, her body shone, reflecting the light from a thousand different facets of the cy-sect cocoons: the crystallescence.

The beauty of it, Karl thought. Did he find it was beautiful? He glanced around the room; the men seemed indifferent. They did not know Sonia. The fast-forwarded video did not capture her humanity. Karl saw the changing light and knew what came next. He slowed the video to real time.

As the sun set, the cocoons split. For one moment, she was a quivering mass. Then her body dissolved into a cloud of plague flies. They rose up from her corpse in a cyclone. Nothing was left. The cy-sects seemed to smell Karl, and a large group swerved, spun and charged at the camera.

Around the lecture room, men leapt to their feet, shouting. There were screams around the building where people were watching in different rooms. Then, silence. Karl looked around and over the crowd of men.

Finally, he thought, they have understood.

Later, Karl wondered why the humans moved so slowly. The population, as a whole, had been told they had to evacuate Domeside, and the lines of citizens queuing to exit through the vacuum tunnels were slow-moving, but good-tempered. Some had refused to evacuate. Most did so at their own pace. The population had been told to leave all but the essentials behind. It was peculiar what some people thought was essential. A mirror, perhaps if you were a model? A rocking chair, ok, maybe it was antique? But a collection of porcelain dogs? The evacuation of the Dome, on the other hand, seemed to be proceeding with military precision. Karl watched as the shuttles flew back and forth with determined speed.

"Where are the Dome Militant going?" he asked Patrice Macey at his side.

"To Space Station 1, and then spreading out to Stations 2 and 3; they have some large transports, but..."

"Tell them they can go to their bases on Sas Darona, I will sort out blanket refugee permissions for them," Karl snapped back.

"I will pass it on." Patrice replied, and he sounded beyond grateful.

They had arrived at the control centre.

"I want to check the traps," Karl said.

"My men have them under surveillance."

"Nevertheless, before I leave."

"Seven poison pills have been found and neutralised; are you sure there were eight?"

"We can't take that chance?" Karl replied.

Karl and Patrice arrived at a desk with four screens, each showing some smaller images. Karl peered from image to image. All at once, one of the pictures turned red and started to flash.

"Where is that?" Karl cut-in.

"It's House Jewel," the analyst replied. "It could be our last poison pill. It could be a false alarm."

"Where is Sayginn?" Karl said.

"She should be back by now," Patrice replied after a short hesitation.

"Send in a cyborg." Karl turned to Patrice: "For God's sake, get them to hurry up the evacuation."

"I will call the driver and get them to come back."

"The Dome is all clear," the analyst confirmed.

"Just get me a cyborg to House Jewel," Karl ordered.

"There's a Borg outside now. But the house has over seventy-five rooms, where do you want to start?"

"Have there been any repairs or decorating done quite recently – say, in the last month?"

"There's the new salon," Patrice said. "They put a new chimney place into the main Salon. I was at the opening, it was smoking."

"Send the cyborg to look at the new fireplace," Karl said.

"The cyborg is there," the analyst said a moment later. "What do you want him to do?"

On the screen, the cyborg examined the fireplace. It was methodical. It checked the front, and then one side and the other. There was a black grille to the right of the fireplace. But nothing moved. There was nothing to see.

"Get him to bang it," Karl instructed.

The cyborg went to touch the black grille. As he did, it dissolved into a cloud of tiny black flies. The grille was not black at all. It was silver.

All at once, there was silence in the control room, and in the silence, they could hear the low hum of the insects over the audio, and then something else. Coming from House Jewel. Girls' voices.

"Get those girls out of there!" Patrice shouted.

Karl did not reply. The swarm was moving, and the cyborg turned to watch it. In the office, Karl and the men watched as the cyborg watched. The flies were drawn to the smell of warm living blood. The girls did not even see them. They dropped their bags. They batted them away, still laughing. The swarm moved on, up the staircase and out through the door.

The girls looked at each other uncertainly, shrugging as they picked up their bags again. The tallest was remarkably familiar, and she was elegant as if walking the catwalk.

"Loulou," Patrice muttered. "Why is Loulou still there?"

On the audio tape they heard her say:

"Ow, I've been bitten." Loulou was pulling back her sleeves. "Ow, those blighters sting."

"What?" Standing beyond the door was Regent Sayginn, then "RUN!" Sayginn screamed even as she slammed the door shut.

"Regent?" Loulou continued to bat her hand ineffectually around her face, even as red freckles appeared on her hands, arms, and across her forehead. "What is that?"

Patrice stared at the screen; he counted at least a dozen bites on Loulou's flesh. Why had she worn a spring dress with no sleeves?

"Was that Sayginn? " Karl exclaimed. He staggered and grasped onto the edge of the table. "Why is she still there? Get me a drone, I need to find her!"

Patrice looked at Karl, then back at Loulou and the flies swarming around her.

"Prime Minister, the drones have found this," an analyst pointed an another screen, it was dark but something twinkled. "It's in the attics of House Jewel, we think these are children, but as you can see it's the advanced stage of crystallescence." As they watched, the shimmering forms of the children started to dissolve and a cloud of flies filled the view. At the far end of the attic was an open window, like an evil mist the swarm wove towards it.

"I have eyes on the Regent, she's on foot, she has a group of people with her." Another analyst said. "She's seen the flies, in fact, everybody." He stopped. On screen what had been an orderly retreat suddenly dissolved into a screaming rout. As the mass of flies curved down to street level, so men, women and children dropped their belongings and ran.

"Where is Sayginn?" Karl asked, his voice hoarse.

"Where is the prince?" Patrice murmured. "Where is King Teodor?"

Chapter 39

Sunset on Earth

"Everyone knows Guy Erma."

On a screen in the corner of the bedroom, Prince Teodor was on the news. They had given him a microphone and installed a podium at the far end of the Buckingham Palace ballroom, for a hastily-convened press conference. Teodor had been speaking for three or four minutes on his captivity and escape from the Dome.

"I knew of Guy Erma, by reputation of course. I had been told there was a superb fifteen-year-old blades fighter in Domeside; I had just never met him. What I had not expected was that everyone else in Domeside also knew Guy Erma. I was, however, glad to meet him on a blades mat. It felt right to meet him for the first time with blades in both hands."

"So, you chose to fight Guy Erma in the Cap of the Dome?"

Footage of the fight had been released by Chart Segat's press office, as evidence that the Dome Militant had 'found' Prince Teodor. Teodor hesitated, then finally replied:

"In retrospect, it was a terrific opportunity. As a direct result, I gained my freedom – for it was Guy Erma who showed me the way out of the Dome. So yes, I was extremely glad to meet Guy Erma; he helped me escape, and now, I must urge all the people of Domeside: you, too, must make your escape. Leave your homes and your belongings, take your children, and yes, your pets, and get out of Domeside as quickly as you can."

"Can we interview Guy Erma?" asked one of the journalists, ignoring Teodor's last remarks. Teodor shook his head and went to apologise. The Regency press team had said categorically that Guy Erma was too unprepared to face the press. Now that he was at the end of his session, Teodor could only agree. It had been a gruelling ten minutes. There was a lengthy list of things he could not say, and it was only through creative phrasing of his replies that he managed to respond to some of the questions at all. However, just as Teodor was about to speak, Guy stepped up to the microphone:

"I will say what Teodor said. Leave Domeside now. It's dangerous..."

Sebastian switched off the screen:

"Brilliant, Guy; not very subtle but to the point."

Guy shrugged, he stood at the window and looked out over the palace gardens.

"Look at the gorans, I had heard they raced them in the gardens, but I did not realise it was so close to the house."

Guy walked out onto the balcony. The palace staff had installed Sebastian and Des in rooms on either side of the bedroom Teodor and Guy shared. The three had discovered the balcony was the quickest and most unobtrusive way to get from one room to another. After the initial euphoria – the running backwards and forwards comparing everything from bathroom fittings to communications hubs – they had settled down to watch the gorans in the garden.

"That's Teodor," said Guy and pointed. "He is riding Blue Barbrina." The enormous ice goran was charging up the avenue of trees at an eye-watering speed. As she came upon the house, it seemed to take all of Teodor's strength and all four of her great paws braking to twist into the sharp bend before racing along the front of the house. There was a thunder of paws under their window. She turned in three huge leaps around a giant chestnut, and then she was running again – gaining speed along the front of the house – before leaping onto the Avenue and disappearing in a gust of shaken branches and leaves. Des and Guy cheered.

"Des?" Guy had had the question in his head for over an hour, looking for a chance to slip it into the conversation. "Des?"

"Yes, Guy."

He looked relaxed and indulgent; Guy decided it was worth a try:

"Do you know who my father is?"

"Guy, I was only a kid when you were born. I'm only three years older than you. Are you jealous of Sebastian?"

"No, not really, it was something Chartsie said, that's all. He said Loulou was my mother. He said that."

"Loulou? She must have been pretty young. But now I think there was some scandal," Des paused, then continued. "They always said Loulou was pretty wild when she was a teenager, trying to make her way up. What did Chartsie say, exactly?"

"He said my life was going to change," Guy repeated.

"Well, he was right there," Des shrugged. "Your life has changed. Anyhow, I should head down there."

"Yeah, right." Guy said uncertainly. *That's not it. He doesn't get it.*

"Look, Guy, Teodor said there were a library and also a collection of news stories. You know the year of your birth. I'm sure there was some scandal way back – it might have been then; it might have been afterwards. But there might be something in the news."

"You think I should look?"

"There's a screen just there..." Des nodded to the small, state-of-the-art comms platform Teodor had in the corner of his bedroom.

Guy nodded as Des headed off, leaving him alone with his thoughts. When he was out of earshot, Guy said aloud to the night:

"Life's not fair. My life is not fair."

This was how Teodor found him, with three screens illuminated with photos and headlines, all dating back sixteen years. Teodor had come back from the stables, taken a shower, and emerged with a towel at his waist. He shook his wet hair over Guy and laughed.

"You should get dressed," Guy said curtly.

"I can't find my shorts."

"What? Seb left your clothes on the bed." Guy pointed to where there were clothes laid out ready.

"Yes, but no shorts. It's ok; I told him."

"You told Seb to go and find your shorts?" Guy asked, incredulous.

"Well, yes..." Teodor hesitated.

"You don't know where they put your shorts?"

"No," Teodor said. The two looked at each other for a few moments, then finally Teodor said, "What? I've always had servants. Why would I know where my shorts are?" Teodor nodded at the screens and asked, "So, what's this?"

The main screen showed an old news story, featuring two pregnant, young women. One of them looked very familiar.

"Well, it's Loulou, she got pregnant at fifteen. Only I thought she was my mum, but here it says she gave birth to a daughter in April of the year I was born. So, well, I think it must be Marline, I mean I think Marline is her daughter."

"So, Marline's your sister?"

"No, no, how could she be? There's no mention of twins. Marline and I were born on the same day, but to two different mothers. I know that."

"You might have been born the year after?"

"So, that would mean I'm only, like, twelve years old. No..."

Sebastian came in, with a handful of underwear and said to Teodor..

"Shorts and vest."

"Thanks."

"Say sorry to Seb. He's not your slave."

Teodor looked a little startled but did not reply, just retreated to his bedside to get changed.

"It's all right, Guy." Sebastian said. "His wardrobe is unbelievable; it's almost as big as one of the showrooms at the Riffaut."

"Why do you need so many clothes?" Guy asked Teodor, who was hesitating over two choices of shirt on the bed. Teodor looked up, stung by Guy's comments, and pulled on the shirt in his hand.

"If you're going to wear that shirt, you need the other trousers," Sebastian said.

"See..." Teodor waved at Sebastian, then said to Guy: "Do you think I like this stuff? I don't want to be a fashion model, but they force me. They say like a million jobs in Domeside depend on me being stylish. So, I have to..."

"Look, don't wear that shirt," Sebastian said. Teodor sighed and threw off the offending item and picked up the other one.

"Do you think I care?" he snapped at Guy. "You, him, Loulou, you all depend on me wearing fashion."

"Not me," Guy snapped back. "I'm Dome Militant."

"Hey, Guy," Sebastian interrupted. "Without Sayginn and Teodor, House Jewel would not have a roof on it."

Teodor and Guy fell silent, eyeing each other up; they looked ready for a fight. Sebastian tried to distract them by pointing at the screens.

"That was a sad story," Sebastian said. "They were both so young. Both teenagers, both models, both got 'caught out' – you know what I mean – during Royal Ascot weekend. They were both underage. Neither should have been working. They both got pregnant."

"How do you know?" Guy asked curiously.

"Well, it's a bit of Domeside folklore. The one on the right is Loulou when she was fifteen; she was dating Erederon. That's when she got pregnant."

"What? Prince Erederon?" Teodor asked sharply.

"Yep." Sebastian smiled at Teodor and added with emphasis: "And the baby was born on the last day of the month."

"Wow!" Teodor whispered.

"Wow! What?" Guy asked.

"If Loulou had given birth to Erederon's son, he would have been lost prince, and he would be two days older than me," Teodor said, then he explained further. "He would have been the next Emperor, well, provided... Well, anyway..."

"Yes, that's why Loulou has always been so famous," Sebastian agreed. "She bore Erederon's lost prince, even though in the end, her child was a baby girl. Dear sweet Marline. who tested negative. Poor lamb."

"My mother was so relieved when Marline tested negative," Teodor said. "I was only young, but I remember. I suppose it was sad for Marline."

"You have no idea," Guy muttered.

"No, that's the sad part," Sebastian said, and they both turned to look at him. "The other girl, now that was sad. She committed suicide. She killed herself shortly after the birth of her baby."

Guy had not looked at the other girl. Now he saw another dark Domeside girl. Her face was very pretty, with a small, upturned nose and a cheeky smile. She looked like someone he might have liked.

...Why did I force her? I promised her we would swap back. I made so many promises, but I lied. Guy remembered Loulou's tears.

"What happened to her baby?"

"I don't know. Maybe he died. Maybe that's why she killed herself. Who knows?"

"He?" Teodor said.

"Yes, another fatherless boy born on Old Fleet Street, what of him?" Sebastian sounded bitter. Guy seemed to slump.

"You ok, Guy?" Teodor asked, then, "Thanks, Sebastian."

Sebastian took one look at Guy's face, nodded a little sadly and headed off.

"I'll call you when the food arrives, ok?"

"Thanks, Sebastian."

As Sebastian left, now fully dressed in coordinated fashion, Teodor sat down next to Guy and took his hand.

"What is it, Guy?"

"It's just that I wanted to believe Loulou was my mother. But if Marline was her daughter, then how could I be her son? We're not twins.

The article says two girls, both pregnant, two kids. One was Marline, one was me. Only my mum committed suicide."

Teodor squeezed Guy's shoulder.

...That was another lie. We lied to protect you... Loulou had said.

Guy was confused now. Loulou had told him she was his mother. So, who was his father?

"We'll have the test results soon enough," Teodor said.

"I don't want to know!" Guy replied, a little too quickly.

Teodor looked at him thoughtfully. If Guy was a lost prince of empire, and more importantly, two days older than him, then...

"No, I don't want to know either!" Teodor said and laughed, and Guy glanced at him – what if anything was funny?

Teodor hugged him. "I must go find my mother; she did not watch me race."

Chapter 40

Political Loyalty

"Karl, tell me that you are not going to do this."

"Just sign it, Nikato. One of us has to stay. You're leaving. I'll stay. She might still be alive. I might be able to save her, Nikki."

"You cannot go into that Dome, not now that plague —," Nikato started to say.

"There's a chance she's still alive. We saw her herding people into the Underground museum, it's cold down there that's enough to keep the flies away. So you see, I have to stay."

"Karl, Mezzatorra was not your fault. This thing going on inside the Dome; it's not your fault." Nikato and Karl were sitting on the back seat of their hover car – with all the windows and doors shut.

"We brought them in, Nikki. There had been no other traffic since the start of the outbreak. They must have been concealed in the crates of Sand Lizards. You know, that famous Sas Darona delicacy."

"Karl, everyone knows how thorough you are. How committed to containing the Sas Darona plague. I thought you would have checked the crates... "

"The Sand Lizards arrived sealed. Sealed by the hunters who captured them that morning."

"These hunters were Sas Darona tribesmen? And you still did not check inside the crates then?"

"It was not a hostile tribe; they always supplied our cases, so..." Nikato shrugged, he seemed a little sad.

"That's how the Dome Militant brought them in, as you said. You said you trusted the tribe, and why not? And why not, if they had been your long-term suppliers? But the tribe must have been connected to the Dome Militant, how else would those poison pills have ended up in the Dome?"

"Yes, but Nikki, on Saturday, when I entered the Dome, I was travelling in the van of an air-conditioning engineer."

"You know, we always own the companies who provide our services, where we can."

"The poison pills were only recently installed in the maintenance and air-conditioning tunnels. The one in House Jewel was only installed yesterday."

Karl felt sick when he thought of Altron, the man he had seen working on the air-conditioning systems. Had they been planting the poison pills, even as he had tried to rescue Prince Teodor? He had known there was something odd about Altron, but poison pills?

"Keep calm you are making connections where there are none," Nikato said soothingly.

"You say that, but eventually, the humans will be looking for those kinds of connections, they will get to us eventually."

"Only if you suggest it as a line of enquiry," snapped Nikato. "And in any case, who would believe it? I mean, why? What motive do we have? Tell me that?"

"You tell me, you're the one who attends the Symposium for Development and Expansion. You know what they discuss in closed sessions of the Zaracan Council. How the humans are too primitive? How the humans are too aggressive?"

"And now you have seen their politics, the poverty, and the sheer depravity of their lives."

"And I agreed with you. The Dodecahedron dome must close, but the empire must fall? Nikato, I ask you: really? We should be doing more to help them. We had a responsibility to keep them safe from the dangers of poison pills."

"Are you saying we had a hand in the actions of the SDLA?"

"Well, somebody provided the explosives that blew open the vault. Explosives that do not exist within the Dodecahedral Empire."

"But the humans trade with others, we know that. The Dome Militant trade with many alien races. And you provided proof that the Dome Militant were backing the SDLA."

"We are responsible for this mess, Nikato. I am sorry, but we are. The monazite-9 rationing. The SDLA. The poison pills. Chart Segat kidnapping Teodor to stop the Dome Debate. It was we who wanted that vote. Not Sayginn. The humans were happy with the Dome as it was."

"Oh, with troops of vicious Battle Borg, toying with and then killing boys for fun?"

Karl said nothing. He was thinking how they should put an extra wall of fire around Buckingham Palace to try and keep it safe. At least they knew the south tunnel from Domeside was blocked by water. That would be an escape route. The rats, cats, dogs, people, – my darling Sayginn – they might make it through that whirlpool. Cy-sects could not.

"Did you do this thing, Nikato? Did you?"

"Karl!" Nikato was adamant. "The humans brought this on themselves. If the prince had not been kidnapped, if the Dome Debate had gone the way we expected, if Chart Segat had been voted out." Nikato paused and said, with emphasis: "Perhaps if you had managed to free Prince Teodor before the Dome Debate."

"That's not fair. I did everything I possibly could."

Nikato held up a hand.

"You do not have to worry whether you brought in the poison pills, whether you failed to rescue the prince. The fact is the council decreed that the Dodecahedron Dome must be closed. The Dome had to close, Karl."

Karl reran his words a couple of times. It was neither a denial nor an agreement. A diplomatic reply if he had ever heard one. What did that mean?

"Good luck in your new posting on Freyne, as ambassador to the Emperor." Karl said. "I will stay here, as Ambassador, to clear up this mess."

"It's the human's mess, Karl."

Karl said nothing; he knew in some circles Nikato's time on Earth would be deemed a success. The Dodecahedron Dome had been closed. The Dome Militant dispersed. So now, it was time for a promotion – promotion to Freyne and the Imperial Court. God help the Emperor Frederon, he thought bleakly. Next, he remembered, it was the Emperor who had organised the kidnapping of his nephew. God help Nikato. Maybe they deserve each other.

"I will say this," Nikato concluded. "Since you choose to stay here, I won't let you die. I will make sure they send you everything you need."

"Not just for me, Nikato, I want to save the people. I will need resources to keep the firewalls burning; if nothing else. There may be famine and other illnesses."

"Anything. Anything you need. You will get it. I will see to it that you have everything you need to save and restore this planet. Afterall, it is the only working democracy in the Dodecahedral Empire. I think that's why we thought it was weak. And yes, I will support you, if you stay here, I will support you and help save this planet."

"We have no choice. We did this, and we killed the old king as well."

"Karl, you don't know that. You're guessing. Listen to me. I will protect the boy king."

"Don't call him that," Karl interrupted.

"King Teodor," Nikato said with new emphasis, "will attend one of our schools. The Council will support that. And he will return."

"Well, that's something. He will do well in one of our schools, I think," Karl replied, trying but failing to hold his sarcasm in check.

Nikato nodded, "He will be a great emperor and an ally."

"Well, that's good." Karl did not conceal his anger. "Shall we go in?"

Chapter 41

A Death in the Family

"Hurry, Guy. There's not much time." Teodor called.

Guy was coming down the stairs with Teodor. Des and Sebastian were just behind, carrying the bags. Four kit bags only and a trip of a lifetime.

"Your Highness," Teodor recognised the egg-shaped medical drone floating towards him.

"Go on, Guy!"

Teodor pushed open the door into the King's office.

"I have the test results," the drone said, as Teodor led him into a small archive, lined with files, a tiny side room alongside the main office. "And I want you to know all the protocols have been followed, all records have been erased, all samples burnt. These are the only two copies."

From the drone, a drawer opened and, inside, were two memory sticks. If all records of these blood tests had been erased, then it meant only one thing.

"So definitely a lost prince, born two days before me?"

"Yes, my king, and a lost princess too."

"Both of them?" Teodor asked aghast. He had thought he would be relieved to see the myth of the Lost Prince materialise into a real person, but this was not one, but two children born of Prince Erederon. He remembered momentarily the photograph of Loulou laughing with her girlfriend, the girl who went on to commit suicide. Why? Teodor wondered. Why did she kill herself when her child could ultimately lay claim to the Imperial Throne?

"Who knows this?"

"The Regent has been notified," the drone said.

"Anyone else?" Teodor asked.

"No one," the drone said. "This is highly sensitive information."

"How can I wipe your memory?" Teodor asked, picking the drone from the air and rotating it.

"Erm," the drone replied.

"You hold extremely sensitive data that has to be erased," Teodor said.

"I will erase my memory; the process will be complete in 10 seconds." The drone paused then, after a few seconds, it powered down. As it restarted, it looked confused.

"Where is the medical bay?" It asked.

"Room B4," Teodor said as he turned to leave. He concealed the tests in his pockets. Two lost princes, who would have thought? He would need to tell Guy of course - but maybe not straight away. He would be in danger, and Marline – he didn't want anything to happen to Guy. But to protect him... "To properly protect them, I will need to be emperor," he told himself, shoving the tests deeper into his pocket.

Next, Teodor checked to make sure no one had seen – and walked swiftly to where they were all looking at the large screen above his father's ('Now mine,' Teodor thought bleakly) desk.

The screen looked like a window, because it was in fact a window into a hospital room. There were people beyond the glass. Guy recognised her first:

"Loulou."

Guy stared at the screen and quickly, his eyes adjusted. He could see she was standing, but only just. Half leaning against a bed, she looked a little flushed and was breathing heavily.

"She's in the quarantine centre in Domeside," Patrice explained. "I am sorry, Guy, but they have confirmed it is plague."

Guy was barely listening. Finally, he asked:

"Was she bitten?"

On the screen, Loulou rolled up her sleeve to show him. Guy stepped closer to the screen. The closer he got, the more it felt like he was, in fact, looking through a window, not at the screen. For a moment, he thought Loulou was just there, on the other of the glass. He went to touch the screen; only the focus changed.

"She has a dozen bites on her neck and shoulders," Patrice said.

"What's going to happen to her?"

"She said she wanted to see you, to speak with you, and then we will end her suffering." Teodor stepped up and took Guy's hand, as Patrice continued: "We will need to end her suffering before the crystallescence."

Guy again put his hand on the screen. Across the city, in the quarantine centre, Loulou also raised her hand. Their two hands matched each other perfectly, as though they touched one last time.

"How long?" asked Teodor.

"Five minutes, ten minutes max. Her bloods... Well, you need to say your goodbyes, and then let me do my job."

"Say something," whispered Teodor. Guy nodded, but what should he say?

"I don't want you to go," Guy said looking at Loulou.

"I don't want to go either," Loulou's voice was croaky. "And I'm sorry I couldn't protect you from Chart Segat. I'm so sorry."

"It doesn't matter anymore. Teodor and I, well, we took his arms. He will never hurt anyone ever again. Not me, not you, not Des, not anyone."

Loulou was sobbing now. Guy could not tell if it was grief or relief.

"Mother, please," he whispered.

"Oh, my son..."

"But Marline. The papers said Marline was your daughter."

"No, I told you. You are my son, but I swapped you. Marline for you, you were swapped just after you were born." Loulou was shaking her head. She looked beyond him: "You have a new king now, a new life, you must forget about me. Forget all about the things I told you. Just forget everything. You have a whole new life. Just take that. Accept it. Forget the rest."

Guy knew at the very last she was trying to protect him. He glanced back at Teodor. Teodor, King of Earth, Son of Empire, the next emperor of Dodecahedral, unless Emperor Frederon had a son. Unless there was a lost prince. Is that what he wanted to be? The lost prince who would replace Teodor as the emperor of all Dodecahedral. For a moment, Guy thought his heart would stop. Through the screen, Loulou was still whispering: "Don't take the tests. Please don't take the tests. Honestly, you don't want to know. You have a new life now. A new life. A new life."

Guy nodded. He wanted to say: But I have already taken the tests. Then with a chill: What happened to the results?

He looked at Teodor once more. Honest, trustworthy and brave. He turned back to Loulou.

"You're right, Mother, you're right. I don't want any of that. I don't want any of that. I am and will stay a Domeside orphan."

Loulou smiled then, and her tears melted away.

"Doctor, I'm ready," Loulou said.

"No, please," Guy begged.

"If I go now, I will save you all." She looked from one to another. "Possibly the best thing I could do. Both of us could do. Please, doctor."

A white cyborg was sent into the vacuum chamber. He pressed a patch to Loulou's arm. She collapsed onto a nearby bed. Monitors on the screen overhead showed her vital signs drop away even as they fell, and the cyborg stretched the woman out on the narrow metal bed that was, in fact, a large tray lying on rollers. With one swift move, the cyborg pushed the body into the incinerator, and the door slammed shut.

Overhead, the screen showed Loulou dead in the incinerator tunnel. The cyborg slammed the door shut. In the red and gold light of the incinerator – her bodies seemed to shine and reflect light from all angles. Then the light started to shimmer. It was the reflection of several thousand wings shaking as they dried. For a moment, the beautiful model looked like a shining multi-faceted diamond statue. The crystallescence. The last moment of humanity of a Sas Darona plague victim. The last moment before the bodies exploded into a cloud of cy-sects, spun outwards in all directions.

Bang... The surgeon had pressed the override button and the tube filled with light and flames.

Teodor clung to Guy, with Sebastian on one side and Des at his back. Guy did not move, nor said a word, but tears streamed down his frozen face. Teodor stared at him, then turned to Patrice.

"You think my mother will be safe in the tunnels?"

"As soon as the situation stabilised we will send in a mission to save her, there will be many people trapped in locked rooms, basements, we will save as many as we can."

"My mother will survive," Teodor said resolutely. "She will lead the people in this most desperate hour."

"But you must leave," Patrice told Teodor. "You must be safe."

"Patrice, I need you to do something for me," Teodor said, still clinging to Guy Erma with one hand, his other was pushed deep into his pocket. "It's very important."

"Anything, my King," Patrice said faintly.

"I want Guy to have a title. He must be Prince Erederon of Earth."

"Are you sure?" Patrice frowned. "Should we not investigate his family?"

"No honestly," Guy interrupted.

"I am sure we should investigate his parents," Teodor replied, with a shake of his head to silence Guy. "But at the right time, but I want him to have the title regardless."

"But Teodor, a title only comes with land."

"Then give him one of my estates, something that will secure him an income. I want this, do you hear me?"

"Teodor, you don't have to," Guy protested.

"Yes, I must," Teodor replied, spinning around to face him. "You must be loyal. Do you hear me? You must be loyal to me. Only me."

Guy stared at him. Why was Teodor standing with his hands in his pockets? What was it Teodor clinging to in his pocket?

All at once, Guy knelt.

"I am yours, my king. My blades, my life, my everything. So, help me God."

Teodor nodded, and drew him up, looking him directly in the face.

"So, help you God, Prince Erederon. I am your king."

"You are my king," Guy replied. He knows, Guy thought. He knows who I am, and when we are alone later, I will tell him I don't want it. I just want to be me. Guy Erma.

"I will not be alone," Teodor said satisfied, turning to Patrice, he added. "I will not rule my people alone."

"No, Teodor, you won't. You will never be alone." It was Karl Valvanchi. "I am the new Ambassador to Earth. I will stay here to fight this plague. I stay behind on one condition – that you leave with Princess Nuria."

Nuria stepped out from behind Karl. She, too, was dressed for travelling – the security drone at her back carried two suitcases.

"We will travel to Zarac 1 to celebrate the fifth birthday of my baby cousin, Karl. Explain to him why his father cannot be there."

Relief flooded over Teodor. Now he knew he was released.

"Take my ring to my son," Karl said. Karl slipped a signet ring bearing the insignia of the Valvanchi house from his hand to Teodor's.

"So, help me God." Teodor replied. The symbolism was clear to all. He and his planets, now all came under the protection of the Valvanchis. He did indeed have the protection of the Zaracan Democratic Union. He nodded.

"What time are we leaving?"

"They are waiting for you now."

Inside the front door, Des and Teodor waited. Sebastian had gone with a tear-stained Guy to freshen up.

"What happened to Chart Segat, did you hear?" asked Teodor.

"They evacuated him with the Dome hospital and clinic teams," Des replied.

"Where will they go?" Guy asked.

"Some are going to Freyne, some to Sas Darona. You heard that Karl Valvanchi has given a blanket evacuation visa for the Dome Militant to go to Sas Darona?" Des said. "Well, thanks to your father, they have excellent facilities there."

"I wish my father had told me more about his plans for Sas Darona."

"It could be a trap, obviously, but Tilson will disperse them on touchdown." Des added. "Remember Teodor – you need the Militants. "And if they are evacuated to Sas Darona with no beers and bars, no girls wearing fashion... All they have to do is train. At the end of the quarantine – well, watch out! Karl's done you a real favour. The Dome Militant have been saved; they will come out stronger in the end, stronger than ever before."

"One day," Teodor replied. "Having the Dome Militant should help me get the empire."

"Dead right," Des replied with a smile.

"I hate being in debt to the Valvanchis, though. And it's about to get worse."

"What else can you do? You need to buy yourself some time. You need four years. Four years and then you will be a man."

Guy had reappeared. He looked pale but resolute. Teodor led him, Des and Sebastian into the ballroom control room where Patrice and Karl looked at many screens showing London and the Dome.

"We've come to say goodbye," Teodor said. "And thank you for staying."

Patrice and Karl bowed their heads.

"Be careful my king," Patrice said. "And Guy too, I mean Prince Erederon. Remember your title and how you have pledged your life to our King." Guy saluted, as Patrice concluded. "Des, Sebastian, good luck. You'll find reward money in your accounts."

"Thank you, sir," Des and Sebastian murmured as one.

"Goodbye, Uncle Karl. I will miss you." Nuria said.

"It's just another battle. I promise I will be victorious." Karl replied.

"You must lead them, King Teodor," Patrice said.

"Go," Karl echoed to Nuria.

Chapter 42

The Dome is Closed

"Patrice, you need to speak to the people," Karl said. "You need to tell the people what to expect and how to fight it. In Domeside, those who have been bitten are now dying. The people have to know what to expect and how to protect themselves."

"Some will survive, surely?" Patrice asked.

"Yes, but still, too many will die. You need to talk to the people."

"What about the Dome Militant?"

"They are helping now; they have taken on Fire Starter duties. I have given instructions to help identify the plague victims, ending their misery. They have set up a processing centre. They have incinerators, and they are also using their flame throwers. But the people need to see you, know that you are involved. You also need to tell them the king and his companions have been evacuated; it will give them hope. Hope that some, at least, will survive."

"Is there anything more we should do, Karl?"

Karl shook his head.

"It's going to be a long night."

"There will be nests throughout the Dodecahedron," Karl explained. "Even though the Dome was given the 'all clear' six hours ago, that is long enough for the cy-sects to build a hundred nests. In fact, cy-roaches have found and reported between four and ten nests in the infrastructure; some are quite small, but some are almost ready to swarm."

"Why four to ten – don't we know for sure?"

"Well, we need verification of a nest, at least two checks, but the cy-sects are attacking the cy-roaches, so even if one roach finds a nest, the second is nearly always destroyed."

"The cy-sects are learning insects," Karl said. "So, we are right to firebomb the Dome."

"I'm not sure about right." Patrice replied.

"How goes the evacuation?"

"Yes, we sounded the alarm about thirty minutes ago; we have sounded them every five minutes so there is no one in the structure who cannot know something is happening."

"Prime Minister Macey, we have alarms sounding at the vacuum port of the Dome Wall."

"On screen!"

Now the screens showed the main square of the Dome. As they watched, a line of heavily armoured Dome Militant infantry charged down towards the Dome Wall. As they watched, guns appeared through the windows and walls from two neighbouring buildings, and suddenly the Royal Guard on the Dome Wall were under heavy artillery attack from a cannon installed on the second-floor workrooms of the Fashion Houses. The people of Domeside were trying to escape.

"They have to hold!" yelled Karl.

"I'll call up the reserves," Patrice added. "All men currently resting must report for duty. Fully armed."

On screen, Dome Militant placed ladders and small pieces of scaffolding to help the men and women of Domeside scale the wall.

"Can men pass through the wall of fire?" Patrice asked.

"With severe burns, yes of course," Karl replied. "But if they are infected, the plague will come through too. The plague flies will be unharmed – they will spread plague across the planet."

"Send in aerial support," Patrice ordered. "This has to stop."

The missile screamed towards the square. There was a warning of a few instants. The Dome Militant seemed to disperse. There was an explosion. As the visibility on the main camera was clouded by smoke, other cameras showed the Dome Militant in full retreat. In fact, the attack on the Domeside wall seemed all but over. When the debris and smoke cleared, Dome Militant and civilian casualties carpeted the square. One cannon emplacement had toppled out of the building; the other still fired, but intermittently.

Patrice stared at the scene playing out on the screens.

"What are we doing? Massacring our people?"

"They're not dead," said Karl. On screen they saw, many of the infantry had survived the blast, the armour they wore having protected them. Others were regrouping all around the side roads and alleyways. "Call in reinforcements. The wall has to hold."

"Put me on the loudspeaker, broadcast this everywhere," Patrice said.

"We have to accelerate the destruction of the Dome," Karl said, "If we can destroy the nests, these people may yet survive – or least have more time to evacuate through safe channels."

"Ten." Patrice Macey started the countdown.

"People of Domeside," Patrice spoke in a clear, determined voice.

"Nine." Karl continued.

"We have to kill the cy-sects which are nesting in the structure..."

"Eight."

"...of the Dome. The cy-sects are in the beams..."

"Seven."

"...so, we will fire the beams."

"Six."

"If we can destroy the cy-sects..."

"Five."

"...we may be able..."

"Four."

"...to lift the quarantine..."

"Three."

"...and free you people..."
"Two."
"You people of Domeside..."
Above them, the screens merged into one display, a large image of the Dome against the darkening early evening sky. "One."
In an instant, the Dome was alight, as the fire blazed down the vertical and horizontal beams of the geodesic structure, so the metal turned from silver to molten gold. So, for an instant, the Dome shone from the inside, like a luminescent golden shimmering apparition. At the apotheosis of the light, they heard a loud wave of deafening cracks, and from the crowds watching in Domeside, screams. The great glass panes had shattered and exploded outwards. A heavy rain of shimmering crystals fell down on Domeside, and the structure passed from gold to red, and then black. Then, there was silence.

The shining geodesic structure, the most famous landmark of Earth, was a charred skeleton – naked of all its covering, and black to its core.

"Well," Patrice said and turned to Karl. "We did what your uncle and your family asked for in the end. The Dome is closed."

Chapter 43

Epilogue

Teodor dreamt of the camp in the snow, the dome-shaped cabins, the light, fast scooters, the yapping, powerful dogs, and the goran cub with ice-white fur and steel-blue eyes. He had known from first sight they would call it Blue.

"Blue Barbrina," his father had said. "In two years' time, she will race at Royal Ascot."

Teodor remembered hugging the cub as it licked his hands and clawed at his shiny weatherproof jacket.

"She likes the reflection," his father explained. "She has seen nothing like that before." They sat in a half-open dome – so-called fire dome – with a raging fire at the centre of a circular sofa. It was the central meeting point and focus of their camp, and a colossal extravagance. Most of the heat and all of the light was wasted across the vastness of the Sas Darona ice cap, and the fuel had to be flown in at great cost. Yet the experience of sitting within its warm glow, while looking out at the polar night, was priceless.

Chart Segat had been there, and he had said, "That's a true champion – the alpha female of her pack. The mother was not pleased to see her go."

"She would be pleased if she knew the glory that awaits her," Teodor said, and then he looked over, "Ah, he's here."

The alien ambassador had arrived, just an hour ago. He had refused to join the Imperial party for the goran hunt the day before. He had arrived today to check that only one cub was being removed.

"Of course, we'll only take one cub," Teodor remembered his father muttering: "I gave my word, didn't I? And we left the mother and the litter unharmed."

They watched as the tall man with the long mane of hair made his way to the fire dome. Teodor had only recently learnt that the Zaracans were telepaths. They rarely displayed their powers among humans, though. Could you tell if he was using telepathy, just by looking?

"Be careful, Serge," Chart Segat said. "I do not trust Nikki Valvanchi. So be careful what you say."

"I have to ask, Chart – there's so much room to spare on Sas Darona. It would be an excellent training ground for your Militants, and I can't see how they would object to us mining for monazite-9. It's a resource they are not even exploiting. If they agree, think of the benefits, the benefits for our future."

His father had kissed Teodor on the head and stood up. His father's bodyguards were the absolute best, carefully selected through repeated competitions amongst all ranks of the Dome Militant. They stood to attention as his father rose, and then shadowed him as he walked forward to greet Nikato Valvanchi. Teodor felt a pang as they disappeared. His father was doing most of the talking. The ambassador just listened, but wasn't that true of all diplomats? Teodor was distracted by a Dome Militant Junior who winked at him as he piled some more logs on the fire. Other Dome men were setting a buffet table for lunch. Sayginn and Deodran were coming across the camp to join him.

"I love him so very much," Teodor confided to Segat. For a brief instant, Teodor saw concern written across Segat's face as he had been watching Serge and Nikato: "Don't you?"

Teodor absentmindedly kissed the goran cub. Its warm softness was always comforting. Segat roughed the animal between the ears, but Teodor had meant his father and nodded meaningfully in the direction where he had gone.

"Yes," replied Segat. "Yes, I love him as much as you do."

Teodor smiled, and then they both stood up to greet Sayginn and Deodran. Deodran sat down quickly next to Teodor, who carefully placed the cub in his brother's lap, still holding it with one hand while his brother kissed and stroked it.

"Thank you, Teo," his mother said. She sat down next to Chart Segat. He reached to take her hand and kissed it, not once, but three times. She playfully pushed him away. They laughed at some secret joke but only for a moment. Now they rose to greet the other barons and guests who were entering the Dome. Teodor saw Bonnie Walesbury approaching; he was already laughing, and then there was a buffet. It was going to be a great party. For one last moment, Teodor looked out over the snow. His father was now quite a distance away, and he was still talking to the tall, enigmatic alien.

❖

"We're screwed," he heard someone say.

The images of the snow camp disappeared, and suddenly Teodor was looking into Chart Segat's face. He could feel and smell his breath on his face. "My boys, I take care of them," he said. Next the lights went out, and out of the shadows, men leapt towards him.

"Remember you are king," his mother screamed but when he turned he saw her naked and embracing Karl Valvanchi.

"No!" he cried for he was falling again, down between the buildings of Old Fleet Street, down the trellis inside the Dome's structure, rolling inside a cocktail table, falling and tumbling, falling and tumbling. It was all pain and darkness. He had scuffed his knees, but when he looked down, his skin had turned black, split with deep cracks, and underneath, cybernetics were revealed.

"I think in this case, we just lie back and enjoy the ride." Who was that?

I have to call my mum, Teodor thought. Why were his hands wet. He saw a Dome medallion splashed with soap suds.

"My Communicator is on the Dome network; they'll track you at once." Oh that was Guy. Suddenly Guy's face twisted with anger and he hissed: "Do you want to be thrown to the Battle Borgs of Dome, to fight for your life?"

"NO!"

Teodor sat up straight and opened his eyes. Where was he? Was it an aircraft, no, a spacecraft. He was in an armchair. A goran rug had been tucked around him. Teodor looked around and saw Sebastian and Des sat on the edge of a large window, looking out into space. They had been laughing, but now both looked at him with concern. What were they doing here? Where was he? Oh yes, on board the Valvanchi flyer. Karl Valvanchi's fifth birthday party. He was travelling to Zarac 1.

"Guy! Teo's awake now." Sebastian called.

Guy was talking with Nuria just a short distance away, now he walked over and sat beside him.

"Bad Dreams?"

'Where are we? Are we safe?'

Teodor sent Guy an abrupt thought message, alongside the garbled images he remembered from his dream. Guy looked at him in astonishment and patted his hand.

'Yes, we're safe. You didn't fall. You escaped. We escaped together. And Des didn't say that thing about Battle Borgs to you; he said it to me. You're just mixed up. And Chart Segat, well, we chopped his arms off. You have to hang onto that.'

'But I felt like I was falling...'

'Carcful, I think SHE can hear us when we talk with our minds.'

Guy motioned to Nuria, stood a little way off, seemingly a little stunned.

Teodor turned to her. The nightmare was fading now. He swallowed once, then coughed as he spoke with his voice:

"How long was I asleep?"

"You crashed out just after we took off." She smiled and took and patted his hand. 'You're safe with me Teodor of Earth.'

He nodded and pushed aside the goran fur someone had laid over him and went to look out the window. "Can we still see Earth?"

"No," Des replied.

"This craft by passed the accelerator and is not using the Star Gates. We're not even sure how it's flying this fast," laughed Sebastian.

"Is that what you meant when you said about enjoying the ride?"

"Sorry, I did not mean for you to hear that," Sebastian apologised.

"But if we only left an hour ago..." Teodor peered through the window. "Which direction is Earth?" Both Des and Sebastian pointed. Teodor looked, but he could see nothing, just a distant star.

"That's not right," he muttered.

"No, it's not," Des agreed. "This is not a long-distance craft. It's small, snug even, for such a long journey."

"Nuria," Teodor called to the girl. "Where are we going?"

"Zarac 1, as discussed."

"And that's seven gates and some seventy-five days away, right?"

"No, not with this ship. As Des rightly said, this flyer is too small for such a journey. We have a universal gate key." she said with a small smile. "It would take one of your ships 75 days, but we will be landing on Zarac 1 tomorrow night."

"As I said," whispered Sebastian, just loud enough for Nuria to hear. "Enjoy the ride."

Teodor watched Nuria blush then frown, fighting hard to conceal her emotions. She was still hiding something. He decided to try a direct question:

"So, are we your prisoners?"

Nuria looked quite shocked. At that moment, Ambassador Nikato appeared at the open door. He gave Teodor a sharp look.

"You boys are our guests. You are not prisoners," Nikato replied. "None of you will be harmed. We will look after and educate you. We will care for you." He gave Teodor such a look that he realised that it was perhaps not just Nuria who had picked up the echoes of his nightmare. Nikato continued:

"And when the quarantine is lifted, you will return to your homes. I hope you will all be stronger and wiser."

'The Emperor said the Valvanchi would betray us,' Guy's thoughts were panicked.

'Past tense, he said the Valvanski had betrayed us,' Teodor replied. 'Something I dare not think about.'

'I never have, nor never will - not now or ever - betray you, my princes!' Nuria cut in, as she approached them. 'So, help me God.' With this last thought, she pressed her hand to her heart.

Guy and Teodor fell apart, aware that they dare neither speak nor think in her presence. Des and Sebastian had closed in to stand at their side. All four scrutinised first Nikato, then Nuria.

"So this is not another kidnap?" Teodor asked and he stamped his right foot, as he always did when he swallowed his anger.

Nikato bowed his head with a smirk, but Nuria smiled brightly.

"Think of it as an adventure?"

She said, and she wrapped her arm through Teodor's and led him to sit at a table were drinks, snacks and cakes were being laid out. Des and Seb followed, but Guy paused to look back one last time at the vast expanse of space, and the one small star that was Sol rapidly disappearing in the distance.

"How will we escape this time?"

THE END?

Now Read On...

First three chapters free

SOLDIER OF EMPIRE

S. A. MELIA

AGE 15

SOLDIER OF EMPIRE

BOOK 3 • DODECAHEDRAL

London's Dying

High above London's Horse Guards Parade, on a tiny 'widow's peak' viewing platform, stood a lone warrior. Tall and slender with pearlescent skin, his hair had grown these past few months; now it fell in white curls across his forehead and down his back in a thick mane. A shapeshifter and telepath, Karl Valvanchi looked out over the burning buildings and was afraid.

Nine months before, a poison pill containing Sas Darona plague flies had been detonated on Fleet Street, and swarms had quickly spread through the City of London's weather dome, the infamous Dodecahedron Dome. The Dome was destroyed in the hope London could be saved, but St. Paul's, the City of London, Spitalfields, and Blackfriars had burnt, and the plague kept coming.

Today the offices, restaurants, and shops of Aldwych and The Strand were aflame. To kill the Sas Darona plague flies, buildings needed to burn down to blackened husks. Yet the flies continued to spawn and multiply, and each day the fires drew closer. What good was this destruction if the plague continued to advance?

Below, his men assembled: twelve handpicked from sixty volunteers. Human survivors had been contacted inside the plague zone. Today, Karl would lead these twelve to save them or, at least, to try to save them.

"No time to lose," Karl thought and set off at a run down the spiral stair. As he did so, his appearance changed. He had started down the steps as an alien prince; when he arrived on the courtyard below, he appeared to be a human Dome Militant warrior.

"Attention!" he cried, and the men in their black and gold uniforms snapped to attention.

"Should anyone wish to step down from this mission, now is your last chance," Karl cried. "No judgement will be made; our mission is inside the fire dome." He nodded towards the shimmering wall of fire before them, pencil-thin yet hot enough to burn the flesh from a human. The fire dome contained the deadly plague. Not one of the twelve moved.

Three small fire trucks drove up, along with twelve Battle Borgs, heroes who had died in battle, resuscitated to live a brief second life as fighting cyborgs. Two men and three of the Borgs clambered aboard each truck. It was time. Karl waved the remainder of the men forward, closed his visor, and twisted his gloves closed on his protection suit. The suit inflated with an outer protection layer of poisonous gas, deadly to plague flies. Nothing else had yet been found to work.

Approaching the shimmering fire, Karl called for the door. A circular opening materialised. Karl jogged on, and at his back, the men inflated their protection suits and followed. The door spiraled wider. The three trucks drove inside the fire-dome and into the plague zone. All checked their helmets and view-screens. Plague insects would show up as green. Nothing. So far, so good. Karl checked the spiral door had closed behind them.

"Onwards," he said.

Karl waved his men forward. The trucks rumbled behind until they came alongside a burning office block. Next door was an antique pub with a pavement double door leading to a beer cellar and basement. Whoever was down there did not have much time before the fires engulfed them.

Four Battle Borgs charged up, carrying a large black box painted with the gold insignia of the Dodecahedron Dome. From the crate, they pulled a synthetic structure and spread it over the double doors. An inflatable dome inflated above the door to create an igloo the size of a room. The inflatable was double lined with its own layer of poisonous gas protection. Karl Valvanchi pushed through a narrow slit. Inside, a small drone expanded into a rail from which hung tightly packed plastic purses that peeled open to become survival suits.

"Secure," cried one man.

Now Karl bent over the double door and pulled it open. He pulled away layers of duvets and blankets taped behind the door and, using a long knife, cut through further layers of winter coats and curtains tacked across the doorframe. Soaked fabrics could protect against plague; it had been discovered, but only provided they stayed damp.

A blade cut up through the fabrics from inside. Karl jumped back. A man's dirty hand appeared. Karl pulled the man out of the tunnel and into the inflatable protection zone.

"There," he said on greeting the first man, and he pointed to the rack of survival suits with clear signs above them for sizes and shapes. The man ran to pull one on. More people climbed out of the cave. Karl helped them up, and he counted them as they came in. He pointed each one to the survival suits.

"Fifteen. We told them fifteen only," he sighed. Beyond, he saw two more families, seven people in total, clambering out of the tunnels and into the protection igloo.

"Ok, wait here," he said. Karl took a moment to check the suited individuals. "You outside. The Dome Militants will show you the quickest route to the safe zone."

"We want to go, too," a boy objected. He did not have a protective suit.

"No," Karl replied. "Wait here. We can get more suits." Karl gave the order even as he pushed the suited survivors through the narrow door and sealed the opening closed.

"We could run," the boy protested. "I'm fast. Fast as Guy Erma, they say."

Karl restrained the boy with a firm hand. "Wait."
CRACK.
From above and to the right came the rumble of collapsing masonry. The neighboring building was dying. One of the Dome Militant fire trucks shot backwards as a flaming window crashed down into the street. Five men, two Battle Borgs, Karl counted. The rest had gone with the rescued survivors, leading them to safety. How long before a drone or a Borg arrived with more safety suits?

The flames danced skywards as the next-door building collapsed in on itself, and a shower of burning paper pages billowed out from a window. Karl winced as they brushed against and even landed on the protective plastic.

Then came the thunder of stone and a shadow. A huge piece of masonry fell directly onto a fire truck, which burst into flames. Instead of fleeing, the Dome Militant ran to heave open the doors on the truck and pull their colleagues free. Three men's protection suits caught fire.

One of the Battle Borgs picked up two burning human soldiers, hoisted them over his shoulder, and then sprinted towards the exit. Their only salvation lay outside the fire dome... if they were fast enough.

Specks indicating plague flies appeared in the corner of Karl's visor. Once again, he counted his seven last survivors and looked in the direction from where the drone and the extra suits would arrive.

All at once, Karl was blinded. Something black filled his view. Then he was aware of the inflatable collapsing around him. Four were trapped inside a blob like inflatable on the far side of a huge flaming beam, while alongside Karl was the boy who claimed to be as fast as Guy Erma, a youth, and a young woman, all now unprotected in the plague zone.

"Run," yelled Karl. The woman ran to climb aboard a truck, despite the flaming debris and rocks exploding near the tires.

"No!" Karl cried. He reached down to grab the woman, only one of the Dome Militant slammed the truck door shut.

Maybe she is right, thought Karl. Locked inside the cab, she would be safe from the plague and perhaps protected from the fire and burning rocks as well. He heard the engine revving up to drive away.

He turned back to see the remaining inflatable had collapsed in on itself, and within, four people were scratching and scrabbling to get out. Two Dome Militant leapt forward, their blades out, ready to set these survivors free. Karl went to...

Another slab fell from the sky. Karl could no longer see either the Dome Militant fighters or those they would rescue.

Then he turned back to see the last truck explode. A Borg was heaving the people from the burning vehicle, including the woman; she ran towards Karl.

Right and left, lines of plague flies swirled in closer, Karl took the hand of the young boy.

"Run."

Looking back, Karl saw the young woman had fallen behind; he waved the others onwards.

Karl sprinted back even as a spiral of plague flies curved down from the right. On Karl's visor, they appeared like green wisps of clouds. The woman looked up. Human eyes might spy flies as dots on the wind. Yet they were difficult to see, but all too easy to hear; every person on Earth now recognised with dread the drone of their approaching wings.

At Karl's side, the woman stumbled and fell. Karl heaved her up. His helmet rang with alarms; his vision a blur of green. Plague flies coiled down to the woman.

Karl watched her bat them away. Red spots like freckles appeared on her face and arms, a multiplicity of bites. All her flesh seemed red and flushed; her eyes bloodshot and bleeding. Too late.

Karl glanced over his shoulder to see the others had made it to the firewall. They had made it, but four others had died in the inflatable, and now so had this young woman.

Could he have saved her?

At his feet, the woman was meta-morphing into hexagonal cocoons. So quick, Karl thought. The crystallescence was supposed to take an hour, now he watched as the human woman was consumed and transformed into a hive in mere minutes.

That's why they are winning, he thought. The flies have evolved. These are more efficient than their forebears from Sas Darona. They convert human flesh to new flies faster. All that remained of the woman was a sprinkling of dust, some last remnant of her bones that the flies had not needed.

The newly hatched insects curled up and around him.

Karl ignored the clock on his visor counting down the minutes and seconds to the breach of his own suit. Instead, he tilted back his head and looked at how the swirl of flies rose like a tornado, and as great trails of plague flies joined the spiral – so the tornado rose higher, until it appeared to brush the very top of the fire dome. A shower of tiny, blackened corpses fell. The plague flies were testing the top of the defensive fire dome, Karl realised, and dying in their attempts to pass through.

How long could the fire dome last? It was alien tech, as were the generators. The fuel, monazite-9, was a rare brown crystal that came from outside the Dodecahedral Empire. So, the people of Earth were vulnerable, their very survival beholden to the goodwill of external powers. Karl comms buzzed. A call from Patrice Mavey, Prime Minister of Earth.

"No sign of Sayginn?"

Karl closed his eyes, grateful that this was the man's first question.

"No," the word seemed to stick in his throat. Maybe his hope was futile, maybe she had died months before.

"NO!" he repeated louder.

"Five civilians dead, six dome militant dead?"

"Six?" Karl repeated; could that be true? "The plague is getting more vicious." He found himself explaining. "The crystallescence is shorter. I have a recording now."

"Good, we needed proof." Patrice replied. "Get out of there, Karl. Teodor will reach Sas Darona tonight. I will call him, make sure he understands."

"Tell him straight," Karl said. "Tell Teodor, he has to secure more monazite-9. No matter the cost."

A Bodyguard's progress

Guy woke to the hum of motors. He blinked a few times as he glanced around the interior of the pod. The cryogenic fluids were draining away, but his eyelids were still heavy with gel. Now, clean warm water rushed in, with jets targeting muscle groups – starting with his calves, then working up his back and arms to his neck. Last of all, his face and hair were drenched in warm soapy water, which drained away with a loud gurgle. Then, the pod door clicked open.

"We have arrived at Sas Darona," a computerised voice said. "Planetary shuttles will be available tomorrow from 1700 hours."

Guy pulled himself up into a sitting position and spat the last gung from his mouth. He stretched his hands. His skin was shrunken and shriveled. Not just his fingertips but also the palms of his hands, and all the flesh of his arms and legs, was as wrinkled as walnut shells.

"Take it slowly," the machine continued. "Try not to make a mess."

A long tube retracted from down his throat; Guy gagged then coughed.

"Any sightings of Scavengii?"

"I am not connected to the command networks," the voice replied.

Guy climbed out of his industrial grey pod – one of six human sarcophagi, set in a pentagonal array linked by a web-like lattice. He climbed down and headed to the showers.

Once dressed, he set off, crunching crackers. He would have preferred hot, buttered potatoes, but according to the science, after six weeks of sleep, one had to start with vitamin biscuits.

Don't get crumbs on the carpet, he told himself. God knows this ship was expensive.

The Emperor's ship, Marsea, was designed in the shape of a serpent, and its long, slim body spiraled through space, providing some gravity to the passengers within. An older ship, she could not use the Accelerator lanes, hence the cryogenic pods. Still, she was beautiful. Two corridors ran the length of the ship. The 'Back Row' was functional, built for staff and security, while the 'Boulevard' was partitioned by large plants, and set with hand-carved wooden furniture. He saw shuttles flying up from Sas Darona; the king's guests, counsellors and petitioners were arriving and soon would take refreshments here, as they looked down on the planet.

Sas Darona, Sas Darona, Pearl of the Galactic Sea – an old-style crooner warbled over the sound system. Below, the green and gold planet filled the view. It wasn't Earth, but it was close, and most of all, there were decent training facilities within the Dome Militant's bases. He pulled his Dome medallion out from within his shirt. He might have outgrown the uniform Tilson had given him all those months ago on Earth, but he still had his medallion. A Dodecahedron crystal full of poison set in a bronze ring carved with words. He rubbed it with his thumb to shine the metal.

Loyal to Empire, Fear only God. Guy muttered the words, then, because no one was watching, he performed a victory dance.

"Tonight, I will be training with the Dome Militant!"

At that moment, one of the bars lit up and a member of the serving staff appeared, hair still wet from the showers. The man started to prep glasses and drinks. It reminded Guy that he should get moving, but he noticed how the waiter wore a red waist coat.

All at once, Guy was assailed by another memory. Almost a year before, Guy himself had been wearing a red-satin, jeweled waist coat as he served drinks. The night he had first seen Teodor, unconscious and imprisoned in the base of a pillar-style cocktail table, his feet bleeding in flimsy golden sandals. Guy had seen and recognised his then prince, now King. He remembered also how the emperor had stared down at him. The memory came with a shudder, how could an uncle do that to his only heir?

At least I got him out, Guy thought. Not that night, of course. But the next night, he and Teodor had raced back to safety at Buckingham Palace, where Teodor had named him his bodyguard and given him the title of Prince of Scotia. Now Guy had travelled with the King to Zarac, then to Demos, and was now on his way with him to the Imperial Court on the capital planet, Freyne. As if visiting Sas Darona was not enough adventure for a boy from the attics of Old Fleet Street... He sighed and breathed in the view for a few more moments.

Just then, a Magpie Ship hove into view. Guy had never seen one before, but the black, bird-in-flight shaped craft with its white and blue markings was unmistakable. Black, white, and blue were the colours of Baron Storm, and similarly, the Magpie was his emblem, since a gigantic strain of these birds was native to their home planet, Stormhome.

That ship is a long way from home, Guy thought. Teodor needed to know. He set off briskly. From the staff pods in the tail of the dragon ship to the Imperial apartments in the serpent's head, it was a mere ten-minute walk, but as he passed inside, it was as if he entered an entirely different ship.

Perched high on a mezzanine, King Teodor was travelling in the Imperial Suite which consisted of a vast bedroom with a bathroom on one side and a dressing room and wardrobes on the other. From there, two wide staircases curved down to a ballroom, flanked by a throne room and several salons. Guy walked to the railing to check. No one in the ball room. He checked again – no one in the throne room or board rooms. Twin globe windows magnified the view and Sas Darona glided across one globe to the other as the ship spun. King Teodor lay asleep in a single gold pod set at the centre of a red rug. Guy went to check.

"Wotcha, Guy." It was Des. Des Parks was a Dome Militant captain, a champion blades fighter, and the person Guy most wanted to be when he grew up.

Next, a side door opened. Beyond was a vast walk-in wardrobe, from where a butler emerged, two jackets in hand.

"Hi, Seb!"

"Hi, Des!"

They slapped hands in greeting, Seb leaned over to slap Guy lightly on the cheek.

"Wotcha, kiddo!"

"What's with the jackets?" Des asked.

"I can't make up my mind. High and mighty," he said as he held up a red and silver uniform, "...or old and stuffy." He raised a tweedy travel suit. "Someone was having a laugh when they picked this lot for him."

"Has he got any blacks?" Guy asked. "He'll be spending a lot of time with the Dome Militant."

"Oh, yes. His 'I am an evil emperor, obey me or die' outfit. Yes, he's got that. It's a new design. But they went over the top with a gold-lined cloak. What's his timetable again?" Guy offered him his screen, but Seb ignored him, checking instead his own gauntlet-style Communicator. "Oh, Storm, Dome Militant, Scavengii. Okay, we'll go Dome Militant Lite. And ditch the gold cloak." He reached back for a black jacket.

A bell sounded.

"And so, it starts... go on you two," Seb muttered as tape measure in hand, he held up and compared two pairs of trousers. "I need to get this sorted."

As Seb tutted and disappeared into a side dressing room, Des and Guy turned to the golden pod set on a red-carpeted platform at the centre of the salon. The lights changed colours as the pod slowly revolved and opened.

The far door flew open, and in strode Commander Tilson, the highest ranked officer of the Dome Militant, with two captains at his heels. He glanced once around the salon, ignored the golden pod, and instead strode over to Des and Guy. Both snapped to attention. Tilson nodded to Des in greeting, but he reached to grab Guy by the front of his shirt:

"Why the hell did you let him spend nine months on Zarac?"

Guy winced – he had tried to convince Teodor to come home.

"Our King did not want to offend the Valvanchi," Des replied in Guy's defense.

"He should have been more worried about pleasing the Emperor," Tilson growled, then thrusting a paper carrier bag into Guy's hands. "Your uniform. Hurry."

Guy nodded. Through the far door came members of the household staff and his doctor. Behind them, two large Magpie warriors entered with an arrogant swagger. They wore bulky space armor together with spears and long blades. What were they doing here? Guy checked with Tilson – there was anger in his eyes, but his face was calm as if he hardly noticed them.

"Hurry," Des repeated, pushing Guy into the dressing room. "He'll need you."

As the door closed behind him, Guy just had time to see Des and Tilson taking their places as bodyguards to their King.

That's my job, he thought. He turned to where Sebastian was hand sewing the hemline of a pair of grey trousers.

"Do you mind?" he said, showing him the jacket.

"Just do it," Sebastian replied. "It's going to be a busy day."

Yes, thought Guy. He's going to need me.

The King Protests

As he woke up, Teodor found himself surrounded by people. They were easing him up out of the golden cryo-pod, wiping his eyes and mouth with a moist warm towel, and holding a robe ready.

"Your majesty. Your majesty. Your majesty."

Their voices were like a chorus of birds chirping at him.

So here I am once again, a king, he thought.

Some people might think he was lucky to be only sixteen and a King, but they never had to wake and search around for a familiar face. Des, his bodyguard, of course, and who was that? Tilson... That's right, the Commander of the Dome Militant. Who else? A Doctor, but not one he remembered – and two Magpie warriors. Magpie what?

"Comms?" Teodor said to Des, still looking at the intruders. He might have expected to see Dome Militant Guards as his security, but not Magpies from House Storm. They were a long way from Stormhome.

He let Des help him climb out the pod, pulled on a dressing gown, then quickly scrolled through the messages. FREDDIE the identifier read. It was the nickname for his uncle, the Emperor Frederon of the Dodecahedral. He clicked it open. It was a voice message, and his uncle was to the point.

"Teo, if you're hearing this, you've arrived at Sas Darona. I've sent Tomas to take care of things, so don't waste too much time there. Get yourself to court. I've attached some photos to cheer you up. Your choice. Just get here soon. Out."

Of course, Teodor did not have an earpiece, so all those nearby heard this, and a few tried to peer at the screen. He quickly thumbed through the portraits, pausing only to briefly check the names – family connections were more important than looks.

"The princesses, the Emperor wants me to marry," Teodor explained, handing the screen back to Des, who scrolled through the images, then shrugged.

"The Emperor wants you to have sons," he said.

"Thank you, Des," Teodor replied tetchily. "My mother said I did not need to marry until I was eighteen."

"You are the King," Des replied.

If Teodor was about to say something, Tilson cut in.

"You should listen to your Emperor," he said. "Your mother has disappeared; your father and brother are dead. You must give thought to your succession."

"Commander," Teodor replied with a nod which was neither yes nor no; instead, he changed the subject. "What plans for the onward trip to the Capital Freyne? How many Dome Militant are you sending?"

"None," Tilson replied. And the finality of his tone sent Teodor's heart plummeting. What was this? No protection for his trip to court. Why?

"Well, if your plans are not finalised, I had promised Guy we might celebrate our fifteenth birthday together on Sas Darona. Did you know our birthdays are just two days apart? In a few weeks, Guy will be fifteen, and me too – just two days later. I plan for us to celebrate together! Maybe a picnic at dawn, overlooking a pride of wild Gorans—"

"The King forgets the Emperor insists he make haste to court," Tilson cut in.

"But if no preparations have been made—" Teodor objected.

"Baron Storm felt the existing force on Freyne would be sufficient," Tilson explained.

"That's barely four hundred men." Teodor had visions of himself arriving at the Imperial Court with a thousand, maybe even five thousand, Dome Militant at his back. "It is not enough men to secure Alma House."

"I think the Emperor intends to give you rooms in the Palace," Tilson replied. "There are no plans to open Alma House at this time. It has not been lived in for ten years."

Rooms in the Imperial Magnolia Palace; Teodor could think of nothing worse. He would have no privacy. The Emperor might visit him at any time. And secret corridors, he would need to get his men to check every wall, every corner, every flagstone for concealed entrances through which assassins or concubines might appear. Even so, how safe would he ever be at the Palace? He was the last of his house. The Emperor's only direct heir, but there were others with claims to the throne, including Baron Storm's four sons.

Unknotting then retying his gown tightly across himself, Teodor remembered his cousins. Each was bright, tall, and strong, only the youngest was younger than him. The competition, his father had once said. And if he had a son, even two sons, would his position be stronger? He sighed and told himself.

I don't want to marry, not like this. Not just to have sons.

"I plan to stay awhile on Sas Darona," Teodor said aloud. "To regain my strength and to check on my people." He was not going to be bullied into going to court unprotected. He would wait here awhile and prepare the men he needed and send instructions ahead to open Alma House. So, what if the house was old? He did not need luxury accommodation; he needed a strong door he could lock behind him at night, and a tight security perimeter. Surely this was not too much to ask?

"Three days is the time recommended as rest between two trips," Tilson replied. "Your uncle said to make haste, and Baron Storm rules your people on Sas Darona."

Baron Storm! Since when did a Baron command a King? Teodor thought, then added aloud. "He was not here when I left Zarac."

"Maybe he might never have been sent, if you had not spent so long among the alien Valvanchis."

There was a catch in his voice which caused Teodor to look at Tilson. He easily read the barely concealed rage beneath the man's placid stance.

"I probably did spend too long on Zarac," Teodor admitted. Teodor had thought he was being so clever. The Valvanchi had no reason to kill him. 'Let us help you reach your potential and keep you safe as well,' they had said. So, they had provided numerous tutors and opportunities to travel. Princess Nuria Valvanchi had been his constant companion, and he had kept in close contact with Karl Valvanchi on Earth, as well as receiving infrequent reports from Commander Tilson on Sas Darona. After his time in the prisons of the Dome, it had felt good. He should have realised things would change in his absence.

"It's not like you had a choice," a voice said. Teodor turned and was relieved to see Guy Erma. He looked sharp too, in a brand-new Dome Militant uniform, only Teodor felt a pang. If Baron Storm controlled the Dome Militant, did Guy report to him now? Maybe he did not realise?

"The Valvanchi are powerful," Tilson agreed.

"I should not have waited on the Emperor's ship," Teodor said. He knew that the Valvanchi could have returned him to the Dodecahedral at any time in their fast ships, but instead, Teodor had waited until the Emperor had sent his own yacht to the last marker, before asking to depart. The point was, not only did he know he could have left - the Emperor, Tilson, and everyone else, knew it too.

"The Valvanchi was not going to let you leave Zarac straightaway. They wanted to hold on to you for a while," Guy said. "If you had started complaining, it probably would not have made any difference. You were right to keep them sweet."

"It's good to have powerful allies," Tilson added, but Teodor had a feeling he did not believe this. In truth, the Valvanchi would not protect him from Baron Storm and his allies – they would see it as an internal power struggle within the Dodecahedral.

"They only really let you go because the Emperor sent a request to the United Races," Guy said, partly speaking to Teodor, but also adding this explanation for the commander.

"I thought he'd be glad that we were back, but..." Teodor glanced past Guy to the Magpie guards beyond.

"When the Emperor wants to strike a blow, the Magpies of House Storm are his fist." Tilson said, as if Teodor did not know this.

Is Tilson right? Guy asked using his thoughts.

Baron Storm had been sent to punish me for my long absence, Teodor replied; he and Guy had the gift of telepathy. During the nine months on Zarac, they had learned to communicate with their thoughts, but only to one another. No one else could hear them. *Probably, they have orders not to hurt me. Probably.*

When will the Emperor would recall them? Guy asked, then seeing the look on Teodor's face, wished he hadn't.

"I will get my Dome Militant back, Tilson," Teodor said, but his voice sounded brittle. *What am I? A boy or a king?*

A King! Guy reminded him.

Teodor passed him his communicator with the photos of the girls on display.

Maybe if I marry well. Maybe if I had sons...

Sebastian coughed loudly as he appeared with jacket and trousers ready for Teodor to dress.

"Gentlemen," Tilson said to his own men but also the Magpies. "We should leave the King to get ready." Teodor watched them retreat. "The Scavengii are coming on board now. You have ten minutes."

"Scavengii?" Teodor asked.

"That's your next meeting," Sebastian said.

"Did you say there was a bath?"

"You've not much time," Sebastian reminded him.

"I'm the King."

Am I really a king? Teodor used his telepathy to ask Guy as he eyed his reflection in one of the long mirrors, a short while later.

Yep, Guy replied with a grin.

Seb had wanted him to wear his blacks, but Teodor had insisted on his royal uniform, the gold and silver his father would wear.

Do I look like my father? Teodor asked.

He reached to touch the rubies of the Roses of England, and the sapphire and diamonds of the Star of Empire. These elaborate badges were the insignia of his rank, King of Earth, and Son of Empire. He smoothed his red jacket. He could not fault the tailoring nor how it was pulled snug to his spine by a pair of matched killing blades.

No-one cares how you look; Guy told him.

Teodor pulled out one of his blades. They had handcrafted gold handles into the shape of racing cats.

I was told these are as strong and sharp as any military blade. Do you think it's true?

Who cares? You won't need them while I'm with you.

Oh, Guy, you always cheer me up.

"So, what's bothering you?" Guy spoke aloud, having noticed how Sebastian was looking sulky knowing they were talking telepathically but also in secret.

"Baron Storm has come here in person," Teodor replied. "All the way from the far side of The Dodecahedral. Supposedly he's here to safeguard Sas Darona and the Dome Militant, but really, he'll want them for himself. He'll want to get rid of me."

Guy frowned. *Would a Baron kill a King and Heir to the Imperial throne?*

Don't worry, I will protect you. I'll protect Marline as well.

"Let's find Marline first," Guy replied aloud.

Teodor did not reply; he walked to the railing. Guy followed, they stood and watched the broken moon rise in one globe window, as a group of magpie ships floated by the other.

Teodor said, "I had not expected a meeting with the Scavengii pirates."

"Probably just want to say hello, sounded like?"

"Any meetings with the Scavengii should involve the Valvanchi," Teodor replied. "Okay, so Sas Darona is on the border of Zarac and the

Dodecahedral, but the planet is under the protection of the Valvanchi. We are bound by their laws. The Scavengii as well. I can't understand why a meeting would take place without them."

You think something fishy is going on? Guy resumed his telepathic speech.

Maybe I should call Nuria, just to be sure? Teodor replied.

"You are our King," Guy reminded him, speaking aloud.

"You're right. It will look bad if the first call I make after six weeks of cryo-sleep is to ask the advice of ..."

I miss her. She was so chatty. So helpful. Teodor thought, then aloud. "Zarac was fun, wasn't it?"

"The travel was good," Guy agreed. "Only, they never shut up about democracy."

"The Imperial family were chosen to represent the Dodecahedral to the United Races," Teodor said. *They were never supposed to rule.*

Tell that to your Uncle, why don't you? Guy replied.

Before or after he tells me who I should marry?

Teodor's eyes were drawn to the three Magpie ships now orbiting the Emperor's yacht.

"I've had no notes for this meeting with the pirates," Teodor repeated. Sas Darona's broken moon swung into view. Shattered in two like a broken egg, so iconic in shape, the moon was recognised throughout the galaxy.

"All I know is that's their lair," Teodor pointed, "that broken moon hides thousands of Scavengii, they say."

"Only a couple of hundred Scavengii at most."

"No one knows for sure."

"You are king, you'll know what to say, you always do."

"You're a Prince of Earth too, Guy," Teodor replied.

Teodor turned then and walked to where Sebastian had left a gilded box on a table. Now Teodor opened the bow and drew out a curved silver dagger. It had a fighting cat with sapphire eyes as the handle, and a luminescent porcelain blade.

"Wear this, Prince Guy Erma; then they will know you are loyal to my house."

"I don't need any blade to prove my loyalty."

"Take it, ok? I want you to have it," Teodor insisted. "I need you, Guy." Why? Wondered Guy. Why did he feel the need to say that?

Negotiating with Pirates

"Boy king, you have not been paying our tolls."

Not polite, Guy thought, as he eyed the pirate with disdain. The Scavengii chief was a vast creature – it wore a robe of orange through which green horns the length of his spine protruded, drawing the eye to their polished sharpness. It had curved claws at the end of his wide hands, and the long snout and sharp teeth of part wolf, part bear. The Scavengii was three metres high and as wide, if not more.

Guy stood behind Teodor, who was seated on a large throne at the far end of a room where over forty Magpie warriors lined the walls. If the white and blue uniforms made Guy uncomfortable, Teodor seemed unhappy with his cousin, Tomas, who sprawled across one of the two smaller thrones. Tall and strong, with a wide, honest face and blond hair, Lord Tomas Storm might look like Teodor's elder brother, but he was his first cousin. Two heartbeats, as they said, from the rule of an empire.

"Who is Tomas Storm?" Guy had asked, as they headed into this meeting.

"There're two." Teodor told him. "The father, the Baron Tomas Storm, he married the Emperor's sister, so he's my uncle by marriage, we call him The Baron. Then his son, Lord Tomas, he is my first cousin. And Tomas is next in line to the throne."

"Not his father?"

"No, the Baron married in, but his son Tomas is Imperial blood."

Hence why Tomas had claimed the second of the three thrones, and his father and uncle stood behind him. Teodor had told Guy there were three younger brothers back on Stormhome. So, Guy reflected, four Imperial princes, all next in line to Teodor.

Teodor seemed very small and alone alongside them. Yet he was the one who must deal with the alien who sat before the thrones perched on a low mushroom-like stool.

"Boy king, you are sending many ships through our space, but you have not sent even one gold coin to your good neighbours, the Scavengii."

Guy thought Teodor should protest at the greeting 'boy king', but maybe it was a fault with the translation machine which sat on the table between them.

He listened as Teodor replied: "They are refugee ships, desperate men, women, and children, fleeing certain death on their home planet, Earth, together with the necessary supplies to house and feed them. Domeside was destroyed. As our neighbours..." Teodor paused before continuing, "I would expect you to understand, and sympathise with our plight."

"Your ships, they are paid for by the United Races?" the Scavengii countered.

"United Races refugee charities make a contribution, but—"

"And you did not think you could spare a few morsels to your good neighbours, the Scavengii. We have children and wives and elders to feed, too. All we want is to be good neighbours," the monster finished with a flourish. "The Baron has paid for his black and white birds."

So, Baron Storm had paid these Scavengii. Guy frowned; that was strictly against the rules of the alien Valvanchi. Surely, House Storm knew the Valvanchi laws. Guy saw Teodor glance back to where Tomas sat behind him, then asked.

"How much is your toll?"

"One gold for every five gold you receive from the United Races," the Scavengii said.

"Twenty percent?" Teodor repeated in disbelief.

That was a lot, Guy thought, a large chunk of the donations. Teodor would never give that much to pirates, would he?

"We only ask the Scavengii to give us free passage for our people to access the refugee camps on Sas Darona. We are not of House Storm, our ships are not warships... well, they *are* warships..." Teodor hesitated, then continued. "If the charities who support us were to learn of this agreement, our funding would evaporate. So, then you would get nothing. And whereas you have nothing to lose, my people will die."

"Who is going to tell the United Races?" the creature snarled.

"You put me in a difficult situation," Teodor replied. "My best friend is Nuria Valvanchi."

Oops, Guy thought, possibly not the most diplomatic thing to say.

Indeed, the name alone appeared to infuriate the Scavengii, who roared,

"You can pay the Scavengii in gold, or we will take payment in blood."

The roar was ghastly, and the smell of its breath fetid, even to Guy – but Teodor, who was closer, did not flinch.

"Are you threatening me?" Teodor asked. "Are you threatening my Dome Militant?" He glanced back to Commander Tilson, who shook his head in a brief 'no'.

What did Tilson mean? Guy wondered. Teodor was also staring at Tilson. Clearly, he too was wondering what the Commander wanted. Finally, he sighed, and bowed his head to the Scavengii. "One moment..."

Unexpectedly, Teodor stepped back. It looked like he was retreating before his alien guest and the creature once again howled in anger.

"Tilson?" Teodor asked.

"The Scavengii are a problem, their ships are small and fast," Tilson said. "A cease fire would be welcome."

Guy was surprised – he did not think the pirate ships were a threat to the Dome Militant fleet. But a cease fire? Were the Dome Militant at war with the Scavengii? What of the Valvanchi protector fleet? Guy saw Teodor frowning.

We SHOULD have been briefed, Guy said using his thought voice. *What are you going to do, Teo?*

"Tomas?" Teodor turned to his cousin.

"Pay them, I would. You can always apologise later to your 'Ski girlfriend."

"She's not my girlfriend," Teodor replied.

"Teo!" Guy cut in, knowing that Teodor would immediately fly to the defense of Nuria Valvanchi. Only that was not the point. Tomas was trying to rial him, and why?

Teodor! Guy was shouting a loud thought voice as he nodded to where the Scavengii had clapped his paws and claws together in irritation at this delay.

Teodor winced, then stepped back to face the Scavengii – he started with a bow of his head by way of a brief apology.

The creature nodded in return.

The King stood a moment, looking at the creature and thinking.

"The charitable donations are not mine to give," Teodor said at last. "The money is destined for the refugees."

"What will your refugees eat, if we take your ships?"

"If you break the rules of Zaracan space, you will face the consequences. Three Valvanchi protector ships guard Sas Darona," Teodor replied. "Also, my ships are protected by the Dome Militant fleet. If you choose to break the Zaracan law, we will defend ourselves, as is our right."

The Alien growled and spat on the floor at Teodor's feet, but he continued.

"So, my answer is 'no'. I will not pay any tolls." Teodor was firm. "But I do ask the Scavengii Congregation, in line with the United Races ruling, please facilitate and respect the ships coming to Sas Darona to support the refugees there."

Teodor stepped down from the thrones, and nodded to Guy, as he headed to leave.

"How about one coin in six?" the Scavengii said, turned to follow – only, two Magpie guards stepped forward to stop him. "Or one in seven?"

Hold on, now the monster wanted to bargain? Guy thought. And why Magpie protection, where are the Dome Militant?

"I have given you my answer," Teodor said. "No tolls."

With a nod to the pirate commander, and a glance to Guy, Teodor strode past the long line of Magpie troops and through the far door.

Once outside, Teodor turned to Guy and complained.

"Why was I not briefed? I should have been briefed." Then looking back. "Now what's going on?"

Both Teodor and Guy watched Tomas rise from his throne and stride towards the Scavengii chieftain. The giant creature bent to listen as Tomas spoke urgently to it.

Teodor went to return into the chamber, only this time the Magpies barred his way.

"What!" Teodor started to say, but just then, the doors opened, and Baron Storm appeared with his brother at his shoulder. Behind them, Tomas was still talking to the Scavengii.

Baron Storm saw Teodor and Guy watching his son, and immediately said.

"Well met Teodor, you've grown. We were sent to escort you. We know you have few ships and need all of them at this difficult time to support your home planet. Hence why we have come. The Emperor is impatient for you to be at court."

As the Baron went to lead Teodor away, Teodor pushed Guy back towards the throne room.

"Watch and listen," Teodor muttered. "Find out what's going on."

Guy nodded – he frowned to see Baron Storm with his arm around Teodor, but now he had orders to check what Tomas was doing.

God, how did life become this complicated.

❖

Now Read on...

Soldier of Empire

Amazon.com

https://www.amazon.com/Soldier-Empire-Sci-Fi-Thriller-Dodecahed ral-ebook/dp/B0C35K8VMX

Amazon.co.uk

https://www.amazon.co.uk/Soldier-Empire-Sci-Fi-Thriller-Dodecahe dral-ebook/dp/B0C35K8VMX

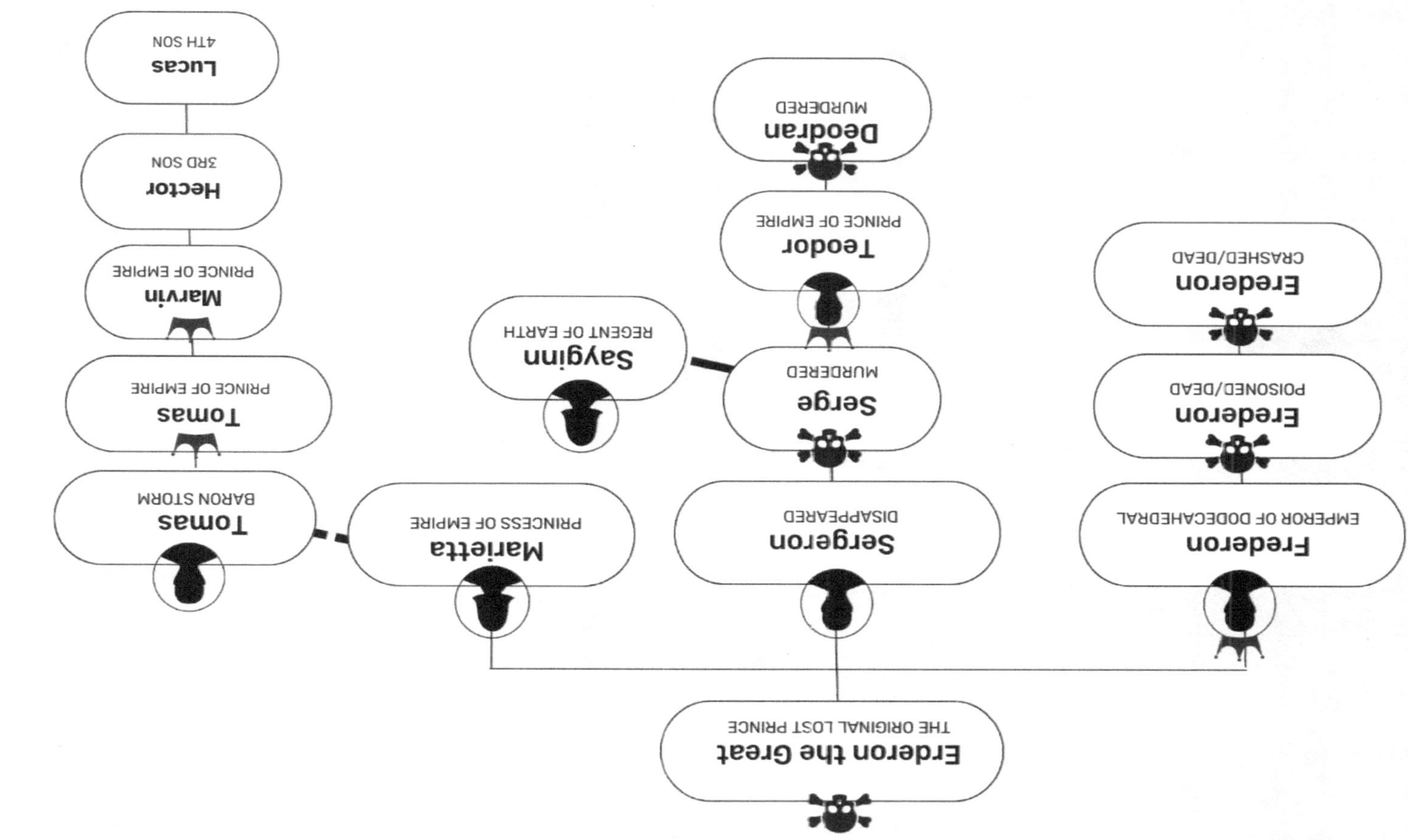

Erderon the Great
THE ORIGINAL LOST PRINCE
Sergeron
DISAPPEARED
Serge
MURDERED
Teodor
PRINCE OF EMPIRE
Deodran
MURDERED
Sayginn
REGENT OF EARTH
Marietta
PRINCESS OF EMPIRE
Tomas
BARON STORM
Tomas
PRINCE OF EMPIRE
Marvin
PRINCE OF EMPIRE
Hector
3RD SON
Lucas
4TH SON
Frederon
EMPEROR OF DODECAHEDRAL
Erederon
POISONED/DEAD
Erederon
CRASHED/DEAD

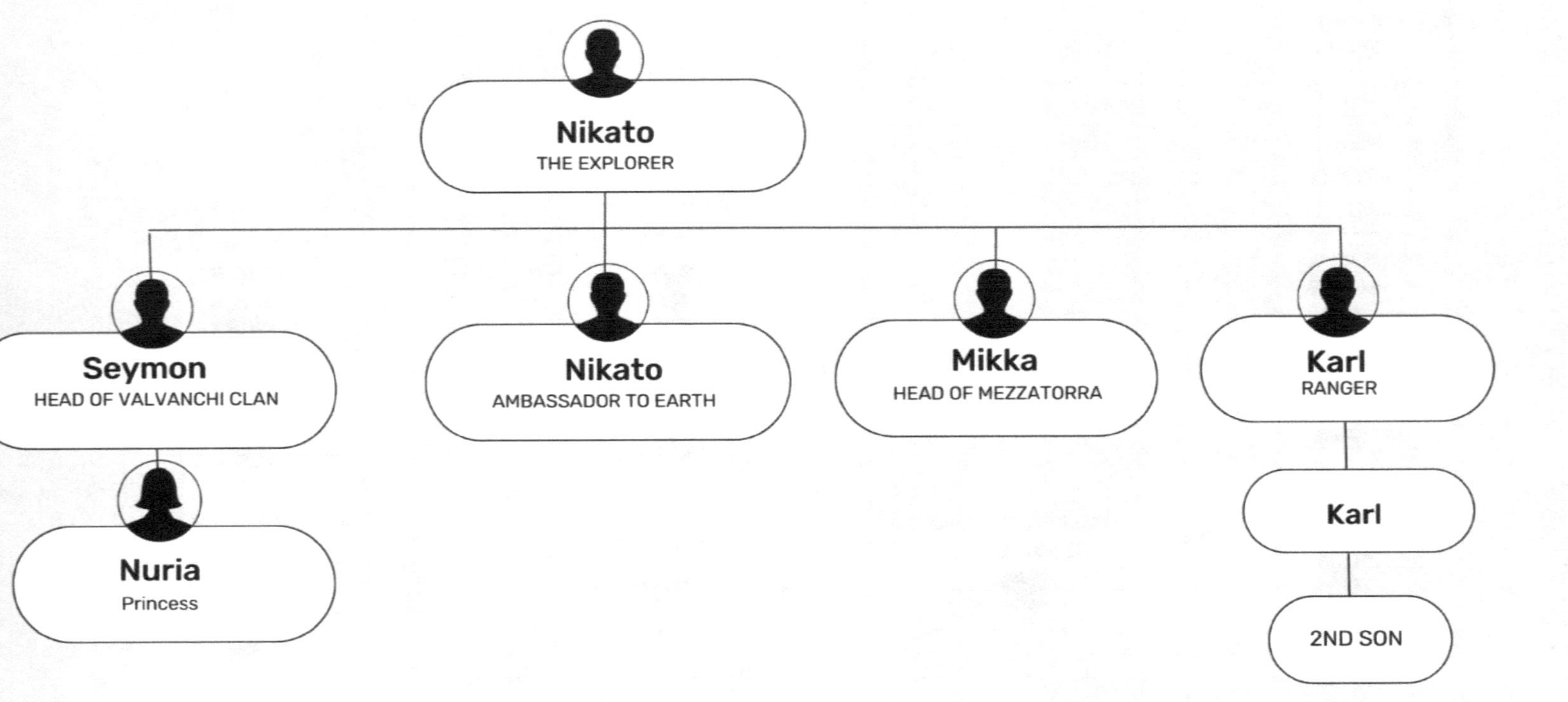

Nikato
THE EXPLORER
Seymon
HEAD OF VALVANCHI CLAN
Nuria
Princess
Nikato
AMBASSADOR TO EARTH
Mikka
HEAD OF MEZZATORRA
Karl
RANGER
Karl
2ND SON

Appendix 1

NAMES AND PLACES

A

AENGUS

One time bodyguard to King Serge, now a cyborg serving in the Royal Guard

B

BARONS

There are twelve barons, one for each of the twelve planets of the Dodecahedral empire. They head up the twelve families, each has a seat at the high council of empire, advisors to the emperor.

BATTLE BORG

The Battle Borgs of Dome were once fighting men who died on duty and were resuscitated as borgs to fight on.

BISTRO JEWEL

A large restaurant-bar in the atrium of the Dome, run as a concession of the fashion house Jewel and as a showcase of their products.

BLACK FRIARS

District of inner London, but also a medieval order of Monks who worked with the poorest in the city. They put together the first brotherhood of Dome Militant, fighters drawn from the poorest men and boys of the city who were then trained and armed and sent to liberate Jerusalem during the Crusades.

BLADES

The Fighting sport of choice of the young men of the Dodecahedral Empire. In duels, two young men face each other within a fighting ring, wearing running/spring blades on their feet and using two daggers – a blade in each hand. They fight three or five rounds. Importantly, if at any time a fighter steps outside of the fighting ring they are disqualified. The winner is the fighter who gets close enough to his opponent to wield a mortal blow. The tradition then is to shout: Do you yield?

BLUE BARBARINA

Two-meter-high racing snow cat originally from Sas Darona. At the time of this story, it is the Regent's best racer, and due to compete in the 3 o'clock race at Royal Ascot.

C
CHARTSIE / CHART SEGAT
Administrator of the Dodecahedron Dome, Mayor of Domeside,
former political ally of King Serge.
COMMUNICATOR
Communication device which includes messages, voice and video.
CREAM CAROLINA
Giant racing cat.
CRYSTALLESCENCE
Last stage of Sas Darona plague when the victim is converted into
crystal-like cocoons, hosts to the plague flies.
CYBORG
Cybernetic man. half-man, half-robot – normal lifespan about two
years. Families will often gift the bodies of their adult children where
they died prematurely to be resurrected as cyborgs. Appears to be 100%
human.
CY-ROACHES
Cybernetic cockroach. half cockroach, half robot – used for
surveillance.
CY-SECT
Cybernetic insect. Genetically enhanced Sas Darona plague fly –
more deadly, faster to breed, quicker to evolve.
CY-WOLVES
Cybernetic wolves. half-robot, half-wolf.
D
DEODRAN
Younger brother of Teodor, Prince of Earth. Died two years before
this story, killed by a terrorist bomb.
DES PARKS
Dome Militant soldier and champion blades fighter.
DODECAHEDRAL
Empire of 12 planets, asteroid mining, gas planets, outposts and
colonies. Dodecahedral claims a 13th planet but is in disagreement with
United Races as to ownership.
DODECAHEDRON DOME
The largest geodesic Dome in the Dodecahedral Empire. Made up
of 12 vast pentagons. It houses entertainments, sports fields, casinos,
hotels, an ancient village square and cathedral, a small port and a
military training facility for 100,000 men and boys.
DOME DEBATE
Debate of whether Chart Segat should continue as the administrator
of the Dome.
DOME MEDALLION
Identification tag worn by the Dome Militant. On one side is the name
and ID, and the motto 'Loyal to Empire, Fear only God'. On the other
side is set a crystal dodecahedron filled with poison, so that a Dome
Militant soldier always has to the choice to take his own life rather than
be taken captive or suffer through severe injuries.
DOME MILITANT

Military unit drawing on the men and boys of the inner-city wards of Domeside. Their uniform is black and gold.
DOMESIDE
Inner-city neighbourhood of London
DOMESIDE EVENING NEWS
Local newspaper of Domeside.
E
EDDIE / EREDERON
Only son of Frederon, emperor of Dodecahedral. Died before this story begins.
ERMA
In Domeside, Erma is given as a surname for boys of unknown paternity.
F
FIGHTING BLADES
Hand-held weapons used in blades fighting.
FIREWALL
Slim wall of dense, intense fire that is used to contain forest fires and Sas Darona plague flies.
FREDDIE / FREDERON
Emperor of the 12 planets of the Dodecahedral.
FREYNE
Imperial Planet, home to Emperor Frederon of the Dodecahedral.
G
GAUNTLETS
Leather arm protectors embedded with three curved blades, worn when fighting with blades.
GORAN
Giant racing cat.
GREAVES
Leather calf protectors embedded with three curved blades, worn when fighting with blades.
GOVE (& JON)
Twin brothers. Geneticists based at Mezzatorra, a centre of research into entomology on Sas Darona. Murdered in raid by SDLA.
GUY ERMA
A 15/16-year-old boy born in House Jewel, good at maths and blades, applicant to the Dome Militant, unregistered, no known father or mother.
H
HOUSE JEWEL
Fashion House, one of the eight houses at the heart of London's fashion and tailoring Industry.
I
IMPERIAL RINA
Giant racing tiger goran, raised by Emperor Frederon.
IMPERIAL GUARD
Bodyguards of Emperor Frederon. Wear the magenta and gold of the Imperial house.
J

JON (& GOVE)
Twin brothers. Geneticists based at Mezzatorra, a centre of research into entomology on Sas Darona. Murdered in raid by SDLA.
JUKE, JUKONA
Market Trader (Fruit & Veg) Domeside. Employs Guy Erma.
K
KARL VALVANCHI
Zaracan alien. Youngest son joined the Zaracan Space Rangers to escape his family's expectations. Commander on Sas Darona
KARL VALVANCHI II
Zaracan alien. Five-year-old son of Karl Valvanchi II, living on Zarac 1 in Valvanchi House.
KARL VALVANCHI CURSE
Though Karl Valvanchi the third is only five years old, there is an old prophecy that says Karl Valvanchi III will never survive to father a son of his own. Thus, giving rise to the Karl- Valvanchi Curse.
L
LOULOU
Model of Fashion House Jewel, probable age 29.
LUCY
Stable girl in the goran stables at Magnolia Palace. Tends to Prince Teodor's gorans.
M
MAGNOLIA PALACE
Emperor Frederon's Palace on Freyne, the capital of the Dodecahedral.
MARLINE
Newest Fashion Model of House Jewel, just had a birthday, age 14.
MEZZATORRA
Research base on Sas Darona.
MONAZITE-9
Precious metal used to create space magnets. Extracted from Samarium. At the time of this story, it was in short supply.
N
NIKKI VALVANCHI
Zaracan alien. Second eldest of four sons and Ambassador to the Freyne Empire
NIKATO VALVANCHI
Zaracan alien. Scholar and explorer first discovered that 13 disparate planets were the remnants of an ancient Empire.
NURIA VALVANCHI
Zaracan alien. Daughter of Syemon Valvanchi, age 13. heir to Zarac fortune.
O
OLD FLEET STREET
Avenue in Domeside where fashion houses Jewel and the Riffaut are located.
P
PATRICE MACEY

Prime Minister on Earth, head of Regent Sayginn's ten-year-old Democratic Government.

POISON PILL

Glass brick containing miniature eco-system where plague flies can live, until released by small explosive mounted on the outside and remotely detonated.

R

RIFFAUT / THE RIFFAUT / HOUSE RIFFAUT

Fashion House, one of the eight houses at the heart of the Freyne fashion and tailoring industry.

ROYAL ASCOT WEEKEND

Festival of Flowers and Fashion. Takes place each spring on Earth.

ROYAL GUARDS

Personal guard to Regent Sayginn. Wear red and silver

RUNNING BLADES

Curved metal extensions that are worn on the sole of shoes during blades combat, but also commonly worn by the soldiers and trainees of the Dome Militant. Running blades help the wearer run faster and further, leap higher and turn tighter. Boys of Domeside such as Guy Erma are rarely seen without them.

S

SAS DARONA

Planet on the outer rim of space, currently under licence for exploration to the Zaracan Democratic Union, also claimed by the Dodecahedral Empire.

SAS DARONA PLAGUE

Plague native to Sas Darona, spread by biting insects deadly to all animal and human species on Sas Darona.

SAS DARONA SAND LIZARDS

Large fat lizards of the Sas Darona savannah known for their fine white flesh.

SAYGINN / REGENT SAYGINN

Queen of Earth, Regent and ruler of six planets in the place of Prince Teodor who is only 13 years old. Probable age 32.

SDLA, SAS DARONA LIBERATION ARMY

A secret army drawing on the native tribes and dedicated to fighting the Zaracans on Sas Darona, supported by the Dome Militant

SEBASTIAN, SEB

Teenage model and impersonator of Prince Teodor, from the Riffaut fashion house, age 17.

SERGE / KING SERGE

King of Earth, husband to Sayginn, father of Teodor and Deodran. Established the Dodecahedral Dome as a place of education and training for the men and boys of Domeside, the poorest quarter of his capital city. Died two years before this story begins.

SNAKE DROID

Weapon in the shape of a snake, a long line of connected bullets ending in an explosive.

SONIA

Young researcher working in Mezzatorra, research base on Sas Darona. Killed by Sas Darona Plague.

ST PAUL'S
Name of ancient cathedral and modern clinic, both located at the heart of the Dome.

SYEMON VALVANCHI
Zaracan alien. Eldest of the four Valvanchi brothers, father of Nuria Valvanchi.

T
TEO / PRINCE TEODOR — 15/16-year-old son of King Serge and Queen Sayginn, and great nephew and only surviving male descendant of Emperor Frederon. King of Earth and heir to the Dodecahedral Empire, goran rider, blades fighter, trained in all necessary skills required for leadership.

TILSON — Commander of the Dome Militant and senior instructor of the Dome blades programme.

U
UNITED RACES — Government body of Known Space.

V
VALVANCHI — Name of a great house of the Zaracan Democratic Union, specialists in diplomatic relations and great explorers.

VALVANCHI HOUSE — Home of the Valvanchis on Zarac 1.

W
WALESBURY (LORD) — Baron of Dodecahedral Empire, resident on Earth. Loyal to King Serge, Regent Sayginn and Prince Teodor.

WHITEFRIARS STREET — Street in Domeside, off Old Fleet Street.

Z
ZARAC — Capital planet of Zaracan Democratic Union.

ZARACAN DEMOCRATIC UNION   Great power of the United Races. Rules / controls vast swathes of Known Space.

ZARACAN — Ancient Alien species, shapeshifters and telepaths

Please leave a review

D ear Reader,

Thank you for taking the time to read Son of Empire. I'm thrilled to know that you made it to the end!

If you enjoyed the story, **I would greatly appreciate it if you could leave a review on Amazon.** Your honest feedback will not only help other readers discover my book, but also encourage me to continue the series. Soldier of Empire is coming soon and Captain of Empire will be available in 2024

Thank you for being a part of this journey with me, and for your support in spreading the word about my work. **I can't wait to share the next chapter of this adventure with you.**

Sally

UK:
https://www.amazon.co.uk/review/create-review/?asin=B0C1T76ZYR
US:
https://www.amazon.com/review/create-review/?asin=B0C1T76ZYR

With Thanks

This series has been a long time in the making and there are many people to thank for their patience and support.

First and foremost, I have to thank my husband David for his endless supply of great meals, and my children Rose and Hazel who have been patient during all the time it takes to 'do the writing', and my parents, Peter and Elizabeth, who inspired and believed in me, and my sister Jane who was endlessly encouraging.

I also have to thank the Hogs Back Writers: Richard Fuller, Alan Findlay, Alison Moulden, Armando Halpern, Charles Burrows, Clare Golding, Debbie Roberts, Douglas Brownlaw, Gabriella Byrne, Hanne Larsson, Jack Laurence, Janine Yiannakis, Jenny Greenland, Joanna Barnard, Kat Guenioui, Kevin Puttick, Laura Bell, Mark Easton, Mary Ellen Foley, Peter Gillespie, Rosemary CassBeggs-Burstall, Sammy Stacey, Tim Ellis and Venetia Maltby. Plus any other past members I may have forgotten.

My writing friends from Hope Cove in Devon: Anne Rainbow, Linda Huckle; Sabrina Spencer; Elizabeth Seal; Sara Martin and Kerry Hadley.

My self-publishing digital tribe: Nick Stephenson, David Gaughran, Mark Dawson, James Blatch, David Cheeson, Alex Newton and Bryan Cohen. Thanks to all you guys.

My editors, copy-editors and proof readers: at Cornerstones, Kathryn Price; on Reedsy, Tim Major, Martha Sprachland, Kankana Basu, Deborah Murrell; Anne Rainbow; and on Fiverr : Sachal Aqeel and Anne Brownlow.

The last and perhaps the most important thank you is to my artist Lazar who has been such an amazing support creating original art to illustrate my words. Thank you Lazar, there is much more to come. Lazar Kacarevic, planet.caravan@gmail.com, artstation.com/boink.

Finally, we got there. Thank You.

- Aliens in Windsor
- Aliens in Sequoia National Park
- Aliens On the International Space Station
- Alien In Mysuru Dasara
- Aliens on Kangaroo Island

Flash Fiction Series by Sally Dickson

- How to write Flash Fiction to Win Competitions
- How to use AI to improve your Flash Fiction
- How to write Genre Flash Fiction

Flash Fiction, Edited by Sally Dickson

- 2024 Farnham Flash Fiction Competition Winners
- 2023 Farnham Flash Fiction Competition Winners
- 2022 Farnham Flash Fiction Competition Winners
- 2021 Farnham Flash Fiction Competition Winners
- 2020 Farnham Flash Fiction Competition Winners
- 2019 Farnham Flash Fiction Competition Winners
- 2018 Farnham Flash Fiction Competition Winners
- 2017 Farnham Flash Fiction Competition Winners

See Amazon Page: Sally Ann Melia

SALLY ANN MELIA

CAPTAIN OF EMPIRE

BOOK 4

DODECAHEDRAL

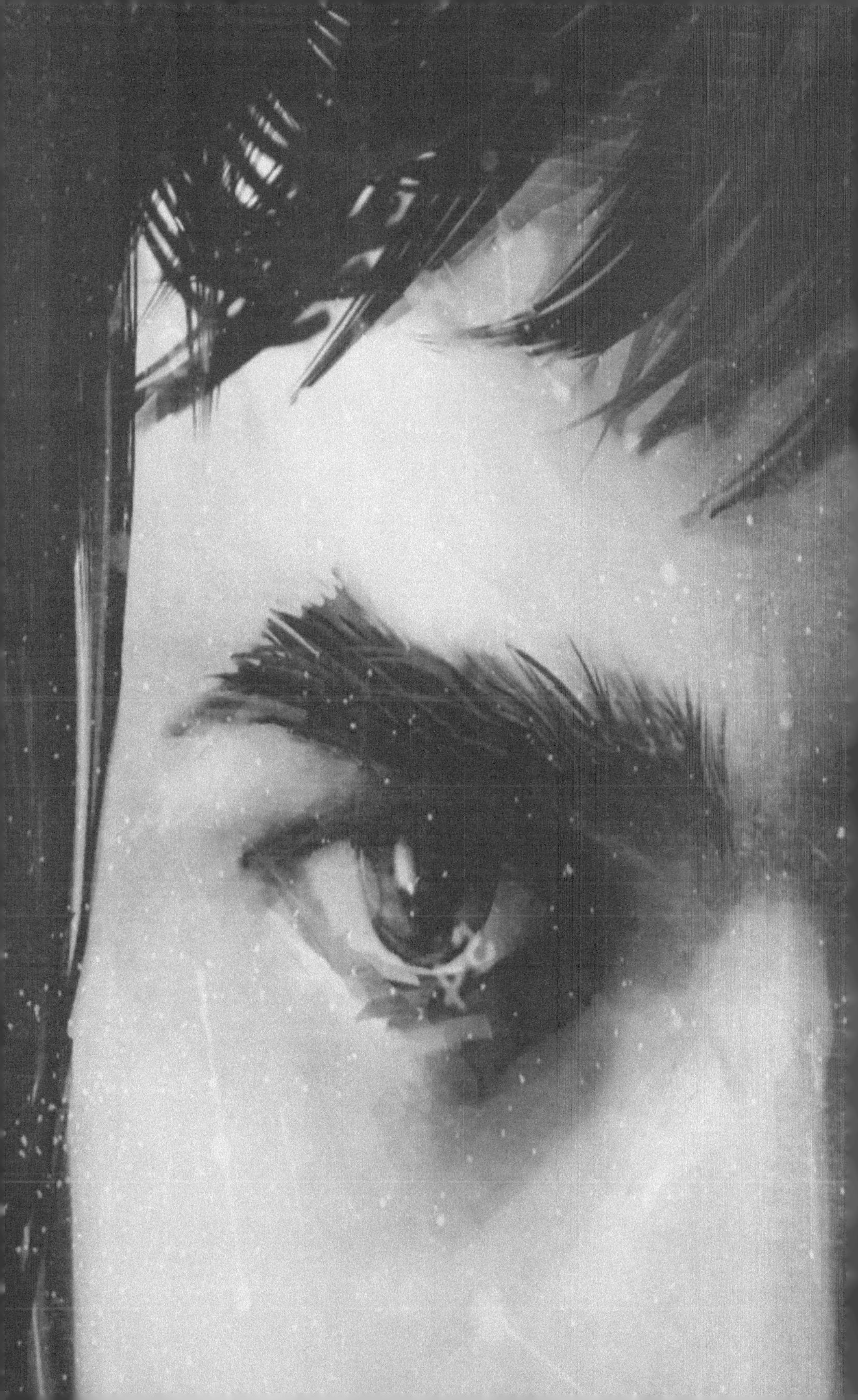